ASCENDANT UNREST

FADED SKIES SERIES - BOOK 2

MATTHEW S. COX

ASCENDANT UNREST

FADED SKIES BOOK 2

MATTHEW S. COX

DIVISION ZERO PRESS

Ascendant Revolution
Faded Skies Book 2
© 2017 Matthew S. Cox

ISBN (ebook): 978-1-949174-44-1

ISBN (print): 978-1-949174-45-8

CONTENTS

[1]

HOPE

Unease had moved into the Baltimore Habitation District. It became the awkward neighbor lurking in every shadow, acknowledged by cautious vigilance and knowing glances among the locals, but never challenged aloud.

Maya let her feet dangle, legs through the bars of the patio deck railing. Seven stories down, the Nons gathered on the street in front of her building in Block 13, the eighth straight day of protests. As if the Authority would care what non-Citizens thought. Every two minutes, a blue four-fanned Authority drone glided by below, sweeping its sensor ball over the crowd, a .50 caliber machine gun serving as a one-size-fits-all approach to every problem from murder to pickpocketing.

Puffs of steam rose from portable cookers, the occasional sniff of chicken, beef, or rat teasing her nose, a too-short reprieve from the moldy smell of a dying city. A man in a tattered olive-drab long-coat brandished a sign demanding 'Dignity for Nons' at a passing e-car. She waved at him, but the man didn't see her.

In the week following the video transmission, the roaring inspiration Maya had stirred in so many that seemed to ignite the world—or at least the Eastern Seaboard—had given way to small pockets of protestors and a quiet, seething tension.

Motivating all those people to stand up to the Authority had been frightening, but she'd do it again. No advertisement she'd ever recorded for Ascendant had ever made her feel so... warm inside. Selling expensive drugs, many with dangerous side effects, had given her a comfortable, if not hollow, life. Selling a demand for justice and respect had given her a sense of satisfaction and hope, but it also came with fear. She'd made herself a target, but *someone* had to stand up to Vanessa Oman, even if that someone was only nine years old.

Genna had been on edge at first, but with no sign of retaliation by now, she'd calmed. Maya had expected the Brigade to whisk her off somewhere to hide as soon as her message ended, but no one had made a move or even discussed it. She couldn't tell if the Brigade didn't expect retaliation, or if they didn't care since she had nothing more to offer them. Fortunate, then, that neither Ascendant nor the Authority came looking for her.

But how long would that last?

Sarah, sitting to her right, leaned forward to watch the people below, pressing her forehead against the bars. Her almost knee-long hair went wherever the wind sent it, a wild tangle of red. The toga-like dress she'd made from an old curtain hung loose on her body, smears of dirt and scrapes visible here and there where skin showed between wraps or through tears in the fabric.

Since the video transmission, the girl had been quieter than usual, and insistent on being at her side—whenever she didn't need to tend to her father. Maya scowled to herself at the thought of a child having to take care of an adult. True, Sarah had her by two years, but an eleven-year-old remained a kid. The man wasn't helpless. He'd lost an arm in the war, but he had a cybernetic replacement. His random angry outbursts at the games he watched frightened her, but thus far, he'd kept his rage focused on the players. The man had never once raised his voice at either of them.

She frowned at a stain on her friend's 'dress.' *He needs to buy her some real clothes.*

"I'll just get robbed again," muttered Sarah.

"Huh?" Maya blinked.

Sarah twisted her head enough to make eye contact. "I see how you're looking at me. You're making that pity face again."

"Sorry." Maya studied her lap, feeling guilty for having a shirt, pants, and sneakers.

She'd left her shoes by the bed, not wanting her friends to feel bad. Few kids out in the Hab had shoes, their parents unable to afford what Foz, the man who operated the nearest store, charged for things they'd grow out of so fast. Her friend Emily's father, Doctor Chang, went to the Sanctuary Zone often enough. That girl had shoes but didn't like them, since 'faeries don't wear shoes.' Sarah's father *could* get her stuff, he just didn't. Pick's older sister couldn't go to the Sanc, but the boy hardly cared about the quality of his clothing. Book, the old man who looked after Anton and Marcus, traveled to the Sanc every so often—probably why the twins always had new-looking stuff to wear.

Maya sighed. She didn't really need shoes inside the building anyway, and it didn't seem likely she'd be going outside any time soon.

"The dosers won't steal this." Sarah fussed with the old, yellowed fabric. "I do miss my camo pants."

"Ask your dad to get you some clothes," said Maya, leaning back.

Sarah shrugged one shoulder. "He won't go to the Sanc. Doesn't trust the Authority at the checkpoint. He thinks they'll either send him back to Korea or shoot him. Sometimes he doesn't realize the war's over." She gazed down, fighting sniffles. "I mean... he said no one *officially* declared the war over. The soldiers decided to go home on their own. Even the bad guys. He believes he'll get called a deserter and be arrested."

"Sorry." Maya put an arm around her.

"It's okay." Sarah wiped her eyes. "He doesn't forget me. When he sees me, he remembers he's back home... and then he teaches me survival stuff."

"I still think he should buy you real clothes." Maya examined one of the safety pins holding the curtain in the general shape of a dress. "I'll ask Mom to—"

"Don't." Sarah gave her a worried look. "Genna doesn't have to take care of me. I'm okay."

Maya opened her mouth to insist but bit off a squeal of fright as a large Authority drone zoomed around the corner, blasting them with a strong downdraft. Sarah clamped her hands over her ears in protest of the loud fans, cringing as the machine flew within a few feet of them and raced off to the right, red and blue lights flashing. Her dress tore in the fierce gale, exposing her right shoulder.

Sarah, shivering, put a hand on Maya's arm. "Shouldn't you be hiding or something? Isn't Vanessa going to come after you?"

"You're so pale." Maya held her friend's hand. "You're not sick, are you?"

"No. I just had a bath." Sarah smiled and stuck her tongue out. "You're too dark."

"Am not." Maya stared at their interlaced fingers, alternating bands of rich caramel brown and cream white.

"I'm teasing. It doesn't matter." Sarah fixed her dress and reattached the safety pin in a different spot.

Maya bit her lip, half smiling. "Well, being too pale can mean someone's sick."

"Don't wanna talk about it?"

"What?"

Sarah leaned forward again to watch the protestors down on the street. "I asked if you should hide, and you changed the subject."

"Like you changed the subject about clothes." Maya poked her in the side.

"Yeah." Sarah's knuckles whitened on the bars of the patio railing as another drone cruised by two floors down. She let off a sigh of relief and slouched when it kept going.

Maya examined her hands. "I used to be jealous of Vanessa. I wanted to look like her. I hated being light. I... thought it's why she didn't like me."

"Sorry."

"It wasn't." Maya shook her head. "She ordered me like a pizza."

"What's a pizza?" Sarah raised an eyebrow.

"You don't know what a pizza is?" Maya gasped. "It's *so* good."

"No. I've never been in the Sanc," said Sarah, sounding blasé.

"It's food that you order from a terminal, and someone brings it to your house. Mostly, it's a big round flat piece of bread with sauce and cheese on it, but you can get like a hundred different things put on it. You pick the options you want, they put it together, and they bring it to you."

Sarah gave her a pitying look. "I know what cheese is."

The girl who'd never had pizza felt sorry for *her*. Out here, Sarah was happy to have food at all. She barely had clothes. Maya thought of her former home, the huge walk-in closet with dozens of outfits, most of which she couldn't stand and had only worn once for a commercial. The Hydra had offered a limitless supply of nutritious—if not bland—meals. Until she'd decided to stay with Genna, her only worry about food had been what type, never *if* there'd be any.

She looked down and picked at her fingernails, tightness building in her throat. Her life up until recently had been safe. Sarah had never known safety. A year ago, dosers had robbed her at gunpoint, stealing the clothes straight off her back so they could sell them and get high. Maya's biggest worry had been whether or not her mother would make time to talk to her. Her bio mother, Vanessa, had caused much of this misery, and Maya, by smiling for the cameras, had helped.

Glum, Maya bowed her head. Two tears jumped from her chin, plummeting toward the crowd seventy feet below. "I'm sorry. I didn't know it was like this out here."

"Hey, don't." Sarah pressed a weak punch into her shoulder. "You're nothing like that woman. I know you're not since you don't want to go back to that nice home." She grinned. "You really don't miss it."

A feeling that had started at guilt became anger toward Vanessa. All those fancy things in that penthouse had never been hers; she'd been simply another possession. Nothing about that place triggered even the smallest bit of regret. For all its wealth, it had no soul. "No. I don't miss it, but I still think your father should get you real clothes."

Sarah pulled her wild hair away from her face while offering a noncommittal shrug. "It's okay. He needs his beer. We get food from the VA, and the rent is covered."

"You *need* clothes. He doesn't need to drink."

Sarah tensed as another drone glided by. Once the whirr of its fans faded into the background noise, she relaxed. "He needs it. When he doesn't have any, he's umm. He's different."

"Sarah..." Maya squeezed her hand.

"No, not like that." She huffed and slouched. "When he hasn't had any beer, he gets creeped out by everything. Super nervous, jumps at every little noise. Thinks the Koreans are watching him. I hate it when he's like that. It's okay if he buys beer. I'll get real clothes when I'm not going to outgrow them. Foz doesn't charge too much for adult stuff."

Maya sighed. "You could at least get a big T-shirt and make a dress out of that instead of a curtain that's falling apart."

"We should go inside before you get seen."

"It's fine." Maya swung her feet back and forth, still staring down at the protestors. "I don't think they'll do anything. The Authority hasn't arrested Vanessa, and it's been over a week. They're not going to. She will say it's all fake, and no one will believe us."

Sarah rubbed Maya's back. "You've given everyone hope. People were like zombies before, but now they're alive. They believed your mo—I mean Vanessa owned the Authority. She's gotta be angry."

"It would cost more to come after me than it would be worth." Maya pulled her head away from the bars and sighed at her friend. "What would she do? Make an example of a little kid? That's just bad PR. She'd much rather I disappear and be forgotten. All she cares about is money."

Maya looked down. Night after night of waiting in that apartment for her mother to come home, hoping she'd spend some time together that didn't involve business, flooded her mind. Vanessa hadn't ever been 'stuck late' at work; she didn't want to see her. She never had.

The memory of that woman's face on the screen in that rathole where the mercenaries had kept her captive filled her mind. Even she couldn't tell if her 'mother' had been bluffing or serious. *Go ahead and kill her. I'll make another one.*

Maya covered her face with her hands and sobbed.

"Hey." Sarah pulled her legs up and wrapped herself around Maya from behind. "Forget that horrible woman. Your *mother* is right inside."

"Yeah." Maya sniffled, wiping at her face, though the tears refused to stop.

She scrambled to her feet, hauled the patio door open, and darted into the apartment, racing across the bedroom, down the hall, and into the living room where Genna sat on the couch. The woman barely got her hands away from the disassembled rifle on the coffee table before Maya leapt into her, face buried against her shoulder.

The sofa smelled of old, damp sneakers mixed with the stink of gun cleaner. A few breaths into sobbing, the chemical scratched at her throat and made her cough.

"Baby, what's wrong?" Genna wrapped her in a firm hug.

Maya clung to the feeling of being wanted, of having a *real* mother. Nothing she'd had inside her Sanctuary Zone penthouse made her feel as good as being able to cling to a mother. Vanessa had barely tolerated holding her hand for photos; she couldn't remember ever daring to attempt an embrace. "Mom."

"Somethin' give you a scare?"

Maya shook her head. "No."

The patio door slid closed with a soft *thump*.

"Well, what's wrong then?"

"I..." She sniffled and smiled. "I'm being silly. We were talking about Vanessa and how she didn't want me."

Genna kissed her atop the head. "Put that sorry excuse for a person outta your mind."

Sarah padded in and sat beside them. Maya squirmed around to face her.

"Sorry for making you sad," said Sarah.

"I made myself sad." Maya leaned her head on Genna's shoulder. "I'm okay now."

Sarah glanced at the table. "Is that a FN-Sabre?"

"Almost." Genna chuckled. "M-17R2. Basically a Sabre though. The only real difference is in the ammo feed mechanism. I think we stole it from them."

"Oh wow," whispered Sarah. "That's the same kind of rifle Dad carried in the war. He said he wished they'd issued the Sabres since the firing contact didn't scum up so much."

"Yeah, they went cheap all right." Genna ran her hand over Maya's hair, making her smile. "Replaced that sucker first thing. Electronics are all custom work. And why do you know so much about guns?"

"The Dad is getting her ready for the next war," said Maya.

Sarah frowned. "Not the next one. The one that's still happening."

"Your father's unit saw some bad times." Genna sighed.

"Yes. He's lucky to be alive." Sarah repositioned a safety pin on her left hip, moving it to a less frayed patch of fabric. "Missile strike wiped out his camp when he was on a scouting mission."

Maya shimmied off her mom's lap and sat between them. "Did Barnes have any good news?"

"Such as?" Genna leaned forward and picked up a rifle piece, which she worked at with a toothbrush.

"Why hasn't anything changed? Ascendant is still there. All we did is make people protest." Maya raised her arms for emphasis and let them drop in her lap.

"Well, the Authority has moved in more officers from other cities to try and prove that Ascendant don't own them. Could be all for show, but I been hearin' whispers that they cleanin' house inside first."

"Anton and Marcus said they got surprised by a blueberry and he wasn't a complete shit to them," said Sarah.

"Were they doin' anything wrong at the time?" asked Genna.

Sarah scowled. "Yeah, being Nons." She pointed at her cheek. "They don't need a reason."

"I wonder if they fired him." Maya clenched her hands into fists, thinking of the blueberry who'd hit Sarah with his rifle.

"Maybe they made him clean all the toilets," said Sarah with a grin.

"Almost time to eat," said Genna. "You're welcome to join us, Sarah. Your father too if he wants."

"I should check on him anyway." Sarah slid off the couch and stood. "He didn't eat this morning."

Genna reached out and grabbed her hand as she walked by. "He keeps doin' that, you best be tellin' Doc."

"I will." Sarah nodded, smiled, and hurried out the door.

Maya picked at the few traces of polish left on her toenails, battling a moment of guilt at her old closet of unwanted shoes. Not that tiny high heels would've done her much good in the Habitation District. The desperate dosers who'd steal the clothes off the backs of the unwary or the defenseless probably wouldn't even bother... no one would buy them out here. Maybe if the Authority changed, they'd do something about people who'd rob street kids for a handful of NuCoin. She scowled at the floor.

"What are you thinkin' about now, baby?" asked Genna. "That glare's gonna light the rug on fire."

"I'm mad at the punks who took Sarah's clothes, and her father. He won't get her any. Wastes his money on beer, and she doesn't mind. She's wearing a curtain she found upstairs."

"That girl's a saint." Genna snapped a small, black piece into a larger section of the rifle with a *click*. "Takes care o' that man like a live-in nurse."

"I thought we were going to change things. The way everyone cheered, it sounded like the whole world was on our side. How can people just not care that Vanessa's setting Fade loose on purpose?" Maya slapped her hands on the cushions beside her knees, creating dust clouds. "She's *killing* people to make money."

"It'll take time." Genna set the rifle down and put an arm around Maya, pulling her close. "Most people out there, they ain't so afraid of the Brigade anymore. They know we're on their side now. And Authority does too. Even Citizens are startin' to resent being under the gun all the time, them armed drones always whizzin' around overhead."

"They need to arrest Vanessa for killing people. The Authority's supposed to protect us, not treat us like prisoners."

"Wasn't easy after the war ended. What little we had left of a government barely held on to itself. Shit, the Eastern Commonwealth States is all we got. You know, before the war, 'state' meant a whole big patch of land, not just a Sanctuary Zone?"

"Yes." Maya fell into the same rote recitation she'd given the e-learn back in the penthouse. "Eastern Commonwealth States consist of New York, Boston, Trenton, Philadelphia, Pittsburgh, Baltimore, DC, Richmond, Charlotte, Atlanta, Jacksonville, Orlando, and Miami."

Genna patted her on the head. "Yep, though Pitts never quite made up their mind if they're in or just allied. But as long as the Authority can keep all the citizens afraid of what's out in the wildlands, people be willin' to put up with a whole lot of badness in exchange for protection. S'long as they think what's *out there* is worse than what they've got inside, the Authority is in control."

"Mom?"

"Hmm?"

"When you found me, you wanted to kill that Authority pilot... aren't a lot of blueberries veterans?"

Genna's jaw tightened. She kept quiet for a moment, stroking her fingers through Maya's hair in a repetitive gesture. "Some, yeah. Lot of 'em are sellouts. Doin' whatever Ascendant wants, not carin' 'bout the oaths they swore. No better'n traitors. The ones here in Baltimore, they a special kinda bad. Was a time I wanted ta kill every damn last one of 'em." Her expression remained intense, the kind of face she'd give someone seconds before punches began flying, though silent tears wet her cheek.

"Are you crying because I made you think of Sam?"

"A bit." Genna glanced down at her, expression softening. "You said 'found you,' not 'broke inta your home and kidnapped you.'"

Maya shook her head. "Nope. This evil woman kept a little girl prisoner all alone in a tower, and made her smile and dance for people. You saved her."

"You..." Genna looked about ready to burst into tears but wound up laughing. "I guess that's one way ta put it."

"Are people here afraid of the wildlands? The AuthNet said that bad people live out there. Cannibals and murderers, and even some old military robots."

"I'm sure they make it sound a lot worse than it is." Genna pulled Maya back into her lap and held her with both arms. "They wanna keep everyone scared. Authority drones still watch over the Habitation District. 'Course, I doubt anyone from the wildlands would bother with us. It ain't like they say out there. Bunch of small towns mostly, anarchists, independents, farmers. Yeah, bandits sometimes, but ain't nowhere near like *they* tell everyone."

"What about killer robots?" Maya held her arms out and mimicked a robot walk.

Genna laughed. "I suppose there could be a few of the KT3s left out there, but the war's over. No one to fix 'em up."

"Why did people let Ascendant take over?" Maya leaned her head back, snuggling.

"Not sure what you read on that computer you had, but no one really 'won' the war. After a time, everyone realized there wasn't much left to fight over. Command on both sides had been more or less wiped out. Soldiers decided to stop shooting at each other. Eventually, we all went home. Hell, the truck I took back to the airfield on my way here had a dozen NoKos on it. Two months before that, we'd have killed each other for wearin' the wrong uniform. On that truck, we all just a bunch o' poor people couldn't believe what our idiot leaders did."

"NoKo? Is that North Korean?"

Genna patted her back. "Yeah. After the war, people wanted order, and they didn't care who wound up in charge as long as *someone* kept things together."

"Before I left the Sanctuary Zone, I didn't really understand the war. It felt like a story."

"Yeah. All things considered, we got a lot more tech left here than I ever expected. A few major cities soaked up people and kinda put themselves back together, but not everyone wanted a government back. People who live in the wildlands decided ta try somethin' different."

"I want something different too." Maya fidgeted with her shirt. "Citizens have too much and Nons don't have enough."

"Now *that* is something to work on. Smart as you are, I'm sure you'll fix it someday."

Maya pondered the idea, daydreaming about a future where the poor weren't so desperate, and the Vanessa Omans of the world didn't treat people like crap for not having money. "We proved she is evil. Why is she still there?"

"Brigade has people inside the Authority, and Harlowe's heard some good things. Ascendant's scrambling to save themselves. I'm sure that bitch is doing everything she can to keep control. She'd have to be a damn fool to drop Fade on anyone, at least for a while. I hope a long while. You at least helped shine a light on that roach."

Maya shivered. "I don't like roaches. We should step on it." She cast a nervous glance around the floor.

"Oh, we will. We hurt them good, but we ain't done yet. And you"—Genna tickled at Maya's sides, making her squeal—"need ta stop worryin' about everything. All you gotta do now is be a kid. This ain't your fight."

Sarah laughed, scooting out of reach as Maya squirmed and grabbed for the attacking fingers, giggling. After a few minutes of tickle war, she lay flat on the couch, winded and grinning. It didn't matter that she'd gone from the luxury of a Sanctuary Zone penthouse to the bleakness of a crumbling apartment building in the Habitation District.

She had a real mother.

[2]

COST BENEFIT

Maya hovered at Genna's side in the kitchen, watching her cut the plastic away from a pack of raw chicken. She peeled off the wrapper, exposing a tile of meat about an inch thick and nine square. BioNatura Corporation grew it somewhere in the Baltimore Sanctuary Zone, but Maya had never seen the raw, packaged form in person before. Whenever she'd had 'real' food instead of a Hydra tray, it had always been at a restaurant. Genna handed her the crumpled up wrapper and dropped the meat onto a cutting board with a wet *slap*.

"Toss that in the bin."

Maya crossed the small kitchen to the trash, staring at the floor in case a roach decided to brave the light. "Does that cost a lot?"

"About two NuCoin a pack." Genna sliced it into cubes, adding the meat handful by handful to a simmering pot. "Fourteen raided a warehouse. Some of it trickled back to us."

"Fourteen what?" Maya wandered back to her mom's side and tilted her head.

Genna chuckled as she dropped the last of the meat into the soup. "Brigade operates in teams. I guess it's like a platoon, but we're not official military anymore. Fourteen's the group who hit the warehouse."

"Why does the Brigade steal food? You said they paid you?"

"Most of my 'pay' comes from the VA. What's left of the old government tryin' ta do right by us vets I guess." She stirred the soup, making appraising faces at it. "That or they want us all close in case they need us. Brigade took that food ta give out ta Frags."

At the word 'Frags,' Maya thought of the people living on the outskirts of the Hab, sleeping in plastiboard boxes. That woman who looked after half a dozen kids already had given some of her grilled rat to Maya without hesitation. Like Sarah, the people out there had all worn old curtains or towels for clothes—at least the ones who had anything on. As soon as the Ascendant threat stopped, she'd start a campaign to help them.

Maya stood on tiptoe to peer into the pot. Watching someone cook for real fascinated her far more than any video the AuthNet had. "Can we get Sarah some real clothes? And shoes?"

The door opened.

Genna smiled and patted her on the head. "I'll see what I can do."

Sarah trudged into the kitchen. Thin and pale, her hair frizzed, she looked like she'd gotten into a fistfight with a dust storm and lost. Fresh tear trails had drawn white lines in the grime on her face. She took a seat by the table, staring at the floor. Her voice came tiny, a trace above a whisper. "Is it still okay if I eat here?"

"What's wrong?" Maya ran to her side.

"Is your father coming?" Genna glanced back and forth between two small bottles before opening one. She sprinkled the soup with whatever it contained, and smiled. At the sight of Sarah, her expression shifted to one of concern. "Faerie?"

"Dad's asleep," said Sarah. "I couldn't wake him up. He's... umm...."

The odor of beer-burp clung to her friend's clothes. Maya folded her arms. "Drunk."

Sarah nodded. Awkward silence lingered for a moment before she rubbed at her arm. "I'll make something for him later."

"Hmm." Genna set the spice down and walked over to pat her shoulder. She tugged on Sarah's 'dress,' exposing the upper part of her arm where she'd rubbed. Having been protected by her improvised garment, the skin remained striking in its paleness compared to the rest of her.

"He didn't hit me," said Sarah in a flat tone. "I'm just itchy." A few seconds passed. She looked up. "I don't have fleas."

"When's the last time you had a bath?" asked Genna.

"A week or two."

Maya tilted her head. "You said you just had a bath."

"They have jokes in the fancy city, right?" Sarah pulled a chair away from the table.

"Or washed that thing?" asked Genna.

Sarah's cheeks pinked. "It's an old curtain. It'll fall apart if I try to wash it."

Genna tested the material between her fingers. "It should handle a wash. Go on and run a tub. Soup'll be a little bit yet. I'll let you borrow one of my shirts 'til yours dries."

"It's okay. I don't wanna be a burden." Sarah looked up with a worried grimace.

"G'won." Genna gave her a light nudge. "No burden."

Sarah looked down. "Okay. Thank you."

"Keep the soup movin', baby?" Genna patted Maya on the head and walked with Sarah into the back of the apartment.

Maya dragged a chair over to the stove, climbed up on it, and pretended to be a witch with a cauldron. A few minutes later, a metal squeak rang in the walls. She looked around, trying to figure out where the sound came from until the hiss of water in pipes made it obvious. Genna returned soon after with Sarah's yellowed curtain-dress, and tossed it in the sink. While Maya stirred, Genna added a pack of pre-cut celery and square potato bits to the soup along with a heavy-handed dose of garlic powder.

"Wow!" yelled Sarah, from the bathroom. "You have bottle soap? Is it okay if I use some?"

Genna laughed. "How else you gon' take a bath without soap?"

Maya kept stirring, basking in the smell of spices and mesmerized by the vegetables swirling around. Genna hand-washed the curtain-dress in the sink. Within seconds, the water turned brown. Maya cringed.

"Ow," muttered Genna. She held the sopping wad of fabric up and pulled out a thin metal rod, which had stuck her in the finger. "What the heck?"

Maya pursed her lips. "Lock pick."

"Girl needs ta be careful where she goin'. Ain't gonna end well she gets caught with that thing." Genna set the pick on the counter and resumed washing. A few minutes later, she'd gotten the improvised garment as clean as possible, wrung it out, and hung it over the back of a chair.

Sarah emerged from the hallway a little while later in a dark green T-shirt that covered her to the knees but left one shoulder visible. The scent of peaches clung to her. She almost looked like a different person with her hair neat, (relatively) straight, and dark from being wet—and not a scrap of dirt anywhere on her. With a nervous glance at her soaked dress, she sat on that chair without leaning back.

"Now that you done in there, goin' ta hang this up ta dry." Genna carried the curtain-dress to the bathroom.

Maya grinned at her.

Sarah managed a weak smile.

"You can use the tub here whenever you want."

"Thanks," muttered Sarah. "Our water heater's busted."

Genna glided back in and portioned out three bowls of soup and some bread before joining them at the table. "You know, you take such good care of that man. It's okay to rest sometimes. I gotta tell Maya she's still a kid. Don't gotta go savin' the world yet. That goes for you too. Spend a little time bein' a kid."

"I guess. I'm just..." She fidgeted at the fabric in her lap. "I don't know why Dad's mad at me."

"Billy needs ta lay off the beer a little, f'ya ask me." Genna dosed her soup with pepper. "He's mad at the whole world. But not you."

"Yeah." Maya nodded eagerly. "Whenever he looks at you, he stops being angry."

Sarah looked up, gave a halfhearted shrug, and started on her soup. "I guess."

Maya blew on the spoon a few times and took her first taste, nibbling on a bit of chicken. Garlic, and pepper flooded her senses. She slurped up two more spoonfuls before taking another breath.

"Looks like I did okay?" Genna winked.

"Mmm!" Maya beamed. "It's good!"

"Yeah, Miss Genna. It's like Sanc food." Sarah's smile radiated guilt, but she kept eating.

"Mom, can Sarah bring some soup to her dad?"

"Sure. I think I got a plastic bowl around here somewhere." Genna glanced at the cabinets.

Maya started to grin at her, but something didn't seem quite right. Like she'd been avoiding eye contact. "What's wrong?"

"Nothin', baby."

"Why won't you look at me?" Maya leaned forward, trying to duck enough to catch Genna's gaze.

"Heh." Genna leaned back, finally looking at her. "I been avoidin' tellin' you somethin' all day, 'cause I know how you gonna take it. It ain't bad news."

The warmth of soup in her belly shifted to discomfort; she tensed, staring at her mother.

"Just a job. Brigade wants me on hand to help out a supply run. We're bringin' Xeno up to Philly. Not too dangerous. Worst part is how long it takes ta drive."

"I wanna go," said Maya.

"No," blurted Sarah, voice raised. "It's too dangerous." Her blue eyes widened, threatening tears. "Please don't. What if they're looking for you?"

Maya frowned. "They know where I am. The Authority isn't *that* stupid. They have to know who I am now."

"They probably do, and they don't care." Genna reached across the table to squeeze Maya's hand. "If they did, they'd have been here already."

Maya let off a sigh of relief.

"Still, she's right. That's a long lotta road. Only way I'd bring a little one along is if the trip was one way, like movin' to a new home. I already talked ta Billy. Says you can stay with them 'til I get back."

"But"—Maya sniffled—"what if something happens to you? Please don't go."

"It ain't dangerous that way." Genna reached over the table and took her other hand, holding them both. "I... we don't think Ascendant is going to come after you, but I'd prefer if you stayed here where the others can look out for you."

Sarah blinked at Genna. "Dad didn't say anything."

He also thought I was his daughter. He could use some Synaptin. She stared at the ceiling, annoyed at herself for the reflexive idea to suggest one of Ascendant's meds. Of course, The Dad *could* use some. Dementia, Alzheimer's, and a handful of other mental issues caused by physical damage to brain tissue showed improvement in seventy-four out of 100 trial patients. Granted, nine suffered drastic personality changes and one went insane, but those numbers had been acceptable for Vanessa.

Why do I keep thinking about drugs? Maya biffed herself in the forehead a few times.

"What are you doing?" asked Sarah.

"Trying to shake out bad ideas." Maya picked up her spoon again.

Genna nodded. "Good. Because you're not going to Philly with me. We'll only be a couple days."

"Did the people in Philly see the video?" asked Maya.

"Everyone in the Eastern Commonwealth States did, baby. We patched it into every screen with a network connection, every handheld, and every transmitter we could find. Hell, we even sent it to California and over to Europe."

Maya's eyes widened. "Do you think Vanessa was using Fade on other countries? They sell Xenodril all over the world." She scowled. "Of course she was. Why else would anyone need Xenodril? There aren't aliens, and the war's over."

"It's good that everyone's sick of war, 'cause that coulda caused 'nother one." Sarah stared into her soup.

"Oh, no." Maya shivered. "Vanessa's going to kill me."

"I thought you said she only cares about money," muttered Sarah.

"If other countries know she used Fade on them to force them to buy Xenodril, they're going to do something bad. And if Vanessa is going to lose her company, she'll go crazy. She'd do *anything* to keep it."

Genna grumbled, shaking her head while muttering, "Oh, bitch, f'you didn't have a hundred damn bodyguards, you an' me gonna have words." Her glare softened when she looked at Maya. "I ain't gonna let nothin' touch you, baby girl. We watchin' them. Right now, looks like they claimin' it's lies, but that data you helped us get is solid 'nuff to keep the Authority interested. I already told Harlowe—shit gets real, the Brigade is gonna hide you so well, even you won't be able to find you."

Maya scrunched up her face. "What? How can I not find myself?"

"Oh, baby." Genna laughed. "Just a figure o' speech. That data we blasted up and down the ECS would've been almost impossible to fake.

People *are* callin' for tearin' the company down, but Ascendant makes a whole mess of vital medicines, so...."

Maya sighed. "Vanessa's the problem, not the whole company."

"Yeah, but she got her talons in deep. And there still lotta 'Thority bastards who oughta be wearin' Ascendant logos." Genna dropped her spoon into her empty bowl, the sharp *clang* startling Sarah. "She'll back offa spreadin' Fade for a while. What I'm worried 'bout is if she gets cornered, would she set off more than a 'light dusting.'"

"Maybe that's why they're hesitating," whispered Sarah. "They believe what you said about her, and they know she'd do something like that—kill everyone to keep her company."

"She would," said Maya, staring into space. "She definitely would."

Genna grasped Maya's hand and gave her a pointed look. "Not your mess, baby. If we ain't fixed it by the time you hit eighteen, then maybe you make it your mess. But now, your mission is to be nine."

Maya fidgeted. "I'm not good at being a kid."

"Huh?" Sarah glanced at her. "What do you mean?"

"I don't understand what the point of dolls is. Or those little plastic things that Pick is always waving around."

"Toy spaceships," said Sarah. "Dolls..." She sighed. "Okay, I'll teach you how to 'girl,' but I guess I have a lot of work to do. We can play that card game too."

Maya grinned.

Genna gathered empty bowls. "All girls don't play wit' dolls, ya know."

"Mom didn't," said Maya, proud.

"Damn straight I didn't." Genna chuckled.

"Ooh!" Maya snapped her gaze from Sarah to Genna. "I know! The reason Vanessa is releasing Fade is so she can make *everyone* buy Xenodril. Only sick people buy medicine. Only vain people buy cosmetic pharmaceuticals. She wanted something to sell *all* the time at a ridiculous price. If we give the formula for Xenodril to another company who sells it much cheaper than Ascendant, she won't make enough money on it and she'll stop."

Sarah slapped her hand onto her forehead. "Ugh. You're right. You do stink at being a little kid."

"That's not a bad idea." Genna nibbled on a fingernail, her face pensive. "Only, we don't got the formula for it, and who knows if that other company would even bother makin' it. If they did, they might be scumbags too and overcharge for it."

"But..." Maya looked at Sarah as if the girl would offer some help, but her friend appeared clueless. "But..." She hung her head. "Making it would be the right thing to do. We send it to everyone. Blast the formula out to the world. If Xenodril is as easy to find as GastrinX, Fade stops."

"What did you just say?" asked Sarah.

"GastrinX. It's an oral antac—I mean, if your tummy hurts, you take it and it doesn't hurt anymore." Maya offered a cheesy smile.

Sarah folded her arms. "I'm not dumb. I just don't know those big words."

"Well, it's not a bad plan, but there's missin' pieces." Genna patted her on the head. "I'll run it up the food chain and see if it sticks. Now, you two go on and play a bit."

"No." Maya ran around the table and grabbed onto her. "I don't want you to go."

"It ain't for a day or two yet. I ain't goin' nowhere tonight." Genna ruffled her hair.

"Maya!" shouted a small voice from the living room.

Everyone turned at the same time to look.

Little Emily Chang leaned in the front door, still wearing the overly fancy dress that made her look like an antique doll. "Mommy fixed the player! It's got movies! Wanna come over and watch?"

The girl's mixture of parents, father Chinese, mother white, had resulted in an utterly adorable seven-year-old. Her endless energy, large eyes, and contagious habit of giggling made her the darling of the building. Maya bit her lip, thankful that awful Mr. Mason had never come anywhere near her. He'd tried to lure Maya into his apartment and had almost managed to do disgusting things to Sarah, but she'd gotten away. Thinking about how the creep had convinced everyone in the building he'd caught Sarah stealing (to explain the bruise he left on her cheek) made her livid all over again. Maya didn't feel a scrap of guilt about planting evidence that probably resulted in his execution for being a threat to Vanessa.

She wondered if Emily had ever felt unhappy with her looks too, being mixed. Then again, both of her parents loved her. That girl never had to wonder what had been so wrong with her that her mother wanted nothing to do with her.

Maya glanced up at Genna, who had a complexion like Vanessa. Maya had spent so many nights jealous of her bio mother's dark brown skin. Too late, she realized her appearance had nothing to do with Vanessa's coldness. *I was being childish. I'm exactly what Vanessa wanted. Not too light, not too dark, a little Japanese in my eyes—perfect for ads. Gotta appeal to every potential customer.* She started to frown, but Emily's catchy smile caught purchase on her lips. *There's nothing wrong with me.* She leaned against Genna, overcome by gratitude.

Genna, assuming Maya's wide-eyed expression asked permission, nodded approval. "All right, but stay inside."

Sarah picked at her borrowed T-shirt.

"S'all right, hon. Your thing's still gonna be wet. You g'won n' keep that shirt long as you need," said Genna.

Maya took a step toward the door, but hesitated. "You're not leaving, are you?"

"No, baby. Not today. Tomorrow late."

Maya hesitated until Sarah took her hand. "Okay."

"Come on!" Emily bounced on her toes in the doorway.

After one last look at Genna's smile, Maya set aside her worry and ran after her friends.

[3]

TOP SECRET

Dreams of talking cars and mermaids who signed silly contracts faded to the cozy bed in which Maya clung to Genna. She yawned and snuggled deeper in the blanket, unwilling to leave her warm nest despite needing the bathroom. The kids had stayed up a little too late, but technical issues had foiled their great plan of breaking bedtime. Less than twenty minutes into the third movie, the old laptop quit. At the time, she'd been more asleep than awake and had only a vague memory of some bald guy with a huge nose ordering a pack of talking yellow pills around. Emily had begged her mother to fix the old computer. Zoe had started looking at it until she realized the time—and chased everyone off to bed.

"Did you have fun last night?" asked Genna.

"Yes. The second movie was silly. What kind of stupid mermaid gives up being a *mermaid* for a stupid boy?"

Genna chuckled.

"The third one got corrupted."

With a yawn, her mother stretched and threaded an arm around Maya, pulling her into a hug. "Corrupt?"

"The file. Zoe said the disk was damaged and the file couldn't read. Then she sent us home."

"Oh. Hmm. You know, it's about time I showed you something. Been thinkin' of it since dinner last night."

Maya sat up. "You're not giving me a gun, are you?"

"No." Genna tapped her on the nose. "And I don't want you handling weapons. Not at your age, and hopefully not ever. Them drones will shoot you for havin' one, even if you don't use it."

Maya furrowed her eyebrows. "Then you shouldn't have one either." She sighed at her lap, staring at her draped arms. "Some of the gang people outside have them. Why don't the drones attack them?"

"They would, if they got close enough to detect it. There's tricks to hiding a weapon. Can't scan through a body, thick enough clothes, aluminum foil, couple other things." Genna sat up and yawned before stretching her arms over her head; her tank top looked new: no stains.

Maya considered Genna's muscular arms, which had been much scarier under the circumstances of their first meeting. She flexed her bicep and frowned. Unlike her new mother, she had spaghetti noodles.

"Hey, when I was your age, I had tiny little arms too." Genna winked. "The military helped me out. Only some of this is natural."

"Graft?" asked Maya.

"Not metal. Artificial muscle bundles. Lucky for me, it'd cost them more to reclaim than they'd be worth, so they let me keep 'em."

Maya pulled her legs up and wrapped her arms around her knees. "I thought the Army gave people metal arms when they wanted to make augments, like, uhh..." She shivered. "Moth."

"That bastard had reconstruction. Only way for him to get those things is if he lost his arms in action. What I got's much cheaper but nowhere near as strong. Still, faster than years of working out. Most of my old unit had 'em. Part of the special operations package."

Maya slid out of bed, frowning at the shape of her body under her nightdress. "I'm always going to be small, aren't I? It's what they made me."

"Oh, I imagine you'll, uhh, fill out in certain ways later on. Muscles, not so much."

A defeated sigh escaped Maya. "Yeah. Boobs sell stuff." She trudged off to the bathroom. "I don't even have an ass."

Genna snickered. "You're nine, hon. Stop worryin' about yo' booty."

When Maya returned to the bedroom, Genna ran to the toilet. Maya traded her nightdress for her black fatigue pants and a black T-shirt before heading to the kitchen.

Genna walked in a few minutes later, dressed as if ready to head out on a job for the Brigade: dark pants, combat boots, dark green BDU shirt over her tank top, and a utility belt. She crossed to the fridge that Zoe had resurrected and pulled some ReadyPak instant waffles from the freezer. Maya couldn't remember where they came from—probably one of the cities up north—but even dirt cheap at three boxes per NuCoin, whoever made them had to be rich. Every Non in the Eastern Seaboard region ate them, sometimes three meals a day.

Vanessa would've fainted in disgust if she had one of these things put in front of her, but Maya didn't hesitate. She loved them, especially when lathered in syrup, and took a giant bite.

"Slow down. Taste your food." Genna winked as she sat with a plate for herself.

When only two bites remained of her second waffle, Maya paused. "Are you going today?"

"Haven't heard yet, but it's possible, yeah."

Maya looked at the bit of golden-brown pastry in her sticky hands.

"Things are changin', baby. Authority's not quite so ready to shoot us on sight now, 'cause o' your message." Genna chuckled around a mouthful. "Can't say I got much love for blueberries. Wasn't easy hearin' you talk 'em up. S'pose you had ta say all that stuff 'bout them bein' noble and shit."

Maya nibbled at the edge of her waffle. "I guess it's because I used to be a Citizen. Whenever I saw them, they were protecting people from criminals. My e-learns taught me about their history and what police were like before the war. I don't like the drones, always watching everyone." She remembered so many mornings sitting by the window, staring down at legions of grey-clad workers shuffling down the street while Authority drones glided overhead. "Everyone's always sad there."

"Just the poor bastards wage slaving." Genna tossed her last bit of breakfast in her mouth. "Finish on up. I gotta show you this. And get your shoes."

Maya looked up mid-bite. "We're going outside?"

"A little." Genna winked.

After finishing her food and washing her hands, Maya trudged to the bedroom. Her black sneakers remained under the bed where she'd left them. Maybe if she said the right thing at the right moment, Genna would change her mind and bring her along. She sat on the floor to put her shoes on, struggling to come up with a good enough excuse to talk her way into the mission. After securing the Velcro flaps, she walked back to the living room where Genna waited by the front door. Her *real* mother led her out into the hallway and went left toward Sarah's corner apartment, but stopped four doors away, right in front of the dead elevator.

"It's broken." Maya glanced at the crumpled steel doors. Black streaks marred the wall above the panel holding the Up/Down buttons, where dark smoke had leaked out from a long-ago electrical fire.

"Right. The elevator ain't worked in years, but..." Genna looked around to make sure no one watched them. "This is our secret. You're not to tell anyone about it."

Maya nodded.

"Both at once, down twice, up twice, and both again." Genna pushed the buttons in that order and a *click* came from the door.

Maya's eyes widened.

Rather than try to pry the elevator doors apart, Genna pushed on them. The right half swung inward, offering a view of a dark shaft. She let it close and pointed at the panel. "Try it."

After a momentary left-right glance to ensure the hallway remained empty, Maya approached the buttons and used both hands to push them at the same time before keying in down, down, up, up, and hitting them together again.

Click.

"Good. This is how our people get out of the building when the Authority locks it down." Genna pushed the door open and stepped past it onto a ladder. "Come on. Might as well show you the rest."

Maya tiptoed up to the edge, worried about a seven-story fall. Then again, compared to flying on the back of an Authority drone, the elevator shaft didn't scare her as much as her anticipation of it had. She peered into the darkness, wincing at the taste of grease and metal in the air. A hint of mildew joined it a few breaths later. Genna's hand at her back guided her to a metal ladder bolted to the cinderblocks. Maya grabbed the rung, cringing at the cold, oily grit under her hands.

When the door closed, everything went black except for a feeble light at the bottom of the shaft. Genna climbed onto the ladder behind her, one rung down. Maya bit back a grunt at being squeezed against the steel, but felt much safer having her mother between her and a blind fall.

"I can't see," whispered Maya.

"Gotta be that way. Any light in here would be obvious to blueberries searching the building. Same pattern works on all the elevators from the seventh floor down. Eight and higher aren't set up since we got no people there." Genna started to climb down, going first.

"Okay." Maya searched out the next rung with her right foot and lowered herself.

"Maybe the day'll come when the Brigade don't need to do this shit anymore, and we can forget about this passage. But 'til that day's here, this gotta stay a secret. It's only for emergencies, like Authority raids. I don't want you playin' in here."

"Yes, Mom." Maya looked around at nothingness as her voice echoed.

They climbed downward for a little while without talking; once her eyes adjusted, the soft glow at the bottom made the walls and ladder visible. Iridescent plastic sheeting with a grid of thin metal wires in it covered most of the shaft.

"What's on the walls? They're shiny."

Genna looked up with a grin. "Good eyes, baby. It's stuff to block wireless signals and the Authority sniffers. They can't see in here 'less they tear the doors off. Weber set all this up."

"Oh... a Faraday cage?"

"That sounds like something one of them said before, yeah. No one in the building except for Barnes and Weber knows this is here," said Genna. "It gotta stay that way."

Maya looked down at her. "I understand. Top secret. You don't even tell new Brigade people until you're sure they're not spies."

"You scary smart," said Genna, a hint of a chuckle in her voice.

The repetitious squeak of boots and sneakers on steel rungs continued for a few minutes, the light increasing the deeper they climbed. Genna eventually stepped onto a concrete floor next to a wall with no door. Maya jumped off one rung from the bottom and landed next to her. While dusting grit from her hands, she gave the blank wall a quizzical stare. A pair of LED bricks on the opposite side hung above the entrance to a tunnel lined with plastiboard boxes, lumber, pipe scraps, and buckets. Distant water drips made the clammy air seem colder.

"There's no elevator door at the bottom?" Maya poked the shielding plastic, staring at the rainbow effect of the light on the metal threads inside.

"We're deeper than the basement now. The other end of that tunnel opens to the outside, near the start of the Dead Space. There's some cots and sleeping bags down here, if we wind up stuck."

Maya leaned to her left and took a step to peer into a shaft with rough hand-cut walls leading away from the small room. It smelled of damp earth and connected to a larger tunnel in the distance with concrete walls. Crude braces made of scrap metal held up the narrow section, failing to instill any sense of confidence. In fact, they made it *more* frightening, hinting that the ceiling would collapse at any second.

"It looks dangerous," whispered Maya.

Genna walked up behind her and grasped her shoulders. "It is, baby. But it beats gettin' caught by the Authority. Don't let me find out you bring friends down here. It ain't for that."

"I understand. I don't even want to go down that tunnel. It looks like it's going to cave in. Pick would just run off down there and get hurt."

"All right. Come on. Let's get on outta this dampness."

"Don't go?" Maya turned around and stared into Genna's eyes. "Please...."

Guilt radiated from the woman's face, but she sighed. "Baby, it's something I gotta do. We're still movin' that Xeno you helped us get to people who need it. Ain't dangerous for me. Worst thing'll happen is a couple of wildland scavvers mistake us for an easy target, but they ain't interested in a real fight."

Maya looked down, lip quivering. "I'm afraid something bad is going to happen."

"It'll only be a couple of days. I'll be back before you know it." She winked. "'Sides, I need ta earn my pay, an' those people need Xeno. I ain't gonna let more people die to that witch."

"What about your veteran pension?" Maya squeezed her tighter.

Face buried in Genna's shirt, she scowled, embarrassed at herself for the sudden bout of childish clinginess.

"Aww, that's barely enough ta survive. Maybe if it was just me, but you seen Sarah. Poor girl's wearin' rags."

Maya frowned. "That's not the pension. It's because her father is spending most of his money on beer. He says Foz is too expensive, but he won't go into the Sanc to better stores."

"I need to have a talk with that man. If I 'member right, we weren't too far off in rank. Pension of his oughta plenty be enough."

"Can I go with you? I promise I'll stay in the truck and keep my head down. If Vanessa *did* want to hurt me, wouldn't it be a better idea for me to be further away?"

Genna picked her up and carried her back to the ladder. "I don't want to take the chance that some wildlander gets a hair up his ass, shoots at the truck, and that bullet finds you." Her embrace tightened, forcing most of the air out of Maya's chest.

"Ngh." She squirmed. "Mom... can't... breathe."

When Genna relaxed her grip and looked her in the eye, tears had wet her cheeks. "I ain't gonna lose another one, you hear me, baby? If word got out we're carryin' Xeno, we might get hit. I don't want you anywhere near that kind of violence. What sort of momma would I be if I brought you into danger? No, baby. Yo' ass is stayin' right here in this building."

Maya crumbled under the weight of the emotion radiating from her and started crying. "But I don't want you to get hurt."

"Shh." Genna patted her back and rubbed her hair. "I gotta know your safe here. Need ta keep my head on what's around us out there, not on if somethin's gonna happen to you."

Wiping her eyes, Maya mumbled, "Okay," in a semi-whine of resignation.

Sitting around waiting for her mother to come back felt all too much like her old life. A couple deep breaths helped get her fear in check. She sniffled. Mom wasn't running off to a boardroom meeting or a fancy vacation in Paris; she needed to bring medicine to people Vanessa sentenced to death for the crime of being poor. Not that Ascendant *wanted* to kill them—much better to give Fade to people who could afford the cure. But not caring about the casualties almost seemed worse than deliberate killing. Her mother had to take this trip because people's lives depended on the Brigade.

Genna boosted her onto the ladder. "Stop at the second door. It's the only one we can open from this side. First one goes to the basement, and it don't open at all."

"How long are you going to be gone?" Maya climbed easy and fast, her eyes having adjusted to the dim light.

"Two days up, two days back. Shouldn't be too long *in* Philly. All we doin' is droppin' off boxes. Nothin' the Authority would even care about. Far as I know, we won't even be goin' inta the Sanc there, so ain't no worries 'bout a checkpoint."

Maya passed the basement door, holding her breath to stop tasting old furnace oil. At the second opening, extra hinges gave away the Brigade's modification. It took her only seconds to find the release catch, and she pulled the door open. She poked her head out into an empty hall, opposite the main stairway no one ever used due to the spoiled milk stink. After making sure no one could see her, she extended her right leg and made the leap from ladder to floor.

"Guess I don't need to explain the latch." Genna stepped out behind her and pulled the fake broken elevator door closed. "There's also a peep hole, but you're not tall enough. Usually, we listen for a bit to make sure no one's out there."

Maya looked left and right down the hall. "No one lives on the first floor, and I didn't hear anything."

"All right, baby. But it's better to take the extra minute to be safe."

She fought the quiver starting in her lip again, and looked down. "You're gonna leave now, aren't you?"

"Leave makes it sound like I ain't comin' back." Genna took her hand. "After Sam died, I gave up on carin' if I made it back from whatever the Brigade sent me to do. Gave up is what I did. Told myself I'd never be in that position again...."

Maya looked up. "When you first took me to that place, you kept standing by that big hole in the wall. I thought you were going to jump."

"You oughta hate me for what I did to you. At least be 'fraid of me."

"I'm not." Maya shrugged. "Does that mean I'm messed up in the head?"

Genna chuckled. "We all messed up in the head in this world. I tried to be so damn *hard* the world couldn't hurt me again, but you got under my armor. I saw the real face of evil on that woman when she said what she said. You gave me a reason to *be* again. Ain't nothin' gonna keep me away."

"Mom!" Maya pounced into a hug.

"After that witch, guess I ought not be surprised you think I'm a nice sort o' person."

"You are." Maya kept clinging, frowning off down the hall. "Vanessa's not even a person."

"I ain't got no excuse for how I treated you that night 'cept I hated Ascendant so much I forgot to be human." Genna shook her head with a guilty sigh. "You saved my life too, and I didn't deserve it. Brought me back from that cold, dark place I'd gone. You right. Sam woulda been pissed at me."

"I wasn't really scared until Vanessa told you to kill me and meant it." Maya tapped the toe of her right sneaker into the rotten carpet. "I was brave 'til then because I thought the Authority would find me." Her voice dropped to an almost-whisper. "They weren't even looking."

Genna's lip quivered and she wiped her eyes.

"You didn't kidnap me from my home." Maya held her head high. "You exfiltrated me from a secure installation and brought me home." She smiled. "How sick is that? Being tied up and stuffed in a bag is like a... *good* memory for me."

"Damn, baby. I'm so sorry." Genna took a knee and stared into her eyes. "None of this is right."

"Stop apologizing. I'm happy here with you. That's why I'm upset you're going to go risk your life."

Genna stood, took Maya's hand, and walked toward the fire stairs to avoid the stink. "Sayin' sorry for the kinda life you had before. No momma oughta treat their kid like that."

"Are you going to teach me how to shoot a gun?"

"I dunno." Genna examined the ceiling. "I'm hopin' by the time you're old 'nuff fer me ta let you touch one, you won't need to."

"Vanessa's got expensive lawyers and lots of money." Maya frowned. "I'll be old like you before she's gone."

Genna leaned her head back and laughed. "Old? Who you callin' old? I ain't even thirty yet."

"Twenty-nine?" asked Maya.

"Eight," said Genna with a hint of haughtiness.

Maya grinned. "To me, that's old."

Genna chuckled the rest of the way up to the seventh floor, and Sarah's apartment. The redhead answered the knock once again wearing her toga-dress-curtain thing.

"Hi," said Sarah. "Uhh, I went into your place to get my dress back. Hope it's okay."

"Hey." Maya waved.

"Of course, sweetie. Your dad here?" asked Genna.

Sarah smirked and muttered, "Where else would he be?" She took a step back, pulling the door open wide. "Yeah. 'Mon in."

The Dad occupied his favorite spot on the well-worn couch, attention glued to the battered flat-panel TV mounted on the wall. Frazzled ginger hair gave him an electrocuted look, and traces of grey showed generously in his short beard. He raised his metal right arm, a spindly prosthetic in no way intended for combat duty. The three-fingered gripper at the end whirred as he waved.

"Gen..." He coughed a couple times and pushed himself upright. "Rollin' out?"

"Billy." Genna nodded once. "Yeah. Gotta pull an escort detail. Basic milk run. Should be back in four days ideal, six days long. Makin' sure you're still up to keep an eye on the little one 'til I'm back."

The Dad wiped his nose with his living hand. "Roger that. Got plenty of rations. Not a problem. Where ya goin'?"

"Op-sec, Billy, you know I can't share that." Genna winked.

Sarah stood at Maya's left, wide-eyed staring at her father, her mouth open.

"Right." He chuckled. "Sorry. Shouldn't have asked. Sergeant Brennan'd tear me a new one if he heard me ask. Hope they at least got a bird or two watchin' after ya. Them NoKos are some sneaky sumbitches."

"Not sure." Genna shrugged. "Low priority mover, so I doubt EUCOM is gonna divert anything our way. Intel says there ain't NoKos within a thousand miles of here."

Maya glanced back and forth between the adults, feeling confused for a second before Sarah's downtrodden expression demanded her attention. "What?" she whispered.

"Yeah, fubar like usual. Them EUCOM bastards don't care every time they pinch pennies, people fuckin' die." The Dad grumbled. "You get back here in one piece, got that?"

"Sure thing, Hawthorne."

The Dad fell back into his seat as Genna turned to face Maya. "Okay, baby. Time for me to get this done. You be good, right?"

"Yes, Mom." Maya shivered. "Please be careful."

"I will, baby. I will. It's—"

Maya put a hand over Genna's mouth. "Stop saying it's easy. Don't jinx yourself."

"All right." Genna laughed. She picked Maya up into a long hug, set her back on her feet, and trudged out of the apartment.

Sarah fast-walked down the hall to her room.

Head tilted in confusion, Maya followed. She crept in the door to find Sarah sitting on the edge of the bed, weeping into her hands.

"What's wrong?"

Sarah looked up. "My dad still thinks he's in the Army. They were talking like they're in France or Germany or wherever. He sounded so... normal. Like he hadn't even had any beer."

"He misses it," said Maya in a soft tone. "He loved being in the military."

"Yeah."

The Dad shouted random half-pronounced insults at the television, as if he couldn't make up his mind what to call someone before bellowing, "You're a bloody bum who cannae outrun a shite floatin' in a pool wit' a rocket up yer ass!"

Sarah blushed. "Sorry."

"It's okay. Ascendant people have said worse things around me." She shrugged.

"I wish he'd talk more to me like he did with Genna. Mostly I get grunts, smiles; sometimes he points." Sarah sat on the edge of her bed, teetering on the verge of another explosion of tears.

"He loves you." Maya sat next to her and put an arm around her back. "He's got mental health issues. When Mom started talking military stuff, it probably triggered some kind of flashback to a part of his head that's still back in time. It's not because he doesn't like you. He can't help it."

Sarah leaned her head against Maya's and wiped at her eyes. "Thanks. Yeah, I guess that's possible. So, what do you want to do?"

The Dad wailed in anguish as if he'd watched a friend die. "Damn idiot! How could ya miss that catch? Stop grabbin' yer balls and grab the one flyin' at yer head!"

"I dunno." Maya tapped her sneakers together, feeling guilty that none of the other kids in the building had any. She thought back to living in the penthouse apartment; she never used to wear shoes inside—mostly since her choice of footwear varied only in the height of the heels. She loved her sneakers and felt bad for doing so. "I asked Genna if she would get you some shoes."

The Dad blurted a series of unintelligible insults at the TV.

Sarah gasped. "That's too much money. I'd be afraid to even wear them. Someone will steal them. Please don't waste her money on me. I don't wanna get jumped. The last time we got robbed, they had a gun—we got lucky."

"How is that lucky? They left all of you naked in the street." Maya blinked.

"If they didn't have a gun, they woulda tried to sneak up and hit me in the head with a rock or something. Then I might've been dead too." She picked at her curtain-dress. "If I look like I got nothin' worth taking, I'm safer. Not even Foz would buy this."

Maya scowled at the floor. "We need to change things. The Authority should protect people from thieves."

"We're Nons. They don't care about us." Sarah scratched idly at her arm.

"You're a Citizen." Maya poked her in the side. "Your dad's a veteran. I *was* a Citizen, but the bitch revoked it. I don't care."

Sarah shook her head. "We live in the Hab. We don't matter. Citizens live in the Sanc. Not like I have a stamp on my forehead that says 'Citizen.' Maybe I'll go somewhere else when I grow up. Like the wildlands."

"What?" Maya gawked. "Are you serious?"

"It's not as bad as they tell everyone. It's kinda like camping. No Authority, no one to bother you. Some people live in small groups out in nature, farming and stuff." She grasped the mattress on either side of her knees, leaning forward, smiling at the ceiling. "Imagine the sun comin' down through the trees, the wind in your hair, not worrying about anyone hurting you."

"Sounds too good to be true. The AuthNet says the settlements out there always fight with each other like medieval days. Some even take slaves. They don't have electricity either. It's really primitive and filthy."

Sarah stopped scooting her feet back and forth on the rug and stared at her. "The Authority just says that to keep everyone scared and in the city. If people knew the truth, they'd all leave."

"People like comforts. Maybe the Nons would be happier out there, and the Citizens wouldn't have anyone left to do the crappy jobs."

"Yeah."

"Could be some truth, too. I don't really think it's safe anywhere." Maya fidgeted at her shirt.

Rapid, soft pounding on the door preceded Pick, Anton, and Marcus shouting, "Faerie!" at the same time. Sarah suppressed an eye roll. Only The Dad and Maya bothered to call her by her real name.

Maya twisted toward the door. "I think they want us to play."

"Okay." Sarah stood. "If you wanna."

"'Kay." Maya pushed herself to her feet and followed Sarah out to the living room.

The redhead leaned over to whisper at her father's ear. He gave her a hug with his non-metal arm, kissing her atop the head, and smiled.

"Stay alert, luv. Donnae go too far."

Maya glanced at the TV displaying the glimmering, flashing spectacle of a football game, happening somewhere in another Sanctuary Zone along the east coast. Players wandered about with no urgency, collecting into some manner of formation. The camera zoomed in on a huge man, about Moth's size but without metal arms. He grinned, pointed at something far off, and threw the ball to a man in white-and-black stripes. She'd heard the suits around boardrooms complain about how only a handful of teams existed now, unlike before the war. They always argued over Ascendant sponsoring the Baltimore team. The voice of Walter Michaelson, a senior VP of marketing, floated by in her thoughts: *Football's good. Gotta keep the commoners occupied.*

"'Kay, Dad," said Sarah. "You need anything 'fore I go out?"

He mumbled and waved his metal arm toward the kitchen. Sarah nodded and jogged to the fridge as the front door opened, revealing the twins, Anton and Marcus, with little Pick beside them. The six-year-old's orb of dark brown hair looked wilder than ever, as if he'd stuck his finger in a power outlet. Pick's olive-drab pants ended in tatters halfway down his thighs, and, like most days, he didn't bother with a shirt. Handprints marked his chest where he'd tried (and failed) to wipe some dark substance away. The twins had almost-matching striped white/blue shirts and beige shorts, clothes they got for their tenth birthday a few weeks ago. Their hair had started to puff up into afros, so odds were high that Book would soon trim it.

The *whump* of the refrigerator door closing came from the kitchen a few seconds before Sarah returned, pulling a beer open on her way across the room to hand it to her father. She started for the door but hesitated when Maya didn't move.

Worry about Genna kept Maya's mood dark; she didn't really feel like going out to play with the other kids. Half of her wanted to go sit alone somewhere, but she didn't want to hurt Sarah's feelings, and having her to talk to *did* make the dread easier to deal with. The boys scampered off, all cheering or yelling, "Come on!"

Sarah stared at her, legs frozen in mid-stride about halfway to the door. Maya caved after a long, pointed look. More for Sarah's benefit, she let the girl take her hand and went with her out the door.

[4]

TRAINING

Maya sat cross-legged on the ground in the parking lot behind the apartment building. An unusually clear sky bathed the area in warm sunlight despite a hint of chill in the breeze. Weeds and grass struggled up from numerous cracks in the paving, trapping the occasional empty cup or plastic carton riding the wind. A hint of Mexican food crossed her nose—probably Pick's sister cooking. Naida could do amazing things with even cheap food, making it a treat whenever her turn to feed the building's children came up. Pick didn't mind it if people used his real name, Ruben, though only his sister bothered. Unlike Sarah, the nickname didn't bug him. Though, it didn't really annoy Sarah enough to complain to anyone other than Maya.

Pick, the six-year-old pirate captain, stood in the middle of his huge, derelict car (pirate warship) while the twins played the part of crew. With near-identical outfits, Maya couldn't tell them apart save for assuming Marcus to be the one who kept looking at her.

Near the left-side fence, Sarah sat on a swing Zoe had made from scrap metal, chain, and a length of cushioned board. Emily's mother fixed things in the building, more out of a mixture of kindness and ability than any reward. Mr. Mason had been the official superintendent, but the only thing he ever seemed interested in putting his hands on were young girls. Zoe did all the maintenance work.

Sarah didn't swing with much effort, though watching Pick and the twins pretend she was a dangerous mermaid chasing their boat did tease a smile onto Maya's lips.

Emily, arms out to the side, attempted to walk while keeping her feet on the narrow trails of grass zigzagging across the lot. Heel to toe, she crept around as if on a balance beam, singing softly to herself.

The whirr of an Authority drone in the distance made everyone pause. Maya searched the sky for it, but the way the fan noise echoed from nearby buildings offered little clue as to its direction.

"Sea dragon!" shouted Pick. "Turn hard left."

"You mean hard-a-port?" asked Marcus.

"Naw, man." Anton shook his head. "Left is starboard."

"Nuh-uh." Marcus pointed right. "Starboard is right."

Anton gestured to the left. "Yeah, starboard is right, as in the right answer for turnin' left."

"I'm the captain, and I say we call left, left." Pick pointed to the side. "Turn 'fore the dragon gets us!"

The high-pitched wail of the drone faded to silence. Since it hadn't appeared, Maya relaxed.

"Hey," chirped Emily.

Maya glanced to her right at pink-painted toenails upon a tuft of brown grass. "Hi."

The younger girl squatted beside her, fancy doll dress rustling. "What's wrong?"

The woeful look on her face made Maya feel bad for causing it. "Genna's gotta drive somewhere far away and it's dangerous."

Emily grinned. "The faeries told me she'll be okay."

Faeries... Maya resisted the urge to roll her eyes. They called Sarah Faerie due to her being Irish, but this kid thought *actual* faeries (tiny people) lived in their building too. Pretending to see them might be one of those 'child' things Maya couldn't quite figure out—or maybe the girl suffered hallucinations. "That's good."

"Genna's tough." Emily lowered herself to sit and stretched her legs out. "Daddy said they're bringing medicine to sick people. They don't gotta shoot anyone for that."

Only if bandits want to steal the Xeno. "Yeah."

The boys erupted in a sword fight, battling imaginary monsters coming up out of the water. A pair of men, gangers by appearance, walking by the rear fence looked in at the sea battle and smiled. Maya watched them until they passed out of sight, confused by thugs grinning at a bunch of kids screaming and waving fake swords. According to the AuthNet, Hab gangs were dangerous and to be avoided at all costs.

"What?" asked Emily.

"Huh?" Maya glanced at her.

"You're making a funny face." Emily crossed her eyes and stuck out her tongue.

"Oh. Those two men look like they're in a gang, but they smiled."

"It's the dosers who're bad," whispered Emily. "The others are nice to us."

Maya sighed in her mind. *Yeah, until we're older.*

"Rubén, *almuerzo!*" called Naida from a window above and behind. "*Entra ahora.*"

Pick paused mid-swordfight, standing on the roof of the car, and looked up toward the building. He cupped his hands around his mouth and shouted, "*¿Pueden mis amigos comer también?*"

"*Si, por supuesto.*" The metallic scrape of a closing window cut the air.

"C'mon," yelled Pick. "Food!"

He jumped to the ground and sprinted into the building with the cheering twins close behind. Maya waited for Sarah to get off the swing and trudge over before she stood. She seemed a little too sad over her father having a lucid conversation earlier. There had to be more going on, but what? Maya forced a smile, despite her worry that something would happen to Genna. Being gloomy would only make her friend's mood worsen. They'd be sharing a bedroom later that night, and when they had a moment of privacy, she'd try to get her to talk.

"Hey," muttered Sarah.

"Hey." Maya put on her drug-advertising smile but only held it for a few seconds. She'd never been genuine on the air, and doing it to Sarah felt even more wrong. "You okay?"

"Yeah, I guess." Sarah offered a halfhearted shrug.

Maya headed for the door, grunting as she tried to haul the old aluminum frame open. Sarah helped, and the metal slid apart with a scrape that made all the muscles in her back lock up for an instant.

Emily ducked under their arms and zoomed into the stairwell. Together, they shoved the door aside and entered the hall, heading for the fire stairs and Pick's home on the third floor.

A *bang* came from the right, inside Mr. Mason's ground-floor apartment, seconds before the door swung open.

Sarah screamed and grabbed on to Maya from behind.

Maya went wide-eyed and stood statue still. *He's back! He knows who I am. He's gonna know what I did.* She attempted to dart to the stairwell before Mason could see her, but Sarah, paralyzed with fear, held her fast.

A man, older looking than The Dad with olive skin, stormed into the hallway. His face had a faint appearance of artificiality, which made Maya suspect he managed wrinkles with the same treatment Ascendant executives used. A hint of silver above his ears put him in grandpa territory. His dark suit and short, neat black hair gave off a sense of wealth. Upon noticing the girls, he raised a quizzical eyebrow.

Not Mr. Mason.

Maya covered her mouth with both hands, too relieved to do anything but breathe.

Shuffling and bumping from the doorway behind the man suggested multiple people moved heavy things around inside.

Sarah, trembling, leaned her weight on Maya, as if only her grip kept the girl from collapsing to the floor. She gulped for air, standing rigid, too terrified to even try to run away.

Emily looked back and forth between them, confused.

"Are you all right, girls?" asked the unfamiliar man. He took a few steps closer. "What are you screaming about?"

Maya puffed up her chest, standing protectively in front of her taller friend. "Who are you?"

The man offered a pleasant smile and gestured around at nothing in particular. "I am Mr. Narov. I'm the owner of this building."

"Oh. Hello." Maya put on her polite smile. "Why are you in *that* apartment?"

"C'mon," whispered Emily before running into the fire stairs.

"The former superintendent will not be returning. We are cleaning the place out." A sneer of distaste curled Mr. Narov's upper lip.

"You saw what kind of pictures he has, didn't you?" Maya narrowed her eyes.

Narov's disgust shifted to suspicion for an instant before he looked horrified. "How did you...?"

Oops! Maya put on her widest-eyed, most frightened face. "Mr. Mason invited me inside. He had a washing machine and wanted to clean my clothes. He said it would be okay if I didn't have anything on while we played video games. I didn't trust him, so I ran away." She wrapped her arms over Sarah's where they encircled her. "He tried to get my friend, too. That's why she screamed. When the door flew open, we thought it was him coming after us."

Mr. Narov's face reddened. "Damn, miserable son of a—" He closed his eyes and let out a slow breath. "I had no idea what sort of man he was. If I'd have known...."

"Was?" asked Sarah in a small voice.

"Yes, *was.*" Mr. Narov gestured at the apartment. "We are cleaning the place out because he died."

"How did he die?" asked Maya.

"I'm not sure. I only received a notification from the Authority because I was his registered employer. Word is that he'd been arrested. I've had investigators going over my records for days now based on whatever that man had been involved with." He pinched the bridge of his nose. "That abomination, his preoccupation with young girls, was icing on the cake. Found that by accident when they were after him for something else. They didn't tell me a damn thing about it, but I doubt they're tearing my offices apart over those images."

Maya shook her head. "They thought he was trying to assassinate that woman who owns Ascendant."

"What?" Narov stooped closer to eye level. "Where did you hear that?"

"People talking." She squeezed Sarah's hand into her chest. "Someone said he had secret information. I dunno. I'm only nine."

Three men in blue-grey jumpsuits exited the apartment in single file, lugging large plastiboard cartons to the front door.

"Well, girls, don't you worry another minute about that man. He won't be back. I'm sorry for not checking up on him more thoroughly. I'll make sure the next super is trustworthy."

"What about Zoe?" asked Maya. "She does all the work anyway. That other man didn't do anything. Did you know there's like a whole wall on the ninth floor that's missing? This guy never did anything to fix it."

Mr. Narov glanced upward. "Ninth? Hmm. No, I never heard anything about a hole in the wall."

"It's more than a hole," said Sarah. "Most of the wall is missing."

"I'll check into it." He sighed. "Again, no one had sent me any word of significant structural issues."

Maya raised one eyebrow. "If you go around back behind the lot you can see inside the ninth floor from the outside. It's surprising the tenth story hasn't fallen in yet. You could probably get more people renting here if it didn't look ready to collapse."

He lowered his gaze to Maya, tilting his head to the side as a look of recognition came over him. She held her breath, dreading how he'd react if he realized who she was. Sarah had ceased trembling but kept clinging to her from behind. His lips parted, but before he could speak, the workers came back in and approached with questioning expressions. Mr. Narov stood back to his full height. "Get rid of everything and spray it down." He suppressed a shudder. "I need to check something upstairs."

With that, Mr. Narov nodded goodbye and strolled off to the main stairwell. As soon as he opened the door, his face scrunched up.

"No one uses that stairway 'cause it stinks," said Sarah, not loud enough for him to hear.

"Are you okay?" Maya turned to face her. "You're still kinda shaking a little."

Sarah bit her lip. "I almost peed when that door flew open."

Maya hugged her. "He's dead. We'll never see him again."

"I can't believe it worked." Sarah eyed the apartment and edged backward toward the fire stairs.

"Yeah... I didn't know the Authority would kill him. Well, I kinda did, but didn't really expect it."

Sarah pushed open the door to the fire stairs. "Do you feel bad?"

"Nope. Not about him."

"Hey, you guys coming?" shouted Pick. "Enchiladas are gettin' cold."

"Yeah!" yelled Sarah.

"Forget him. Pretend like he never existed." Maya grinned and ran up the stairs, pulling Sarah by the hand.

CHICKEN ENCHILADAS MADE ODD NOISES FROM THE DEPTHS OF Maya's stomach. The cloying, something-like-rotten-egg smell that pervaded the basement didn't sit well with a recent meal. She stood on a box to reach the controls of an old cabinet-style arcade game where she controlled a stick figure in the middle of a room. Alien robots came trickling in from doors at the four sides with increasing speed, and if any reached her character, she'd die.

At a pause between levels, she glanced at the tunnel of old kitchen ranges, fridges, washers, dryers, appliances, junk, ceiling fans, and furniture that led to the exit, all stuff from before the war that the building management kept on hand as replacements. Of course, most of it had sat down here too long to be of any use.

On her left, Sarah sat on a chair in front of a driving game, another old arcade machine Zoe had resurrected, titled *RoadBlasters*. The cheesy digital engine noise blurred into the continuous drone of alien robots and the *bleeping* of her laser gun. Sarah cheered as a little flying thing swooped in and dropped a roof-mounted machine gun on her car.

An hour or so into playing the robot game, Maya noticed a pattern in the way the enemies entered, and started firing at doorways before they appeared, timing it so her laser blasts reached the openings as soon as the threats came on screen.

Pick flopped on his chest behind them, atop the squarish patch of carpet where multiple layers had been stacked to create a soft place to play. He had his box of comic books close at his side and balanced his chin on both hands while reading one.

Marcus and Anton sat in the square as well, backs against a few rolls of carpet Zoe'd set up around the edges. The twins had evidently eaten too much, and lay there holding their bellies rather than hit the ping-pong table or air hockey machine like they usually did.

Emily sat in a nest of pillows at the corner of the carpeted area closest to the arcade games, playing with a bunch of dolls. That *still* didn't make any sense to Maya, but listening to the girl pretend voices for each plastic toy did make her smile a little. Before she could wonder if she somehow failed at being a little girl because she saw no purpose to dolls, the robots started attacking again.

"Shit!" yelled Sarah, seconds after a digitized explosion noise. She thumped her fist on the console next to the steering wheel. "That car rammed me on purpose." Grumbling, she poked the start button, slammed the 'shift' to the bottom, and stomped on the pedal.

Marcus appeared at Maya's side, watching the screen. He stood close enough for her to feel his body heat and radiated awkwardness. She found it amusing but concentrated too much on the game to smile. It didn't take long for him to relax, and he gawked at the screen.

"Oh, wow! You're on level thirty-six!" He twisted to look back at his brother. "Anton, check this out! Maya's on thirty-six!"

The ten-year-old grunted like an old man as he stood, still with a hand on his gut, and wandered over. "Damn... she's good at this."

"There's a pattern," said Maya. "The bad guys always appear in the same sequence, but the door it starts from changes. Like if it starts at the top, they spawn two top, two right, one bottom, one top, one left, then two each from top, left, right, bottom. After that, the start door changes but it's the same pattern."

"Awesome," said Marcus.

"You gonna kiss her?" asked Anton.

"Better question would be if I'm going to punch him," said Maya.

"Ooh!" Anton cringed, grinning.

Marcus looked much the way a deer might two seconds before being hit by a giant truck. "Eww, no."

Maya tapped the joystick to fire lasers, two down, two left, two right, one up. Her thoughts matched the 'eww no' part, but she didn't say anything. She'd watched enough adults around the Ascendant offices to understand at least on an intellectual level that someday she'd probably feel different about boys, but for the time being, she prepared to pound a fist into his lips if they got too close.

"Aww, we all know you like her." Anton gave him a playful punch in the shoulder.

"We wanted ta go scavvin'. You wanna go?" Marcus smiled.

"Hope we find 'nother smashed drone," said Pick. "That was cool!"

"No it wasn't." Maya took advantage of a level break to shoot him a glare. "Those drones are dangerous."

"Thirty-seven! Holy crap!" shouted Marcus.

"Even Emily never got past level five." Anton patted Maya on the back. "You're kickin' ass."

"That game is stupid," muttered Emily. "It's just stick figures."

Sarah twisted herself to the left, leaning as she pulled a hard turn. She downshifted and stomped the brake. A less-loud digitized explosion sounded, and she laughed before cranking the wheel to the right and accelerating. "Missed me, bitch."

"So can you go?" asked Anton.

"I don't think I'm supposed to go outside." Maya tensed as a robot got close; she mashed the button as fast as she could move her hand, barely managing to avoid death. "I, uhh... guess I gotta ask Sarah's dad."

"He'll say yes." Pick pushed himself up to kneel, sitting back on his heels. "He thinks it's 'good training' for us."

Sarah crashed her digital car but didn't pound the game, instead slouching in the seat. Maya glanced over, worried at her friend's deflated posture. In that two-second distraction, a robot exploited the lapse in her laser barrage and got her.

"Aww, damn," said Marcus.

After the death animation, the game prompted her to enter her name for the number one high score. She tapped in 'MAY' and hit the button to save it.

"Damn, ain't no one ever gonna beat that score." Anton patted her on the back again.

"We'll be okay. There's more blueberries around." Pick climbed over the wall of rolled carpet around the square play area and walked up behind them. "And Faerie's gotta gun now."

"It's not a gun. It's a Hornet," mumbled Sarah.

"Same thing." Pick held his hands up as if holding a pistol. "Take out bad guys with it and you don't gotta feel bad for really hurtin' someone."

"Them shits hurt, Pick, but she won't kill no one." Marcus whistled. "Saw a blueberry nail some guy with one. Dude crapped his pants right there."

"Eww," said Emily.

Sarah turned ninety degrees in the chair to face everyone. "I don't wanna shoot anyone with it 'cause they're gonna remember and come after me. Better we just run."

"Still, you should bring it case we get cornered again." Anton's faced darkened with blush. "Sides, Marcus saw a hole inna building what wasn't there before. We gotta check it out 'fore someone else finds it."

"A hole?" asked Maya. "If it's falling apart, we shouldn't go in there."

"No, a little hole." Marcus held his hands close. "Like a drone crashed."

"So?" asked Maya. "Those are too dangerous."

"Aww, yeah. We gotta!" Pick bounced on his toes.

Anton shook his head. "Not one o' them drones. Like the type they use ta carry stuff from Sanc to Sanc."

"Come on, you gotta go with us." Marcus smiled.

"I gotta ask permission."

Sarah looked down. "He'll say okay. Pick's right. He thinks it's training."

Mom wouldn't say yes. Or would she? If they were gonna come after me, they woulda done it by now. If she really believed I'm in danger, she wouldn't have gone with the Brigade.

"Okay, but we shouldn't stay out long." Maya looked at Sarah. "Unless you think we should stay inside."

"It's been quiet. C'mon. Gotta get my bag." Sarah headed for the maze/tunnel of junk.

"Be right back," said Maya.

She followed Sarah to her apartment on the seventh floor. The Dad slept in his chair, an empty beer can a short distance from his hand on the rug. He didn't reek of alcohol, so she figured he'd just been tired.

Once in her bedroom, Sarah hiked up her dress, holding it under her armpits with no trace of hesitation or embarrassment. She grabbed a black nylon holster from the closet and attached it across her stomach with a click strap before stuffing the pistol-shaped Hornet in it and letting the fabric fall down to conceal the stunner. She'd become so skinny, the device didn't appear obvious under her clothing.

It hadn't been that long ago that The Dad ambush-trained the pair of them on how to use it. His voice narrated in the back of her mind, explaining how the Hornet could fire stun darts at distant threats or be used as a close-defense weapon with two metal prods above and below the barrel. That it held thirteen darts on a full magazine seemed like an unlucky omen.

Maya tapped her sneaker on the rug, contemplating taking them off, but wanted to keep them—especially since they'd likely encounter roaches. What was the point of having shoes if she couldn't wear them? After having all her clothes taken at gunpoint, Sarah had to be traumatized, expecting dosers around every corner waiting to do it again. *Maybe she's making it sound worse than it really is?*

Sarah grabbed the fanny pack she kept her lock picks in from under the bed and put it on before adjusting her dress to somewhat hide it. "Ready?"

"Almost." Maya took a knee and pulled open the Velcro on her left sneaker.

"I'm not jealous. Keep them on if you want. I don't think anyone's gonna steal from *you* after your face was all over the Hab." Sarah smiled. "It doesn't bother me that Genna got you shoes, or Emily's got a fancy dress, or Book gives new shirts and pants to the twins three times a year."

"Does he make them dress the same on purpose or do they like to?" Maya re-secured the Velcro and grinned.

Sarah giggled. "I dunno. C'mon. Better go quick so we can get back inside before it's dark."

"Why do they want me to go? I'm not really good at scavving." Maya led the way across the apartment to the front door.

"Numbers." Sarah picked up the empty can and carried it to the kitchen.

Maya went out into the hall. "Huh?"

"One kid alone is asking for trouble. Two kids isn't as bad, but still risky. Three, less chance someone will try something. Four, even less."

"Oh." Maya bit her lip. "That's kinda scary."

"It's the dosers and the weirdos we have to watch out for. The gangs don't bother kids. Oh, and those creepy Jeva people will grab kids too, but most of us are too old."

Maya blinked, thinking back to the two she'd run into. "Really? They seemed nice. Little dumb and weird, but nice."

"You're too old to just grab." Sarah shoved open the fire stair door and started down. "They take like *little* kids so they can fill up their heads with that crap about their talking statue and some invisible man in the sky who loves us all. Like anyone would believe that crap if they didn't grow up hearing it all the time. Dad says they gotta 'program them young.'"

"Oh. Well, they *did* try to talk me into joining." Maya laughed. "I almost pity them."

"Huh? Pity?"

"Feel bad for," said Maya. "Kinda like how I do for eleven-year-olds who don't know what pity means."

Sarah spun and gave her an intense hurt look for a second or two before she crossed her eyes and raspberried. Maya couldn't help herself and giggled.

Both laughing, the girls rushed down the stairs together.

[5]

GOODWILL

The boys plus Emily met them in the foyer between the main stairwell and the hall to the parking lot by the super's apartment. A man in a blue-grey jumpsuit carried a spool of red hose in from the street, unwinding it as he went. He glanced at the kids only enough not to step on any of them and disappeared into Mason's former apartment.

Pick tried to step on the red hose, but didn't weigh enough to crimp it.

"What they doin'?" asked Anton.

"Spraying to get pervert off the walls," muttered Maya.

"Huh?" Anton looked at her.

"Disinfecting," said Maya. "The guy who used to live there is dead."

"Mason?" asked Marcus. "That dude was a major creep."

"Yeah." Anton nodded. "Book says it ain't good ta talk bad 'bout a dead man, but good on that guy bein' dead."

"Who?" asked Emily.

"No one," said Sarah. "Come on."

"Rah!" Pick yelled and darted out the front door.

The twins followed. Emily dashed after them with Maya and Sarah behind. More people than usual walked outside Block 13, some in a hurry to get wherever they were going, others loitering, and a handful still protesting Ascendant control of the Authority. Four-fanned blue drones as big as motorcycles glided overhead, electronic eyes constantly observing. Their presence had definitely increased since she'd first arrived here when she barely saw one in the span of a week. Whenever a drone got close, Sarah hunched a little forward, trying to hide the Hornet.

"Relax," whispered Maya. "It's not obvious, and they're not illegal."

"That doesn't mean they won't take it away from a kid." Sarah picked up her pace not to fall too far behind the others. "Slow down, Ruben. Don't spread out so much." She put a hand on Emily's shoulder.

"Can't believe Zoe let her go with us," said Maya. "She's little."

"I'm eight," said Emily. "Pick's only six, and you're nine. If I'm little, you're little too."

Maya couldn't argue that. *And I'm sure the faeries told her we'd be fine.*

"Besides, the faeries said we'd be okay." Emily smiled.

Maya grinned to herself.

"Hey there," said a loud man on the right. "Well, heck. It *is* you."

The kids all froze in place as a shaggy brown-haired guy in a long olive-drab coat walked out of an alcove between two high-rise buildings. He zeroed in on Maya and ambled toward her. Pick zipped into his path, as if his scrawny little self would slow the guy down. Anton and Marcus moved behind him, protectively in front of Maya.

Sarah squeezed her hand. Emily smiled at the man.

"Easy." He raised his hands. "No trouble from me, just wanted ta thank her for sayin' what we all been thinkin' for so long but no one had the balls to say."

"Hi," sing-songed Emily, waving.

"Hello there." The man grinned at her.

The boys relaxed, evidently regarding Emily's trust of the man as some manner of supernatural asshole-detector.

"You kicked a nest o' hornets there, kiddo." The man extended his right arm. "Nice work."

Maya stared at him for a few seconds before her fear ebbed enough for her to remember that sometimes people shook hands, though never had anyone bothered with a small girl. Usually, she got ignored, head-patted, or nodded at. "Thanks." She tentatively accepted his handshake, prepared to yank her arm back if he tried a grab and run, but he let go after a few seconds.

"You've got us all fired up now. 'Course, some don't think you're real... or really out here with us." He stuffed his hands in his coat pockets. "Never thought I'd see the day. Damn good of you, child. Name's Rusty." He pointed over his shoulder with his thumb. "Live in this one here, fourth floor number six. F'ya ever need anythin', ya let me know."

"Thanks. I'm sorry things aren't changing faster." She sighed.

"Not your fault. Don't blame the match 'cause the wood burns slow." He winked, chuckled, and backed up to lean once more on the wall. "Keep yerselves safe."

The kids resumed their walk, once again with Pick in the lead.

A block and a half later, they overtook a young woman with light brown skin a touch fairer than Maya's. A black poncho covered most of her, though she had her hood down and an air-filter mask with slow-blinking blue lights dangled loose around her neck. She glanced up as the faster-moving children passed her on both sides. After a double-take, she jogged to keep up.

"Maya?"

She looked up at the woman, more likely an older teenager. Sensing gratitude in the stranger's expression, she nodded. "Yes. Hello."

"Wow, you're such a little thing. You looked bigger on the screen. Hey, you know, I like that baggy shirt and pants look way more than those stupid glittery dresses they used to make you wear."

"Uhh, thanks," muttered Maya, hooking her thumbs in her pants pockets. "Most people out here don't care *what* they wear—they just want to *have* clothes."

"Aww, this ain't the Dead Space. Girl gotta have a little style." The woman winked. "You all dressed up like a little revolutionary, ain't ya." She made finger guns at nothing. "You hear what's goin' on in the Sanc?"

Maya's interest in the conversation bloomed. "No?"

The woman's eyes went wide as she thrust both hands into the air, fingers splayed. "The Authority goin' crazy in the Sanc, tryin' ta prove 'Cendant don't own 'em an' shit. Ain't so many drones now, lotta blueberries. Some of 'em are even talkin' to Nons."

"Dat's 'cause them drones is all out here in the Hab," muttered Marcus.

Sarah smirked, eyes narrowed with doubt.

"I tend bar at HiveMind—oh wait, you's little. Probably not know what that means. Forget it."

"I'm nine, not stupid." Maya smiled. "I know what bars are."

"Yeah, even Pick knows what bars are," said Anton.

"Like on a jail?" asked Emily.

Sarah snickered.

"Aww, ain't she adorable." The teen patted Emily on the head. "So, like I hear people talkin'. They investigatin' yo momma's company fo' real now."

"Vanessa is not my mother," said Maya in a flat tone.

"Sorry." The woman winced. "Say you fo' real walk away from all that money to slum it out here with us?"

"Unless you're hallucinating me, I fo' real did."

Sarah giggled.

Maya sighed. "Sorry, that was snotty. You mentioned Vanessa and I...."

"S'awright." The woman patted her back. "Good on you for what you done."

After a wink, the woman turned and went back the way they'd been walking. Maya relaxed. Perhaps Genna had a point. Change came slow. She'd imagined that after her video message played, Vanessa would get arrested, or Ascendant would collapse, or *poof*—everything would be perfect. Evidently, Emily wasn't the only little girl in their building who believed in faerie tales.

Pick took a right at the next corner, brazenly walking past a cluster of seventeen-to-twenty-something gang punks lounging on steps leading to an elevated courtyard in front of a former office tower. Maya's chest tightened when the crowd took notice of their group, but none gave them more than a cursory 'oh, just some kids' glance.

An open door to a dive bar three buildings later let scraps of conversation into the street. Men discussed a conflict between the Authority and Ascendant security teams that escalated to a fistfight. One man said some of the security forces got arrested; the other didn't believe the Authority would dare.

Maya slowed to keep listening, but Sarah pulled her along, whispering, "Don't fall behind. You don't wanna get caught alone."

The redhead seemed to mother the group like she took care of The Dad, and occasionally whisper-shouted at Pick to slow down. Maya looked around at streets and alleys, sometimes worried dosers would mug them all for everything they could sell to score some chems, and sometimes wondering if Sarah's experience had left her paranoid. Granted, a pair of dosers had tried to rob her and Genna almost two weeks ago, but they had been in the Dead Space at the time.

She grinned at the memory of Genna beating the snot out of them.

"There." Pick pointed up.

A high-rise much taller than their apartment building caught the waning late afternoon sunlight, gleaming harsh orange. Maya squinted against the glare, but after a few seconds, made out an irregular hole close to the top. Something had struck the building between two windows hard enough to smash through the wall and wind up inside. From the ground, she guessed an object about four-by-four feet.

"C'mon!" yelled Pick.

Despite an approaching e-car, the boy sprinted into the road, making Sarah scream at him. He jumped up onto the hood of an abandoned wreck a good three seconds before the functional car went by. The driver shook his fist at Pick, his yell reduced to an unintelligible murmur by the closed windows.

Sarah held Emily back by the collar of her dress and looked for more traffic. The twins checked for approaching cars too, rushing across afterward. Pick jumped from the hood to the street when they went by, and sprinted past them to the main entrance, a heavy-looking set of double doors. Pick struggled but couldn't budge them. Anton used both hands and got the door to move.

As soon as it opened, a woman's repetitive moaning became apparent, mixed in with "yes," "oh, that's the spot," "faster," and louder wails that failed to form words.

Sarah's face went beet red.

Anton and Marcus covered their mouths to stop from laughing.

Pick glared at the twins, clear in his intention to punch anyone who dared make a remark about his sister, who worked as a prostitute.

"What's happening to her?" Emily turned to look up at Sarah. "Is she bein' hurt?"

"Umm, no. Don't worry about it." Sarah covered Emily's ears and walked her to the stairwell door on the far side of an elevator cluster.

Not one of the old lifts looked functional. Junk packed the dead end of the elevator alcove: shopping carts, green plastic trash bins, cardboard boxes, and busted up furniture, among smaller debris like bottles, cartons, and paper cups.

"Is anything still gonna be there?" asked Marcus in an unenthused tone. "People be livin' here, maybe they found it."

"No one *lives* here," said Sarah. "We walked far enough to be out of the Hab. This is abandoned. That, uhh, woman. They just came here to, uhh, not be outside."

Maya grabbed the stairwell door and hauled backward, dragging it open with both hands.

"Whoa," said Marcus.

"Damn," muttered Anton.

Pick laughed.

"Poor man," said Emily.

Maya peered around the door. A skinny twenty-something man lay naked on the floor with a needle hanging out of his arm. A trail of drool leaked from the corner of his mouth, matching paths of snot dribbled from his nose. Maya stared at him until she perceived his chest moving with breath.

"Is he dead?" asked Anton.

"No. He's high. Took too much and passed out." Sarah pushed Emily onto the stairs.

"Someone took all his stuff." Marcus bit his lip, eyeing the area nervously.

"Maybe he didn't have nofin'." Pick stepped over the man without looking.

Maya moved around the door and pulled it closed behind them. "He won't bother us. None of us have anything that would fit him."

"He's a doser," said Sarah. "He'd take our stuff to sell so he can buy more drugs."

"They can't all be that mean." Maya hurried up the stairs.

"He's a *doser*." Sarah added a bit of urgent whine to her voice. "The chems control his brain. It's not like they actually think about anything.

He'd probably try to put Pick's shorts on and not know why he couldn't get them halfway up one leg."

"If he tries an' takes my pants, I'ma pee in 'em."

"Nasty," muttered Marcus.

Maya laughed.

Over many sets of switchback stairs, they found mostly debris from crumbling walls and little human-created trash. At the twenty-seventh floor, Anton pointed at the door.

"We should"—he gasped for breath—"check this one. Place"—he wheezed—"got thirty floors, looks about where"—he coughed—"it hit."

Sarah sat on the steps. "I need a break."

No one protested.

In a few minutes when she'd gotten her breath back, Sarah grabbed Pick's shoulder. "There's dosers in this building. I don't want any of you running off. We stay together. I swear, if anyone does something stupid, I will never go scavving with you again."

"Don't be mean," muttered Pick.

"She ain't bein' mean." Marcus nodded at Sarah. "She bein' smart. Tryin' to protect us."

"We should bring an adult when we go scavving," said Maya. "It's dumb to be alone out here."

"We're not alone," said Pick. "We're together."

"Grown-ups don't got time to do scavvin'," said Anton.

Maya swallowed a knot of worry. "Genna would come with us."

"Yeah, but she don't gotta job," said Pick.

"She does, but not like people who go to a place every day at the same time," said Emily. "Mommy might help us too. She works in our building. She's gonna be the new super!"

"New?" Marcus blinked at her. "I thought she already was."

Emily shrugged. "It's what she said. It's 'fishal now."

"Let's get out of here. I want to go home," said Maya.

"We can't go back yet, we haven't found anything." Pick waved his arms.

"I don't mean right this second. I mean I want to get home as soon as possible, so hurry up." Maya stood.

One by one, the kids got up and proceeded past the doorway into a hall with relatively intact carpeting. An odd stale smell reminiscent of petrified bread hung in the air. Drab beige walls held light fixtures that looked like upside down clam shells at even intervals. From her countless hours surfing the AuthNet, she remembered enough pictures to guess by the décor this had been a higher-end apartment building before the war. Pick started to sprint for the first open door, but caught himself after three steps. He gave Sarah a 'see, I'm not running off' stare while pointing at it.

When the group reached that apartment, he peered inside. The place looked like some gang had thrown one hell of a party. Graffiti covered everything, including the ceiling. Beer cans littered the floor along with crumpled paper and plastic bags.

Maya stood with her feet together, arms tight at her sides, staring at the ground. If a roach showed itself, she'd be ready to run.

"This ain't it," said Marcus. "Wall's not broke."

"I know." Pick hurried to the far wall, and a sliding glass patio door covered in spray paint. "Wanna see what side we're on."

"Don't go out there," said Sarah. "The deck might break."

"'Kay. I just wanna see." Pick grunted, fighting the sliding door. He found the lock, flipped it, and pulled the door open enough to stick his head out. "The deck won't fall if I step on it."

"*Don't* go out there!" yelled Sarah.

He looked back with a big grin. "It won't fall if I step on it 'cause it already fell."

Sarah half threw Emily into Maya and ran over to grab Pick. "Get away from the—eek!" She pulled him back from the patio door, which opened to nothing but air.

Maya held on, keeping Emily from going over to check out the view. Sarah made an alarmed squeal when Marcus approached, but he only grasped the handle and pulled the sliding door closed. At the *click* of the lock, Sarah let go of Pick and swooned to her knees.

"Are you okay?" Maya walked over to her.

"Yeah. I don't like high places."

Maya tilted her head. "You weren't scared on my porch."

"Your porch has a railing, and we live on the seventh floor. This is the *twenty-seventh*." Sarah stood.

"This is the right side. Prob'ly four or five 'partments that way." Pick pointed to the right.

"Not checking all the rooms?" asked Maya.

Marcus grinned. "Thought you's in a hurry to go home."

"I am, but you like scavving."

"We been here before, couple times. Only comin' back here 'cause of that new crash." Marcus put on a reassuring face. "We ain't so far from the Hab that it's too bad here. We spent a couple days checkin' this place out 'fore you showed up. Ain't like dangerous people from the Dead Space come this close."

"Hey, a balloon!" cheered Emily, pointing at something under the crushed sofa.

"Don't touch that," yelled Sarah.

"Aww." Emily whined.

"Someone else has put their, uhh, lips on it. You will get sick." Sarah took her by the hand and pulled her to the door.

Maya peered at the limp scrap of beige-yellow stuck to a cushion. She recognized latex, but the glove only had one finger. Also, it seemed an ugly color for a balloon. With a shrug, she followed the group into the hall, past four doors and a giant spray-paint mural that attempted to depict Vanessa Oman being shot. A tangle of shapes underneath formed such a stylized effort at lettering she couldn't make out what it tried to say. The twins backtracked when they caught her twisting her head to attempt reading it.

"They wrote 'F Ascendant,'" said Anton.

"Oh." Maya nodded. "Yeah. F Ascendant."

Pick turned the knob on the next door on the left, causing the door to swing open hard enough to knock him on his butt and let a strong wind into the hall. Maya squinted and guarded her face from a pelting of grit. Undeterred, the boy leapt to his feet and pointed inside, letting off a whoop of victory as his puffy brown mane whipped about.

"Yes!" shouted Marcus.

The boys ran inside.

"Stay away from the hole!" yelled Sarah.

Maya crept in last, still cringing from the gale. The apartment stank like wet dog. Small black footprints formed on the pale beige rug wherever the kids stepped, street dirt washed away by a saturated carpet. The kids fanned out to either side, giving Maya a view of a long, rectangular craft slumped in the middle of the living room, surrounded by chunks of brick, cinderblock, and drywall. It lay at the end of a gouge in the rug, having slid to a halt about fifteen feet from the smashed wall.

The pale green drone had a rectangular shape with an aerodynamic tapered nose and mostly flat rear end. It matched her estimation of size, as big as an e-car. Six broken struts jutted out from the frame, one at each corner and two at the midpoint, though the fans and their shrouds were missing. Both sides bore a simple black stripe with 'IPS' in plain block letters.

"It's a drone all right, but where the fans at?" asked Anton.

Maya walked into the stiff gust, her hair whipping about, and circled the crashed machine. "Probably sheared off when it hit the building. Bet the fans and stuff are all over the ground outside."

"Sheared?" asked Sarah. "Don't pity me."

Maya giggled. "They broke off when it hit. The body is tougher and shaped like a spear, so it made a hole in the wall, but the fans were weak so the wall won."

"Uhh, 'nuff school," said Anton. He crouched by the back end and fiddled with something. "Hey, Faerie, can you open this? It's locked."

"This transport drone is the property of Interstate Parcel Service. Unauthorized tampering is a violation of the law," said a recorded female voice.

Sarah crept around to the rear and gave the hatch the once-over. The wind kept throwing her hair forward over her face. "Probably. It's a physical lock." She gathered her unruly mane, stuffed it into her dress, and pulled a couple thin rods from her fanny pack. "Anton or Marcus, watch the hall. Pick, keep quiet."

"Okay." He jammed his finger up his nose.

Maya stood behind Emily, arms wrapped around her.

The howl of the wind filled the otherwise silent apartment. Pick wandered over to the hole, leaned out, and spat. Sarah yelled at him to get back, but he lingered until his missile hit the ground.

Emily twisted to look at Maya. "Are you holding me like a doll because you're scared or because you don't want me to get into something dangerous?"

"Yes," said Maya. "And you look like a doll."

"Oh." Emily smiled. "I like this dress."

"Your parents get you nice clothes, but you always wear this same dress."

"I like it."

"Did they get you shoes?" asked Maya.

Emily nodded.

"Why don't you wear them? Think they'll get stolen?"

"Faeries don't wear shoes. It makes them too heavy to fly."

Maya giggled. "But you can't fly."

"I'm trying to learn, and if I'm too heavy, I won't know if it works." She raised her arms as much as Maya's grip permitted, and let them fall.

"Dosers won't steal her dress because it's *too* fancy. Foz can't sell it 'cause no one will buy it 'cause they'd all be afraid of it getting stolen," said Anton.

"That doesn't make any sense. People don't steal it because it'll get stolen?" Maya scratched her head.

Pick climbed up on top of the drone, triggering the recording to announce again.

"Get down," said Sarah, her concentration on defeating the lock making her voice monotone.

"This one's broken. It won't fly away and 'splode." Pick held his head up in triumph.

Maya shifted her weight from leg to leg. "How long is this gonna—?"

"Got it!" Sarah stuffed her tools back in her hip satchel before pulling a small handle that made the entire rear end of the drone open like a hatchback, revealing a bunch of boxes inside. "Ooh. There's stuff!"

The kids swarmed the drone, reaching in and unpacking boxes as fast as they could get their hands on them. Maya grinned, surrendering to the elation of discovering unclaimed property. She couldn't quite make up her mind if it counted as stealing, considering it had crashed and been left here. Not like they'd broken into a place. Still, even if it did fall under the label of theft, a corporation could bear the loss. They hadn't raided the storeroom of a person trying to survive.

The first white plastiboard cube Maya pulled out had markings for Medela Biotech Miami on the outside. According to the print at one corner, it held a hundred bottles of Paratab. She skimmed the label until she hit the word Paracetamol. *Oh, pain pills.*

"What's that?" asked Sarah. "You're studying it like it's gold."

"Uhh, looks like a common pain medication. Like for headaches and stuff." Maya set it on the floor.

"Oh, Foz'll buy that right up." Anton grinned.

Medela Biotech Miami... Maya traced her finger back and forth over the carton. *Wonder if they'd make Xeno?* While the others continued unloading the drone, Maya slipped a single bottle from that case and pocketed it after making sure the label had an address for the company on it.

A squeal of delight came from Pick. He held up a box full of mini-computers.

"What are those?" asked Marcus.

"Games!" yelled Pick.

"They're minicomputers. Almost everyone in the Sanc has them," said Maya. "You can call people, take pictures, play games, hit the AuthNet."

"Oh." Pick frowned. "I thought they were game machines."

"They kinda are, but not like a console." Maya unpacked ten other cubes of the same pills and decided to push the one she'd opened to the side. "We should keep one of these for Doc."

Emily picked it up. "I'll carry it."

The boys stacked boxes once they'd cleaned out the drone and surveyed their haul of headache pills, minicomputers, and accessories (headphones, protective cases, and charging plugs). Marcus ran deeper into the apartment without warning. He returned a minute or so later with a bundle of white cloth, which turned out to be a bedsheet and a fitted sheet.

"We can make Santa bags." He set the sheet flat and stacked boxes on top of it.

Soon, Anton and Marcus each struggled with a giant sack over their shoulder, and Emily carried the box of pain meds destined for her father's clinic. Going *down* the stairs didn't exhaust everyone, even with the burden of their plunder, though they stopped about halfway and again at the bottom to rest their hands. The passed-out naked man remained as they had found him, flat on his back inside the ground-floor landing.

"Ow." Anton kneaded his hands. "These shits is heavy. Carryin' em all the way home is gonna suck."

"Yeah," muttered Marcus.

"Hey," said Sarah. "Idea."

She darted over to the dead end and dragged a shopping cart out of the pile of junk.

"It ain't all gonna fit in that." Marcus rubbed his hands on his khaki shorts.

"There's tons of them," said Sarah, while trotting back to get another one.

"Two oughta do it." Marcus opened his bundle without hesitating and tossed boxes one by one into the cart.

Emily clung to her precious store of meds.

After packing two wagons overflowing, Sarah used the sheets as covers so no one would be able to tell what the kids had collected. She even added a few pieces of broken appliances from the pile in the back.

"What's with the crap?" asked Pick.

"To make people think we're just a bunch of kids collecting trash no one wants." Maya smiled.

Sarah grinned at her. "See, you're not bad at scavving."

Amid the clatter of old wheels, the kids pushed the shopping carts down the hall, out the front door, and along the street. Whenever one of the pieces of camouflage trash fell, Pick scrambled to collect it and stick it back in place. Maya kept her head down, hiding her face behind her hair. With any luck, a bunch of street kids with junk would be functionally invisible.

Sarah walked at the rear of the procession, one hand under her dress, likely on the handle of the Hornet. Every so often, she bit back a yelp when she stepped on something painful, her attention too focused on possible threats to watch the ground. Maya pushed aside an upwelling of guilt at having shoes by promising herself she would make sure Sarah got some.

Despite the increased number of people out and about as they returned to the Habitation District, due mostly to day workers on their way back from the Sanc, no one paid much attention to a pack of grungy kids pushing two shopping carts that appeared full of broken toasters, lamps, and chair pieces. Pick impressed Maya when he started bragging about how cool their pirate ship would be after they got all this new stuff on it.

"Keep moving. You guys are too young," said a man from a doorway on the right.

"Do we look like we're trying to go in?" asked Sarah.

Maya glanced over at a big man in a black leather vest, no shirt under it, leaning on the wall by a bar full of weary-looking people. He pushed himself off the building and leaned toward Sarah, who stood her ground and met his glare with an equally defiant glower. Marcus and Anton jumped, flailing in their failed effort to decide between running or looking brave.

The man laughed at her lack of fear and leaned back against the wall. "Say hi to your old man, eh?"

Maya resumed breathing.

"Yeah..." Sarah sighed. "Sure."

Maya kept glancing back at the guy as they walked. Once they'd gotten far enough away, she scooted close to Sarah and whispered, "Who was that?"

"Friend of Dad's. He teases me like since I'm Irish, all I wanna do is drink beer and am tryin' ta sneak inta his bar before I'm old enough."

"Oh."

A minute or two passed without words, the din of commuters mixed with the rattling of bent wheels.

"It's not," said Sarah, her tone flat.

"Huh?" asked Maya.

"Funny."

Maya couldn't think of any reason her being Irish would make her want beer, never mind the insensitivity of The Dad being *too* fond of it. She shook her head. "No, it's not funny at all."

A hint of a smile peeked out from under a waterfall of red hair. Pick let out a yell of alarm and rushed around to the lead cart, bracing his body against the nose end to keep it from tipping into the street. Marcus grunted with the weight, but regained control. A left turn and most of a block later, Foz's place came into view.

Metal mesh with quite a few dents covered the two giant windows of the storefront. Neon lettering spelled out 'The Emporium' in bright green letters in the right side pane. Both windows looked in on shelves full of whatever stuff Foz found or bought from people, behind a horse-shoe enclosure of metal fencing around an empty area in the middle.

The innermost portion of the open hall had a counter enclosed in a protective barrier of thick, transparent plastic coated in smears of an oily residue. Pegs along the rear wall held several pale grey hooded ponchos with breathing masks. Behind the bulletproof window stood an older, pale man with unnaturally black hair in a wild spray, attention glued to one of two ultrathin television screens hung near the ceiling on either side of the counter. The display he watched showed football; the other had a woman with coffee-toned skin in a bright red dress droning on and on about financial markets and some big deal that happened in the Trenton Sanctuary Zone.

Maya squinted at the unkempt man, not at all trusting him. *That has to be Foz.*

The air smelled of electronics and coffee, tinged with a heavy fruitiness that defied explanation. Sarah grunted as she shoved the second wagon over the lip in the doorway. Pick grabbed the front end and pulled. At the clatter of shopping carts, the man behind the counter looked away from the game. A coffee dribble darkened the front of his peach-colored button down shirt.

"Hmm?" asked Foz. Cottony eyebrows climbed his forehead at the sight before him. He waved his hand in a shooing gesture. "Don't deal in junk, kids. Take that mess somewhere else."

Sarah skirted around the carts and glided up to the window. "The junk is a decoy so we didn't get robbed comin' here. We found good stuff."

"Good stuff, huh?" Foz leaned on the counter. "All right. Let's see."

Maya followed, stooping to pick up a safety pin that had fallen from Sarah's dress.

Foz took a hit from a vape wand and exhaled a cloud of fog against the inside of the barrier. The twins and Pick removed the junk from the first cart and Sarah pulled away the sheet. She held up a box of microcomputers while Maya showed off a case of the pills.

"What's that in the white box?" asked Foz.

"Nine cases of Paratab. It's a Paracetamol-based pain medication," said Maya. "Each box has a hundred 250-count bottles. It's a fairly standard OTC pill, probably about $12 a bottle off the shelf."

"Hmm." Foz stared at her, his left eye twitching. After a moment, he leaned up to the barricade. "Let me see the minicoms."

Sarah moved the box closer.

"BSZ news back now, live with Vanessa Oman, embattled CEO of Ascendant Pharmaceuticals," said a woman's voice from the television.

Maya snapped her attention to the screen on the right. The same woman in red had moved to the side of the image, while a box containing Vanessa's artificial smile appeared in the blue field beside her. Text along the bottom of the screen read 'Elsa Saeed - BSZ Newsroom.'

"Thank you for being with us today, Miss Oman," said the reporter.

Vanessa offered a quick nod.

"Let me start off with the question on everyone's mind. What is your reaction to your daughter's apparent involvement in the recent disinformation efforts by the Brigade?"

Vanessa put on a somber expression. "Oh, Miss Saeed, I had hoped never to have to reveal this publicly, but recent events have made it necessary. Maya Oman never existed."

Maya clenched her hands into fists and glared at the screen. Sarah's discussion with Foz faded into background noise.

"I'm sorry? Never existed?" The reporter raised both eyebrows.

"Yes." Vanessa shook her head, eyes downcast. "It would've been the best part of my life if I had a real daughter, but unfortunately, the girl you've all been watching over the past few years was created by our marketing department. She's little more than a computer-generated actor."

Maya snarled, trembling with rage. Vanessa's casual dismissal of her existence didn't come as any surprise. Being left alone all the time, without even the effort of a goodnight vid call, had long ago proved the woman didn't really want her. The lame attempt to act sad at her 'daughter not being real' went too far.

"That's bullshit!" shouted Maya.

Emily gasped, mouth agape.

Foz stared at her; after a second or so, the vape wand fell from his lip. "What are you talking about? These things *are* difficult to sell out here."

Sarah blinked. "What?"

The twins and Pick got the giggles.

"I see," said the reporter.

"As realistic as she appeared to be, that child is purely a product of computer imagery. These terrorists somehow managed to gain access to our files and reproduce her for their own purposes."

"You're saying Ascendant suffered a network breach?" Miss Saeed leaned back, eyebrows still high.

"I do not believe so. More likely a disgruntled former employee smuggled the files out." Vanessa's 'don't cross me' smile returned. "Our network is impervious. We have the best security in the world."

"No you don't," yelled Maya. "Head walked right in and took over that drone!" She looked at Sarah. "She's lying!"

"You said a bad word," whispered Emily. She shivered, worried about getting in trouble for hearing it.

The reporter glanced at something in her lap. "The allegations that Ascendant has been releasing the Fade virus on purpose have proven surprisingly resilient to being disproved. Do you have an official statement?"

Vanessa rolled her eyes and made a dismissive wave, as if having heard ludicrous gossip. "Clearly, the terrorists are attempting to destabilize order in New Baltimore. No one knows where Fade is coming from, and any rumors that my company has anything to do with it are a laughable smear. It is beyond my imagination how anyone could even consider that as a possibility."

"But the Authority is investigating?" asked the reporter.

"Yes, they are. I would not expect them to take such a serious accusation lightly in the interest of public health. When they realize the Brigade terrorists are responsible, you can be certain that appropriate action will be taken."

"You're so full of shit I can smell it from here!" shouted Maya.

"Maya..." Sarah rushed over and grabbed her by the shoulders. "Forget her."

She couldn't tell at what point rage had turned into crying. "She's such a liar."

"Stop swearing," whispered Emily. "You're too little."

"And as a good faith gesture, Ascendant is distributing Xenodril free of charge to New Baltimore's Fade wards."

"What about us?" shouted Marcus.

Sarah pulled Maya into a hug, but she squirmed enough to keep watching the TV.

"Some are asking why Ascendant hasn't taken that step before." Miss Saeed looked up with a faint grimace, as if she'd been afraid to ask the question and dreaded the response.

Vanessa's fake smile didn't crack. "Goodwill in light of extenuating circumstances is goodwill, but a company must remain profitable or *all* the medicine stops."

The reporter bowed to Vanessa. "Very understandable. Thank you so much for your time, Miss Oman." She shifted her gaze to the viewer. "Stay with us. When we come back after these messages, we'll have an exclusive interview with Jake Cruickshank, the man who has ventured into the wildlands over a hundred times and managed to return in one piece."

An image of Maya in a glimmery cyan dress appeared on the screen, an Ascendant ad for Panmax, a diabetes cure that only killed four of every thousand people who tried it.

"I hate her." Maya wanted to hit something but had an armful of Sarah. "She's such a liar."

"I won't tell on you." Emily bit her lip and swished side to side, making her dress flare. "If anyone asks me if you said bad words, I can't lie."

Sarah gave Maya a squeeze and leaned back to make eye contact. "Don't let her bother you. People won't believe her. Of course she's going to say it's a lie. That's what criminals who get caught do."

"Okay then." Foz cleared his throat. "Comes out to $60 for the lot, which is $8 each for the six of you."

"Ooh." Sarah grinned.

The boys seemed excited, though Marcus watched Maya.

"No." Maya shook her head. "Are you serious? $60? The pills alone have a retail value of..." She thought for a second. "About $9,600, if you sell 'em at $12 per bottle. And knowing this place, you'll charge at least $20. You should give us at least $800 each for just the meds, plus whatever the minicomputers are worth."

Foz's face reddened; his mouth opened in shock, and he twitched. It took him a few seconds to stop making faces as if she'd walked in on him in the bathroom. He cleared his throat again. "Well, you have to understand that not many people out here bother with headache pills. I'd be lucky to sell them at all. I've no guarantee they'd move before they expired."

Maya folded her arms. "They've got a few years... and I'm sure you'd pull them right off the shelf as soon as they're old."

"The most I'm willing to offer is $200 each. I still need to pay someone to unlock those minicomps before they're any good to anyone. If that's not acceptable, I suppose you could cart all this stuff to the *other* pawn shop in the Hab." Foz tapped his chin. "I don't imagine you'll be interested in selling it in the Sanc, seeing as it's stolen."

"There's another pawn store?" Emily blinked.

"It's not stoled," said Pick. "We found it. Smashed drone."

"No, that's the point," said Anton with a frown. "There ain't no other store. We ain't got no choice."

"Deal," said Sarah. "$200 each." She leaned close to Maya and whispered, "He knows we have it. He'll hire thugs to steal it if we leave an' try to sell it ourselves."

"Fine," muttered Maya.

"All right then, form a line." Foz pulled the retractable drawer in.

The kids queued single file, and one by one retrieved handfuls of NuCoin from the bin.

Maya counted forty-five. "Wait." She looked up. "How many coins did everyone get?"

"Lots," said Pick.

"Umm?" The twins sifted their pile. A moment later, they looked up. "Forty-five."

"You all got the same amount," said Foz.

Emily pulled at Maya. "My turn!"

"Except"—Maya leaned up to the bulletproof glass—"the amount is wrong. Forty-five NuCoin is $173... actually $173.25. The exchange rate is $3.85 per NuCoin. $200 would be fifty-one-point-nine. We may be kids, but we're not *that* dumb. You're already robbing us at $200 apiece. At least keep your word. It would cost you more time to count out change than just round up to fifty-two NuCoin each."

Grumbling about smart-ass kids, Foz doled out more coins, bringing everyone's handful up to fifty-two.

Marcus and Anton bought a giant box of candy each for two coins. Emily held her money tight to her chest, smiling.

Pick pointed at a flower pendant hanging on a shelf inside. "How much is that?"

"It goes with your eyes, Ruben," said Anton in a feminine voice.

"Shut it, Ant. It's for Naida."

Foz glanced at the necklace. "Eight coins."

Pick nodded, and dropped the money in the drawer. Foz pulled the necklace down off its peg and put it in a small box, which he passed out via the drawer.

Sarah tucked her NuCoin in the fanny pack with her lock picks and zipped it. "You gonna buy anything?"

"No," said Emily. "Gonna give it to Mom."

"What about you, smart girl?" Foz raised an eyebrow. "Anything here you like?"

Maya pointed at Sarah. "Do you have any shoes that'd fit her? Or clothes?"

Sarah blushed. "You don't have to use your money on me."

Foz shook his head. "Got some, but they're way too small for her, or too big. There's a nice new set of sneakers prob'ly fit him"—he gestured at Pick—"if he don't mind pink."

Pick raspberried no one in particular.

"Uhh. I got nothin' kid-sized, but maybe look at T-shirts." Foz pointed at a rack.

They spent a few minutes examining a pitiful selection while Sarah tried to pull her away, insisting Maya not spend money on her. Most of the shirts had holes or bloodstains. Two bore prints of nude women, and one had 'I fuck on the first date' in white block letters on a plain black shirt. That one made Sarah drag her away.

"Stop. I'm fine. Dad will get me something."

"Want some?" Marcus held his box of candy out to Maya. Red, green, orange, yellow, and white capsules radiated a generic fruit smell.

"Thanks." Maya gave Sarah a guilty look, Marcus a genuine smile, and helped herself to a modest handful. She tossed a green one in her mouth. A somewhat-hard shell gave way to gummy green apple inside. "Mmm!" Her eyes shot open wide.

"Never had 'em before?" asked Marcus.

She shook her head, unable to get her teeth apart fast enough to talk.

"That. Was. Awesome." Anton patted her on the back. "Best scav ever."

Pick jumped on Maya from behind. "Yeah! She gotta come wif us alla time now. We got all the money! She talk smart ta Foz so he don't cheat."

"We should get home. It's almost dark," said Sarah.

Foz gestured at the window. "Get them carts an' that junk outta here."

Grinning and chewing on the sticky, fruity mass, Maya helped collect the scrap appliances. Once the kids finished gathering the mess, the twins pushed the shopping carts outside and abandoned them at the mouth of the first alley they found. At Sarah's urging, the group ran down the street to their building as fast as their legs would carry them.

[6]

CHEESE SANDWICHES

Maya sprawled on the floor, gazing over her array of old cards spread out on the grimy beige rug. Some of them had tooth marks, small tears, dents, and water damage. Illustrations depicted fantastical creatures, resources, magical items, and spells she could use to take away the other player's life dots. She'd initially thought magic and monsters to be silly, but playing this game with Sarah had changed her mind. It had become fun, and that first half-played game they'd left on the floor when Maya decided to run off and get Genna back had forever burned it into her psyche. She couldn't even think about these cards without remembering how guilty she felt at leaving without at least telling Sarah what she planned, and how afraid she'd been at the chance she might not come home again.

Despite that, the game was fun.

Except for whenever it reminded her of that night.

Maya lay on her stomach, feet in the air as she surveyed the spread, noting that she could at any time steamroll Sarah's meager setup in one turn and win. Since they planned to be in for the night, she'd stashed her sneakers under the bed. Her friend didn't seem to be *playing*. More like randomly tossing cards around. Sarah sat cross-legged on the far end of the card sprawl, staring at the ones in her hand and rearranging them every so often.

"Ya useless bastards," shouted The Dad over rapid metal clicking. "I coulda caught that with this piece of shite roto-rooter I've got for a bloody 'and!"

"What's wrong?" asked Sarah. "You could've beat me six turns ago, but you're just building up. Trying to set a record for how much negative life you can give me?"

Maya put her seven cards on the floor, face down, and propped her chin up on both hands, tapping her fingers at her cheeks. "You're not really even playing. It wouldn't be fair."

"Ach!" roared The Dad. "That's it! Bet he shite himself with that hit! 'Bout damn time!"

Sarah looked down. Her lip quivered, but she kept quiet and collected.

"I'm scared too. Vanessa said I never existed... what if that means she wants to kill me?"

"That's not it." Sarah looked up. "If she came after you, everyone would know you're right. It's smarter for her to lie and say you're not real."

"Oh come on!" shouted The Dad. "You call that defense? Me bloody daughter coulda knocked him on his ass!"

Maya looked at the door. "Does he yell all night?"

Sarah put a card down, a use-at-will spell effect that did one point of damage to every creature in play as well as both players for every point of mana she allocated to it. "Only when his team isn't winning. I think it's like a special game or something. For a trophy. So he's extra angry."

A heavy *thud* shook the apartment. Maya jumped, but Sarah didn't even flinch.

"What was that?" Maya stared at the door.

"The footrest hitting the wall." Sarah put down a land card. "Don't worry. He only beats up the furniture. He won't hit us. Go."

"Useless bunch of morons!" shouted The Dad. "Is that a defensive line or synchronized diaper changin' at the old folks' home?"

Maya picked up her cards. "We should start over. This isn't a real game. It's already escalated to stupid and the draw deck is almost gone."

"So end it," said Sarah, sounding utterly bored. "If you attack with all your creatures, you win."

"You have tons of land out." Maya gestured at her cards. "You could kill all my creatures and both of us with that disease card. You didn't use it on your turn, so you're letting me win."

"Sorry." Sarah started to lose her fight not to cry. "I'm worried."

"Worthless fu—" The Dad lapsed into wet coughing.

"You've been kinda sad for a while now. What's wrong?" Maya tilted her head.

"It's okay. I don't wanna make you sad too."

"Fine." Maya waved her hand at the cards. "I attack with everything."

"Twenty-one-point plague." Sarah tapped the disease card. "We're both dead."

Maya laughed.

"What?" Sarah squinted at her.

"That's the best ending for a game like this. We were both trying to lose." She put her cards down and crawled around to kneel at Sarah's side. "Please tell me. Don't keep it all inside."

The Dad's coughing started up again, louder.

Sarah stood. "It's Dad. He's getting sick and he won't go to the VA clinic. I need to check on him."

She hurried out of the room. Maya followed her down the little hallway past the bathroom and closet and over to The Dad, who sat on the couch, bent forward, coughing, live hand over his mouth, a little blood seeping between his fingers. His skin looked paler than usual, and a thin layer of sweat covered his face, neck, and living arm. His coppery hair and stubble had grown more grey and wild.

Maya stopped a few steps back, eyeing a new smudge on the wall above the upside-down cushioned footrest that had been hurled across the room. Above it, the television showed a paused football game, a drone-eye view of players that looked more like a video game than reality.

"Dad?" Sarah put a hand on his back, rubbing and slapping as he coughed.

He mumbled, coughed, and waved his metal arm at the kitchen. "M'awright, fetch me a towel, hon."

Sarah ran to the kitchen.

Maya rolled the footrest onto its legs and pushed it back over to its place near the chair. The Dad coughed a little more, much quieter than he had been, and gave her a nod of thanks. His breathing had a whispery, wheezy quality, louder at the end, and he seemed to be inhaling rapid, small breaths.

"Here." Sarah rushed over and handed him a towel.

He wiped his mouth, chin, and hand free of blood, and flopped back looking exhausted and smiling at her. "Thank ye, hon."

Sarah leaned over him and fussed at his hair. She took the towel and dabbed his forehead. "You really should go to the VA."

"Bah." He rolled his head to the right, dodging eye contact. "Won't do any good. 'Sides, they'd get me at the gate an' then you'd be on your own."

Maya fidgeted. *She's pretty much already on her own.*

"I'll make you some soup." Sarah dropped the towel in his lap, pushed off the chair, and headed to the kitchen.

The Dad raised the metal hand as if to protest but let it drop without saying a word.

After a few awkward seconds, Maya offered a cheesy smile and padded through the archway after her. Sarah's back end stuck out of a low cabinet by the sink, inside which kitchenware clattered. Soon, she extricated herself holding a medium-sized pot with a wooden handle. She stood, set it on the e-stove, and grasped a plain white can labeled 'beef soup.'

Maya sat at the table.

"This won't take long," muttered Sarah as she dumped soup into the pot. "We can play another round if you want."

"Okay." Maya swished her feet back and forth.

The Dad looked like the actor from the Davomex-EN ad. Cured of lung cancer after a two-week regimen of 'easy to use auto-injectors you can administer from the comfort of your own home.' *Maybe that guy wasn't an actor? Sometimes Vanessa's medicines work.* She again glanced over at Sarah, who stirred at the soup. Ascendant probably made some astoundingly expensive treatment that could fix whatever he had. It didn't seem right to tell Sarah 'well, all he needs to do is get *blah* and he'll be fine.' Davomex-EN if cancer, Alveo-4 if asthma, Vitaboost to get rid of his fatigue, and maybe some Myomega to get his soldier's physique back in a few weeks of pill-taking. Her voice chattered away in the back of her mind, scraps of lines she'd had to memorize for ads.

Sarah abruptly fast-walked out, startling Maya into wondering if she'd somehow eavesdropped on her thinking and got upset.

A moment later, she came back down the hall carrying an olive-drab blanket, which she tucked around The Dad, trying to make him comfortable. He murmured at her while smiling. She whispered, and he shook his head. Sarah bounced on her toes, whispering again with a hint of pleading whine.

"Mmm... think about it." He let his head go back and closed his eyes.

He's getting sick fast. Maya bit her lip. *When Mom's home, I'll ask her to drag his butt to the VA.*

Sarah plodded back to the stove and resumed stirring the soup. For a few minutes, the apartment hung in deathly silence save for the soft scrape of a plastic spoon on aluminum. A sniffle escaped, and she lost the battle to keep from crying. Still warming the soup for her father, Sarah leaned against the stove and wept as quietly as possible.

"Hey." Maya slid from the chair and moved over. "He's gonna be okay."

"No he's not," mumbled Sarah. "He won't listen. Doc's already done as much as he can do here. He said Dad needs to go to the VA in the Sanc, and he won't. Dad says he's just tired, but it's more than that."

Maya put a hand on Sarah's shoulder. "I think he's got lung cancer, or something like that. There's a bunch of meds that can fix that. One of the ads, the man looked worse than your father does and he got better in a couple days. He's a vet, so the Authority will pay for it."

"He got exposed to something during the war. When I was little, he told me he'd get sick someday. Dad knew I'd still be a kid when he..." She let go of the spoon, bracing her hands on the stove.

"He's not gonna die." Maya hugged her tight. "There's treatments they have now that no one expected would be around when the war ended."

"I know." Sarah sank to her knees and sobbed into her hands.

Maya looked back and forth between her friend and the living room, feeling helpless. Everything she tried to say only made Sarah more upset. She dropped to kneel beside her and held on. "Sorry. I don't know how to be comforting. My babysitter was an AI. Please stop crying. I'm sorry if I said something wrong."

"It's not that." Sarah sniffled and wiped her nose on the back of her arm. She fixed Maya with a stare that hurt like a knife to the heart. It took her a moment to find the voice to whisper, "I think he *wants* to die."

Maya grasped her friend's hands and gave her the stern look of a parent laying down the law. Anger that The Dad could put his daughter through such pain when he didn't have to pushed aside her insecurity. "As soon as Mom is back, I'm going to make her drag him to the VA. Try going in there and telling him not to retreat. What kind of soldier abandons his daughter? You're only eleven. He can't stand down yet."

"Okay." Sarah nodded, wiping her face. "Okay...."

The soup burbled and popped.

"Oh!" Sarah jumped up and got the spoon moving again. "I hope it didn't burn."

Maya sniffed. "Doesn't smell like it."

"Dad doesn't trust the VA doctors. He thinks they'll 'do something to his brain' and make him into someone else."

"A lot of soldiers have mental issues. He's seen some bad things."

Sarah glanced at her, sighed, and hung her head. "He's not *that* nuts. He just doesn't want to tell me that he thinks they'll take me away from him."

"Maybe before the war. There's not enough government left to do that anymore." Maya smirked. "I tried. Called and emailed everyone I could think of to report Vanessa for neglecting me, but nothing ever happened."

"Duh." Sarah rolled her eyes. "That woman *owns* the Authority too. No way would they dare." She stood on tiptoe to grab a bowl from a cabinet over the shelf and transferred the soup into it.

Maya furrowed her brow. "I never even thought of that."

"Just a thought. I dunno for sure." Sarah turned off the stove before carrying the soup to the living room.

The Dad grumbled but begrudgingly tolerated her sitting next to him on the sofa and feeding him. Maya hovered at the archway between kitchen and living room, watching. Seeing a girl Sarah's age mother her own father awakened a malignant sense of jealousy that her friend had such a deep emotional bond to her parent. She couldn't blame Sarah for how her life had been any more than she could blame herself for Ascendant poisoning people with Fade. Rather than dwell on being jealous of her friend, she let the sight of them intensify her need to have her mom home.

Maya daydreamed about clinging to Genna, savoring every minute they were given together. A momentary pang of doubt as to whether her motherly feelings toward Maya went as deep as Sarah's and her father's evaporated when she remembered what the woman looked like after fighting Moth. Had Genna not cared, she would've run before subjecting herself to that monster.

"I got it. I got it," muttered The Dad. "You g'won eat your own dinner. Yer too skinny."

Sarah squealed into a giggle as he tickled her side.

He took the bowl in his metal right hand and continued tickling at her with his living one until she scampered off to the kitchen, laughing. At the archway, she stopped to catch her breath and collected her hair out of her face.

Maya grinned.

"Want soup? Or I think there's some quick-mac left." Sarah crossed the kitchen to the cabinets. "Might even have some tuna blast too."

"Tuna blast?" Maya raised an eyebrow. "Orange label? With like, umm, a cat on it?"

"Yeah." Sarah nodded. "They're single-serving casseroles."

Maya pushed off the wall she leaned on and walked up behind her. "That's cat food."

"Cat food?" Sarah gave her a quizzical look.

"Yeah. Food for cats. People aren't supposed to eat it."

Sarah smiled. "That's silly. Stop teasing me."

"In the Sanctuary Zones, there's different food meant for pets. It's not as high quality as people food."

In a feat that seemed previously impossible, Sarah became paler. "You're not kidding? But... Foz sells it as tuna casseroles." She grimaced. "I kinda like it."

"Foz." Maya frowned. "He probably buys it in the Sanc and sells it out here for three times the price. I don't think it's dangerous, just *eww*." She grinned. "Got any cheese sandwiches left?"

Sarah's mood slam-shifted to laughing again. "Two whole cabinets full of them."

"We could have those if you want."

"'Kay." Sarah opened a door below the counter all the way on the left and pulled out a brown plastiboard box. She opened it and claimed four packets before shoving the box back in and nudging the cabinet closed with her foot. "Guess you like these things too?"

"They're okay, and you don't have to cook them."

"Oi, girl. Grab me a brew, what?" called The Dad.

Sarah smiled and handed Maya the sandwiches. "Wanna play another round? We can eat in there."

Sarah retrieved a beer from the fridge and carried it over to The Dad. Maya headed into the hall toward the bedroom, marveling at the dense white squares inside clear plastic pouches that bore more resemblance to bathroom tiles than sandwiches.

A *pssht* and *crack* came from behind her as a beer can opened.

"Thanks, luv. An' yer friend gotta point. Ain't time fer me ta stand down yet."

Sarah squeaked.

Eep! Maya halted, clinging to the sandwiches. *He heard us?*

"F'ya want me ta, I'll see what them mind-thievin' fools in white coats have ta say."

Sarah burst into tears, saying, "Yes, Dad" over and over.

Feeling conspicuous, Maya continued to the bedroom. She dropped the sandwiches on the rug and gathered all the cards into a dozen stacks small enough to shuffle. A few minutes later, Sarah bounced in, red-eyed but smiling.

"He's gonna go to the VA!" She flopped to sit and grabbed two piles, which she shuffled.

"That's great! Tomorrow?"

"Maybe. If Zoe will watch you. He doesn't wanna drag you to the Sanc in case there's... issues. I think he'd rather wait for Genna to come back." Her expression lit up with happiness. "He's gonna go!"

They spent a little while shuffling, restacking, and reshuffling their decks. Eventually, they each drew a starting hand. Maya examined her cards, put them down, and grabbed a sandwich packet. She looked it over but didn't do anything until Sarah picked one up. Out of the corner of her eye, she watched her friend squeeze the small capsule along one edge until it broke. Some chemical agent inside caused the white parts of the tile to inflate like a sponge, becoming bread.

Maya broke the ampule in her packet and waited until her sandwich stopped growing. The expansion stretched the plastic, designed to unfold and make a pull-strip available once it had reached full size. As soon as she tore it open, the bedroom filled with the smell of fresh-baked bread. Or at least some chemist's idea of what fresh-baked bread shoved straight up someone's nose smelled like.

Still, the sandwiches proved oddly tasty. Maya had grown fond of the sponginess in the bread, even if the cheese didn't have much flavor. Their next game was cutthroat; Sarah tried not to let her summon any creatures, and Maya returned the favor. They picked at each other's health pools little by little for the better part of an hour. Maya had three life dots left, Sarah four. Either one of them could lose to one lucky draw.

Maya stared over her cards, trying her best old gunslinger squint.

Sarah narrowed her eyes, though her lips couldn't quite stay straight. A hint of smile kept creeping in at the corners.

Shuffling in the hallway preceded the rather loud sound of The Dad pissing.

Maya giggled, biting her arm in an effort to keep quiet.

"He never shuts the door," whispered Sarah, her face almost as red as her hair.

Snickering, Maya pulled her next draw and got a four-point creature. She played it. "That's embarrassing."

"Ooh." Sarah play-scowled. "You think I'm gonna let you do that? Counterspell!" She waved a blue card at her. "Spell failed."

Maya growled at the ceiling but couldn't stop grinning as she moved the monster to the trash pile.

"That's not embarrassing. One night, he had so many beers, he walked right in when I was taking a bath. Didn't even notice me."

Maya gasped. "He didn't!"

"Sure did," yelled The Dad. "Pooped too. Stank so damn bad it drove her clean outta the bathroom covered in suds."

Maya shifted her eyes toward the door.

Sarah covered her mouth and nose with both hands. "I can still smell that."

A flush echoed in the hall.

"He can hear us," whispered Maya. "He probably heard everything we said in the kitchen."

"Yeah. He's trained as a scout. And he's paranoid." She pulled a card, rolled her eyes, and played another land.

"I'm not paranoid," said The Dad, hovering in the doorway. "I'm observant and vigilant. 'Mon, you two. Bed time."

"'Kay." Sarah put her cards down.

After hitting the bathroom, Maya rummaged one of Genna's T-shirts she'd been using for a nightgown out of the plastic bag she'd brought for her extended sleepover. She slipped her shirt off, tossed it down next to the bag, and pulled the huge T-shirt on, which draped down past her knees. Sarah returned from her trip to the toilet as Maya shoved her black fatigue pants down and stepped out of them.

Sarah hopped into bed and crawled against the wall.

"You're going to sleep in that?" asked Maya.

"This is all I have. When it's warm, I don't wear anything to bed, but it's kinda weird to do that with a friend sleepin' over."

"Don't you have a nightdress?"

Sarah looked down, ashamed. "No."

"The Dad should buy you some clothes instead of so much beer," whispered Maya.

"He needs it. It's okay."

Maya climbed onto the bed, crawling over until she stopped nose-to-nose with her. "No, that's not cool. You're always taking care of him like a nurse or something. He should provide for you."

"I don't mind, really." Sarah broke eye contact, fidgeting at her hair. "We don't have a lot of money. He's on a military pension."

"Cheese sandwiches." Maya smiled.

"Heh." Sarah looked back up, grinning. "Yeah. Too many cheese sandwiches."

Maya rolled onto her back and settled into the mattress, staring at the ceiling. "I'm going to use some of my scav money and get you a nightdress."

"I can buy one myself. I got scav money too." Sarah poked her in the side.

"But it won't be a present then." She smiled. "I wanna give someone a present. When's your birthday?"

"I dunno. Sometime in April."

"You don't know the day?" Maya rolled her head to the right and gawked at her.

"No, but Dad always does something corny the first week, so it's probably like the first to sixth or something."

Maya gave her a raspberry.

"What?"

"I'll be ten before you turn twelve. My birthday's in November. The fourth. I hatched in 2084."

"Hatched?" Sarah's eyebrows drew together.

Maya pushed aside the wave of anger that tried to rise. "Vanessa had a doctor grow me in a tank because she didn't want to lose time from work having me and then taking care of a baby. I don't remember it, but I found emails on her computer. She only took me home after I didn't need diapers anymore."

"That's so sad." Sarah held her hand. "Sorry."

Maya looked up at the ceiling again. "I don't miss her. She's a horrible person, and my *real* mom is going to make sure she can't hurt anyone else."

The Dad coughed a few times, but quieted, and the low murmur of football resumed. He even made an effort to reduce his streams of obscenities whenever the game went against his team to a low murmur.

"You really don't miss that place?"

"No. It was like jail. I never even saw other kids. Never had any friends." She squeezed Sarah's hand. "I'm glad you're my friend."

"Me too." Sarah stretched and yawned. "We should probably stop talking before Dad gets mad and yells."

"Okay."

"Night."

Maya closed her eyes and squirmed in an effort to get more comfortable. "Night."

[7]

A NIGHT DISQUIET

Worry that something would happen to Genna circled Maya's head. Fear wet the corners of her eyes, brought a lump to her throat, and kept sleep at arm's length. Sarah seemed to drift off fast, but soon stirred and rolled toward her, reaching one arm across her chest. Whether she wanted to be protective or seek comfort, Maya couldn't tell. This new world she had chosen to live in offered far greater warmth and happiness, but also insecurity—a world that Sarah had always known.

It came as no surprise the girl could zonk out so fast, accustomed to the idea that anything could happen in the Habitation District, and the Authority *might* care. Her friend would probably never trust the Authority after the way they'd treated them here. The time the blueberries had come looking for Maya and left everyone zip-tied to fend for themselves had been something like the eighth time Sarah'd gone through that, but fortunately, only the first time they'd hit her.

Maya tapped her foot on nothing under the sheet, trying to understand how the same blueberries who'd been so cruel to Nons, even the kids, could've been enraged at the contents of Mr. Mason's terminal. They had assigned precincts, so it would have been all but guaranteed that the same group who'd left her and her friends in plastic handcuffs had been the same ones who beat Mason bloody during his arrest. If they thought all Nons 'criminals waiting to happen,' why did those disgusting images bother them so much?

A brief memory of how terrified she'd been that Mr. Mason would return from work and find them all helpless brought the taste of cheese sandwich back to her mouth. Would he have been so brazen as to walk in, pick up the girls in full view of the boys, and abduct them? She sighed. *No, the man was a coward. He wouldn't want witnesses.*

Sarah murmured and cuddled tighter.

Dolls, teddy bears, or anything of the sort had been a mystery to Maya. Her former home had been so austere it could've passed as a demonstration unit for prospective tenants. Having Sarah squeezing her like some overgrown stuffed animal did make her feel somewhat better, and lessened her worry that Genna would get hurt enough to let her eyelids become heavy.

The apartment hung in deathly silence. Her head felt detached from her body, as if floating off.

Thump, thump, thump. "Quiet down in there," muttered The Dad on the other side of the wall.

Approaching sleep backed off, leaving her fully awake. Maya rolled her eyes. *We couldn't be any quieter unless we stopped breathing.* She scowled at the wall. *He's probably hearing the rats two apartments over.*

Drone fans approached outside the window.

Maya pulled the sheets up over her head, scooting down to hide.

"Mmm?" whispered Sarah. Moonlight striking the white sheet illuminated the small igloo of bedding. "What?"

Wide-eyed, Maya pointed toward the window and whispered, "There's a drone outside."

The buzzing became louder and faded, grew louder again, and trailed off the other way.

"It sounds small," whispered Maya.

"Rat killer?" Sarah yawned.

The Dad bumped the wall again, though the single, softer thump most likely happened by accident while he tossed and turned. A minute or so later, he grunted. The squeak of a door came from the hallway, and shuffling went by their room. After the *clank* of a toilet seat, the echo of nocturnal urination came from the hallway.

Sarah grinned.

"It's *so* loud!" whispered Maya, also smiling.

"Yeah." Sarah put a hand over her mouth and giggled.

That got Maya laughing. She bit her arm to muffle herself.

When The Dad farted, Maya wanted to laugh aloud so badly she cried. Sarah made a gagging face before muffling herself in the pillow, shaking the whole bed with the giggles. The echo of peeing ceased.

Bweee. Bweee. Bweee.

The electronic beeping from the other side of the wall killed Sarah's smile as fast as a light switch. She shot upright, a look of pure terror on her face.

Maya, not quite done laughing, glanced up at her. "He set his alarm for the middle of the night?"

"No." Sarah put her hand over Maya's mouth and whispered, "Someone just opened the front door; we need to hide." She leapt over Maya and pulled her out of bed, heading for the closet.

"No," rasped Maya, setting her heels in an effort to resist being dragged. "That's the first place they'll check."

Sarah searched around for a second before diving at the closet and grabbing the Hornet pistol.

The Dad grumbled something unintelligible and ran by, heading to his bedroom.

Maya crept up to the door and peered into the hall. Two men in black with facemasks had entered the apartment. One stood in the center of the living room with a small rifle pointed in the general direction of the hallway while the other one edged up to the kitchen.

No! Maya rolled away from the door, back to the wall, hoping they hadn't seen her.

Sarah backed out of the closet, holding the yellow-and-black striped gun.

"We gotta run!" whisper-yelled Maya, running over to grab Sarah.

The Dad glided past the door, fired a rapid barrage from his rifle, and shouted, "Sons um bitches! P'rim-ter breach!"

Maya screamed and clamped her hands over her ears as the rapport of gunfire smashed the silence. Puffs of white dust burst out of the wall by the door. Sarah tackled her to the floor and crawled back against the bed, dragging her.

"Think ya kin sneak me?!" shouted The Dad during a brief pause in the firing.

Sarah pushed Maya down. "Stay here."

As soon as the girl took a step toward the door, Maya sprang up and grabbed her from behind. "No!"

The Dad roared in pain and broke into coughing, though his gun kept going off.

"Dad!" screamed Sarah. She thrashed, trying to get away from Maya.

Maya refused to let go but lacked the strength to stop her friend from dragging her to the doorway. They caught a fleeting glimpse of The Dad taking cover at the corner, shooting down the corridor, blood oozing from his back.

Muzzle flare flashed in the living room, and The Dad ducked a spray of plaster.

Sarah froze, trembling on her feet.

"Grr!" Maya snarled, wrapped herself around Sarah's middle, and hauled her across the bedroom to the window. "Fire escape!"

Sarah looked back and forth between the window and the door. "But...."

"They'll kill you!" Maya shook her. "We have to run!"

As if on cue, a bullet burst out of the wall above them in a spray of plaster dust.

Maya shoved the window open and climbed out onto the chilly metal fire escape. She turned back to help Sarah, but the girl stared at the doorway, sobbing. "Sarah! Come on! We gotta run!"

The *snap* of a nearby ricochet startled a high-pitched scream from Sarah. She leapt up and through the window. Maya hugged her for a split second before running to the stairs. The entire metal scaffold along the side of the building clattered with their meager weight, threatening to break off. With gunfire still raging overhead, Maya scurried down the first ramp to the sixth floor, rounded the railing, and came eye-to-camera with a drone the size of a housecat.

"Shit!" screamed Maya.

Sarah crashed into her from behind, almost taking her off her feet.

I knew it! Maya's anger flash burned, consuming panic and fear. The drone would trail them outside. The window on that level had been left open, the apartment below Sarah's unused. She climbed halfway in before she realized Sarah had continued past her to the next set of stairs.

"Here!" she yelled.

Her friend backpedaled, shrieking and waving her arms at the drone as if it were a giant wasp. Maya jumped down from the windowsill, stepping on something hard that crushed into slime. The drone glided up to the window as if it would follow them straight inside. Without bothering to look, she grabbed the first object she spotted, an old trophy of some kind, and threw it at the buzzing annoyance.

The block of wood and crystal clipped the drone's left side, sending the small remote camera into a spin. It bounced off the metal gridding of the sixth-floor fire escape and tumbled out into the air over the street. From the pitch change in the fans, she figured it recovered in a few seconds.

Sarah came in the window head first, slithering forward until her hands touched carpet.

When Maya took a step back to help her up, she again stepped on something hard that burst into a patch of slime. "There's a lot of roaches in here, aren't there?" She didn't look down.

"Daddy!" whimpered Sarah. "They shot him."

"They're gonna shoot us too. We don't have time to be sad right now." Maya grabbed her by the hand and ran.

Somewhere between nine and fourteen roaches died to her bare feet between the back bedroom and the front door. Maya squealed in disgust for the whole sprint, and continued gagging as she ran down the corridor to the elevators.

"What are you doing?" whispered Sarah. "They're broken."

Maya punched in the code on the up/down buttons, and shoved the fake elevator door open inward. "No time to explain." She grabbed Sarah and pulled her into the doorway. "Ladder. Down. Go!"

Without a word, Sarah extended her leg to the ladder and nervously shifted her weight onto it. Maya bounced on her toes, gaze locked on the stairway behind them, dreading those men would show up before she could get out of sight. Sarah needed to move faster. As soon as the girl went down a rung, Maya jumped in and slammed the door behind her.

"Gah!" Sarah wailed. "It's dark!"

"Shh! If they come looking, they'll hear us," whispered Maya.

"I'm scared," whispered Sarah.

"It's okay. We're safe in here. We don't have to break our necks. You can climb slow, just stay quiet."

"'Kay."

The tromp of boots echoed in the shaft from above. Maya peered into the dark, imagining the two men going right past the elevator without giving it a second look. The dented and warped doors had been good enough to fool the Authority for years. If *two* men went by, that probably meant that Sarah's father... She swallowed the lump in her throat. *Maybe it's a whole team, or they backed off. The drone saw us go out the window. They didn't need to keep shooting at him.*

Minutes passed in a gradual descent. Her feet stuck to the rung from the bug guts on her soles, but she kept quiet. Too much adrenaline in her system made worrying about cockroach germs trivial. Eventually, the glow from the weak LEDs at the bottom lifted the elevator shaft out of total darkness, and Sarah moved faster.

At the bottom, Sarah stepped off the ladder into a spin, surveying the chamber. "What is this?"

Maya wiped her feet on the concrete after she got off the ladder. "You can't tell anyone about this. It's top-secret Brigade stuff. Only for emergencies."

"What are we supposed to do now?" Sarah, shivering, stared at her.

The older girl appeared frightened, small, and vulnerable standing there in the dim light, a far cry from the little mother who always looked out for the smaller kids. The sight of her lost and confused, clutching the Hornet to her chest like some twisted child's toy, broke Maya's artificial courage. She clasped her hands over her mouth and wept.

Her tears got Sarah's flowing.

Maya hurried over and held on. The girls clung to each other, shaking in the dark with a gentle side-to-side rocking, chins resting on shoulders. Every so often, the noise of someone moving past one of the elevator doors made her twitch. Eventually, crying gave way to staring into space.

"Why did the Authority try to kill us?" whispered Sarah.

Maya sniffled. "They aren't Authority."

"Who are they?" whispered Sarah.

She shivered. "I don't know. Bad guys."

They didn't look like anything she'd ever seen before. Not military, not Ascendant, not Authority. Clinging to Sarah, Maya gazed up at the damp, moldy ceiling.

A forgotten, crumbling tunnel didn't feel like such a scary place after all.

[8]

BEE STINGS

On a cot beneath the ground, under a coarse wool blanket, Maya and Sarah held each other, trying to stay quiet and motionless.

A cluster of camping beds and locker cabinets lined the walls of a larger tunnel beyond the dangerous narrow section that appeared ready to collapse, where the Brigade had tunneled from the bottom of the elevator shaft into an existing subway or sewer. There, they had created a small sanctuary.

Maya stared at the wall, rubbing Sarah's shoulder whenever she cried and staring over her at the wall during stretches of silence. She jerked awake with a start, realizing she'd passed out at some point. The gloomy space robbed her of any sense of time. Sarah had gone from hugging her chest-to-chest to mostly lying on her back with one arm across her forehead. The girl's hand had turned black from the filthy ladder. Maya watched her breathe, battling a growing sense of guilt that what had happened to The Dad had been her fault.

"What time is it?" mumbled Sarah, not opening her eyes.

"I don't know." Maya pushed herself up to sit and looked around. "There's no clocks down here."

"I think I fell asleep." Sarah moved her arm from her forehead to rest at her side.

"Yeah. Me too, but it could've been only a few minutes."

Sarah yawned. "I don't think so. I gotta pee real bad."

"Mmm." Maya pulled the blanket aside and got up. She frowned at her T-shirt nightdress and scratched at her shoulder where it peeked out the neck opening. "That man...."

"What man?" Sarah sat up and swung her legs over the side.

"The one we saw leaving Mr. Mason's apartment. He looked at me weird. I think he knew who I was."

"So?" asked Sarah. "Everyone in every city knows who you are."

Maya waved her hands on either side of her head for emphasis. "No, I mean he recognized me and probably sent those guys."

"Why would he do that? He seemed to get mad about Mr. Mason." Sarah stood and looked around.

Maya forced herself to sit up and let her feet dangle over the side of the cot.

"Can we go back up?" Sarah bit her lip. "I wanna find Dad."

"I dunno. They might be waiting for me. That little drone." Maya shivered. "There's a way out at the end of the tunnel. They won't be watching that."

Sarah wandered to the left, deeper into the dark. "They shot him."

"I still heard him cursing when we went out the window. The drone saw me. Those guys probably ran after us and left your dad alone."

"You think?" Sarah made a sudden turn and jogged a few steps to an exposed toilet against the wall. She lifted her dress without hesitation and sat.

Maya whirled away. "Uhh, I hope so."

"Sorry. I couldn't wait. What's a little lack of privacy after being shot at?"

Maya let out a sad chuckle but still didn't look.

Once the (sort of) flush happened, Maya slid off the cot and walked over to take a seat on the toilet, grateful the lack of light hid all the frightening details of what she must be touching. Sarah hovered protectively close.

"Maybe we should stay here until Genna comes back?" asked Sarah. "Is there food?"

Maya hopped back to her feet, taking a moment to wipe imagined contamination off the backs of her legs before reaching up to the improvised flush valve. "I don't think so. If they stored food here, there'd be rats. Maybe those ration things, but I don't think people are supposed to camp in this place for days. And if those men are waiting for us, I have to warn Genna and the others before they go inside."

Sarah looked down.

"And find an Authority officer to get help for your dad."

"What?" Sarah gawked at her. "They'll just finish him off if he's even still alive. And it could've been them last night!"

"No. Blueberries wouldn't have snuck inside at night. They'd have kicked down the door and walked right in—after locking down the whole building. And they hate guns more than they hate Nons. Don't forget your dad's a veteran. He's still a Citizen. They'll care." Maya grabbed her hand. "Come on."

"Veterans are allowed to have guns," said Sarah.

"They are?" Maya glanced at her.

"Yeah. That's what Dad says." Sarah stuffed the Hornet under her dress. Without the holster, she kept her hand on it so it didn't fall. "Someone will *definitely* want to steal this."

Chunks of concrete littered the tunnel ahead, with the occasional bit of pipe or cluster of plastic bottles for variety. Maya stepped with care, wary of putting her unprotected feet down on something sharp. It made her think of the first time Genna wanted to carry her into the Hab, worried she'd cut herself on glass or something.

"Ow," said Sarah. "You're gonna break my hand."

"Sorry." Maya stopped squeezing so hard.

"I'm scared too." Sarah wiped her nose on the back of her left arm but didn't let go of Maya's hand. "Dad was gonna go to the VA. He's too sick to get shot."

"Getting shot sucks no matter how sick you are or aren't."

Their voices echoed off the mold-stained walls, devoured by the darkness in front and behind. The deeper they went, the heavier the stink of mildew and dirt became. Feeble LED bricks gave off only enough light to reveal the walls and some of the bigger rocks in the way. The passageway took on a gradual curve after several minutes of walking. A cluster of metal cabinets on the wall bore labels reading 'High Voltage,' 'Maryland Transit Administration,' and an inspection sticker dated June 2031.

"Wow, this is long," said Sarah. "Are you sure there's an end?"

"Genna said it goes to the outside. It's how they escape the Authority. You can't tell anyone about it. She made me promise not to tell anyone."

Sarah squeezed her hand. "Sorry."

"No way was I gonna leave you there. Mom can yell at me all she wants. Getting shot at was an emergency." Maya stopped, bug-eyed. "Oh, shit."

"Stop swearing. You're too little."

Maya turned her head slow, looking up at her with dread in her eyes. "I think they wanted to *kill* me. They were shooting into your room."

"They fired at Dad. If they wanted to hit us blind, they'd have gone full auto."

"'Kay." Maya swallowed hard, not quite believing that but finding it more appealing.

"Look." Sarah pointed.

A thin rectangle of daylight ahead suggested the presence of a door leading outside. Around it, down-angled shafts of sun illuminated swirling particles of dust. Without another word, Maya hurried up to a jog, tugging Sarah along until they reached a metal-and-wood barricade braced against the floor by thick beams that blocked off the end of the tunnel. At its center, a steel door with a push bar had been mounted to a hand-built frame. The soft moan of wind emanated from the other side, raising rattles and clinks from all the junk. A faint breeze slipped past the gap around the door, brushing her face with fresh air.

Maya gave the bar a shove and the door opened with a scrape. The sudden bright light made her squint at a huge crater of dirt and concrete chunks, strewn with old furniture. From where she stood, the ground continued downward in a bowl shape, pale swirls of dust appearing and vanishing in the breeze. A pathway of dumpsters, ladders, and desks led up to the ground surface on the right side of the collapse. At the far end, the mammoth shapes of two decrepit boilers slept like long-dead dragons under a layer of silt.

"There must've been a skyscraper here." Sarah looked straight up. "Dad said some of the old subways had stations right in the basements of important buildings. Guess this one blew up, or a bomb hit it."

Maya stepped onto the soft dirt and let the door close behind them.

Corrugated steel on the outside held some mismatched pipes and scrap metal, making the exit appear like an impassable wall. She studied the area until spotting a potential route to the top, beginning with a giant transoceanic shipping box half-buried in the rubble. From there, a pathway formed of ruined furniture, concrete slabs, trucks, and other junk spanned almost halfway around the circular basin on its way to the surface.

She held her free arm to the side for balance while descending the hill, and hurried to the cargo box. Sarah released her hand for the climb since she didn't want to let go of the Hornet.

Maya shimmied up the ladder to the top, then scrambled over a few concrete slabs to a dumpster. After crossing that, she traversed a 'bridge' made of three office desks in a row with short jumps between them. Another concrete slab formed a ramp up to the roof of a half-buried box truck it partially crushed, the vehicle's nose long ago vanished under the collapse. At the front end, she climbed the dirt burying the cab, crawled through a scary maze of sharp rebar spikes jutting from concrete fragments, and dropped down onto a debris-free dirt path that spanned the last thirty feet to the surface. She paused to catch her breath, winded from the arduous climb. Sarah seemed to appreciate the break as well. A few minutes later, they walked side by side along the soft trail.

At street level, Maya entered a 'room' formed by three crumbling walls without a roof. Their height varied, but the lowest point reached about the middle of where a second story would've been—too high to go over. Copious amounts of graffiti decorated the naked cinder blocks. The smell of burning wood and burned meat hit her hard enough to draw forth a cough.

A group of older boys sitting around an array of old chairs, sofas, and benches all looked at the two of them.

Glints and spots of color from the ground brought her attention to hundreds of discarded autoinjectors and plastic sheets used to hold drug derm patches. The youngest had to be about eighteen, the eldest perhaps a few years older. Four of the seven wore bright yellow jackets with hoods; the others sported the mismatched scraps of Dead Space dwellers. One man's clothing consisted entirely of a jock strap, a football helmet, and pink sneakers. Most had a half-awake glaze to their eyes, and two suffered persistent full-body twitching.

All of them looked like trouble.

Sarah climbed over the edge of the broken floor slab and stood behind her.

The walled-in area had once been the ground floor of a building. Other than going back down into the crater, the only exit sat to the right, where a former doorway (sans door) had been enlarged by someone bashing out a few cinder blocks.

Don't even talk to them. Maya offered a polite 'excuse me' smile, grabbed Sarah's left hand, and started moving at a brisk pace toward the doorway.

A man in one of the bright jackets drifted into her path. The right side of his head had been shaved bald. Black hair from the left half hung down to his belt. "Well, look at that."

Maya halted, gaze darting between the doser and the doorway behind him. "Sorry for walking into your place. We're lost. Just going to go home now."

The others ambled over, forming a human wall in front of them.

Jock Strap hefted a metal baseball while staring intently at Sarah. He sniffed, huffed, and took on an almost dog-like posture. "We fightin' 'em?"

"Take their shit," said another man in a yellow coat.

"We ain't gonna get much. Just a shirt and a rag." One of the twitchy guys, with short blond hair, rubbed his finger back and forth under his nose. "Almost ain't even worth it."

"If we can sell it, it's worth it. We'll get a couple bucks for their shit." A guy with a scraggly sorta-beard and a permanent nosebleed took a step closer, making a 'give it here' gesture at Maya. "Come on, rat. Let's have it."

"Wait, wait." A tall, skinny man with no shirt, prominent ribs, and a milked-over left eye pointed at Sarah. A few scar lines left hairless trails in his four-day beard. "Let 'em keep the rags. We can sell them bitches to DeeDee."

Twitchy laughed. "Hah. Take the rags too. They won't need 'em at DeeDee's."

Half-Hair scrunched up his nose. "DeeDee? Naw. That redhead's flat-chested. Don't even have fuckin' bee-stings yet."

"You sick bastard." The oldest, a ginger-haired man with a beard down to his crotch, threw a bottle at Milk-Eye. "Even that crazy bitch won't make these two work yet."

Jock Strap grunted, clenched the bat, and kept eyeing the man next to him. "Fight? Fight?"

"How old you is?" asked Milk-Eye.

"I'm nine, and she's eleven. Too young for prostitutes." Maya glared at them.

"Ehh, DeeDee might take 'em. Keep 'em 'til they old 'nuff ta work," muttered a guy with a shaved head.

"Redhead's close enough," said the youngest of the dosers. "I'd hit that." He raised a small device to his mouth and inhaled hard. Once a momentary convulsion passed, his eyes crossed. All the veins in his face and neck stood out as his skin reddened. "Oh... yeah."

"Dude..." Twitchy stared at him. "That ain't cool."

A handful of the other dosers edged away from the youngest, varying levels of disdain in their glares.

Jock Strap glanced back and forth between the group and the youngest. Wild eyes and a confused expression made him look like he *really* wanted to wallop someone with his bat.

"I'm gonna be sick," whispered Sarah. "Let's run back down."

"I have some money at home." Maya tried to tap into Vanessa's haughty confidence to stop herself from shaking. "I'll make you a deal. You let us leave. One of you comes with to make sure we get home safe, and I'll give you ten NuCoin. That's way more than you'd get for selling our clothes."

"Bullshit," said Half-Hair. "You had that much coin, you'd 'ave more than a ratty old shirt on."

"We're wearing crap so cretins like you don't rob us. I know who DeeDee is, and I don't want to become a harlot."

"Not gonna be no harlot." The youngest kept staring at Sarah. "You's gon' be a pros-a-toot."

"They're the same thing, idiot," said Maya. "And I don't want to be either one."

"Too bad for you then, eh?" Half-Hair lifted a handgun from his belt. "Now, you two are gonna do what you're told. Don't make me have ta get nasty. DeeDee'll take nice care of you 'til you're old enough to earn your keep."

Maya looked at Sarah, fear plain in her expression. *How much do they think that woman will pay him for us?* "All right. Fine. I'll pay you thirty NuCoin."

The dosers laughed.

Half-Hair gestured around at the others. "Hey, Possum. You still got those cuffs? These two look like they're gonna try an' run, deprivin' us all of our finder's fee."

"Possum gets caught so much he's got a private cell," said Milk-Eye.

Some of the men scowled at the girls, as if their refusal to be sold to DeeDee equated to stealing the dosers' drugs.

"Uhh." A skinny twenty-something in a shredded black coat patted himself down. "Think so, but I ain't got a key."

Half-Hair laughed. "Key's DeeDee's problem. Fix 'em together at the ankle so's they can't run."

"Over here, sweetness," said the youngest doser, waving at Sarah. His eyes vibrated from whatever drug he'd taken, seeming ready to pop straight out of his skull. "I'll carry that one. She won't get nowhere." He winked at her. "Lemme see them bee stings."

Half-Hair fidgeted, looking decidedly uncomfortable. A man in a yellow coat behind the youngest muttered something to him, which seemed to frighten the man. He took a step back from Sarah.

"I don't wanna show you any bee stings." Sarah ceased trembling and stared at Half-Hair. She let go of Maya's hand and reached under the folds of her curtain-dress. Her expression hardened. "But I'll let you see my Hornet sting."

She yanked the stunner pistol out from under her dress and shot Half-Hair in the face. The glow-tipped silver dart embedded itself a finger's width to the left of his nose, glowing and sizzling. Sparks wrapped around his entire head; foam sprayed from his mouth as his eyes rolled up, consciousness lost before he even started to collapse. Sarah fired another dart at the man beside him, catching him in the right pectoral. Electric blue flashes danced across his fluorescent yellow jacket. Body rigid, he slammed into the ground like a board, flat on his front, and convulsed.

"Fight!" roared Jock Strap, raising the bat.

"Go!" shouted Sarah as she took off running.

Maya sprinted after her, leaping the stunned doser and ducking away from grabbing hands. Seconds later, another guy in a yellow coat caught up to them. He grabbed a fistful of Maya's T-shirt at her back and got his other hand on Sarah's hair. She twisted around and jammed the Hornet into his arm, triggering the contact-stun electrodes. The doser careened over sideways into a rolling wipeout, cradling his arm and wailing.

With open space ahead, Sarah poured on speed and ran screaming down the street.

Hoping someone with a scrap of decency might hear, Maya followed suit, letting off a loud, clear shriek but not quite managing to turn it into the word 'help.' She strained to go faster as Sarah pulled a frightening distance ahead. Having spent her life surrounded by danger, her friend's body was no stranger to hauling ass. Maya had done more running in the weeks since her abduction than the preceding nine years put together and struggled to keep that pace for more than a few minutes. Only her desperate panic at being sold into prostitution kept her going.

Scenery blurred by in a meaningless haze. She pushed, motivating herself by combining the memory of when Genna's mercs handcuffed her leg to a bed frame with the nightmare scenario of Mr. Mason finding her like that. What awaited her at DeeDee's sounded much the same. Maya belted out another scream and ignored everything except for the patch of red hair in front of her.

Sarah slowed a little, allowing Maya to catch up, but kept going for two cross streets before veering around a dead car. She jumped over what might have been a fridge and swerved around a hard left turn into an alley, startling a group of pigeons to wing. Frags sleeping or drinking booze occupied a row of large plastiboard boxes lining both sides of the alley. Few of the men and women paid attention to Maya's screaming.

At the end of the block, Sarah grabbed the corner of the building to go left, ducking under a huge neon sign full of Chinese symbols. They darted through a cloud of steam billowing from a metal shroud on the wall into the scent of chicken broth. Sarah hesitated at the door as if she contemplated going in for help, but a cluster of young Chinese men with guns gave her warning stares, as if the girls had interrupted some secret meeting. She leapt away with an "Eep! Sorry!" and sprinted off down the crumbling sidewalk.

Maya glanced back at the crash of the dosers barging past the Frags in the alley. She let out a frightened shriek and ran into Sarah's back, pushing her to run faster. Four blocks later, her friend made a sudden left turn into another alley where her stride broke; she loped to a halt against a crumbling building, gasping for breath and choking. Maya stumbled up beside her and slumped against the brickwork, wheezing. Sarah trudged a few steps more to scoot around behind an old wash-er/dryer unit, where she collapsed with her back to the wall, Hornet in her lap, and hands over her face.

Maya flopped next to her, barely able to breathe.

They sat for a few minutes, trying to muffle their desperate gulps of air. Eventually, Sarah's expression brightened from 'about to cry' to 'trying not to laugh.' "Did you see the face that guy made?"

"Yeah!" Maya giggled into her hands. "I bet he shit himself. I can't believe you shot him."

"It's just a stunner." Sarah coughed, gagged, and choked a little. "I can't believe I did too. He had a real gun. He could've killed me."

Maya coughed into her hands. "My lungs are on fire."

Sarah nodded, wheezing.

The clamor of men running echoed off the walls.

"Shit," muttered Sarah.

Maya overacted a gasp of shock at her friend using a swear word.

In the span of a second, the hide-or-run decision flashing in her eyes went in favor of run, and she sprang to her feet, dragging Maya along. The dosers had entered the alley, alarmingly close to where they'd been hiding. Fear destroyed the pain in her legs, and on a burst of second wind, Maya scrambled to keep her balance. Sarah's hand closed around hers like a vice, a silent affirmation that they'd either both get away or both get caught.

At the end of the alley, Sarah headed left.

The girls rounded the corner and stumbled to a stop in the middle of another crowd of older teens lounging around on derelict vehicles or car seats set up in the middle of the road. Maya's attention leapt to a young man with cherry red hair, the same man who'd killed a guy in the apart-ment they'd been scavving, the one who joked about shooting Pick—*little kids make the hardest targets.* On the left, leaning against an upside-down pickup truck, stood the man with a tattoo of a grinning horned skull over his sternum. He still had the airbrushed violet strip across his eyes and the leather jacket. At the sight of the girls, he grinned.

Sarah stared around at the gang punks before glancing at the Hornet, but didn't raise it.

The dosers spilled into the street behind them.

Maya glanced back over her shoulder at the druggies, then at the punks in front of her. Trapped between men wanting to sell her to a woman who'd force them into prostitution and men who'd probably shoot them for target practice, she pressed herself tight to Sarah's side. Every ounce of her wanted to scream "Mommy," but Genna couldn't hear her.

[9]

CHERRY RED

Staring from dosers to gangers and back again, Maya squeezed Sarah tighter.

The guy with the purple across his eyes had to be over six feet tall, and more than one handgun lurked in the space under his black leather jacket.

"Hey there." Cherry Red tilted his head back in a brief nod of greeting, his gaze on Maya. His raspy voice reminded her how he'd berated the man they'd bound with duct tape, the man they'd killed after the kids had left the apartment.

The big guy with the tattoo pushed himself off the car and stood upright. "I 'member these two. Hidin' in our place."

A faint whine leaked from Sarah's nose.

Half-Hair stumbled around the corner behind them, staggering up to the rest of the dosers. Blood ran down his cheek from where the Hornet dart had nailed him, and he still didn't appear to have full control of his legs—the left wouldn't bend at the knee. He clutched his handgun in an arm as stiff as a two-by-four, twitching and emitting gurgles while glaring at Sarah.

Jock Strap raised the bat and started to rush at her, but two other dosers in yellow coats grabbed him.

"No, man," said one. "We need 'em alive or there ain't no money. There ain't no money, there ain't no Fume."

"Oh..." Jock Strap lowered the bat and inhaled hard, as if taking a hit. His face twitched as the daydreamed rush of drugs washed over him. "I like Fume."

Maya thought back to how the gang punks let her and the other kids leave *before* they murdered Dave. She decided to take a big chance and darted forward, pulling Sarah by the arm, scrambling up to stand in front of Cherry Red. "Help us, please. These guys want to steal our clothes and sell us to DeeDee to be prostitutes."

"Huh?" Cherry Red looked from Maya to the dosers. "The fuck's wrong with you? They're like *little*."

Hope bloomed in Maya's heart. She scooted around behind him and pointed at the youngest doser. "That one wanted to have sex with Sarah, and she's only eleven."

"Back off, street meat," said Half-Hair, shuddering as he raised his paralyzed right arm, the gun held mostly sideways. His body jerked and trembled. No matter how hard he tried, he couldn't keep himself from swaying.

Cherry Red—and all eight of his friends—pulled guns, except for the big guy with purple on his face, who whipped out a pair.

Sarah gawked at Maya, glanced at the gang punks, then stared back at her with a 'holy shit' expression. The dosers had one gun, Half-Hair's, to the ganger's nine. Dosers who only carried bats, pipes, knives, or hammers appeared to lose some confidence, except for Jock Strap (who held his bat up as if he could swat bullets out of the air with it) and Half-Hair, who struggled to point his gun at Cherry Red.

"This ain't your shit," said Half-Hair. "Them bitches is ours."

Cherry Red glanced down at the girls. "They ain't bitches yet. Look like a couple little kids to me."

"We found 'em first," said the pervert, pointing at Sarah. He flinched, swatted at nothing, and wiped his hand over his face several times fast. "Money's ours."

"Hmm. I don't see any tits there." Cherry Red leaned closer to Sarah.

She leaned back and whimpered, "Please don't."

He shifted his gaze up to her eyes, winked, and whispered, "You two get down," before raising his voice. "End 'em."

Maya dove to ground as gunfire exploded overhead. She crawled a short distance to the left and hunkered down for cover behind a rusting derelict car, hands over her ears. Sarah scrambled over and clung to her. They huddled as low to the ground as they could get, screaming as a fusillade of pistol shots thundered. Maya shrieked (not that anyone noticed over the gunfire) when a hot, spent casing landed on bare skin a few inches above her knee. She swatted it away and looked up. A puff of dust burst from Cherry Red's left arm as a passing bullet gouged the sleeve of his leather jacket.

Another shot hit the car with a *clank*, sending bits of white glass washing over them like a rain of small diamonds.

She sucked up a lungful of air that reeked of cordite and screamed again, squeezing herself against the old tire. Sarah pulled her close, trembling. The barrage ceased in a few seconds, leaving her scream clear and loud. Maya's yell trailed off to silence when her lungs ran out of air.

Cherry Red's voice came from right above her. "S'all good now."

She lifted her head, sending a cascade of glass bits tumbling from her hair. The gang leader bled a little from the graze on his shoulder but didn't seem bothered by it. Other gang members converged on a spread of beer cans laid out on an old car trunk, which they hastily packed into a box.

"Dude was fucked up," said a man behind Maya, the likely source of the hot brass. "Could barely hit the car. Bet he took some good shit."

"He dosed Hornet," said Maya. "Right in the face."

Sarah reached up, grasped the top of the car door, and pulled herself into a squat, staring silent and wide-eyed through the shot-out windows at the carnage beyond. The girl said nothing, but didn't have to. Maya didn't want to look at what had become of the dosers and shook herself to get rid of the rest of the glass, keeping her eyes on the road.

"Hey." Cherry Red picked her up by a hand under each arm, carried her a few steps, and set her down on clear pavement. "Watch yer step. That's glass."

"Drones are comin'," said Tattoo.

"Yep." Cherry Red returned to the car and carried Sarah to safe ground. "You two best get on outta here 'fore the Authority shows up."

"Thank you." Maya smiled.

"Bah." The gang leader waved her off. "Can't say no ta some target practice. 'Sides, you got some righteous friends, Maya."

She blinked. The shock of being recognized faded in seconds. Of course, her face had been *everywhere* with the Brigade video. Did that make her part of the underground? Had she become a criminal? The gang gathered their beer and ran into an alley across the street from the one the girls came from.

Sarah clutched her hand again and pulled her along at a run, continuing in the same direction they'd been going before. She headed for an open doorway a short distance later, entering a dusty room filled with shelves and mannequins. Once inside, she slowed to a silent walk around the sales counter toward the rear of the building. Maya followed, peering back over her shoulder every few seconds at the unmistakable whirr of Authority drones that had no doubt sensed the gunfire.

Yellowed paper crinkled underfoot in a narrow corridor leading from the front room to a plain white door at the end, with a tiny bathroom on the right most of the way toward the end. A pile of porcelain chunks remained where someone had smashed a toilet. The likely culprit, a sledgehammer, lay on the floor nearby. Spiders scurried up the walls, and a few four-inch roaches emerged from a stack of boxes to investigate what disturbed their home.

Maya shied away from the bugs, bumping Sarah in an effort to nudge her faster. The door at the end opened with a spray of peeling paint, revealing a small office containing a single desk, a pair of filing cabinets, and a ceiling fan with beard-like strips of dark grey dust dangling from the blades. The air smelled (and tasted) like wet socks that had been sitting for a few days. Sunlight leaking past slats in the rotting ceiling painted bands of glow in the floating haze.

Maya inched in, threading her feet between piles of rocky debris and rusting cans. Sarah pushed the door closed behind them and turned a deadbolt.

"We're too close," whispered Maya.

Sarah led her behind the desk and crawled into the hollow beneath it, between two sets of drawers. "They'll be looking for anyone running. We aren't faster than drones. We didn't do anything wrong. If the

Authority comes in here, stay quiet. If they find us, we'll say we heard guns and hid."

"Okay." Maya nodded. "That sounds like something little kids would do."

Sarah grinned for a second, then looked sick. "Ugh. They shot them all."

"You have glass in your hair." Maya scooted around to face her and got to picking the sparkling fragments away one by one, tossing them aside.

"I'm so scared." Sarah bit her lip. Again, she lost her little mother bearing, looking more like a terrified six-year-old. "I want my dad."

"Everyone had to hear them shooting. Doc Chang is right downstairs on the sixth. He definitely heard the guns going off. The men saw us go out the window so they left, and Doc would've helped your dad." Maya kept picking bits of automotive glass out of Sarah's thick hair. "Those men are probably still watching our building. They had a little drone. It's probably still there looking for us. If we go back, someone else could get hurt."

Sarah's lip quivered as tears slid down her cheeks. "W-what about that Barnes guy?"

"He went with Mom." Maya gave her a once-over, finding no more sparkling bits. She frowned at the curtain-dress, wide strips of pale skin visible where safety pins had stretched. "Your dress is falling apart."

Sarah shrugged one shoulder, seeming unconcerned.

"Minute..." Maya repositioned safety pins, moving them to non-ripped spots and tightening the fit of her friend's improvised garment. The yellowed former-curtain fabric had gone brittle in spots. Of course, to buy something to replace it, they'd have to get home to the money. After some minutes of pulling her fingers through Sarah's hair, a sparkling not-diamond fell from Maya's head and landed between her knees. "Ugh. Glass in my hair still. Check me?"

"Sure." Sarah smiled back at her.

Cross-legged, Maya turned to give Sarah a clear look at her hair, rested her elbows on her knees, and mushed both fists into her cheeks. Bit by bit, Sarah cleared glass from her wild black mane.

"Your hair is so pretty," said Sarah. "At least when we're not running for our life. I'm jealous. Whenever it's really humid out, I turn into the frizz monster. Yours is always so straight."

Maya almost giggled. "Umm, so do I. The straightening isn't natural. Well, I mean it is... but my genes are custom ordered. I think the hair is Japanese or something. I like yours more. I'm going to let mine get that long now. Always wanted to, but the bitch wouldn't let me. Had to stay perfect for the camera."

"It's long because I can't pay anyone to cut it and I keep forgetting. Sitting on my hair all the time isn't fun."

"Oh, you gotta keep it." Maya gasped. "It's *so* pretty that long."

"I dunno. Maybe." Sarah picked and plucked, hunting for glass bits.

While her friend worked, thoughts of what to do came and went. Home offered both the best and worst option, the most feeling of safety, but also the greatest risk—at least until Genna returned. Her mind went blank. Every few seconds, she flinched at a strand of hair pulling tight, but remained quiet. Sarah eventually shifted from removing and tossing glass bits to combing with her fingers.

Amid the meditative silence, her eyes started to close under the soothing gesture.

"I think we should go home. We can sneak up the alley out front. There's a lot of awnings and fire escapes there, so it would be hard for a drone to see us before we see it."

Maya pushed herself back from the edge of sleep. "I guess we can look, but we have to be careful."

"It's better than running into the wrong people out here. We're too far away from the Hab."

Getting closer to friendly, or at least more civilized areas sounded like a good idea. Those men who broke in at night would probably hesitate opening fire on a pair of kids in broad daylight with Authority drones in plain sight.

"Think it's safe to go?" asked Maya.

"I don't hear any blueberries. I bet they're not in a hurry. They saw a bunch of dead Nons. I bet they're more pissed that someone has guns than people died."

Maya crawled out from under the desk and stood. "Not sure those dosers counted as people."

"Ouch," said Sarah.

"They were going to *sell* us to a prostitute lady." Maya approached the door and put her ear to it. "They stopped being people when they thought that was a good idea."

Sarah flared her eyebrows with an eye roll. "Okay. Good point."

After listening for a few minutes and not hearing any armored boots tromping about, Maya undid the deadbolt and pulled the door open enough to look out. The old clothing store remained as empty as it had been earlier. Not wanting to deal with roaches, Maya sprinted down the hallway to the big showroom. Sarah walked, giving her a quizzical look.

"Bugs." She shivered.

"We already stepped on like a hundred of them."

"Eww," whispered Maya. Her feet felt slimy all over again from the mere thought.

Sarah crept up to the door, gave a quick left-right glance, and waved for Maya to follow.

They walked down empty streets littered with vehicles, about one in six a working e-car, the rest long dead husks riddled with bullet holes. Twice, they crossed the street to avoid packs of older teens and adults hanging around porches of decaying buildings. Much to her relief, they got no more attention than passing glances.

A couple blocks later, Sarah took a left onto a street that had more-intact buildings. The line where the official Habitation District started looked obvious even without the signs, a glaring difference about nine blocks ahead. On the near side of the 'border street,' the high-rises crumbled, many missing large sections of wall or whole corners. Less than thirty feet away across the road, the towers didn't appear too much worse than they had before the war. Patches of modern repair work showed bright grey against the darker original construction. Intact buildings stretched side to side as far as they could see, like a wall keeping out the decay of abandonment.

Sarah walked faster, likely pulled by her need to find out what happened to The Dad. Maya held on to her left wrist with both hands, her gaze fixed on the approaching (relative) cleanliness. They crossed a handful of streets, evaded a man with a shaved head in purple robes, and strayed into the road to get around a hotdog wagon with a sidewalk-clogging line. The sight of it made her think of 'nutrient tubes' and those crazy Jeva cultists. Sarah picked up speed when they came within one block of the entrance to the Hab.

No Authority officers staffed the checkpoint, a good sign. Three portable combat barriers, their dark blue metal scuffed and scratched, blocked the street between two booths, the whole thing surrounded by concertina wire. Perhaps the officers who'd normally stood guard there had been diverted to the scene of the doser shooting.

With a muffled yelp, Sarah stopped short when three blueberries wandered out from a side street at the edge of the Habitation District and strolled back to the checkpoint.

"Don't stop. Don't act scared," whispered Maya. "Just ignore them. We don't matter. We're just some street kids."

Her grip on Maya's hand tightened, but Sarah kept going, eyes downcast. The Authority officers conversed in voices clipped off with short bursts of static from their helmet speakers. Apparently, they shared The Dad's love of football. None even glanced at the girls as they hurried around the barricades and entered the Habitation District. Sarah headed to the right and jumped out of the road onto the sidewalk without breaking stride.

The number of people increased the farther they went. One or two approached as if to beg, but retreated without much protest after getting a good look at them. Sarah kept the Hornet hidden under her dress, her head swiveling in a constant process of scanning their surroundings. A man climbing out of an e-car waved to Maya and grinned. Several steps later, a woman in a grey poncho and an air-filter mask coming the other way paused long enough to say, "Right on, kid."

Here and there, other people recognized her and offered waves, smiles, or raised fists in gestures of solidarity. Fear that more dosers or less-friendly gangs would find them faded. All she'd have to do here is scream 'help,' and it seemed likely ten or more people would come running. Her timid posture gave way to a confident stride, which Sarah sensed and matched.

Five blocks deep into the Hab, Sarah pulled her to a stop. "We're almost there. Left two streets ahead and down another three. If they're looking for you, we should start being sneaky now."

"Okay."

They cut left into an alley. Maya stared up past fire escapes laden with drying laundry, small grills, and an old person or six. A wrinkled man with streaks of yellow in his waist-long white beard. He stared down at them from a third floor patio shelf and took a long pull from a non-electric cigar. Age had weathered his features to the point Maya couldn't tell if he squinted out of suspicion or poor vision.

What little sky peeked between the fluttering linens, awnings, and patio extensions appeared drone free. Pigeons perched everywhere from the first to tenth floors, sat on wires, or milled around on the ground. The ballsy creatures walked right up to her as if expecting to be fed.

Sarah stopped a minute or so later at the end of the alley. She clung to the wall and peered around the corner. Her stomach growled.

"What?" Maya leaned up behind her and caught a whiff of food. Fried... something. Her mouth watered. It had to be well past noon, and neither one of them had eaten since the previous night.

"'Mon," said Sarah, pulling her around the corner. "Let's go scrapping."

"Scrapping?"

The building they'd been hiding by turned out to be a small restaurant, the source of the wonderful aroma. Two huge windows offered a view of a dining area full of booth seats opposite a counter where a man sat on a padded stool, back to the door. About a third of the booths had people sitting in them.

"It's free food," said Sarah.

She pushed the door open and walked in, heading to the left, past two empty tables and a couple in the middle of their meal. A plate with a scattering of fries and a bit of hamburger bun, as well as an untouched stack of lettuce/tomato/onion, sat on the fourth table. Since no one sat there, Sarah hurried over and divided the remaining fries as close to in half as possible. She pointed Maya at one pile and stuffed the other stack in her mouth.

Maya gawked.

Still chewing the fries, Sarah took one piece of tomato, and half the lettuce, and jammed it into her face.

Maya hesitantly picked up a cold fry and nibbled on it. "Someone else ate this."

"Smf?" asked Sarah. She swallowed. "So? Ours now. They don't want it."

"This is scrapping?" Maya picked up the other tomato slice with two fingers. It had no bite marks, so she gave it one.

"Yeah. They're just gonna throw it out." Sarah took two gulps out of a cup, and left the rest for Maya before moving to the next table.

Overcome by hunger, Maya cleared the plate and grabbed the cup. Water.

"Hi," said Sarah to the man seated at the fifth table. "Are you done with that? Can I have it?"

"Sure, kid." The short scuff of a plate sliding on table followed.

Maya put the empty cup down and hurried to Sarah's side. The plate in front of her held a few bread crusts and a half-eaten quarter of a sandwich. She broke it apart and gave Maya the slightly bigger piece.

The smell made it easy to forget some total stranger had bitten it before her, and Maya gobbled up the turkey, toast, lettuce, and something trying to be bacon. Someone cleared their throat on the other side of the place, sounding annoyed. Sarah ignored it and helped herself to a pile of potato chips on another plate at an empty table across the aisle from Turkey Sandwich Man. Maya gulped down her share and rushed over to feast on chips beside her friend.

"Hey," said a deep voice, above and behind them.

A firm hand landed on Maya's left shoulder.

Sarah let out an "Eep," spraying crumbs.

"What are you two doing?" asked the man.

Maya twisted to peer up at a large-framed man in a white apron over a blue flannel shirt. He had a few extra pounds on him and drooping jowls that gave his face a raindrop shape—much wider at the jaw than the top of his head. His clothes reeked of fried food so much she almost bit him.

"Uhh...."

Sarah went platter-eyed. "We're just asking for scraps. Please, we're no trouble."

"Where's your parents?" asked the man in a stern tone.

"I don't know," said Sarah, lip quivering.

"My mother had to go on a job that takes a few days. She's coming home soon."

The man pulled them along, ushering them to the end of the row.

With a shake of his head, he let go and gestured at the last booth seat in the corner. "Sit here an' keep quiet. I'll fix you some proper food."

Sarah blinked. It took a second for her to recover from her astonishment. "Thank you!" She bounced on her toes, grinning and crying.

"Yes. Thank you." Maya beamed. "Sorry if we're a little dirty. Bad guys tried to kidnap us and we've been hiding all day."

The man frowned. "The damn hell is wrong with people?" He sighed. "Got four of my own or I'd offer ta take yas in. Least I can do is give ya a decent meal."

"You're nice." Maya smiled. "When Mom comes home, she'll pay for our food."

He smiled like he didn't really expect anyone to show up with money, then walked off through a flapping door into a kitchen area, still grumbling about the state of the city.

Sarah crawled onto the bench seat against the wall. Maya scooted in beside her. Their perch offered a view of the entire room, except for where the dining area bent around the corner to the left on the far end of the counter. Still, the front door sat nine tables away directly in front of them. No one could walk in without being obvious. The wall by the window afforded a little concealment from the outside, helped along by a dusty plastic rhododendron and a fern, and the man who owned this place made her feel safe enough to relax.

Her feet hurt. Her legs ached. Her heart almost slowed back to normal.

"What are we gonna do?" asked Sarah.

"Eat," said Maya.

"Butt." Sarah poked her in the side. "I mean after."

Maya leaned against Sarah and held her hand. "I'll think of something."

[10]

ROAD WARRIORS

The restaurant owner returned carrying two plates, each holding a burger and a portion of fries. Both meat patties had a suspicious, perfect roundness, which told Maya they'd come from the Sanc, most likely artificially grown beef, since the only cows left roamed free, away from civilization. It struck her as odd that the elite in New Baltimore Sanctuary Zone regarded real meat as an expensive delicacy, but in the wildlands, people had gone back to farming. Out there among the 'savages,' keeping live animals for food had once again become commonplace. In the supposedly horrible, deadly, unlivable wildlands, people thought nothing of eating a steak that would cost someone $600 here.

All thoughts of economics and ridiculousness blanked from her mind when she got a whiff of the food placed in front of her.

"Go on, eat up." The man smiled. "You both look like you could use a decent meal."

Sarah murmured gratitude around a mouthful of burger.

"Thank you for being nice." Maya smiled at him and picked up hers.

Like a pair of starving dogs, the girls attacked their food. Maya inhaled the first half of the huge hamburger before slowing down enough to taste it. After a few breaths to let her stomach settle, she munched on fries between mouthfuls of beef. Despite feeling full, she kept going until she licked meat juice and salt from her empty plate.

"That was *so* good," whispered Sarah. "Okay, so what do you wanna do? We could sneak down the alley and check the place out. If we don't see anything, go in?"

Maya sucked at her teeth, trying to dislodge a stuck bit of meat. "Maybe. What if we told the Authority and asked them for help?"

"No." Sarah frowned. "They'll arrest us for bothering them. Or just zip-cuff us and leave us with our hands tied to our feet in an alley because it's funny."

"They didn't do that to me when I told them about the creep." Maya raised an eyebrow. "You can hide and I'll talk to them."

"No. We need a new plan. I don't trust them." Sarah gave her a pleading stare. "Please."

Maya tapped her fingers on her knees, racking her brain for something that didn't involve walking straight into a trap or involve blueberries. Maybe the restaurant owner would let them stay here until Genna came home?

"Ready?" asked Sarah.

Maya scratched at her overfull belly. "I can't move yet. I don't think it's a good idea to go back so soon."

"I gotta find my dad." Sarah looked down at her lap, picking at her fingernails. "I need to know if he's okay."

The urgency in her voice made Genna's absence hurt even more. "He wouldn't want you to get hurt. If those men are still watching, they might just shoot us. I'm scared."

"We have to do *something*. We can't just sit here all day."

"I know. I know." Maya grasped her hand. "What are we going to do? We're a couple of little kids. Barnes and Weber are on the same trip as my mom. Book is too old to fight. Doc doesn't have any guns. I don't want to be responsible for anyone else being hurt." She choked up. "I'm..." *Cough.* "Sorry about." *Sniffle.* "Your dad. It's my fault."

"You didn't know they'd come after you." Sarah picked up the cloth napkin and wiped Maya's tears. "We don't know that they even came after you on purpose. Maybe they just wanted to rob us, or grab a couple of kids." She shivered.

"They had a drone," said Maya in a quiet, guilty tone. "I'm sure they were looking for me. They broke into the apartment on purpose. If your dad didn't have that alarm...."

"Yeah." Sarah squeezed her arm.

Maya jumped as the door opened; her body tensed, preparing to run. A man in an olive-drab poncho walked in, pulled down an air-filter mask, and cleared his throat a few times into his fist. An explosion of shaggy brown beard hung from his face, merging with his unkempt hair. Green camo pants swished as he approached the counter and took a seat at a stool. The sight of the scruffy veteran triggered a memory:

Pope.

The ex-soldier/hermit had offered to help her if she ever needed it.

Guys trying to kill me counts as needing help.

Of course, he lived way off in the Dead Space, so getting *to* him could be more dangerous than going home. That it seemed a better option made her wonder if she'd allowed herself to get too scared to think straight.

"I got an idea." Maya turned in the seat to face Sarah. "When I was trying to get Genna back from the Authority, this guy found me. His name is Pope, and he said if I ever needed help, he would."

Sarah bit her lip, looking disappointed. After a second, she took a breath. "Okay. Umm, where is he?"

"Near the Spread. He lives underground in old tunnels."

Sarah blinked. "Are you serious? That's out in the Dead Space. There's like cannibals and crazy people there! Dosers stealin' my clothes is bad enough. I don't wanna die." She pulled Maya into a tight hug. "You got *so* lucky going out there. You could've been killed."

Maya looked down. "I know. Every time we play those cards, it reminds me how stupid it was of me to go. I always think about how scared you must've been when you woke up and I was gone. When I got lost, I was really sad that we might not get to finish that game. I should've told you."

"And I would've made you stay."

A weak smile curled the corner of Maya's lips. "That's why I didn't tell you."

Sarah sighed.

"We can follow the road this time. It shouldn't be too dangerous if we stick to the highway. All the bad people are hiding in the ruins or the grass."

"No way. Missy Hong is out there and she's got enforcers with guns. They'll definitely sell us to DeeDee."

"She won't. I met her." Maya shook her head. "She's actually nice. She gave me food. A dumpling."

Sarah gawked at her. "But she sells like *all* the drugs in Baltimore."

"Pope will help us. Come on." Maya started to slide out of the booth seat. "We'll have to find a place to sleep once. It's not too bad."

"But..." Sarah pulled her back. "Walk for two days? Are you nuts? Genna will be home by then. We should just hide somewhere and wait."

Maya exhaled. Worry got her hands trembling. "If those men are still there, they will come after us. What if your dad is hurt? We can't just sit here."

"Not fair." Tears ran down Sarah's face, but her expression remained serious. "I dunno. It's too dangerous out there."

"What if we walk back home and get grabbed or shot?"

Sarah bit her lip, eyes shifting side to side. "Mmm. I dunno."

"Okay." Maya nodded once. "We'll try sneaking up without getting too close and look. If those men are there, we'll go to the Spread."

"All right." Sarah frowned.

Maya slid to her feet and approached the counter where the large man stood. "Thank you for the food. As soon as I can get home safe, I'll come back and pay you for it."

"Aww, don't worry about it, hon." He smiled. "You already helped us all. Things're changin'. Took a lot o' nerve ta do what you did. More on 'count o' you knowin' exactly what that witch is capable of."

Maya shivered. *Yeah. That's the problem.* "Sorry. I thought it would be different."

"Oh, I'm sure you did. Things aren't always as simple an' easy as they seem to a kid, but don't lose hope. You kicked that stone down a hill. It'll hit the bottom eventually."

If it doesn't run me over. She offered a nervous smile. "I hope so."

"Thanks for the food." Sarah smiled up at him.

He nodded. "You two stay safe."

"We will," said Maya.

She headed out the door and turned right, walking among pedestrians going the other way, mostly adults all in similar dull grey ponchos and air-filter masks. The Ascendant-controlled media had conditioned everyone to believe the air carried billions of bacteria and other pollutants. After realizing the truth, it all seemed like lies so no one would question it when they got sick. Seeing so many people with them on made her question the wisdom of breathing without one, but then again, they all worried about catching Fade, and Maya knew exactly where that came from.

And being vaccinated didn't hurt.

"Go left up there," said Sarah, ducking under an armload of plastic crates carried by a fat Chinese guy.

She pointed at an alley on the opposite side of the street about halfway up the next block, full of awnings and patio porches covered in laundry. Perfect cover from flying eyes.

"Okay." Maya stopped once they'd gone far enough to be able to see into the alley. She hid between a pair of parked cars, looking high and low for any sign of a small, black drone. Seeing none, she started to cross the street.

A split second after her toes touched blacktop, an e-car careened around a corner toward her, tires squealing. Sarah screamed and pulled Maya back onto the sidewalk as the sedan whipped past her, half a meter or less from clipping her. The car skidded in a swerve and came to a halt in front of a noodle restaurant at the corner adjacent to the alley. The driver, a reedy young man with a shotgun, in jeans and black leather jacket, leapt out and ran into the place, leaving the car door open.

"Idea!" shouted Sarah.

She dragged Maya into the street, sprinting for the car. Inside the restaurant, the driver pointed his weapon at the owner, Mr. Nori. The middle-aged man rambled in frenetic Japanese, pretending not to understand English. Maya halted, staring at him with one hand on the door, the other on the side of the car. She hesitated, wanting to find the Authority so the poor man didn't get hurt. Sarah grabbed a fistful of Maya's T-shirt, pushing her up into the car, accidentally exposing her butt to a brief cold breeze.

With a squeal, Maya leapt forward, crawling on all fours over the driver's seat to the other side. Sarah jumped in behind her, tossed the Hornet on the floor by Maya's feet, and slammed the door. She stared at the instrument panel with an 'okay, now what' face.

"Do you know how to drive?" Maya blinked.

"Umm. Not really. Just that game in the basement. How hard can it be?"

Maya gulped. "Judging by the number of explosions, I'd say pretty hard."

"That's a game. There's no aliens shooting at me here. I just gotta put the lever on 'R'." Sarah pulled the gearshift back and stepped on the accelerator. The car lurched to the rear, swinging around in a sharp turn that tossed Maya into the dashboard. She scrambled to hold on to anything, but couldn't get a grip on the smooth, dusty plastic. Sarah's hands slapped the wheel as she tried to straighten out, but they backed into a parked car with a loud *bang*.

The impact threw Maya against her seat.

Inside the noodle bar, the driver whirled toward them, his expression one of complete shock. The instant his attention left Mr. Nori, the restaurant owner pulled a handgun out from under the counter and shot the younger man repeatedly in the back. Three streams of blood sprayed from his chest.

The would-be thief fell to his knees, teetered for a second, and went over forward onto his face.

Maya screamed and cowered down so she couldn't see out the windshield.

Sarah stomped on the accelerator, her knuckles white on the steering wheel. The e-car hesitated for an instant before taking off with a jolt like a truck had hit them from behind. They scraped another parked car and caromed away, sliding closer to the center of the road. A man with a dog on a leash shouted and dove for his life. Sarah let out a sharp, short, "Yeep!" as she swerved to avoid the animal.

Maya got her arm up before her head bounced off the window, and clung to the handle on the roof while bracing one foot against the dashboard.

They ran over a bag, which burst into a cacophony of cluttering and banging on the undercarriage. Cans scattered into the road behind them.

The car emitted a faint electric whine, but the noise of its motors remained quieter than Maya's panic-stricken breathing. Sarah's concept of 'straight' appeared inconsistent with reality; parked cars along the right drifted closer and closer.

"Left! Left! Left!" screamed Maya.

She overcorrected and started to fishtail, bouncing Maya off the door. They shaved the side-view mirrors off three cars parked on the left side of the street and again bounced into the middle of the road.

"I think I'm getting the hang of it. It's way more sensitive than the game," said Sarah. "Game's pedal is just drive or stop. If I push this one too hard, we go too fast."

Maya stared at her, speechless.

"Where should I go?"

"There's a highway to the Sanc. I remember seeing it on my right when I was walking out to the Spread. We should be able to see where we need to go from the road."

A few minutes later, and by some miracle without an Authority drone chasing them, they left the Habitation District behind. Sarah leaned forward, gazing toward the distant glow, hunting for the same long highway that all the commuters took to the Sanc. Sarah managed a passable right turn once they reached a place where the buildings crumbled. Dozens of plastiboard boxes littered the street, along with upwards of thirty children and a handful of adults. Only about half of them had even attempted to scavenge clothing. A cluster of grime-encrusted children swarmed around the road chasing a dingy soccer ball.

Sarah screamed and stomped on the brake with both feet.

That time, Maya had expected it and caught herself before she sailed into the windshield.

Kids scattered like roaches in the light, scrambling into their plastiboard homes or hiding behind dumpsters. Once the kids cleared, Sarah nudged the car up to a bit faster than a person could jog, and slalomed shopping carts, concrete dividers, other ballsy children who seemed unafraid of a moving car, and one angry-looking old man with a skirt made out of shag carpet and a necklace of DVDs. He whacked the car on the roof with a length of pipe when they passed.

"I don't see it." Sarah turned left onto a deserted stretch of street, empty except for a dusting of concrete rubble that had fallen from nearby buildings.

A block and change down, a missing high-rise on the right offered a break in the concrete canyon and a view of the highway Maya had been thinking of. "Over there!" She pointed at the road leading out across the wide-open nothing toward the Sanctuary Zone. From here, the fancy Citizens' city looked like a gleaming silver castle set upon a foggy moor, studded with winking lights.

Sarah turned and drove into the gap, unconcerned at the lack of roadway. They left the paving with a double *ka-thump* of rubber on dirt. Maya held on tight as the car rocked side to side over the uneven terrain. Sarah seemed to get a thrill out of navigating between piles of rubble and sped up even more.

"This is much cooler than the game!"

"Yeah," said Maya, deadpan, "but the game won't kill us for real if you crash."

Sarah cringed, flashing an 'oops' smile. "Sorry. But there's no Frag kids in the way here."

"Right..." Maya rolled her eyes.

"Hang on!" yelled Sarah when they reached open field after the swath of ruin.

She stomped on the accelerator, leaving the sprawl of the once city-center behind. A two-minute drive over bumpy grassland ended with a loud *bang* when they hit the edge of the highway and caught a few inches of air. Maya screamed, clinging to the handle above the window as the maneuver bumped her head on the roof and drilled her into the seat again. Tires squeaked with another hard leftward swerve. Sarah lined up with the road and mashed her foot down on the pedal again.

"See? That was easy," said Sarah, grinning.

Maya sat motionless for a second, grateful at no longer being thrown around like a rock in a clothes dryer. She stared at the oncoming road until something didn't feel right, then glanced out the passenger side window at a double-yellow line. "Umm, Sarah?"

"What?"

"You're in the wrong lane. We're supposed to be on the right side of the middle line."

"Oh, crap." She veered into the other lane with only a little fishtailing. "Are we in trouble?"

"Yes, but not with the Authority. We could've hit someone head on." Since the car traveled straight and wobble-free, Maya shifted onto her knees and looked around for a chasing drone, but the skies looked clear. With a long sigh of relief, she rolled around to sit normally and pressed both hands over her heart. "No one's chasing us."

Sarah sat tall, both hands on the wheel. "No two days of walking now."

Maya glanced at her. "Did you have to pull my shirt up? You made me moon everyone."

"That was an accident. I just wanted to shove you in the door since I didn't think you'd get in if I just said 'get in.' You're too much of a good girl to steal a car." She grinned.

"You're so sure?" Maya folded her arms. "We have a good reason, and that guy *was* robbing Mr. Nori's. He probably stole this car. So we didn't steal it. We found it."

Sarah leaned close to the wheel and peered out over the endless open nothing. Far to the left, scraps of crumbled buildings and the scar tissue of once-city formed a grey murk across the land. Maya remembered her last trip out here, square in the middle of that ruin, on foot, with nothing but a silk nightie on. She frowned at Genna's T-shirt.

"I'm going to start sleeping with pants on. And shoes."

Sarah spared a half-second glance. "Why?"

"Because I keep getting attacked at night and stuck out in the middle of nowhere with nothing on."

"You don't have nothing on. You've got a shirt. *I* got stuck with nothing when those dosers robbed us."

"I mean sleep stuff. Nightdress. Not supposed to go outside like this."

Sarah corrected a slight drift, re-centering them in the lane. "How many nights do you go to sleep and nothing happens compared to how many times something happens?"

"A lot. I've only been kidnapped twice. And once wasn't *that* bad. It was a little scary when Genna tied me up, but I'm not mad at her."

"Dad ties me up sometimes too," said Sarah.

Maya blinked, turned her head to stare, and blinked again. "What? Seriously? That's like *way* weird."

"Survival training. In case we get taken as POWs." Sarah again stretched up to study the land outside. "What are we looking for?"

"Survival?" Maya continued gawking.

"Yeah. Wanted me to learn how to 'escape and evade' if we get captured by the enemy. You know how he gets about training. No way to tell him it's pointless. He doesn't understand the war ended." She frowned. "Didn't help much. He made me practice escaping rope, and the Authority has zip ties. I couldn't get loose when the damn blueberries got me."

"They knocked you out."

"I mean the other times." Sarah frowned.

"That's, umm, not normal. What kinda parent ties their own kid up?"

Sarah looked at her. "Ask Genna."

"Ouch." Maya cringed. "But I wasn't her kid then. I was 'a Citizen brat.' She thought I was as nasty as Vanessa. And she cut me loose as soon as we got to that room."

"No one's as nasty as Vanessa." Sarah shook her head.

Maya folded her arms. "Yeah."

A few minutes later, Sarah gazed left and right. "It's all open space. What are we looking for?"

"Keep going." Maya pointed forward and left. "It's out that way in the fog. Stay on the road now, please. Have you ever seen the Spread?"

"Not up close. Just from the ninth floor, but it's so far away it's just a spot of color."

Another car emerged from the fog up ahead and zoomed by in a flash of headlights and blue, heading back toward the Hab.

"You're doing well." Maya wrapped herself around the seat, staring backward to watch taillights recede. "Whoever that is thinks you're driving okay."

"How do you know that?"

"They didn't stick their middle finger out the window at us."

Sarah laughed. "So what's the Spread look like?"

"Lots and lots of trailer boxes stacked on top of each other. Right in front of it is this little town. That's where we need to go."

"Pope is at the town?"

"No." Maya twisted around to sit normally again and pulled her legs up, heels on the edge of the cushion. "He's out in the grass. But I know how to get there from that place."

"Okay."

They drove in silence for some time. Guilt, worry, fear, and hope sat like stones in Maya's gut. Sarah played with the car, poking buttons and dials to see what they did, and occasionally steering around pretend hazards like in the arcade game. She made machine gun and bomb noises for a little bit while pushing nonexistent buttons on the wheel. Maya kept her gaze locked on the fog, wondering how long they'd have to drive to cover the same distance that took her two days on foot. When she spotted a puddle up ahead in the oncoming lane, Sarah veered for it, causing Maya to scream as water splashed over the windshield.

"What?" Sarah corrected back into their lane. "It's a power up."

"It's a puddle! In the wrong lane!" Maya stared at her, not blinking for a moment. "If another car is coming, they will hit us and we'll die. As fast as you're going, they'll find us in the trunk. Of the *other car!*"

"Sorry..." Sarah shrank a little. "Trying not to think of Dad, so I was pretending to be playing *RoadBlasters.*"

"That's okay... just stay out of that lane."

Forty-six minutes after leaving the Hab according to the dashboard clock, the multicolored rectangular shapes of the Spread's towers emerged from the mist off the road to the left.

"Sarah?"

"Hmm?"

"Thanks."

Sarah looked over at her. "For?"

"Trusting me. I know you wanted to go check on your dad, but you went for the car."

"I... know it's too dangerous back home. The car just happened. It was there." A moment of silence stretched between them. "I'm afraid to go back too. I think Dad's not going to be there."

"Sarah?" Maya peered at the rapidly approaching Spread.

"Huh?"

"How fast are you going?"

She studied the instrument panel. "Umm. Either 108 or eighty-four circle eff."

Maya leaned left. A large 108 sat in the middle of the dash, with a smaller 84°F at the top left by 'e-motor temp.' Her chest tightened. "Please slow down. We're doing a hundred and eight miles an hour. If you hit something, we're going to die."

"Right." Sarah raised her leg but hesitated before simply stomping the brake like she always did with the game. She eased her foot down.

The car pitched forward. After the initial jerk, she relaxed even more and bled off speed.

"How fast should I go? I guess it wasn't that bad since you weren't scared 'til you looked at the number."

"Umm. I dunno, like fifty? You gotta slow down anyway, we're almost there. Tell me when it says like thirty or less."

Sarah stared at the speed, her forehead almost touching the wheel.

"Sarah, Sarah, Sarah!" yelled Maya.

They ran over a furry lump.

"You just re-killed something."

The redhead looked up. "Eep. Sorry. I was watching for the thirty."

"You gotta watch the road *and* the speed." Maya raked her hands through her hair. "Ugh."

"That's hard! How can I watch them both?"

Maya held her hands up in a helpless shrug. "I dunno. I'm nine! I've never tried to drive before. Ask Mom." Light from the settlement flickered in the foggy distance. "Here. Turn left here. Go off the road."

Sarah obeyed in an instant, pulling hard to the left and tossing Maya once more against the door.

Horn blare came out of nowhere as an oncoming car materialized from the mist almost the second they crossed into the wrong lane. Maya screamed, but the other driver swerved into the right lane to clear them.

The car bounced off the paving onto dirt.

"Is he holding his finger out the window?" asked Sarah.

Maya clutched her chest, staring wide-eyed at her friend. "If I spend five more minutes in a car with you driving, I'm gonna be as pale as you."

"Huh?" asked Sarah.

A cluster of ramshackle buildings emerged from the fog, the outermost portion of the Spread. Old cargo containers as big as semitrailers lay in scattered groups, stretching into the distance, many converted into homes. At the center, the wide one-story brown building with a bright neon sign reading 'The Devil's Hangover' glowed like a lighthouse in a stormy sea.

"Forget it." Maya took a few breaths. Despite the car jostling about, she sat up. "There. That's Diego's place. Drive up to that. We can leave the car there."

Sarah nodded, smiling. She slowed to 10 MPH—and drove straight into the wall.

A purple neon light in the window above where they struck the building sputtered and died. Something inside hit the ground hard enough to hear the *bang* from the car.

Sarah, still clutching the wheel with both hands, looked over at Maya. "Oops."

"I said *up to* it. Not *into* it." Maya grabbed the shifter and pushed it to park.

"Sorry. I was watching the speed thing, making sure I didn't go too fast. The building snuck up on me."

Diego raced out the front door with a metal baseball bat in hand; he looked ready to kill someone. At the sight of the girls, his rage evaporated into bewilderment. He stood speechless, waist-long black hair hanging straight. Maya flashed a cheesy smile. His mustache had grown a little. With a tank top on, he didn't have such a feminine silhouette, though he still reminded her of the guys from that ballet show she'd been dragged to a few years ago.

Maya pushed the button to turn off the e-car and got out. "Uhh. Hi, Diego. Sorry about that. My friend's still learning how to drive."

A *whump* came from behind as Sarah closed her door. "Sorry for hitting your place."

"What the hell, kiddo?" Diego ran his hand over his head, scratching at the back. "What are you two doing driving? And who's piece of shit is that?"

Maya glanced back at the car: missing both side mirrors, scratched, dented, and battered. The rear quarter panel and bumper had fallen off at some point, and a splatter of red, chunky goop covered the right passenger side door. She cringed at the gore, about to scream, until the scent of tomato sauce made her remember the bag of cans they'd run over.

"Wow. Umm." Sarah walked around the back end and stood at Maya's side. "I maybe bumped a couple things."

"Some guy already stole it," said Maya. "He was robbing Mr. Nori's place with a gun, and we, umm, well, we had to get out here fast and... yeah."

"You in trouble again, *cariña*?" Diego rested the bat across his shoulder.

"Yes. Some men broke into our apartment in the middle of the night. I don't know if they were trying to kill me or kidnap me, but we got away. I need to find Pope."

"Genna okay?" Diego's eyes widened with worry, though his brow hardened.

"Mom's busy with a mission." She bounced on her toes. "I need to find Pope. Is he here?"

"No way. That man and me don't see eye to eye. Far as I know, he's still in his little mole hole."

"Okay." Maya faced the wavering tall grass. "Can we leave the car here?"

Diego walked around to the driver's side door. "Sure, but I'm gonna back it out of the wall."

"It's not *in* the wall," said Maya. "Just touching it."

He lowered himself into the car. "How long you gonna be? Someone's gonna run off with it."

Maya bit her lip. "Not long. I hope."

"'Kay, well, I'll do what I can ta watch it for you, but if the shit is gone, don't be surprised."

"Thanks."

"You kids need anything? Food?"

Maya shook her head. "No thanks. I'm still full..." She spun around. "Got any pants or shoes our size?"

"Naw. I give 'way all the kid stuff to the poor bastards livin' out there." Diego nodded toward the Spread.

"Wait." Sarah ran to the car, yanked the passenger door open, and grabbed the Hornet from the floor. "Almost forgot this."

Maya waved to Diego. She looked around at the grass one more time to get her bearings, then walked following instinct, chasing the shadow of a memory etched in fear and desperation. The whole time she'd been out here before, her gut had been twisted in a permanent knot of worry over Genna. Not knowing if she'd been killed had been worse than if she'd found her dead.

Tears in her eyes, she turned and hugged Sarah, overcome by the realization that her best friend had to be holding back the same dread—and had decided to help her get out here rather than rush back to her father's side.

"What?" asked Sarah, hesitantly returning the embrace. "What's wrong?"

Maya pulled back, sniffling, and resumed walking. "I know how you're feeling about your dad. I felt the same way the last time I was here, not knowing about Genna after the Authority got her."

Sarah opened her mouth but closed it without saying anything, then glanced away and down, wiping at her face.

"Pope will help." Maya strode faster, headlong into a sudden stiff breeze that rustled the meadow grass and whipped her hair.

"I trust you," said Sarah in such a small voice her words almost drowned in the howling gale.

A few minutes of walking away from Diego's, they slogged through grass up to Maya's chin. In her memory, the trip from Pope's entrance hatch to the place hadn't taken *that* long, and paralleled the road. About twenty minutes of walking later, she reached a familiar spot; at least it looked like the place they'd been when she witnessed Brian meeting with the Authority. She clenched her hands, unsure how angry to be with him. He'd gotten Genna arrested and Sarah clubbed with the end of an assault rifle. His tip brought down the Authority on their building, but he hadn't intended them to take Genna. For all he knew, Maya had been kidnapped and forced to stay. He might've thought he helped her, plus the reward for his family.

Assuming, of course, Vanessa would've paid anything.

"Where is it? Everything looks the same." Sarah walked forward while doing a full circle turn.

"I think we're close. Look for a round hole about this high." She tapped her leg below the knee.

Maya looked back toward Diego's, a small presence in the distance.

When they'd started walking here, she didn't remember seeing it at all. She sighed in disappointment. "Never mind. We're not far enough yet."

"Okay." Sarah sniffled.

Keeping the road in view to the left, Maya hurried forward. She couldn't quite get up to a jog while fighting the tall grass, but she tried. As best she could remember, they'd walked almost two hours. In hindsight, driving straight to the tunnel might have been a better idea, certainly faster. Although, the car probably couldn't handle all this grass. She knew the way there on foot from the Devil's Hangover, and doubted they'd even be able to spot a low-lying sewer access tunnel from a moving car. Not to mention, Sarah probably would've crashed into it.

Eventually, she couldn't see Diego's bar any longer and searched in earnest for the tunnel opening.

"Hey," said Sarah, not quite at full volume. "Is that it?"

Maya looked where she pointed: a trail in the grass like something or someone had walked there recently. On a burst of hope, she darted forward, grabbing and pushing at the endless piles of green vegetation surrounding her. Sarah followed close behind, single file.

When the concrete square with the metal disc in it came into view, Maya had to bite her forearm not to cheer out loud.

Yes! She whirled to face Sarah. "We found it!"

Maya grabbed the handle and tugged, but only made the metal rattle. She set her feet and pulled with her whole body. For all her effort, she succeeded only in making her fingers hurt. She let go before they fell off. "It's stuck!"

"It moved a little. You're just weak."

Maya gave her a raspberry.

"We should try together. I'm weak too." Sarah flexed her unimpressive biceps.

She set the Hornet on the concrete and they both grabbed the cover plate.

Grunting and straining, they managed to lift it out of the hole and drag it aside, exposing a vertical shaft with a ladder.

Maya rushed around to that side and backed into the opening without hesitation. "Come on!"

She ignored the cold metal underfoot and climbed as fast as she felt safe doing, reaching the dry tunnel in about half a minute. Sarah descended more cautiously and seemed out of breath by the time she reached the bottom.

They stood in a weak shaft of light coming down from above, the tunnel around them midnight black.

"It's so dark," whispered Sarah, her voice echoing.

"Yeah. Pope had a light. It's okay. I remember the tunnel. There's only one way to go here. When we gotta turn and stuff, there's light."

Maya took Sarah by the hand and walked to the right, reaching out to brush the wall. After a few minutes of being dripped on and stepping in freezing puddles, Maya stubbed her toe on the floor.

"Ow." She stopped and reached a tentative probing foot out. The ground sloped upward at a curve, which had to mean she'd hit an elbow bend in the old sewer. "Right turn."

She followed the contour of the pipe, walking in the lowest part. Fifteen steps later, light appeared on her left, revealing an S-shaped switchback in the concrete tube. Minutes of being in total darkness had allowed her eyes to adjust, so even that weak light gave her the confidence to hurry up to a brisk stride. Ahead, passages diverted left and right as well as continuing straight.

Pope's markings near the ceiling in chalk helped her navigate the series of tunnels, turn after turn, in the dark. The last time she'd been here, he'd carried her, which made the trip feel much faster than walking it herself. The fourth passage led to a tiny room with ancient metal boxes on the walls full of dials and dead lights. From there, a narrow corridor connected to a larger office on the other side. A single doorway opened to a larger, square-walled tunnel that contained the remnants of train tracks.

She remembered approaching that door from the other side and turning right to go in, so she headed left, gaze upturned in search of more chalk marks. An arrow pointed left at a fork. Sarah clung to her from behind, trembling at the echoing darkness.

"Don't be scared. I remember this place."

Sarah sniffled. "'Kay."

Another mark pointed to the right at a wider fork. Maya hurried up to a light jog as her feeling of being near the end grew. Soon, they emerged in a chamber where a flat area abutted the tunnel with the broken tracks. Grinning, Maya hurried to the edge and pulled herself up.

"This is it!"

She remembered the green cot, rat dinner, and the little metal table with three chairs. A row of military-style trunks sat in front of a long locker cabinet opposite the cot. In the far left corner, a toilet perched on a spur jutting out from a vertical pipe, shrouded by a hint of broken wall.

Sarah ran for the toilet.

"Pope?" asked Maya, wandering closer to the cot. "Pope?" she repeated, louder.

"Do you think he's gone?" asked Sarah.

Maya looked at her in horror, never even having considered that he might not be here anymore. Her friend sat on the bowl, high enough off the ground that her feet dangled. "Uhh. I don't know."

"It's okay."

"He could be out hunting." Maya cupped her hands over her mouth and yelled, "Pope?"

Her voice echoed a few times before fading to the silent symphony of endless dripping.

"Why does he live underground like this? It stinks here." Sarah jumped down, adjusted her dress, turned to reach for a handle, and froze. "Whoa. Where's the thing?"

Maya pointed at a valve sticking out of a narrower pipe above the toilet. "He made it himself. Gotta turn that."

"Oh." Sarah stood on tiptoe to reach a small metal wheel. She opened the valve and running water flushed out the bowl. Satisfied, she closed it with a painfully loud *squeak*.

"Is it okay if we wait for him a little?" Maya approached the bathroom.

"Yeah. I'm tired anyway. That was a long walk." Sarah wandered over and sat on the edge of the cot. Soon after, she let herself flop backward, arms to the sides, feet still on the floor.

After using the toilet, Maya curled up beside her on the mildew-smelling cot. She pulled a coarse green blanket over them both and cuddled together. "We need a blanket. It's cold and wet down here. We could get sick."

"Mmm." Sarah'd already slid half into sleep, clearly exhausted from the ordeal of the past twenty-four hours.

Maya reached an arm across her friend. She snuggled close, staring into the dark, determined to stay awake watching for danger. Maybe Pope had moved to that room she'd helped him open by crawling through a pipe since it had a lockable door. Once Sarah had rested, she'd try to remember how to get to that chamber. Worry that he might not even be there caused a lump in her throat to swell, but she swallowed it thinking of Diego. If they couldn't find Pope, she'd take Sarah back to The Devil's Hangover, and they'd hide there until Genna came home.

[11]

WALK RIGHT IN

Maya snapped awake at a sharp jab in the side. Sarah elbowed her again, twice fast, and emitted a faint nasal whimper of alarm. Maya pulled the blanket down from her face as she raised her head, blinking away the heaviness of sleep. A glint drew her attention to the corner by where the room gave way to subway tunnel.

The business end of a giant rifle covered in strips of tattered olive-drab cloth pointed at the bed.

"Eep!" yelled Maya. "Don't shoot us!"

"Aww shit," muttered a man. "Kids."

The rifle lowered, and a figure in a green poncho covered in similar strips of cloth walked out from behind the corner. Round goggles sat on his forehead, exposing eyes ringed by cleaner skin than the rest of his face. A spray of pewter-grey hair around his mouth stretched with a grin.

"You just waltz right inta a man's home?" He chuckled, walking over and setting the rifle on the table. "Cripes. Saw somethin' movin' in my bed. Sorry for scaring ya."

Sarah let out a heavy sigh and went limp, staring at the ceiling.

"Pope!" Maya flung the blanket aside, leapt to her feet, and ran to him, ready to tell him about everything that had happened. The instant she clamped her arms around him, the feeling of being safe again shut her brain down, and she burst into tears.

"Oof." Pope caught her with his left arm while shrugging a backpack off his shoulder and slinging it onto the table. "Hey, easy. It's okay. You're okay."

She looked up at him but couldn't do anything but babble while crying. Her want to tell him about Sarah's dad, about the men who tried to kill them, the dosers, even watching that guy they took the car from get shot dead, all crashed together and tumbled out of her mouth in a series of incomprehensible noises.

Pope picked her up and moved to sit on one of the chairs by the table with her in his lap. She let her head rest against his shoulder, covering her mouth and nose with both hands in an effort to collect herself.

Sarah sat cross-legged on the cot and pulled the blanket around her shoulders like a cloak. She looked forlorn and frightened, a kitten abandoned on the side of the road with nowhere to go. Maya clenched her jaw against the crush of guilt that The Dad had been hurt because of her. How could she have been so foolish to think that video wouldn't have had serious consequences, or that she could simply walk away from Vanessa? When Sarah looked at her, Maya wept harder.

"I'm sorry," she mumbled.

"Well, this is going to be a heck of a tale I bet." Pope leaned to the right, trying to catch Maya's eye. "Who's your friend?"

"Sarah," said Maya in cry.

"Hello, Sarah. I'm Pope."

Her cheeks did something that might've been an attempt to smile. "Hi. Are you a priest?"

He chuckled. "Naw. Just my name."

"That's an odd name." Sarah reached a hand up from the blanket and pulled her hair out of her face.

"Army. Everyone uses last names there. My parents called me John; friends, Jack. No one's much called me anything for a couple years except Diego, and I won't repeat his name for me to you two."

Maya sat up. "Will you please help us? You said if I ever needed help I should find you. We came here looking for you and you weren't here and I didn't know what to do and we were so tired we just sat on the cot and I didn't even wanna fall asleep."

"Whoa, slow down. Aye. Right, I did say that. What sorta fix you got yourself into this time?" He winked.

She swallowed hard and took a breath. "Genna's away taking Xeno to Philly. I was staying with Sarah and her dad. Men attacked us at night and tried to kill us. We ran away. Her dad got shot... We're afraid to go back because I think those men are still watching the building. They had a little drone." Maya held her hands about cat-length apart. "It was hovering by our window right before the men broke in, and it chased us outside."

"Men tried to kill you?" Pope's eyes narrowed.

"Umm. I think it's because of that video. I—"

"I saw it." He nodded once. "Hard to miss. You walloped that hornet nest good. That stuff you said 'bout what the Authority ought to stand for got heard by the right people. Lot of eyes in a lot of places they haven't been in too long." His expression hardened. "So what'd these guys look like?"

Fleeting images played a slideshow in her memory, but the fog of terror left them blurry. "They had black on. Helmets, masks, stuff on their face. Not Authority."

"Hmm. Could just be mercenaries. You sure they were trying to *kill* you?"

"Bullets came through the wall," said Sarah. "But Dad was shooting at them. He has an alarm on the door."

Pope's silvery-grey eyebrows climbed. "He have training?"

Sarah nodded, letting the blanket fall and gather around her waist as her posture relaxed. "He was LRRP/D working with the 7th Cav around Pujon. He survived a missile attack on the camp and only lost his right arm."

"Damn. Pujon was a horror show." Pope shook his head. "Glad to hear he got out. Did he get a piece of them?"

"The Koreans or those men?" Sarah shuffled her feet back and forth on the concrete.

"The ones who came after you," said Pope.

Maya looked up at him. "They were after me. Her dad got hurt because of me."

"No." Sarah sprang from the cot and ran over to stand nearby, hand on her shoulder. "He knew about the video. Genna asked him to watch you because he's Recon, but...."

"But?" asked Pope.

"He's sick. Like an old man, but he's only thirty-four." Sarah's lip quivered. "He was gonna go to the VA too. He's been afraid to, but he changed his mind 'cause of what Maya said. An' now... now he's d—"

"We don't know that." Maya reached up and grasped Sarah's hand where it rested on her shoulder.

"Right. So where do I fit in to all of this?" asked Pope.

Maya pulled her stare away from Sarah's eyes and gave him an earnest look. "We're afraid to go home in case those men are watching for us. Mom's going to be back soon, and if we're not there, she's going to freak out."

"She's not gonna be too happy that you came all the way out here again." Pope lifted her onto her feet and stood. "S'pose you haven't eaten yet. I'll grill up some rats and we'll get going."

Out of nowhere, a thought frightened Maya into squeaking.

Pope and Sarah glanced at her.

Wide-eyed, she pointed at the tunnel. "Oh, crap! I totally forgot about that place you asked me to help you open. I thought you were gonna stay there. We could've been waiting here forever."

"Ahh, that bunker." Pope chuckled. "Didn't work out. Remember the body we found?"

She shuddered. "Unfortunately."

"Well, figured out how he got dead. Place's ventilation system is shot to hell. Loads up with toxic fumes from the battery and power capacitor."

She stared at him. *He didn't know that when he asked me to go inside.*

"So, yeah... I'm still livin' here. Now, time for you two ta eat something."

"We have a car," said Maya. "It's by Diego's. Might get stolen if we don't hurry."

"A car?" Pope blinked. "Who drove you out here?"

"Me." Sarah raised her hand. "It was a bit different than *Road-Blasters.*"

He shook his head. "I'm not sure if that was actually safer than the two of you walking here."

"You can drive on the way back if you want," said Sarah.

Pope gave her a stern look with a playful smile. "Yeah, that's not up for debate."

She tilted her head. "Can I ask you a stupid question?"

"Go for it." He rummaged his backpack, removing a few dead rats, which he set on the table.

"Why do you have grey hair but you don't look old?"

Maya couldn't help herself and giggled.

Pope opened the lid on a large white box with a glowing blue light on the front. Ice lined the inside; he dropped the rats in one by one. "Just lucky, I guess."

"You're not old," said Sarah.

"Depends. You think forty-one's old?" He shut the cooler.

"Yeah, but I'm nine," said Maya.

"Not like *old* old. Book is *old*." Sarah fidgeted.

"Right." Pope grabbed his rifle. "Get the sense you're in a hurry. 'Less you'd rather eat first."

Maya shook her head. "Too worried to be hungry right now an' we can eat at home if it's safe. Can we go now?"

Sarah's grateful smile eased her guilt.

Pope hung his backpack on a peg, slung the rifle across his back, and headed toward the tunnel. "Let's go then."

After Sarah grabbed the Hornet from the cot, he led them back down the weaving tunnels. Maya had to work to keep up with him but didn't complain or protest, barring a grunt of exertion or two. When they reached the point where the round concrete tunnel became pitch black, he flicked on a flashlight. Numerous turns and passages later, a shaft of daylight illuminated a section of old sewer tunnel in front of them.

Pope overacted a sigh of disappointment, gesturing at the bright cone shining down from above. "You left the tunnel open."

Maya raised her arms a little and let them flap against her sides. "Sorry. We could barely move the lid."

"You're one determined and resourceful kid, Maya." He chuckled, shaking his head, and climbed up out of sight. Maya followed, raising a hand to guard her eyes from the blinding glare in the opening above.

Sensing her friend's eagerness to go home, she let Sarah go next, then scampered up behind her. Pope reached down and lifted Sarah up and out, doing the same for Maya when she climbed to the top. She squinted, cringing at the painful light for a little while until her eyes adjusted. The tunnel had been so dark, even a glum, grey day hurt.

The heavy, overcast sky seemed to leech the color out of the world, but fresh air on her face brought on a wave of energy and made the idea of a two-hour walk a welcome one. She turned in place, gazing up at the vast expanse of silvery-dark clouds. The Hab sat too far away to even show as a darkening in the haze.

Both girls jumped at the *clang* of Pope reseating the cover over the shaft. The sound hit her in the lungs like a physical blow. Maya managed to keep from screaming and stared at him. He patted her on the head.

"Holler if I'm going too fast." He frowned at her feet. "You two need some shoes."

"See?" Maya made bug-eyes at Sarah. "I have some, but they're in the bedroom. We had to run fast."

"Ground's pretty tame from here to the Spread. Worst part is the grass. Stay in my trail, it'll be easier."

Pope took off at a brisk stride that forced Maya to jog. With him plowing the tall grass aside, crossing the meadow *was* easier, but after only a few minutes, she started to lag behind. Sarah tolerated the pace better: longer legs, and she'd had a much more demanding life. Pope slowed enough to keep her fast-walking, a pace she found much easier to hold.

"That message of yours made it to the whole Eastern Seaboard," said Pope some minutes later.

"Yeah." Maya jumped over a small puddle. "They told me."

"They're auditing the Baltimore Authority. You got the attention of the provisional governor."

"What's that?" asked Sarah.

"They still haven't figured out how to arrange stuff. Provisional governor's the one in charge of the Eastern Commonwealth States. Basically tryin' to keep the US together. Provisional means as soon as they figure out if they're going to have a president and stuff again, he's no longer in charge."

"Oh," said Sarah.

"I thought Vanessa would be gone." Maya frowned. "She's still there, like nothing we did mattered."

"That woman had Baltimore so tight under her thumb I'm amazed the Authority is even investigating at all." Pope laughed. "Gotta be a political crapstorm flying around behind closed doors."

Maya trudged over bent grass for a few minutes, dreading and looking forward to being home in equal parts. "I know it doesn't make financial sense for her to come after me, but I'm scared. I got this idea to protect everyone. Only problem is it's hard. I want to give the Xenodril formula to another pharma company. She's only releasing Fade because no one else has Xenodril."

"Makes sense. Got the formula?" asked Pope.

"No." Maya sighed. "That's the hard part. But it's in their computer."

Pope chuckled. "Planning on walking in and taking it?"

"No, not again. I think Zeroice can get it for us. Mom's going to ask her boss about it when she gets back."

"Hmm. I imagine if hackers could've gotten it, they'd have it already. Ain't much out there that's as valuable as that."

The urge to cry squeezed at her throat. She stared down as she continued to follow along in his trail. Her defeated slouch brought her head below the level of the grass, leaving her walled off from the world behind the unending green. *Dumb. Yeah. If he could've stolen that formula, he would've done it already. Like I needed to suggest it.*

With each passing minute, the constant fast pace sapped her energy and made talking at all less and less appealing. The rhythmic *swoosh-crunch* of Pope's march and the rustle of the grass everywhere around her conspired with her waning energy to make time blurry. The occasional buzzing insect cruised by, disturbed to wing by their encroachment. She didn't even bother swiping at the bugs that landed on her unless they remained for more than six steps.

Eventually, Sarah's gait became as much a stagger as a walk. She put on an angry face and kept going, even faster. Maya pushed herself up to a jog.

A short while later, Pope stopped and whistled. "Wow. What did you two do to that car?" asked Pope. "Looks like you drove through downtown Songnim during the third bombardment."

"She learned to drive from playing a video game," said Maya.

Sarah shrugged. "We got here, didn't we?"

"So how did you two wind up stealing a car?" Pope swatted a few bugs from his fatigue pants as he emerged from the tall grass into the sandlot around the Spread.

"Someone else stole it," said Sarah. "Guy ran into Mr. Nori's noodle place with a gun to rob it. We just hopped in the car and took off."

Pope laughed. "Imagine the look on his face when he ran outside with the money and his car was gone."

"Mr. Nori shot him," said Maya, a fatigued wheeze in her voice.

"Oh." Pope shrugged. "Well, run into a store waving a gun, expect to be shot at."

He hopped in behind the wheel, sniper rifle wedged atop the passenger seat with the butt on the floor and the barrel jammed into the roof. "Not going to drive straight up to your building. If it's being watched, I don't need them seeing us coming. Also, don't want a bored blueberry giving me attitude over who's car this is."

Maya climbed in back. The cushioned seats felt *awesome*. She melted into the upholstery and gasped for breath. Sarah rolled in next to her, pulled the door closed, and flapped her dress to fan air at her chest. One safety pin went flying into the front seat.

"Hey," shouted Diego from the door, a shotgun not quite aimed at the car.

Maya grumbled at having to move but leaned up to the door, opened the window, and waved. "It's okay. We're back. Thank you for keeping the car safe."

He tilted the shotgun back across his shoulder and nodded, a trace of an evil eye sent Pope's way. "*De nada.* You two be careful."

The car felt like an altogether different creature as Pope backed around a k-turn and pulled away from The Devil's Hangover. No herky-jerky acceleration and no being thrown into the door. After a momentary pause to watch for an approaching car, he pulled onto the road leading back to the Habitation District and leveled off at 80 MPH. Parts of the car's battered shell rattled in the wind.

"Guess I was doing it wrong," muttered Sarah.

Maya took her hand and smiled. "You got us here."

Her friend returned a sad smile and looked down at the Hornet in her lap. It made Maya think of The Dad coming out of nowhere and teaching them both the basics of handling it. She closed her eyes and wished for him to be okay.

The drone of tires on paving proved mesmerizing, though Maya couldn't sleep. Her legs ached from fatigue, but her brain raced. A few minutes into the trip, an Authority drone went by overhead. It paid them no mind, racing back along the road toward the Sanctuary Zone.

It seemed silly for the law to care about stolen cars. People who took cars outside the protection of the Citizen areas did so at their own risk. Maybe inside the Sanc they'd track one down, but out here? The owner had likely written it off. As far as she knew, most of the cars on the Eastern Seaboard were made in Pittsburgh. She'd only seen a handful of Nons with vehicles, and based on their clothes, they probably had decent-paying jobs. People who made Citizen wages but wanted to pay as little rent as possible often lived out in the Hab. Most of the Nons in the Hab took buses. Chances are, their stolen ride had been expensive; she considered trying to give it back to its owner by way of turning it in to the Authority, but the idea died with the side mirrors. Even if they returned it, they'd get in a ton of trouble for the damage.

Grey clouds overhead darkened as they approached the Hab, but fortunately, the world remained dry. Most people feared the rain, for they thought it pulled Fade from the clouds and brought it to Earth. Old rumors of aliens seeding the sky and government cover-ups struck her as silly, yet according to Barnes, some people still believed invaders from another world and not Vanessa Oman made them sick. Maya scowled at the window, disgusted at people who could stare clear evidence in the face and *still* cling to their previous wild theories. Weber thought they'd simply gotten used to Ascendant being the 'protector' and rejected the accusation only because it scared them to have to think for themselves.

Her spiral of anger, frustration, and helplessness stalled as a stiff deceleration slid her forward. Pope pulled off the road and drove for a short distance over uneven dirt before bringing the car to a stop behind the ruins of a one-story building next to a giant yellow M sign. Darker spots formed words where the crumbling bricks hadn't faded so much from the sun; the shadow of where old lettering had once been read 'I'm lovin' it' above a dried bloody smear.

"This is as far as the car goes." Pope hit a button and the console went dark. "Battery's about dead anyway. Remind me which building's yours?"

"Block 13, ninth apartment building on the right," said Maya. "It's the only one on that street that's got two little patches of fake grass in front of it."

"All right. Come on. Stay behind me." He got out of the car, pulling the rifle into a ready grip.

Maya crawled to the front and slipped out after him. Sarah followed, pushing the door closed with a soft *whump*. Pope approached the corner and peered around at the alley beyond. Maya crept up behind him while Sarah rushed over to put her back to the fragment of wall, Hornet pointed up in a two-handed grip. He waited a few seconds before continuing, crossing the street to the right while heading for an alley half a block down.

Following another short survey of the area, he advanced again. Two blocks later, he ducked into an alley on the left rather than take cover at the corner. Maya hurried after him and bit back a yelp of surprise when he stopped short and grasped her shoulder. Sarah ran into her from behind.

"All right. You two stay here. The building's over there. I think you had the right idea. Pickin' up a RCSU on the scope."

"A what?" whispered Maya.

"Remote, umm, combat surveillance unit," said Sarah. "That little drone."

Pope's intense 'in the zone' expression softened to allow a fleeting smile. "Not bad." Game-face returned in an instant. "Sit tight. I'll come get you when it's clear."

"Okay." Maya sat on the street and huddled against the wall.

"Better idea." Sarah pointed at a big yellow plastiboard carton among other trash that had collected on the opposite side of the alley by a dumpster. "Concealment."

Maya got up and followed her over. Someone had arranged a tiny, improvised mattress inside made of scrap denim, wadded paper, and a ratty blanket. It stank like moldy clothes but didn't make her want to throw up. She crawled inside, tucking herself against the rear corner while Sarah backed in and pulled the flap closed, guarding the entrance with the shaking Hornet.

"You okay?" Maya scooted closer.

"Scared." Sarah looked down for a second before making eye contact. "About Dad. He was so sick and weak. I'm afraid I'm going to find him..."

Maya put an arm around her. "Your dad's a good soldier, like Pope."

"Thanks, but Pope's a Ranger. Dad just scouted. His job was not being seen. Pope's a killer."

"Well." Maya raised her head. "Those assholes shot your dad. We need a killer."

Sarah chuckled with a sniffle. A single tear crept down her face.

A *pop* came from the distance, as if someone had whacked a board with a hammer.

Maya tried to lean past to look outside, but Sarah pushed her back.

"Don't. I think he just shot someone. He's got a silencer."

"That wasn't silent." Maya glanced at the inch-wide opening in the flap. "It was kinda loud."

Sarah whispered, "It's a *lot* louder without one."

"Oh." Maya sat back on her heels, hands squeezing her thighs. Pope shooting at someone proved she'd been right to avoid going home. Worry at who else those men might've hurt while searching the building for her brought shivers.

Minutes passed in silence.

Sarah tensed at the scuff of shoes approaching. Maya pressed forward, eager for the safety of having Pope nearby again.

The flap of plastiboard pulled away fast, revealing a shaggy, brown-haired man in a grey poncho with a weathered face. A caustic ambiance of cheap alcohol, vomit, and piss flooded their little hideaway.

Maya leaned back with an "Eep!"

Sarah pointed the Hornet at him, inches from his nose. "We don't have anything you can steal."

"Whoa!" The man flinched backward hard enough to fall on his ass. "Easy there, girlie. You's in me house."

She kept the yellow-and-black striped pistol trained on him. "Sorry. Some people are trying to hurt us, so we had ta hide."

"Aww." The man coughed as he shifted from sitting to all fours and crawled closer. "Who'd wanna hurt a pair o' little ones?" He glanced at the tip of the Hornet. "Yer so sweet and friendly."

Maya pulled her shirt up to cover her mouth and nose, trying not to obviously gag with him watching.

"We're not alone," said Sarah. "My friend's dad is coming back for us, and he's a soldier."

The man flashed a mostly toothless grin. "No need ta get all like that, girlie. Ol' Farnham here ain't gonna hurt yas. Fact, I'll help ya hide." He turned his back to the giant carton and sat on the street, leaning against it. "Jus' an' old drunk sittin' by his home."

Ugh. He stinks. Please don't stay there. Maya's eyes watered. She grasped Sarah's dress at the back of her neck and pulled her close enough to whisper, "Pope's not my dad."

Sarah lowered the Hornet and glanced back at her with a feeble smile that couldn't quite climb out from under her worry about The Dad. "You act like he is, and he's trying to protect you."

"Us." Maya hugged her from behind, mostly to use her friend's hair as a filter to breathe through. "He's protecting both of us."

Another short silence passed.

"So, who's after yas?" asked Farnham. "Skeevers tryin' ta steal yer rags, er 'Thority catch ya doin' somethin' ya shouldn't?"

"Sorta," said Sarah. "Dosers did try to grab us, and the Authority hates us 'cause we're Nons."

Farnham let off a wheezy chuckle. "Desperate bastards tryin' ta swipe them rags o' yours. Can tell yer new out here. Gotta set up a defense."

"Defense?" asked Maya, barely able to speak without choking on the fetid air.

"Yep. No one will take my threads." He tugged at his battered poncho as if he wore a thousand-dollar suit. "Alls ya gotta do is throw up on yourself a couple times, rub some alley water inta yer clothes, and yer be left alone."

Maya turned her head to the side and dry heaved.

"I'd rather not have clothes," muttered Sarah.

Hand over her mouth, Maya nodded. *Yeah. Me too. I can't breathe.* Pushing at Sarah's back, she whispered, "Air."

"We have to hide," mumbled Sarah.

"So where's this, uhh, 'father' of yours?" asked Farnham. "You sure he's gonna come back?"

"He's real," said Sarah.

"Mmm." Farnham chuckled into a coughing fit. He extended a small bottle of brownish-red liquid over his shoulder into the box. "Thirsty?"

"No thanks," said Sarah.

Maya shook her head, not wanting to open her mouth to speak. Again, she nudged at Sarah. "Go. I can't breathe."

"That's how them skeevers feel when they come ta take mah stuff." Farnham laughed.

With a whine at her friend's refusal to move, Maya curled up and buried her face in two handfuls of her T-shirt. No trace of hunger remained. As one minute stretched into the next, sitting trapped in a confined space filled with such stench made the idea of being chased by men with guns sound like a better option. Only, in order to leave their carton, she'd have to *touch* the man outside.

Maybe if I stop breathing, I'll pass out.

"Hey, man. Spare a coin?" asked Farnham.

"Morning, friend," said Pope. "I'm lookin' for a pair of kids I left 'round here. I sincerely hope you can give me good news."

"Hey, easy, man. Bloody knife ain't ness-sary."

"Pope!" yelled Sarah. She pushed the plastiboard flap open and clambered out over Farnham.

Maya cringed against the side of the box, but desperation for clean air overwhelmed her disgust and she darted forward, managing to only brush the man with her side.

Pope towered over Farnham, holding a large combat knife tinted red. His rifle hung across his back, barrel pointed down. At the sight of the girls, he pulled the blade between two fingers to clean it, and slid the weapon into a belt sheath with a *click*. Maya ran to him, as did Sarah.

"This guy giving you any problems?" mumbled Pope.

"No. He lives here." Sarah shook her head. "He helped us hide."

Maya gulped at clean air, hanging on Pope's left arm.

"'Preciate it." Pope tossed the guy a couple NuCoin, took the girls by the hand, and walked with them to the end of the alley. "You were right, Maya."

She gulped. "What happened?"

He led them around the corner, walking casually. "Found two mercs watching the building. They aren't goin' to be a problem for anyone anymore."

Sarah leapt over a puddle. "Did you shoot them?"

"Naw. Too loud and messy."

"We heard you shoot," said Maya.

"Drone was hanging around the top of your building. It's in pieces now." He winked.

"Who are they?" asked Maya, her gaze bouncing back and forth from Pope's face to the ground so she didn't step on anything sharp.

"Were," mumbled Sarah.

"Not Authority. Didn't look like Ascendant either. No markings or insignia on 'em anywhere. Probably freelancers. Found a bag with some, uhh, stuff in it. Pretty sure they weren't trying to kill you."

"Stuff?" asked Maya. "I may be small, but I'm overly mature for my age. You can tell me."

He chuckled as they rounded another corner onto the street where they lived. "Looked like a kidnap kit. Chloroform, rag, short lengths of rope, blindfold. Probably some outside party thinking they'll get money from Ascendant for grabbing you."

Maya rolled her eyes. *Yeah right. That woman doesn't pay ransoms.* "Idiots."

[12]

ATTACHMENT

Sarah took off running as soon as their building came into view, a red-haired missile weaving among a few grey-clad pedestrians. Maya walked faster but didn't want to let go of Pope's hand. Her friend zoomed across the tiny front yard and disappeared into the main entrance.

A plain silver van parked on the opposite side of the street and a little ways down sent a shiver down her back. It stood out for being new. Had they tried to go straight home, they would've been caught.

They only wanted me, but probably would've hurt Sarah.

She scowled at the van, absent even the little pity she'd had for the dosers who'd wanted to sell them to DeeDee. Whoever lay dead inside, she felt only relief that Pope had killed them. He hurried toward the building, earning a few odd looks from passersby, most of whom moved to give him distance. It took a few seconds for her brain to acknowledge a thought other than the need to catch up to Sarah.

"You're not hiding the gun?"

Pope walked fast, with a forward lean that suggested he'd have knocked people out of their way if he had to. "Nah. Authority's got a problem with small weapons, stuff you can hide. Plus, they're sympathetic to an old vet livin' out in the Dead Space. Doubt they'd let me carry it into the Sanc, but ain't no chance of that."

"Why?"

"I'm allergic to livin' under an army of remote-controlled fifty-cal machine guns and a surveillance state. Like askin' mice to live in a house built by starving cats. Sometimes I wonder why we even bothered fighting North Korea. I came home to live in it."

"Oh." At the steps, she finally released his hand and flung herself at the door. Grunting, she pushed it open and hurried in.

The main stairwell echoed with the slam of a door, suggesting Sarah tolerated the stink for a faster way up. Maya cringed, expecting the reek of spoiled milk to make her throw up, but after Farnham, it didn't even register. Then again, perhaps her nose had died.

She raced up the stairs. Pope followed at a light jog.

Around and around she went, up to the seventh floor. Maya sprinted down the hallway to Sarah's apartment at the left corner. She skidded to a stop, clinging to the doorjamb.

Sarah knelt in the middle of the living room, sobbing into her hands. Shell casings and blood splats littered the rug, but the lack of a dead body offered some hope. The amount of blood didn't seem enough to indicate anyone here had died. Plaster dust tinted the interior hallway floor white, and a few bloody handprints marked where The Dad had made his stand. Dots of sunlight glimmered on the wall past the corner, holes from bullets that had invaded their bedroom.

"Sarah?" Maya hurried over and knelt by her.

"He's gone!" wailed Sarah, wrapping her arms around her and bawling.

Maya held on tight. *Gone dead or gone not here?*

A rustle and clatter at the door preceded Pope entering with his rifle across his back, pistol at the ready. He swung his weapon toward the kitchen for a brief sweep of his eyes before fast-walking to the inner hallway.

Sarah stopped crying only long enough to gasp for breath and wailed again.

Guilt kept Maya's tongue still, and she soon inherited her friend's tears. Unable to speak, she swayed side to side in a gentle rocking motion. Pope returned to the living room, gun lowered. His expression didn't offer much other than the likelihood the apartment held no threats. He lingered on his feet for a little while as Sarah continued bawling, but eventually took a seat on the sofa, leaning his rifle against the wall in easy reach.

"They killed him," blubbed Sarah.

"We don't know that," said Maya, patting her back.

"He'd be here. Where is he?" Sarah gestured around, sniveling. "They killed him and someone took his body."

Pope leaned forward, forearms across his knees. "There's blood on the rug back there, but it don't look like enough for a man to have bled out."

"Huh?" Sarah sniffled and twisted left to look up at him.

"Your old man took a hit or two, but I don't think they killed him." He nodded toward the hall. "There's a damn lot of blood inside a person. Dead people make much bigger puddles."

Sarah lowered her hands from her face, arms falling limp in her lap, and gave Maya a hopeful, pleading stare. "If he's alive, where is he?"

"I don't know."

"Someone's gotta know something," said Pope. "You two got more dirt on ya than I crawled in at Songnim. Why don't ya clean up and we'll go 'round asking who heard what." He headed for the couch.

"Okay." Sarah wiped her face, stood, and walked down the hall to the bathroom door. "I want my dad."

Maya followed, keeping her hand on her friend's back. "We'll find him. Ugh, I still smell that guy in the alley."

"You can go first," said Sarah. "Our water heater's crappy. It'll take like an hour to get warm again."

"But..." Maya cringed. "You smell like him too. Ugh. Rock, paper, scissors?"

Sarah seemed to become even paler, staring at a spray of blood on the wall. "I dunno if it's too weird, but if you want..." Her face tinted with blush. "We could both clean up at the same time. I don't really wanna be alone now."

Maya blinked. "Umm."

"Yeah. That's weird, huh? We're not *little* kids. Well, you kinda are." Sarah looked down. "It's okay, you can go first."

Maya watched her friend shivering for a few seconds before pushing her embarrassment aside. How different could it be from changing gowns in front of an entire production crew, plus whatever incidental employees walked in to ask for Vanessa's input on something? "Okay, you look scared, and I can't make you wait hours stinking like that man. Soldiers shower together, right? Be right back. I wanna get my clothes."

Sarah nodded.

Having no desire to put the same filthy T-shirt nightdress back on, Maya ran to the bedroom to collect her black shirt and fatigues. She hurried down the hall and ducked into the bathroom. Seafoam green tile surrounded the tub, matching the sink and toilet. The room appeared in better structural shape than the one in Genna's apartment: no cracks, no mold, and only a couple of missing tiles. A thick brown bathmat offered a soft place to stand while she peered around at an utter lack of supplies. Genna at least kept a few different hair products as well as some 'womanly things.' The Hawthorne bathroom had one bar of soap, but the towel on the bar appeared almost new.

Sarah closed the door and secured the deadbolt.

She's afraid he's like Mason. That man tried to trick her into taking a bath. Maya decided not to say anything and let Sarah's trust of Pope evolve the same as hers. After all, Maya's first thought at seeing him had been 'eep, please don't kill me.' Sarah turned the water on, adjusting the hot/cold spigots and testing the stream with her hand until she found a good balance of temperature. Once satisfied, she pulled her makeshift dress off and draped it over the front of the sink.

With the door closed, the reek of Farnham coming off Maya's T-shirt filled the small bathroom and made her feel even stickier, killing the last of her hesitation. She wriggled out of it and winged it into the corner before stepping into the tub and sitting in the rising bathwater, back to back with Sarah. She picked up handfuls of warm water and poured them over herself. Soon, Sarah closed the faucet and the bathroom hung in silence, save for dripping and sloshing.

Sarah's intermittent sniffles echoed as she ran the lone bar of soap around her body. Maya waited patiently, rinsing off as best she could without it, frowning at a mess of bug bites on her legs, no doubt from the walk in the meadow. After a few minutes, Sarah handed the soap over her shoulder. Maya washed herself for about ten minutes until Sarah asked for the soap again. They wound up passing the bar back and forth as needed.

Before long, they sat in brackish charcoal-colored soup.

Sarah opened the drain. "The water's so black."

"Yeah," said Maya. "All the dirt we washed off is getting all over us again."

"I'll run another."

Maya availed herself of a little brush, trying to erase the grime outlining her finger and toenails as the last of the filthy water disappeared. Sarah flipped the drain shut and ran more water, turning the hot all the way open. The second tubful wound up being a few degrees warmer than chilly. Not pleasant, but nowhere near cold enough to send Maya out of the tub shrieking.

"You should ask Zoe to fix your heater," said Maya.

Sarah sniffled, running the bar of soap up and down her arm. "Dad was going to."

"Oh." She let out a silent sigh, grateful Sarah couldn't see her annoyed expression. What else had that man kept putting off?

A while of quiet soap trading later, Sarah used a beat-up plastic pitcher to pour water over Maya's hair. Once she'd scrubbed the stink of Farnham out of her head, she twisted around and helped Sarah wash her hair. They sat in silence for some time after, dripping, neither talking. This moment together in the bath offered a sense of security and comfort. Despite their being finished, Maya had little urge to go anywhere.

"We're going to turn into prunes," muttered Sarah a few minutes later.

"No we're not. We can't become fruit."

Sarah chuckled and stood. "It means get wrinkles and stuff from being wet."

Maya waited for her to get out of the tub, then scooted back to open the drain before standing and stepping over the tub wall. Once she bad both feet on the plush bathmat, Sarah draped a towel over her shoulders from behind.

"Thanks." Maya started drying herself, but hesitated once she noticed Sarah standing there with her arms folded, dripping and waiting. *They've only got one towel?*

She surreptitiously sniff-tested it, unsettled that she might be using a towel that had seen The Dad in places no person would want to. It didn't smell bad. Probably clean. She dried off quick and handed the towel over before stepping damp into her black fatigue pants. Sarah gave her a forlorn look as she dried herself.

"I'm going to get you some new clothes." Maya grabbed her black shirt and wriggled into it. "I mean some *actual* clothes. You're wearing an old curtain. I won't listen if you say don't."

Sarah wept into the towel.

"Stop it." Maya put her hands on her hips. "You're always taking care of everyone. It's okay to let someone help you."

"That's not why I'm crying." Sarah looked down. "Those men tried to grab you and you're more worried about my crappy dress."

"Those guys are dead. I'm not afraid of dead people." She looked down and flexed her toes. "Be right back."

Maya hurried to the bedroom in search of her shoes. To her relief, they remained half under the bed where she left them. She flopped seated on the floor and pulled them on. Sarah appeared in the doorway, again in her curtain-dress, looking sad and a little annoyed.

Isn't she going to wash that? It still stinks like Farnham. "What?" whispered Maya.

Sarah's eyebrows furrowed. "He's sitting in my dad's spot."

"He doesn't know that. If it bothers you, ask him to move. He won't mind." Maya bit her lip. "Are you going to wash that?"

"No. The fabric is old. Some of the curtains where I found this got wet and they fell apart." Sarah looked down. "It's a silly thing to ask him to move. Dad's not here now."

"It's not silly if it's making you sad. I'll ask him." Maya brushed past her and started down the hallway but jerked to a halt at Sarah's hand on her shoulder.

"Don't bother him. He's been nice to us. It's okay." She sighed. "I'm just...."

Maya nodded. She opened her mouth to ask about food but froze when a knock sounded at the front door.

Sarah dragged her backward to the room.

"Calm down!" whisper-yelled Maya. "Bad guys don't knock."

"Hello?" called a woman. "Sarah? Maya? Are you in there? It's Zoe."

The girls exchanged a momentary stare of relief before rushing together down the hallway.

Pope had pulled his rifle across his lap, not quite aimed at the door.

He shifted his attention to Maya as they came barreling into the living room, headed straight for the door. Sarah stopped two steps short, hands clasped to her mouth and shivering with anticipation.

"Zoe!" chirped Maya, opening the door.

The woman's green eyes lit up with relief. Light brown hair hung in an unkempt leonine mane down to her elbows, obscuring a dark stain on her powder-blue sweatshirt. "Oh, thank goodness you're okay!" Her enthusiasm stalled as her eyes shifted toward Pope. "Who's that?"

Sarah zipped up behind Maya. "Where's my dad?"

"He's a friend," said Maya. "He helped me when the Authority had Mom."

"Ma'am." He left the rifle on the couch, and walked over to offer a hand. "Name's Pope. Live out a ways north. Givin' Maya here a little help with her rat problem."

"Rats?" asked Zoe before grumbling. "I just can't keep up with the little bastards." She shook hands. "Zoe Chang. We live a floor down."

Pope quirked an eyebrow.

Zoe laughed. "Married name."

"Not four-legged rats. Mercenary rats." Pope pointed a thumb back over his shoulder. "They had a midnight visitation from some not-quite angels. Maya didn't trust coming back here, and she was right. Couple of miscreants were watching the front door."

"Where's my dad?" asked Sarah.

Zoe nodded to Pope before taking Sarah's hand. "We heard the gunfire and saw men dressed like soldiers roaming the hallways. Mike came up to check as soon as we felt safe enough to open the door. Your father's been shot, but he's at a medical facility in the Sanc. He's a veteran, so they'll treat him. Mike did what he could, but we don't have the greatest supplies here. Your father was kinda weak. Mike's pretty sure he, uhh...."

"Has cancer," said Sarah, eyes downcast. Sadness lasted only seconds before she got angry. "He didn't wanna go for treatment."

Maya fidgeted. "Metavil or Alveocor both work for lung cancer, but they're expensive. Xenodril's cheap next to them."

"That's not the problem," said Pope. "ESC government will cover a vet's medical bills, but it takes so damn long to get approval for them to pay out, most of us don't even bother."

"He should've gone to the VA a long time ago. He's too stubborn." Sarah looked ready to hit something in anger, but wound up crying into her hands.

"It'll be okay." Zoe squeezed Sarah's shoulder. "You've been taking care of him for so long you haven't been allowed to be a child. It's not your fault. The man was, umm, set in his ways."

"He's not dead!" yelled Sarah. "Stop talk—please stop talking about him like he's dead."

Zoe bit her lip. "Sorry. I just don't want you blaming yourself for how sick he'd gotten."

"It's my fault," said Maya. "Those men wanted me. He got shot protecting me. I don't understand. Vanessa wouldn't waste money on revenge. She wouldn't even pay a ransom to save me."

Sarah stood in silence for a little while, a look of painful insecurity on her face, before quiet tears flowed. Her expression remained stoic, but her voice had no strength. "He was gonna die soon anyway. He wanted to. If he didn't have me, he would've killed himself."

Sniffling, Maya clamped her arms around Sarah. "Being careless about his health and wanting to die aren't the same."

"So, you're...?" Zoe peered at Pope.

"Evidently the guy keeping an eye on these two until her mother comes back."

Sarah looked up at him. "Can we go see my dad? Please?"

"The Sanc is under lockdown right now. There's some rioting going on, and I've heard rumors that the Authority is fighting itself. You know, the ones Vanessa bought and paid for with the blueberries from out of town." Zoe shivered with worry. "Mike's still stuck there after takin' Billy in."

"Who's Billy?" asked Pope.

Zoe gestured at Sarah. "Her father."

"They won't let me in to see my dad?" asked Sarah, her expression heartbroken.

"They're not letting anyone in or out. I..." Zoe shrugged. "Maybe if you found a blueberry with a soul and made that face you're giving me now they'd let you in, but I wouldn't count on it."

"Thanks for helping her dad," said Maya.

Zoe smiled. "Oh, that's all Mike. I hid in the bedroom with Emily.

We had no idea what happened. Em was sure the Authority was coming to arrest everyone. Speaking of Em, I should really get back home."

At the word 'Authority,' Sarah scowled.

"Sarah's water heater doesn't work. Can you look at it sometime?" asked Maya.

"Sure, sweetie." Zoe winked.

"Right. We'll be here." Pope eased the door closed as Zoe walked off, and locked it. "Figure I'll stick around at least 'til your mother gets back. Gonna grab a couple zees so I can keep alert when it gets dark. You two stay inside, and wake me up if anything strange happens."

Sarah glared, seeming ready to lash out. Maya braced for the shout of 'you're not my dad,' but her friend's defiance melted away, and she slumped in a defeated slouch.

"Yes, sir," said Maya.

Pope reclined on the sofa, rifle over his chest.

"C'mon," muttered Maya. She tugged Sarah by the hand into the kitchen and went for the drawer of cheese sandwich packets. "Mom can sneak us into the Sanc. Soon as she's back, we'll go see your dad."

Sarah sat at the table, staring at the plastic-encased square in front of her while Maya brought three of them to Pope.

"Hey." Maya pulled a chair around to sit beside her. "He's okay. He's in the hospital. We're safe."

"But what if they come back?" Hands in her lap, Sarah picked at her nails.

The strong scent of imitation fresh baked bread filled the air when Maya opened her sandwich. "They can't come back. They're dead."

"You know what I mean." Sarah reluctantly picked up her packet and crushed the capsule inside. "Mercenaries get paid. Someone hired them to take you."

Maya hesitated, sandwich less than an inch from her mouth. "Someone's stupid then. They should know that woman won't pay them."

She bit off almost a quarter of the sandwich in one chomp. While chewing in silence, watching Sarah nibble, a guilty realization dawned. It didn't feel like that long ago that Sarah had invited herself in to meet 'the new kid.' Maya hadn't had a friend before; she'd never even been in the same room with another kid. As soon as Sarah had peeked in, Maya had been so terrified at the thought of interacting with other children she'd almost run and hid in the bedroom. The warmth that had radiated from this girl when they'd first met felt at that moment like a fist in the stomach.

Before the lump in her throat grew too fat to talk around, she muttered, "I'll go back down the hall if you want. I understand if you're afraid of being around me."

Sarah looked up, blinked, and stared at her. "No! Don't you dare run off alone!" The mini-mom sternness returned to her eyes. "And we're not allowed out. Pope said to stay inside."

Tears welling, Maya dropped her half-sandwich on the plate and clung to her friend. As awkward as sharing a bath had been, afterward, Sarah had become closer to family than merely a friend.

Maya had no idea what the future would bring, but she knew that no matter what fate held for her, she wouldn't have to face it alone.

[13]

A MORE PERMANENT FIX

Maya went to bed fully dressed, shoes and all. Despite Pope planning to be up all night on watch, Sarah put the Hornet under the pillow.

They'd spent the rest of the day keeping away from windows and generally being quiet so Pope could sleep. Zoe dropped by again with Emily in tow and worked for a few hours patching bullet holes in the walls. She'd even replaced a blown sensor on the hot water unit that made it register 'full' at only a quarter capacity. Sarah had been too unsettled by the blood in the carpet, so Maya had spent her evening scrubbing after a little coaching from Zoe on how. Emily and Sarah collected shell casings and bits of drywall big enough not to need a broom. By the time Zoe left, the living room and hallway had dozens of fresh plaster spots, and the apartment smelled like rug cleaner.

The sense of safety Maya felt with Pope watching over them, and the relief at knowing he'd killed the men who attacked, let sleep come easy. Vaguely aware of Sarah's arm around her middle, she lay on her side, annoyed at the sunlight for knocking on her eyelids. Her head felt as heavy as stone, and she had no desire to move.

A gentle touch brushed hair from her face.

Maya murmured and snuggled tighter into the pillow.

"Wow. Someone's sure tired."

The almost-familiar female voice needled at her, triggering a fight between heavy sleep and her need to understand why she recognized this woman.

A gasp puffed at the back of her neck. "Maya!" shouted Sarah. Small hands shook her from behind. "Maya, get up!"

Alarm exploded in her brain. Maya shot upright, searching for the source of danger. In seconds, the fog of sleep drained from her consciousness and the blurry figure hovering over her clarified into Genna. A swath of olive-drab at the door became Pope.

"Mom!" Maya dove into a hug.

"Hi," said Sarah.

Genna sat on the edge of the bed with Maya in her lap. "Oh, baby. Pope told me what happened. Dammit. I shouldn't have gone off yet. Stuff hasn't cooled off enough."

Maya grinned, elated at having her mother back. Her surge of joy ebbed at the earnest look on Sarah's face. "Can we go to see Sarah's father?"

"Not sure what the situation at the Sanc is like yet, but we will definitely go as soon as we can. Give Barnes and Weber a little bit to wrap up and we'll get a handle on it."

Maya nodded. "I was worried about you. Like, a lot."

"I'm sorry, baby. We all gotta do stuff that's scary. World won't make itself a better place. We had a pretty easy run. Didn't even get shot at once." She chuckled. "Philly's a bit of a mess though. People are pissed about Fade. That PR bullshit ain't holdin' no tack with them people. They all believe you, knowin' Ascendant did it on purpose. There's been attacks on medical clinics as well as Authority officers."

"Oops," deadpanned Maya.

"Barnes wanted me to ask if you'd do another video. Something to send out a message the Brigade ain't no enemy of the Authority. We need to tell people that most of the Authority are veterans who remember what they fought for. Yeah, it's true the ones around Baltimore aren't too much different from Ascendant thugs, but people as a whole gotta know their opponents are the Vanessa Omans of the world and the corporate machines they run."

Maya blinked. "But you hate the Authority."

"Oh, baby..." Genna rocked her. "I hope you never know the kinda rage that losin' a child can cause. I watched Sam get sicker and sicker and couldn't do a damn thing about it."

"But, you're technically a Citizen, right? Because you're a veteran?" Maya tilted her head. "Why didn't you take him to the VA?"

Genna's expression darkened, though her anger didn't feel directed at Maya. "Was with the Brigade already. That hacker you found hadn't wiped my records back then. I knew I'd get nailed as soon as they looked me up in the system to verify the VA claim. Went anyway, even wit' Harlowe and Barnes tellin' me not to." She let off a somber chuckle. "I was too pissed off to think. Didn't care what happened ta me, long as Sam made it. Damn, I was furious wit' Barnes an' them too, thinkin' they wanted Sam to die. They's right though. Got there, they took Sam into 'nother room 'for a checkup.' Blueberries showed up real quick. Since my ass was suspected Brigade, they didn't bother haulin' me to jail. We just went right out back the hospital. Put me up against a wall and planned on shootin' me. Only, they brought Sam out too. Figured he was old enough to be Brigade. Asked me if I wanted to watch him die, or if I'd rather he watched me go first."

Sarah gasped, covering her mouth with both hands.

"Soulless bunch of cock—" Pope eyed the girls. "Miserable bastards."

Maya squeezed her. "That's horrible!"

"I hate blueberries," said Sarah. "They're all bastards. Before you got here, I tried to tell one what Mr. Mason did to me, but he thought I was lying. Said he'd arrest me for bothering him if I didn't go away."

"What did he do to you?" Maya gawked.

Sarah gave her a blank look. "I told you already. Tricked me into his apartment for, uhh you know. He hit me when I tried to run away and he told everyone he caught me stealing to explain why I had a bruise on my face." Her voice shrank to a tiny sound. "He didn't do what he wanted to. I got away."

"Girl, you shoulda told me. I'da believed you." Genna patted Sarah on the head.

"Sorry. You were kinda scary after Sam was gone." Sarah offered a cheesy smile. "Always felt like you wanted to kill everyone who looked at you."

Genna patted Sarah on the shoulder. "S'okay. At your age, I'd have been afraid of me too."

"All right," said Maya. "I'll make the video. Not all the Authority are assholes. Just the ones Vanessa bought."

Sarah blushed.

Genna pulled Maya up a little and gave her a light swat on the rear end.

Wincing, Maya rubbed the spot. "Really? The stuff Ascendant's done and you're mad I said a bad word?"

"You're nine. I'll let a 'shit' go every now and then, but the rest of 'em are waitin' for at least fourteen. An' I don't wanna hear no F-bombs outta you 'til you're eighteen."

"Heh." Pope chuckled. "My mother would *still* throw a fit if I swore, even now."

Maya narrowed her eyes at Genna. "You do realize that 'don't wanna hear no' is a double-negative, which basically means you said you want to hear F-bombs."

"Smartass." Genna hugged her a little too hard. When she let go enough to look her in the eye, tear trails ran down her face. "What all happened here?"

"Mercenaries," said Maya. "They broke in at night, but The Dad had an alarm on the door. They started shooting at each other. We tried to use the fire escape, but a little drone came after us, so we went in a window one floor down and, uhh, it was an emergency."

Genna nodded, glancing at Sarah.

"I won't tell anyone about it," whispered Sarah.

"It's okay, baby." Genna kissed Maya atop the head. "Your friend's done a couple errands for the Brigade. She know what secrets are."

Relief stole all the strength from Maya's muscles. *She's not mad!* Cuddling closer, she continued telling the story of how they'd run into the dosers, the gang, gotten free food, and 'borrowed' a car to get out to Pope. "Did he tell you the rest?"

"Yeah." Genna shivered, eyeing the spots of white plaster.

"They didn't want to shoot us," said Maya.

Pope shoved off the wall and walked a few steps into the bedroom. "I think if they'd wanted to kill you, they could've sprayed at the wall. Both of 'em had night vision setups, and the drone controller had thermal as well."

"You still don't know who?" asked Genna. "Other than mercs?"

"Nope." He shook his head. "Maybe Ascendant threw a little money at grabbing her, maybe it's someone else hoping to cash in."

"Vanessa wouldn't pay a ransom for me." Maya absentmindedly rubbed her left ankle, scrunching up her face at the memory of the mildew-mold smell of the building where Genna's group of mercs had taken her. "She wouldn't waste money on kidnapping me. She wouldn't even turn on the lights."

"Huh?" asked Sarah. "Turn on the lights?"

"The place I used to live. It was always dark because she didn't want to pay much for electricity. She said it would keep me safe by making bad people think I was a decoy android."

"Some people oughta not be allowed to have kids." Genna rocked her.

Sarah started to sniffle but quieted when Genna put an arm around her.

"I thought Zeroice would be able to get the Xenodril formula so we can give it to other companies... but I guess if he could've taken it, he would have done it already and gotten rich." Maya sighed. "I don't think that plan's going to work."

"Well, I still gotta talk to Barnes and them 'bout it. Sure it won't be simple as you're thinking, Zeroice walking right in and taking it, but the idea's got some merit. Don't give up yet. The Brigade's got more resources than one lone hacker."

"Okay." Maya smiled.

A small chance offered a lot more hope than no chance.

[14]

THE SPARK

Bizarre dreams filled Maya's head in which she rode an Authority drone like a flying horse while Sarah sat behind her, zapping bad drones out of the sky using a magic wand. Far below on the ground, Vanessa ran away from them, summoning wave after wave of blueberries to kill them. The dream had a video-game quality, with little balls of energy instead of bullets and people disappearing instead of dropping dead.

Great discomfort in her bladder dragged Maya to consciousness in the middle of the night. She squirmed, stuffed in a sleeping bag with Sarah on the floor of Genna's room. The bed hadn't been big enough for all three of them, and she couldn't make her friend stay on the floor alone. Sleeping in her day clothes felt weird, but she didn't quite trust her safety to change into a nightdress. For comfort, she'd taken her sneakers off but left them in arms' reach. If something happened *again* to make her flee in the middle of the night, dammit, she would at least *carry* them out the door.

A little wriggling got her out of the bag without waking Sarah. She grasped the edge of the bed to stand and froze when she realized Genna wasn't in it. Murmuring voices filled in the silence created by her shock. Biting her lip at the need to pee, she padded into the hallway and forced herself to go past the bathroom.

Genna and Pope sat on the couch, talking about their respective times in Korea during the war. He mumbled in Korean while mimicking dropping something and running away, which got Genna laughing so hard she almost failed to keep quiet.

Momentarily forgetting the urgency that had awakened her, Maya crept to the end of the corridor and hid at the corner, watching them.

"Poor bastard never went near another e-grill after that." He chuckled. "Damn, got the oddest craving for a Hite."

Genna gagged. "Seriously? You drank that stuff?"

"Haven't had a beer since I got back."

She shot him a playful look. "Maybe you oughta stop livin' in a cave."

"Didn't use to think there's much left to bother giving a fuck about. 'Til I ran into that li'l girl of yours." Pope grinned. "She's gonna be a handful in a few years."

Genna sighed, a trace of sadness in her eyes. "In a way, it kinda makes karmic sense. That bitch took Sam away, so I got Maya. Only, it don't feel like revenge. For one thing, that kid didn't deserve her life, and another, that woman don' miss her. Ain't really revenge. Just did it for her, ya know."

"Yeah." Pope put his hand atop hers on the sofa cushion between them. "Lot of us came back from the war with a hardened nugget of coal in here." He knocked on his chest with his other hand. "That kid's got a way of turnin' things back."

"Hah." Genna rolled her eyes. "My ass was full charcoal for a while there. Maya slapped me upside the head." She sighed before smiling at him. "Suppose she had that effect on you too."

"For a little thing, she's got nerve. First time I saw her, she's ready to go storm the Sanc all by herself. Figured her just a kid with rage issues. I shoulda damn stayed with her but, bein' the grumpy old bastard I am, I actually let her go inta the Spread on her own. Figured she'd get disappointed pretty quick and come wandering back. Couldn't sleep. By the time I unfucked my head, she's zooming off in the air on a goddamned drone." He shook his head. "I for sure thought I killed her by not stopping her."

Maya bounced on her toes, desperate to pee but she *had* to keep listening.

"That kid..." Genna shook her head. "She ain't my blood but it don't feel no different. That why you're still here? Figure you didn't wanna make that mistake again?"

"Something like that." Pope smiled.

"Something?" Genna raised an eyebrow.

Pope leaned back, thumb to his chin while looking at her as though he admired some piece of artwork. He said something in Korean that made her blush and flash a playful grin.

They're going to kiss!

"Before you answer that in English," said Pope, "we have an audience."

Maya gasped.

Genna leaned forward, staring at her.

"Sorry. Sorry. Sorry," whispered Maya. "Gotta pee. Heard voices. I'm going back to bed now."

She hurried to the bathroom, trying to fend off the giggles. *He's gotta be psychic. How did he know I was there? He didn't even look!* After some much needed relief, she tiptoed to the bedroom and crawled back into the sleeping bag. Sarah offered so little reaction to the disturbance that Maya hovered a hand by her mouth to make sure the girl still breathed. Satisfied her friend remained alive, she closed her eyes.

THE NEXT DAY DRAGGED ON IN BOREDOM. THEY SAT AROUND FOR A while before Sarah got up and started cleaning, complaining that not doing anything kept her worrying too much about her father. Maya decided to help while Genna and Pope discussed the situation with the current unrest in the Sanc. She filled him in on how bad it had been in Philly. It seemed the discontent among the population had finally spread to Baltimore despite Vanessa's attempts to undermine it. Hearing that even Citizens believed her made Maya's heart swell with hope. Of course, Ascendant's release of Fade hurt everyone, not only the poor.

Late in the afternoon, Genna ducked out to get food, leaving Pope to watch them. Maya didn't worry *too* much since the men who'd shot up Sarah's apartment didn't know Genna from a rock. She returned in a little under an hour. Maya poked her head out of the bathroom, where she'd been wiping down the sink. The scratch of Sarah scouring the bathtub continued behind her. Between the two of them, they'd gotten most of the black gunk off the tiles.

Genna stopped by the archway to the kitchen, a cloth bag hanging from her grip, and grinned at her. "You two tryin' ta tell me somethin'?"

"No, we're just bored. Sarah gets sad if she's bored, so she's teaching me how to clean. Can we go to the Sanc yet?"

"Not yet, baby. Still a mess. I'm gonna have a chat with Barnes after dinner. We might be able to take an alternate route in."

"What's that?" Pope walked up to Genna.

"Food. Gotta cook it."

He smiled. "Want some help?"

Genna blinked. "You cook?"

"Mostly rat these days, but I ain't afraid of a stove."

Maya grinned at the way they looked at each other and returned to her sink cleaning. Soon, the smell of garlic overcame the cheap green disinfectant solution they'd been using on everything from windows to the toilet. The girls ran out of places to scrub not long after and flopped next to each other on the bed to rest.

"I thought all the apartments were the same. It's weird you've only got one bedroom," said Sarah. "Ugh, my fingers are all wrinkly."

"Cleaning was *your* idea." Maya grinned at the ceiling. "I thought it was weird that our patio is attached to the bedroom and not the living room like your place."

Sarah threaded her fingers behind her head. "Yeah, that is weird."

"Wonder why." Maya yawned. "Wanna play the card game?"

Sarah shrugged. "I dunno. They're in my room."

"I can get them if you don't wanna go in there."

"It's not that. I'm not afraid of going back there. I'm just... ugh. That would require walking." She laughed. "I'm tired."

"I repeat." Maya raised an arm, pointing skyward. "It was *your* idea to clean everything."

"Girls?" said Genna. "C'mon an' eat."

Maya got up and plodded to the door. When she noticed Sarah hadn't moved, she marched back to the bed, grabbed her by the arm with both hands, and pulled her seated. Laughing, Sarah got to her feet and followed to the kitchen. Pope and Genna sat across from each other at the square table. The girls took the remaining two seats, where steaming plates of spaghetti covered in red sauce waited for them.

"Ooh!" Maya jumped into her chair.

"What is it?" Sarah tilted her head.

"Spaghetti," said Maya. "I love it!"

"You've had this before?" Sarah sniffed at it. Seeming pleased, she picked up her fork.

Maya attacked her plate. "Yeah. I used to get delivery a lot."

"Delivery?" Sarah gave a forkful a test lick. "Oh, it *is* good."

"Umm." Maya felt a sudden sense of embarrassment at her former privileged life. "In the Sanc, there's these restaurants that bring food to your home. You can order over the AuthNet and either a person or a drone shows up with the food in like half an hour."

Sarah didn't react much more than a nod of 'oh okay' while she chewed.

Genna's spaghetti put Pizza Galaxy to shame. The reason sat somewhere between it not being made in vast quantities, not sitting around until ordered, and her mother cooking it. She fought the urge to inhale it like a tiny woodchipper.

"Hmm. Guess it's okay then," said Genna.

"Mmm!" Maya nodded.

"Yeah," said Sarah. "It's a lot better than cheese sandwiches."

"So are my boot soles," muttered Pope.

Genna glanced at him.

"Than those damn VA cheese sandwiches." He chuckled.

Sarah shot him a hurt look. "I kinda like them."

"Oh, you poor, poor child." He patted her on the head.

A little while later, Maya sat back, feeling stuffed. "That was awesome."

Genna grinned. "I'll clean this up when I get back. You two did enough cleanin' already."

"Back?" Maya sat up straight. "You're leaving again?"

Genna stretched across the table and clasped her hand. "Ain't gonna be gone long. Meeting with Barnes and them. Jack's gonna stay right here with you."

"Jack?" Maya couldn't help but grin. "Okay."

Pope chuckled as Genna pursed her lips and couldn't seem to look at him.

A small knock came from the door.

Maya got up.

"Wait." Pope raised a hand. "Let me."

He stalked out of the kitchen, drawing the combat knife from his belt and holding it behind his back. Genna moved to the kitchen arch, watching left down the hall toward the bedroom. She pulled a handgun from her thigh holster and raised it at the bedroom.

Braced against the wall by the front door, Pope eased it open an inch. A second later, he relaxed and took a step back, keeping the knife hidden.

Pick, in his tattered knee-length khaki shorts, waved. "Hi. Is Maya here?"

"You hurt, boy?" asked Pope.

"No. It's sauce." He rubbed at a blotch on his bare chest. "Naida made burritos."

Genna holstered her sidearm and walked out into the living room. "Hello, Ruben. What's up?"

"Hi, Miss Genna." Pick waved. "Book's gonna read stories tonight. Can Maya go?"

Pope tucked his knife back in its sheath and gave Genna a raised eyebrow.

"'Nother ol' vet. Lives on the ninth floor. Bunch of headware. He's got like a thousand e-books in his skull. Reads the tame ones to the kids sometimes." She beckoned Maya with a wave. "Up to her. Long as you kids stay inside the building."

"I can go with her," said Pope.

Maya looked at Sarah. "Want to?"

She replied with a halfhearted shrug.

"A story will help you stop worrying for a little bit. Mom's going to talk to Barnes like right now to see if they can sneak you in to visit your dad."

"Okay." Sarah pushed herself upright and collected plates.

Pick bounced from leg to leg in the hall. "Come on, he's gonna start soon."

"We're coming." Maya waited for Sarah to put the dishes in the sink and walked with her to the door.

Pope followed without his rifle, which he'd probably left in the bedroom closet. Pick raced off to the fire stairs. Maya knew her way to the room where they all gathered to play with the plastic spaceships and other action figures, so she didn't bother running to keep up with him. She walked up two flights to the ninth story, smiling to herself that her sneakers would protect her from the squishy carpet. At the door, she stopped short, gawking at a bare concrete hallway blotched with black and green stains. The stink of mold remained noticeable but no longer overpowering. "Wow."

"What?" asked Sarah. Before Maya could answer, she emerged from the door and stared at the discoloration. "Oh wow. The rug's gone. And eww."

"Yeah."

"Smells like outside," said Pope.

"There's a big-ass hole in the wall," said Sarah, holding her arms out. "Whenever it rains, the whole ninth floor gets wet."

Unfamiliar men's voices emanated from the doorway to the story room, slowing Maya's approach to a cautious creep. One emitted a frustrated sigh.

"I'm just sayin' you shouldn't be having kids around here for at least two weeks 'til we finish. And there's a good chance we'll be fixing the walls so all this space is going to go back to being three apartments."

Maya poked her head in the doorway.

Book stood by the concrete 'table' near the room's center with a pair of men in white jumpsuits and yellow hardhats. Three other men in similar outfits explored the edge where the enormous hole yawned out to the world. Anton, Marcus, Emily, and Pick sat on the floor near the interior wall, recovering the toys from a pile of swept dust.

"Damn," muttered Pope. "You're right. That is a big-ass hole. Amazing the upper floor hasn't fallen in."

Book chuckled, shaking his head. Little lights blinked and fluttered from a thin metal strip mounted to his skull over his left ear, tinting his grey hair blue. He patted his generous belly and nodded. "I still can't believe you guys are actually here to fix that wall. It's been like that since I moved in here, and that's going back a while." He took notice of Pope and offered a raised hand of greeting. *"Buenas tardes, amigo.* Good evening, friend."

"Hey," said Pope. "You must be Book."

The men shook hands. "Enrique, but yeah, the kids call me Book."

"Maya," said Anton, his voice raised.

She pulled her attention away from the adults and walked over to the toy-rescue operation. "What happened?"

"You're okay!" Marcus leapt to his feet, grinning.

"Are you gonna kiss her?" asked Emily.

Maya leaned back.

"Uhh..." Marcus froze, a trapped expression on his face.

Emily smiled at Sarah. "Sorry your dad's sick. Mommy said he's okay. She called Daddy before." She sighed, her mood shifted sorrowful in the span of a single breath. "They won't let him come home."

Sarah lowered herself to sit cross-legged and gestured at the pile. "So what happened?"

"Workers thought our stuff was garbage." Anton scowled at the men, recovering an old x-wing toy with a missing canopy. "They just sweeped it all here."

"Swept," mumbled Maya.

"All right, all right," said Book. "We can relocate story time. We used this place on account of it havin' so much room."

The worker on the left blinked at him as if he'd said something stupid. "On what planet does letting kids play on a ninth floor slab with no wall seem like a good idea?"

"They like the view." Book grinned. "And they ain't dumb enough to walk off the edge."

Gunfire erupted outside; a few rapid shots echoed from the building across the street, along with several startled screams.

Three of the workers by the edge leapt back and hit the ground. Maya startled and jumped. The other kids froze like statues. Book started to head for the edge, but Pope put a hand on his shoulder.

A series of shouted curses came interspersed with more gunshots and the smash of breaking glass. The telltale whirr-whine of an Authority drone grew louder.

"Drop your weapon," said a deep, quasi-electronic voice.

"Fuck you!" shouted a man, before a rip of automatic fire.

The drone fan noise increased in pitch; the heavy *blam-blam-blam* of a machine gun started but cut off with a resounding crash. Tires squealed and a deep *thud* sent a palpable shockwave into the floor.

Sarah darted to the open edge, waving her arms for balance as she stopped with her toes an inch from freefall. She leaned forward and stared down.

"Dammit, kid," yelled a worker. "Get away from there!"

"Sarah!" bellowed Pope. "Get away from there and come over here."

The loud, parental tone made her jump back. She looked about ready to burst into tears but fast-walked over to him.

He grasped her shoulders and stared into her eyes. "What are you doing?"

"That man is right outside. He shot down a drone and ran into our building. The blueberries are already here." Sarah shivered, sniffling. "Can we please hide?"

"Oh shit," muttered Book. "Here we go again."

"Come on." Sarah looked at Maya. "We can hide in that, umm." She bit her lip. "Place."

Maya swallowed hard. Genna told her not to tell anyone about the elevator escape route, but if the blueberries left everyone restrained and more black-armored mercenaries showed up, they'd be dead.

Emily pounced on Anton and bawled.

"The, umm..." *No! The doors on this floor don't work.* "We gotta go down two floors."

"Attention residents of Block 13, Building C-11. This is an Authority lockdown. All persons within are to remain in their present location. Anyone attempting to flee is subject to disciplinary action. Anyone found in the hallways will be assumed to be fleeing."

A blue four-fanned Authority drone hovered up to the massive hole, bathing everyone in the glare of a blinding spotlight mounted to a swivel under its nose.

Sarah clung to Pope, emitting a soft, nasal whine.

Book held his hands up. "Everyone stay calm. Just let them do what they have to do."

Maya crept over to Pope and Sarah. "They're not looking for Brigade this time, just that guy who was shooting."

"They don't care." Sarah, red-eyed, scowled at the floor. "Any excuse to be mean to us. They do it every time. Dad got angry once when I was eight and cursed them out. They arrested him and left me tied up on the floor. No one found me for a whole day."

Pope patted her back. "You gotta know how to talk to them. Be surprised how much an old war story will do for you." He winked. "Don't be afraid."

The tromp of boots grew loud in the hallway. Everyone fell quiet.

Two blueberries walked in, carrying compact assault rifles, though they didn't aim directly at anyone as they swept their gaze over the room.

"Everyone over there. Line up." One gestured at the wall by the pile of dust and toys.

Pope picked Sarah up and carried her; she trembled too much to walk. Maya followed close, keeping hold of her hand. Emily held up her hands like someone being robbed at gunpoint. Pick and the twins trudged to the wall. The five workers and Book followed. Everyone formed a single-file line. Maya refused to let go of Sarah's hand, still clutching it in both of hers. The older girl trembled, her fearful gaze locked on the Authority officer.

The other blueberry approached and lifted his visor, exposing his face. Maya recognized him in an instant: Hammond. The one who'd punched Baxter for hitting Sarah. As soon as she made eye contact, she smiled at him. The warm reception appeared to catch him off guard.

"It's okay." Maya pulled on Sarah's arm. "He's the guy I told you about. He got pissed at that other asshole for hitting you. He's nice."

A look of recognition dawned in Hammond's eye.

At the word 'nice,' Marcus and Anton gave her a 'say *what?*' stare.

His partner, who hadn't opened his visor, pointed with his left hand at the children. "Stay put." He approached Pope. A device in his left hand chirped, and he spent a second glancing at small screen. "Hmm. John Pope huh? Staff Sergeant US Army. Been a long time since we ran you in the system."

Sarah clung to him, staring at the blueberry.

"I'm not a people person," said Pope with a smile. "Been living out in the Dead Space."

"What's got you back here?" asked the blueberry.

More heavy footsteps echoed below; Maya pictured armored Authority officers swarming the entire building. She hoped the ones who found Arlene and her two-week-old son weren't assholes, but it wouldn't bother her *too* much if Brian got a little roughed up.

"Monthly supply run. Ran into this kid." Pope hefted Sarah. "Chased some dosers off her and she needed lookin' after. Her dad's in the VA care facility. Figured I'd stick around 'til he got back. You serve?"

"Yeah. Thirteenth Armored. We repaved most of Pyongyang." The blueberry chuckled.

Pope nodded. "Yeah. You boys were pretty thorough there."

"What unit?" asked the blueberry.

"1/75 Ranger Battalion. My ass was all over that damn peninsula." Pope smiled. "217 confirmed, but that's just my rifle. Didn't bother counting the knife work."

The blueberry leaned back. "Damn. Look, man. We're just after some shithead lightin' up drones for the lols. Took a couple pops at one of our guys too."

Pope held up his right hand. "Right on. Nail that idiot."

While his partner gave Book and the workmen a cursory check, Hammond waved at Maya, beckoning her over. Sarah emitted an uneasy whine from her nose. Maya reluctantly released her friend's hand and approached him, arms straight at her sides.

"You all right, uhh, *Lisa?*" asked Hammond.

"Yes, sir." She smiled a little. "Thanks for sticking up for Sarah."

He raised his handheld as if running a scan on her. "Guess we weren't chasin' our own tails last time, were we?"

Maya grimaced. "No, sir."

"Hmm. I heard a bunch of stuff about you. Guess things have a way of getting worse on the grapevine."

She bit her lip, tapping one sneaker on the ground. "I may have been a little bitchy to some officers in the past. Probably the same ones who are in trouble now."

"So you really chose to stay out here instead of going home?" He scratched at his eyebrow.

"This is my home now. Vanessa doesn't want me. Some mercenaries kidnapped me and tried to get a ransom. They vid-called her to prove they had me. Put a gun to my face. Vanessa told them to go ahead and kill me since it would be cheaper to 'grow a new one.'"

He cringed. "No shit. Damn, I heard that woman was a piece of work, but what the f..."

"I know 'piece of work' means bitch." She smiled. "But you can't call her a bitch, or you'll insult bitches. That stuff I said about her releasing Fade to make people buy Xenodril is true."

"Yeah. We all saw those files. Things are, uhh, kinda interesting now. Look, for what it's worth, sorry for the rough treatment last time. Sarge saw some bad shit during the war, and he's convinced everyone out here's got a hand grenade with his name on it. Baxter always was an ass. Wish he got worse than what he did for hitting your friend, but at least he got something. Wasn't even for that too. Heard the request came from the very top."

Maya's eyebrows shot up. "What did they do to him?"

"Booted from the Authority, lost his citizenship. He's a Non now. Not sure where he went."

Could he *be the guy who sent the mercenaries?* She dismissed the idea. Officially, he'd been dismissed for being rude to one of Vanessa's employees. *No way he could find out it was me who faked her complaint email.* "Wow."

"Yeah. All right, well, if you're actually happy here. I suppose after that video, there's not much going back for you." He shook his head.

She smirked. "You think?"

"Got that feeling when no 'go get her' order came down the pipe. All right, go on back over."

She nodded and hurried back to stand against the wall by Pope.

Hammond approached the residents and grasped a case on his belt.

"Please don't tie me up!" wailed Emily, jumping to her feet. "Please!"

Anton and Marcus glared at him but didn't appear ready to put up a fight. Pick hung his head in defeat. He tried to look tough, but his eyes reddened.

Sarah whimpered.

"Everyone stay calm." Hammond removed a little black box, about the size of a deck of playing cards, from the case and held it up. It sprang open at the corners, revealing itself to be a tiny drone. Two bright dots appeared on the front as the fans came to life and it hovered up from his palm. "There's no need for that. Used to be SOP for everyone's protection. New policies, and new toys. No one's going to be restrained unless they give us a reason to."

Sarah let her head sag against Pope's shoulder, exhaling a sigh of relief.

"'Kay." Emily sniffled and sat back down, hugging her knees to her chest and shivering.

Hammond pointed at the drone. "Everyone sit still until this thing flies away. This is for your protection as much as ours. It will let us know if anyone tries to leave this room."

Muted gunfire came from somewhere below.

"That's our cue." Hammond pulled his visor closed and jogged out.

His partner followed, and the armed drone that had been hanging by the hole in the roof dropped straight down. The high-pitched buzz of four one-inch fans filled in the silence after the clamor of boots on concrete stairs faded.

"Can we talk?" whispered Anton.

"Don't see why not." Book smiled. "Impression I got was just not ta leave this room."

"He said sit still," said Pick. "My butt itches."

Pope, Book, and two of the workmen chuckled. Emily scrunched up her nose.

Sarah squirmed, so Pope set her on her feet. She peered past at Maya, astonishment clear on her face. "They didn't cuff us."

"No..." Book's eyebrows climbed. "They did not. Talked to us civil even." He laughed, a deep baritone that made the little drone pivot toward him. "Almost like our little friend here really was the spark of change."

Maya grinned.

After a few minutes of silence, Book started 'reading' out loud from a story. He enthralled the kids with a tale of a pair of boy detectives in mid-1800s London investigating a mysterious figure haunting their boarding school. The story held the attention of the workers as well, once they got over the oddity of a variety of different voices coming from a seventyish man. Whenever he narrated character dialogue, electronics in his throat changed his voice to match. Maya couldn't reconcile the voice of a small girl coming out of Book, so she closed her eyes to imagine the scene. About forty minutes later, echoed shouts rose from the street along with the distant *slam* of van doors. The minuscule drone emitted an electronic chirp, rotated to face the hole in the wall, and flew out before diving toward the road.

"Well, that's an hour I won't get back," said one of the workers.

"Hey wait," asked the short guy in the hardhat, staring at Book. "What happens next? Is that kid gonna find the secret door?"

Maya laughed.

Pope sat on the floor, still holding Sarah, who shivered, still stunned that the Authority hadn't restrained anyone.

Book continued the story while the men in white jumpsuits resumed their survey of the damaged wall. Pope and the children settled in to listen. It seemed the plan to relocate the story room would be postponed at least for one night.

THE FINAL NAIL

With some reluctance, Maya changed into her nightdress to sleep. She squished herself into the sleeping bag with Sarah, on the floor next to Genna's bed. At least the nightgown made the cozy accommodations more comfortable. Despite the close quarters, she had a feeling that sleeping in a forced hug made Sarah feel better. Pope had the couch all to himself.

In the morning, Maya woke first. She dragged herself out of the sleeping bag, waking Sarah, who didn't much move. Before even going to the bathroom, Maya changed into her fatigues and shirt. Sarah trudged into the bathroom as Maya left and headed to the kitchen.

Genna portioned out a breakfast of Megawaffle, an overly sweet cereal that resembled tiny waffles fused in pairs with a dark brown 'maple' layer between them. Maya munched spoonful after spoonful, still not used to the odd aftertaste of boxed milk. The plastic carton of cereal had been permanent-markered at the top left corner with 1 N/C. Maya quirked an eyebrow at the writing.

"What? Something wrong with the cereal?" asked Genna.

"It's okay. I'd say it's too sweet, but I don't want you to think I'm complaining. Any food we get out here is good." She pointed at the marker. "Who wrote on it?"

"Someone stole a truckload of it and they're selling it here for one

NuCoin a box," said Sarah without looking up from her bowl. "This stuff's like six bucks normally."

Genna nodded. "Probably. Didn't ask where it came from. Was still sealed, so it's all good to me."

Pope slurped the last traces of milk-like-product from his bowl.

"You're finished already?" Maya gawked at him and then Genna as she tilted back hers.

"Army habit." He chuckled. "Havin' more than two minutes for a meal still feels like I'm taking forever."

She slurped up another spoonful. The overwhelming amount of sugar made it difficult to eat fast.

"So..." Genna patted the table. "Our mutual friends are going to contact Zeroice and see what he thinks of your idea. Harlowe got pretty angry."

Maya shrank in her seat. "Sorry."

"Oh, not at you." Genna winked. "Angry that we hadn't thought of trying to make the formula public before. Everyone's been so convinced of Ascendant's untouchability that no one dared suggest something like that. He said this could put the final nail in Fade's coffin—if we can pull it off."

"Yes!" Maya grinned. After another spoonful, she looked up. "Can we go to the Emporium and get Sarah some clothes? All she's got is what she's wearing."

Sarah's cheeks reddened. "You don't gotta waste money on me. Dad'll get me something in the Sanc when we go to visit him."

"You could use some shoes too." Pope ruffled her hair. "Lucky you haven't gotten sick from an infected cut."

"I'm used to it. I've never had any shoes. Dad says it's not worth the money since I'd just outgrow them before they wear out. And people will steal them." Sarah pushed cereal around her bowl. "It's all right. I don't mind."

"Billy drinks most of his veteran's pension." Genna leaned her chin on her fist, a smirk of contemplation on her lips as she watched Sarah eat.

Sarah glanced sideways at her with a momentary scowl. "He's not trying to be mean. He thinks I'll stay inside and be safe. Foz charges too much for everything. I can wait."

"I have money," said Maya. She explained the scav. "It's in the bedroom in one of your socks under the dresser. I want to pay that man back for feeding us too."

"Foz won't overcharge me." Genna laughed. "We'll go talk to him soon as we get back from meeting Barnes. Pope's agreed to hear him out. Maybe even stick around."

He yawned and stretched, making his chair creak. "Hole in the ground's nice for privacy, but hot running water has its perks."

Genna exchanged a surreptitious glance with him and smiled.

Pretending not to notice the way they looked at each other, Maya finished off her cereal. "When are we going?"

"Our meeting is downstairs. We're not leaving the building. You two are to stay inside until we get back. The longest we should be is about an hour"—she shifted her gaze to Pope—"unless he's full of questions."

"Okay." Disappointed, Maya stared at her lap.

"I mean that. You two stay inside. Don't go out and don't open the door for anyone but us. Weber's watching the front, so if anyone shows up we don't expect, we'll come running."

"Yes, Mom," said Maya.

"While we're down there, I mean to get a good answer outta Harlowe about the Sanc." Genna squeezed Sarah's shoulder. "If there's any possible way to get you in there to visit your father, we'll go in a couple of hours, 'kay?"

"All right. Thanks." Sarah almost smiled. She collected the bowls and spoons and carried the stack to the sink to wash.

Maya picked up a towel and stood beside her.

Pope retrieved his rifle from the bedroom before following Genna out.

"I wish she would stop saying mean things about my dad," muttered Sarah.

"Sorry. She's not saying it to be mean. It is a little weird that he won't buy you important stuff like clothes."

Sarah handed her a bowl. "He did. I kept having my stuff stolen. He told me not to go out and scav, but I didn't listen. Those camo pants I liked, he just bought 'em like three days before the dosers robbed us. He got pretty mad at me, yelled, 'You must like not havin' any clothes. Zat why all yer wee friends call ya Faerie? Since ya like it so much, ya can stay that way for a little while.'"

"Wow. That's mean." Maya frowned. "Was he drunk?"

Her face reddened; she leaned both hands on the counter. "No!"

Maya worked the towel around the bowl in silence and set it on the table, planning to drag a chair over to the counter and climb up to put all four away at once.

"Maybe." Sarah bowed her head. "He might've been a little drunk—and angry. He always gets angry when someone tries to hurt me. I think he was mad at himself for not being out there to protect me." After a minute of silence, she sighed again. "Okay. He was a lot drunk."

Maya put an arm around her. "He's trying to do the best he can."

"Yeah," said Sarah, the onset of cry in her voice as she worked the cloth around the next bowl. She didn't speak for a little while. After handing the bowl into Maya's waiting towel, she wiped her face and stood straight. "He forgot about it the next morning. I guess I should've asked him, but I didn't want him to get mad again. He's sick and he doesn't need to worry about me being stupid."

"How are you stupid?" Maya frowned, and dried the bowl.

Sarah pulled the third bowl into the water. "I should have stayed inside where it's safe, not gone out where someone could've robbed me. I found this curtain in a room on the tenth a couple days later. I didn't wanna bother him."

Maya blinked at her. "You ran around naked for days?"

"No." Sarah gave her a look as if she'd said the dumbest thing in the world. "Only one. Second day he told me to put on one of his army tees. I wasn't allowed to leave the building with it."

"We can't spend our whole lives inside, worrying about who might hurt us. The Hab's not that bad." Maya set the bowl on the stack and waited for number three. "You're doing it right. You don't go out alone, and you got the Hornet now."

"I guess. Most of the dosers stay in the Dead Space."

Someone knocked on the door.

Maya spun to look out the archway at the living room. Sarah froze. Four seconds later, Maya made a 'shh' gesture at Sarah.

"Hello?" said a man. He knocked again. "Maintenance crew. We're working on the building and need to check all the apartments for structural integrity."

Maya thought about the men fixing the gaping hole in the wall on the ninth. That the building owner kept his word about repairing the place shocked her. She didn't want to be rude, but Genna told her not to let anyone in. Better they think no one home.

"Hello?" More knocking.

"No one's there," said another man. "Fuck it, just go in."

Shit! "Wait," yelled Maya. She trotted into the living room. "Can you come back in like two hours?"

"Hey kid," said the first man. "We just gotta look around at the walls. Be in and out in five minutes tops."

She snarled under her breath. "Umm. I'm really sorry, but I'm not allowed to let anyone in."

"What, you got left home alone?" asked the second man.

Crap. She cringed. "My mother's right downstairs. She'll be back soon. You should come back when she's home."

"We're in a hurry, kid. Gotta survey the whole damn building." The lock clicked open.

Maya gasped and took a few steps back as the front door swung inward, revealing a pair of men in white workers' jumpsuits with yellow hard hats. The closer guy had a bit of grey hair poking out over his ears and his pale face sported a few days' worth of beard stubble. The man behind him, more muscular but shorter with a buzz cut, pushed a cart into the apartment. Various tools and little handheld meters littered a bin on the top level, and a huge plastiboard box on the lower shelf bore a 'CenCor Networks' logo. A bit of wire stuck out of a hole at the top.

"You shouldn't just walk in like that." Sarah hurried over, putting herself in front of Maya.

The tall man stared around at the ceiling while walking deeper into the apartment. "You won't even notice we're here. Just gotta check for damage."

Maya spun to keep staring at him as he passed, fuming at being ignored, but intimidated by his height.

His partner pushed the cart in a little further before grabbing a brick-sized black box from the top and calling, "Hal," before tossing it.

Hal looked back in time to catch the device.

Maya twisted to glare at the shorter man for a second before taking a step after Hal. "You can't just walk into someone's home."

"Sure we can." Hal pushed a button on the box. "It's in the lease contract. Landlord access for maintenance needs."

"Gah!" yelled the other man.

Maya whirled around.

The worker had grabbed Sarah from behind, holding a white rag over her face. She'd gotten a healthy handful of his testicles and squeezed for all she had. Maya screamed as loud as she could and jumped at him, trying to pull his hairy arm away from her face.

Hal grabbed Maya, crushing a wet cloth over her mouth and nose. Tears sprang from her eyes at the fumes, and a burn like alcohol fire ran up her nostrils. She gagged and coughed, panic rising at her inability to breathe. Instinct took over; she stopped trying to pull the man off Sarah and clawed in a frenzy at the arm holding her, but he refused to let go. Sound melted into a murky morass, and her muscles stopped listening. Dingy green carpet met her cheek and faded to blackness.

[16]

NEGOTIATION

Mouth dry and head pounding, Maya awoke flat on her back staring up at a clean ceiling of Washington blue. Dizziness lingered, and her effort to sit up manifested as a feeble side-to-side squirm. Softness beneath her suggested she lay upon a bed with her legs bent at the knee over the edge. A sour, chemical taste remained on her tongue, and her limbs felt heavier than they should be. Warmth beside her made her roll her head to the left.

Sarah, awake, lay close enough to touch shoulders, tears running down the sides of her head. Maya tried to sit up, but tight cords squeezed at her wrists and ankles. Her hands, bound behind her back, had gone numb from her weight pressing on them. She pushed herself up to sit and slouched forward, staring woozily down at her bare feet poking out from the floppy leggings of her fatigue pants. Despite the quiet murmuring of multiple strange men nearby while she found herself tied hand and foot in an unknown location, she grew angry at being stranded without shoes *again*.

"I am so fucking tired of being kidnapped," muttered Maya.

"Genna's going to spank you for cursing," said Sarah, sniffing. "She said no f-bombs 'til you're eighteen."

Maya lifted her head. The workers' pushcart stood parked at the foot end of the bed. Beside it, the giant plastiboard box lay on its side, top open, with a fake length of wire attached to a plastic guide. Instead of network cable, it held a large quantity of nothing. Those men had to have stuffed them in the box and rolled them right out the front door—past Weber. She contemplated screaming, but these people didn't bother taping her mouth shut, so they obviously didn't care how much noise she made now.

A small table between the beds held a lamp, a non-video phone, and an alarm clock that displayed 7:18 p.m. Maya stifled a gasp. *We've been unconscious all day...* She swallowed hard, hoping they'd only lost *one* day. The oddity of waking up in the early evening made her feel disjointed from time, unable to tell what day of the week it was. *Chloroform wouldn't have knocked us out that long.* Her heart raced in fear at the thought these men had likely injected her with some drug to keep her out cold. She twisted side to side, checking her arms for any sign of needle marks, but didn't find anything obvious. Having no idea what they dosed her with gave her a case of the shivers that wouldn't stop.

She winced, testing the binding at her wrists. The men had used rope, which pinched the more she squirmed. Sarah, aside from her soundless weeping, looked in control of her emotions. Her shoulders twitched side to side in an almost imperceptible continuous motion.

A fortyish man in a grey suit paced around the far side of the room beyond a second bed. One cheap-looking desk and an entertainment center sat against the wall to the right. From the lack of dirt and peeling paint, and the pleasant floral scent in the air, she figured they'd been brought into the Sanctuary Zone already and wound up at a hotel or something.

"What is taking Ruiz so damned long?" asked the man in the suit.

Hal, having traded his worker's outfit for a dark turtleneck sweater and black fatigues similar to Maya's, occupied a wingback chair near the window. He shrugged. "You didn't hire me to be a psychic. Are you expecting an answer or just wasting oxygen?"

The other 'workman' emerged from the bathroom, chuckling.

Music with a strong Asian influence, rendered on wind chimes, emanated from Grey Suit. He took a minicomputer from his pocket, poked its screen, and held it up to his head. "Miss Shen... Apologies for the delay."

A feminine voice murmured, indistinct.

"Of course. Yes." He glanced at Maya. "Gut says yes, but Ruiz isn't here yet with the PMRI."

Shen? Maya squinted. Something sounded too familiar about that name. She leaned forward, turning her head to put an ear toward the man in the suit, straining to listen in.

"... going wrong ... absolute certainty ... as soon as you're finished."

"Of course. I'll call you as soon as humanly possible," said Grey Suit.

That woman's voice made Maya think of a boardroom, but she couldn't put a face or identity to her.

She bent forward, examining her feet. Black cord as thin as her fingers wound about her ankles, but her pants got in the way so she couldn't get a good look at how they tied it. Maya grumbled as she squirmed her legs back and forth in protest of the rope. "You're wasting your time."

None of the men even looked at her.

Maya twisted left to check on Sarah. The girl continued to stare at the ceiling with a look of intense concentration. Sensing Maya watching, Sarah shifted her gaze to lock eyes with her and offered an apologetic lip bite.

"What?" whispered Maya.

Sarah looked at the ceiling again and resumed squirming.

"What?" whispered Maya, louder. When Sarah didn't react, she faced the room. "What do you want? Who are you?"

Hal's minicomputer emitted plink noises like glass crystals tapping together. His face flashed with a rainbow of colors. A moment later, the device said, "Level four," in an inhuman, deep voice.

Grey Suit continued pacing. His expression said he wanted to be here almost as much as Maya did.

"Argh!" Maya struggled at the ropes, rocking side to side and swinging her legs up and down. "Stop ignoring me!" She scowled. "My mother is going to rip your balls off."

The short 'worker' chuckled. "Good luck with that. Hal's ol' lady has 'em in a jar."

"Your little sister would say otherwise, Mike," said Hal in a conversational tone, still tapping gems on his screen. "And that precious little redhead over there already tried."

Grey Suit stifled a chuckle while Mike scowled.

Sarah's concentration lapsed long enough to show a hint of a smile. Maya shot her an intense look, trying to get her attention and at least an answer. A gap in her curtain-dress where two safety pins struggled to keep it from unraveling exposed a strip of her pale, white stomach, rising and falling with her hard breathing. The girl looked beyond terrified, but she kept her attention on the ceiling, as if refusing to look at any of the men might make her situation not real. Maya twisted and pulled at her arms, hating her tiny wrists that Vanessa probably ordered like a pizza topping. The email said Vanessa had chosen her eye shape from Japanese DNA, her sylph's build from the Sudan, and her complexion a mixture of several ethnicities. Only thirty-something percent of her genes came from her biological mother. *Vanessa's more my cousin than my mother.*

Headlights washed over the front window as a car came to a stop with a faint *squeak.*

"It's about damned time," said Grey Suit.

Mike opened the door, admitting a dark-skinned man with a dense helmet of black hair and a thick mustache. He entered carrying a silver metal briefcase with a red cross on both sides over the unoccupied bed, where he set the case flat.

"Sorry about that, Mr. Winnow." The man Maya assumed to be Ruiz flipped open the latches on the case. "Got stuck behind a goddamn emergency cordon. Some asshat threw a Molotov at an Ascendant clinic."

Maya leaned back, fighting the ropes, as Ruiz pulled a device from the case that resembled a giant ray gun. "What do you want? Why did you kidnap us?"

"Make sure it's her," said Winnow.

Ruiz walked up to Maya and pointed the thing at her. His face lit up from a small screen on the back end. He fiddled with buttons for a few seconds before lowering his arm. "Yeah. It's her. Or at least it's a live kid. No android."

"You're wasting your time," said Maya. "Vanessa doesn't care about me at all. You won't get any money out of her."

"We're not here for a ransom." Winnow walked up to stand beside Ruiz, his shimmery suit swooshing with his motion.

Sarah froze. What little color she had disappeared. "Please don't make us do sex."

Hal grimaced. "Relax kid. That's not happening."

"What?" Maya stared at him, still fidgeting at the rope. "Why did you take us then? What are you going to do?"

Mr. Winnow gave her a blasé look. "We had to be sure you weren't an android. I'm rather allergic to nuclear radiation."

"You know the decoys don't have nukes, right? Vanessa's far too cheap for that. Plus she doesn't trust electronics in case one shorted out and went off." She gasped as her continued effort to escape caused the rope to pinch her. "Ow. Dammit. Untie me right now!"

"Still bossy I see." Mr. Winnow removed a small black case from his suit jacket pocket. "This is not about a ransom. You are in Vanessa Oman's will to inherit the company should anything... unfortunate happen to her."

Maya shook her head. "I don't even *want* the company. All I want is for them to stop using Fade on innocent people."

"You really believe that about Fade, don't you?" Mr. Winnow unzipped the case and removed a syringe.

"What is that for?" Maya leaned back. "And yes. I believe Vanessa has released Fade to make money. Those files are true."

"Guns are so messy." He examined the syringe in the light. "This won't leave any blood to clean up."

Maya almost wet herself at the realization the man intended to kill Sarah if she didn't cooperate. She pulled as hard as she could, but the rope binding her arms refused to break. Sarah grunted and squirmed with renewed effort.

"No! Please don't!" said Maya, adding a trace of whine. "You don't know Vanessa. She disowned me after I made that video. I'm no one to her now. I got kidnapped once before and she told them to go ahead and kill me—with me watching. I'm out of her will. I'm not even a Citizen anymore."

"Tragic, really." Mr. Winnow frowned. "And yet she has not removed you from the will."

Maya growled. "In case you idiots hadn't noticed, I walked away from Ascendant. I'm living out in the Hab with the Nons because *I don't want* Ascendant. I *hate* Vanessa. You don't have to threaten Sarah to make me sign it over. You can have the stupid company. I don't want anything to do with it."

Mr. Winnow raised an eyebrow. He cocked his jaw to the side, measuring her with a stare.

Her heart thudded in her chest; she couldn't stop shaking. That he hesitated at all gave her hope. The man clearly hadn't expected that. "I'm nine years old. Even if Vanessa died today, I wouldn't really have control of anything for another nine years. A trustee would manage it. I'll sign it over. I only want one thing."

Mr. Winnow looked her up and down as she wriggled. "You're hardly in any position to negotiate, Maya."

"The only thing I want is for Ascendant to stop releasing Fade. Think about it. If the company stops covering for Vanessa and blames her for the Fade, then *stops* using it, the Brigade won't have any motivation to cause problems. Public opinion of the company will bounce back as Vanessa takes all the fallout."

Mr. Winnow patted her on the head. "That's quite clever, and not at all a bad idea. You're only forgetting two small things."

Maya shrank away from him, terrified and furious at being tied up in equal parts. "W-what?"

He gave her shoulder a comforting squeeze and pushed her over to lie flat. "Ascendant is not, nor ever was, releasing Fade, and Maya Oman never existed. She's only a computer simulation created for marketing purposes. We also weren't going to threaten your friend. This needle isn't for her. As long as you live, you represent an obstacle to our goals." He lowered the syringe toward her neck.

She struggled and screamed, trying to lean away from the point.

Sarah pulled her legs up, rolled to the side, and mule-kicked him in the hip hard enough to make herself slide off the bed. The hit knocked Mr. Winnow two steps to his left. He recovered his balance and lunged at Maya again, ignoring the floundering redhead on the floor.

"Wait!" screamed Maya. She forced herself to keep thinking. If she breathed too hard, she'd be sitting in piss. "It won't do any good to kill me. Vanessa will just make another one!"

Sarah rolled around and tried to bite Winnow on the leg.

Hal gestured at her, not taking his eyes off his game. "Mike...."

The shorter man stormed over and grabbed Sarah. She growled and thrashed, but couldn't escape his grip before he tossed her face down on the bed and pounced on top of her. She screamed into the mattress, unable to budge with a grown man's weight pinning her.

Winnow grabbed Maya by the throat, needle poised. "What do you mean by 'make another one'?"

"I-it's what she said to the other mercs." Maya trembled; streams of hot tears ran down her cheeks to the mattress. "I don't have a father. She ordered me from a gene clinic. Her egg, custom genetic profile to make me pretty for commercials. She'll just do it again and throw up a wall of bullshit until the next 'daughter' is old enough. Please don't kill me. Please! I swear I'll sign the company over to you. You need me as the oldest heir."

"Come on, man. Kid's got a point," said Ruiz. He fidgeted with his necktie. "Bad karma offin' a kid anyway. She's so little. Do we really gotta—?"

The windows exploded inward with a shower of glass fragments; flashes of muzzle flare lit up the night outside in time with a rapid series of gunshots.

Hal's head burst like a melon struck by a train. His minicomputer tumbled to the floor and spoke again in the demonic-deep voice, "Level complete."

"Fuck!" roared Winnow, grabbing the back of his leg and collapsing over sideways.

Mike stopped holding Sarah down and pulled a handgun from his coat. He dove to one knee between the beds, using the empty one for cover, and fired at someone outside.

"Motherfuckers," screamed Genna.

"Mom!" shouted Maya. "Mommy!" She burst into tears. "Help! They're gonna kill me!"

Winnow got back upright; blood stained his left pant leg.

Maya grunted and swung her legs up, mashing both feet into his nuts.

He grunted and stumbled back, raising his fist as if to jam the needle into her heart—only he'd lost the syringe.

Boom.

A fraction of a second after the deep rapport outside, a blast of blood burst from the center of Winnow's chest with a wet *splat*. He gawked at the wound and collapsed. Maya hurled her weight to the right, rolling aside to avoid having a dead man land on top of her.

"Shit!" shouted Pope, outside. "Incoming!"

Car tires squealed, and a floodlight lit up the smashed windows.

An angry, grunting nasal-roar came from Genna.

"Stay down," yelled Pope.

Mike popped up, aiming. He let off a shot; the bark of his gun so loud it seemed to compress Maya's brain. A chatter of automatic fire came from outside, sending Mike into a jerky dance. Gurgling, he careened over sideways.

"Mom!" screamed Maya, lying on her chest. She refused to look at Winnow and shimmied backward off the mattress until her toes touched carpet.

Sarah rolled onto her back and kicked her legs out to fling herself to her feet, hopping around in an effort not to fall over.

Men in whitish armor rushed in, aiming submachine guns around at the dead men. A few 'just to be sure' bullets perforated corpses. One man headed for Maya, another, Sarah, who screamed and tried to hop away, but the man scooped her up. The other tossed Maya over his shoulder like a duffel bag and carried her outside.

"Mom!" shouted Maya. "Help! Put me down! Let go of me!"

Sarah grunted and growled in the arms of the man behind her. The two armored figures not carrying them pointed guns toward a shot-up car on the left. Genna popped up from behind the hood with an assault rifle, but before she could get off a shot, both men fired at her.

A noise like a stepped on goose came from Genna as she collapsed out of sight. Her rifle landed on the hood and slid, abandoned, to the sidewalk.

"Mommy, no!" shouted Maya, along with an explosion of tears, squirming, and growling. "You assholes! You shot my fucking mother! Get off me!"

Shouting degenerated into wailing as the man carried her to a waiting car and tossed her in the back seat before slamming the door. She squirmed around, trying to get her hands on the lever to open it. The driver side door opened and Sarah flew in headfirst, her face landing in Maya's lap. The man slammed the door behind her and opened the front.

A loud *boom* came from the direction of the shot-up car, and one of the men staggered forward with a neat fountain of blood gushing from the side of his helmet. He fell against the car, blocking the window by Maya, and collapsed.

"Go, go, go!" shouted another.

The man who'd tossed Sarah jumped into the front seat and stomped the accelerator before he even closed his door. Squealing and smoke filled the air as the car swerved onto the road. Cursing, the driver pulled a hard right turn that hurled Maya into Sarah. Another harsh maneuver seconds later threw Maya into the door and sent Sarah crashing into her. They slid across the seat and mushed against the other side when the man jerked the wheel to line up with the road. Sarah bounced away and landed on her back across the seat at her left.

Maya, tears streaming from her eyes, wailed and bawled. She saw Genna go down over and over and over in her mind. "You bastards," she muttered. "You fucking bastards." Sorrow gave way to pure rage, but the brute force anger of a scrawny little couldn't defeat nylon cord. Livid at being tied, she kicked the back of the passenger seat again and again while screaming curses and incoherent wails of sorrow.

Nothing mattered now. They'd killed her mother. Maya didn't care how foolish or unlikely it would be for a girl her age to end Vanessa Oman. She resolved to make that bitch pay for Genna's death—or die in the attempt.

[17]

BEST FRIENDS

Rage faded to an exhausted slump a minute or so later in the back of the speeding e-car. Maya curled against the seat, angrier than she'd ever been but still crying quiet tears. Her legs ached, her hands and feet had gone numb, and her skin burned under the rope.

"Maya," whispered Sarah.

Maya stared into space, daydreaming about the shocked look that would be on Vanessa's face when she barged into her lavish office and shot her.

Sarah grunted, acting like the car's motion flung her against Maya.

A hand grabbed her arm.

At the painful squeeze, Maya glared at her. She almost lashed out, but Sarah pulled her right arm out from behind her back and wiggled her fingers. Only red marks remained around her friend's wrist—no cord. Using her body to hide her task from the driver, she cleared the rope from her left wrist and chucked the tangle to the floor before mushing herself against Maya and attacking her bindings. Something scraped over and over at the knot between her wrists.

"How did you do that?" whispered Maya.

"Shh."

The car skidded around a left turn, earning horns and beeping from at least three people he cut off. Once he straightened out again, he slowed, perhaps in an effort to drive casual.

Maya tensed, waiting for the feeling of tightness in the cord to lessen.

"Don't be stupid," whispered Sarah, lips close enough to kiss her ear. "Pretend you're tied still."

She wanted to jump into the front seat and kill this man for shooting Genna, but Sarah was right. He had armor, and she didn't even have a weapon, much less the strength of an adult. Maya nodded.

The scratching stopped, and Sarah wormed a finger around for a few seconds and tugged. The rope let go. Maya pulled her hands free but kept them together behind her back. Sarah stared between the front seats at the road. As soon as the man tapped the brakes on approach to a red light, she overacted being thrown to the floor. Out of sight on the ground, she untied Maya's ankles in a few seconds, using a single pointy lockpick to attack the knot, before freeing her own legs.

After stashing the little rod back in her curtain-dress, Sarah climbed, grunting and squirming, up into the seat, pretending to be tied.

Maya gave her a 'now what?' look.

Sarah mouthed 'next red light.'

Maya nodded.

"Oh, shit," muttered the driver. "What is that thing doing?"

The high-pitched whine of drone fans approached from behind and left. Sarah looked over her shoulder but cringed away as strong light flooded the car.

Maya huddled behind her friend, peering out the window at a dark blue Authority drone overtaking their car with ease, its .50 cal machine gun trained. It skimmed low, barely a foot above the roofs of passing cars. The armored man kept looking back and forth from the rearview mirror to the road ahead. He accelerated.

So did the drone.

"Fuck is wrong with them?" mumbled the driver.

He tapped a finger on the wheel and took a sudden right turn, swerving with a fishtail that narrowly avoided sideswiping a line of parked e-cars. The drone kept going straight, unable to follow without crashing into the building at the corner. Before the man could finish laughing, the drone emerged from a side street two blocks behind them.

Maya squirmed up to look out the rear window. Sarah did the same.

Shoulder to shoulder, the girls gasped in unison as the drone tilted forward and gained on them.

"Is it gonna shoot us?" asked Sarah.

Maya slid down, rotating to face front. "How should I know?"

Sarah lowered herself.

"Dammit! What the hell?" grumbled the driver. "Damn blueberries forgot who they work for."

Two more small sedans skidded into view from the left, adding to the chase. Identical to the one Maya rode in, they also had white-armored men driving. She stared at the cyan accents on the shoulder of the man in the front seat. *Ascendant security? But why?*

The drone raced up alongside their car, the tip of the machine gun inches from the driver's side window. A voice emanated from a loud-speaker. "Stop the car or be subject to annihilation."

Maya blinked. She knew that voice. *Zeroice!*

"Stupid bastards overstepping their power," mumbled the driver.

"You're about to overstep a giant machine gun to the face," said Maya.

He slowed and pulled to the curb.

The instant the car came to a complete stop, Sarah climbed over Maya's lap, pushed the door open, and dragged her out.

"Hey!" shouted the driver.

Fans whirred higher as the drone popped up over the car to 'look' at the girls. Sarah screamed as if the gun would fire on them.

"Wait," rasped Maya. "It's—"

Sarah dragged her into an alley at a full sprint.

The machine gun went off in the distance.

Maya twisted back to look, stumbling into a loping run. The drone appeared to be firing on the approaching cars; a huge blast of orange muzzle fire burned into her retinas. Sarah kept pulling, dragging her down the alley. Multiple shadows slithered over the wall, filling her head with visions of armored men coming after them.

"The drone's friendly!" shouted Maya. "Zero hacked it!"

"There's more coming!" Sarah's feet hit the wet paving with sharp *claps*. "I don't wanna get shot."

The hand squeezing hers could've belonged to a tiny cyborg. Maya tried to keep up, mimicking Sarah's stride. Another alley later, they raced into an open-air bazaar. Dozens of carts hawked wares ranging from treats to jewelry to drinks and even clothes.

Fragrances of perfume, Chinese food, searing meat, coffee, incense, and frying chicken came and went as they darted among people. Except for one guy who gave Sarah a healthy shove while muttering 'damn pickpocket,' everyone else ignored them. Maya wanted to scream back at the idiot how no one could pick a pocket while running at full speed, but the man disappeared in the crowd before she could take a breath.

After crossing the courtyard and ducking into a side street, Sarah pulled her into a cramped alley full of dumpsters and loose trash. Something caught her eye and she made a sharp right turn, skidding to a halt in a squat past the second set of trash boxes. She pointed at a narrow slot in the curb and pushed Maya toward it.

"In there. Go! They're coming!"

Panic overrode reason. Maya stuck her feet in the storm drain and slid forward. She hung by her fingertips for a second until she noticed a rung on the wall and stretched to get her foot on it. Sarah scooted through and dropped, ignoring the ladder, and landed in a tumble about eight feet below.

Maya hurried down a series of metal bars stuck in the concrete wall like staples. As soon as her foot hit wet dirt, Sarah grabbed her hand again and pulled her into a concrete tunnel half the size of the tubes comprising the Jigsaw River. Despite being smaller, the place still made her think of Pope. She flashed back to him shooting the one Ascendant soldier in the helmet, and then the two cars coming after them. Did they kill him too? Did he run?

No... he wouldn't have just let them take her.

Sarah stopped at the end of the tunnel and spun around before climbing down another ladder into a cistern chamber. Crying and shaking from grief, Maya followed her to a small platform overlooking a huge area filled with brown water. A thin layer of dark grey silt coated the dingy concrete slab, tinted green with moss at the waterline.

Her friend crumpled in a heap, out of breath and shivering.

Maya fell to her knees, sat back on her heels, and bawled into her hands.

Sarah pulled her into a fierce hug. Gasping for breath, she didn't try to talk.

"They killed her," sniveled Maya. "They shot her. It's my fault."

"It's not your fault." Sarah took a few breaths. "The only ones whose fault it is are those guys who kidnapped us."

Maya looked up. Sarah's reassuring blue eyes and hopeful expression made her sob harder. "Your dad's my fault too." She wailed for a while, unable to talk.

Sarah squeezed her, rocked her, and rubbed her back until she calmed.

"I shouldn't have stayed with Genna. I should've let her take me back to Vanessa and lie, say she rescued me. I should just go back to Vanessa and let her use me. I don't want anyone getting hurt."

"No way!" Sarah put her in a headlock and raked her knuckles back and forth over Maya's head. "Not happening."

"Ow!" Maya pushed at her but couldn't escape. "Stop!"

"You're my best friend, and best friends don't let each other do dumb things!"

Maya pulled at Sarah's arm around her neck. "She's just going to keep hurting everyone around me."

"You don't even know it was Vanessa. Those guys were trying to take Ascendant *from* her. She didn't do that."

Drips and *ploinks* echoed in the massive chamber around them. Maya scrunched up her face, breathing hard, scowling at nothing in particular. She coughed on air that tasted like wet dirt.

"You're right. My dad should've bought me clothes before beer. He should've done a lot of things he didn't do."

Maya gawked at Sarah. Hearing the girl admit that felt like a knife in the heart.

"I keep trying to take care of everyone. I didn't know how to handle someone trying to take care of me, especially a younger kid." Sarah looked down, tracing lines in the silt with her finger. "Dad loves me. I know it. He's just got problems, and he can't deal with a lot of things. I'm not going to let you be stupid."

Maya sniffled. "I've never had a best friend before. Never had a friend before really. Not 'til I ran away and met you and Marcus and Anton and Pick and Emily. What's a best friend?"

Sarah held out her hand. "It's kinda like being sisters, only we didn't have the same mother. Well, maybe not exactly. Sisters fight more than best friends do."

"Really?" Maya took her hand.

"Yeah. Naida has a sister. Pick says they hate each other."

"That's sad. How can sisters hate each other?" Maya squeezed Sarah's hand. "Best friends."

"Best friends." Sarah grinned. "Dunno. He said something like his grandmother likes the younger sister more than Naida and they fight all the time. Maybe 'cause Naida's a... you know."

"Oh. Well, I'm never gonna be a prostitute, so if we were sisters, we wouldn't have to hate each other." She wiped tears from her cheeks. Though her heart remained like a lead weight inside her at the loss of Genna, she couldn't cry anymore. "What are we gonna do?"

Sarah took a deep breath and let it out slow. "Hide here 'til they stop looking for us."

"Then what?"

"We'll figure something out."

Maya frowned at her feet. "I left my shoes behind again."

Uncontrollable giggles crippled Sarah for a few minutes. "Next time someone grabs you, ask them to let you get dressed." She pantomimed being chloroformed. "Wait, Mr. Kidnapper, let me put my shoes on."

Maya punched her in the shoulder. "I am *so* sick of being kidnapped. I'm going to make it stop."

"How?" asked Sarah, still trying to stop laughing.

Eyes narrowed, Maya picked up a small rock and threw it into the water with a *plop*. "I'm going to kill Vanessa."

Sarah gasped. "Remember that whole part about best friends don't let each other do dumb stuff?"

"Yeah."

"That's dumb."

Maya leaned her weight back on her hands. "Maybe. But putting a bullet in her stupid face will make me feel better."

"I don't think you can kill anyone." Sarah put an arm around Maya's shoulders. "You're too sweet."

"Am not."

Sarah grinned. "And you can't stand looking at people getting shot."

Mr. Nori shooting the punk leapt into her mind. She cringed. "Okay, so I won't shoot her." Tears started again. "But she killed my mom."

In her friend's comforting embrace, Maya surrendered to grief, unable to do anything but cry.

ORPHANS

Cold concrete, dank dripping, and time chipped away at Maya's simmering anger. The men who'd attacked them at Sarah's apartment had probably intended on killing her too, or taking her to be scanned and shooting her after they scanned her to make sure they hadn't grabbed a decoy android.

A momentary flash of the man with the needle leapt across her memory, startling a shiver out of her. Eyes clamped shut, she grabbed her neck where he'd almost stuck her. She couldn't dredge up an explanation for how she'd stayed so calm when Genna and the others abducted her from the penthouse she'd spent most of her life in. Perhaps believing that Vanessa would bring the power of Ascendant and the Authority to save her and she only had to buy enough time to be found had given her courage at first.

Courage that shattered with four words—*I'll make another one.*

At first, she'd picked up on Genna's heartache at losing her son and tried to leverage that for pity, but the instant she'd seen Maya's reaction to being thrown away, Genna had gone from kidnapper to mother and almost gotten herself killed protecting Maya from Moth. She *had* gotten herself killed trying to rescue her from these people, some internal coup going on at Ascendant. A coup she'd probably started with her video, or at least emboldened. Maya wrapped her arms around her legs, hiding her face against her knees.

With the adrenaline of abduction, gunfire, and running fading, the reality of what had happened crept over her shoulders like a leaden blanket. Genna, her mother, died twenty feet away trying to save her.

Maya sobbed.

Sarah rubbed her back.

She tried to distract herself by analyzing why the two fake workers hadn't just shot her in the apartment. Maybe they feared getting caught or truly believed those decoys carried nukes. Maybe neither man had the stomach to kill a little girl. Why did they have to scan her? If they were worried about an android, they should've known they got a real kid when chloroform worked on her.

Oh, those androids would've faked it. They're designed to be kidnapped.

All she had wanted while trapped on the bed in that little motel room was for Genna to kick in the door and save her. Sorrow twisted her thoughts; the idea that her mother had shown up there only because Maya wanted her to brought crushing guilt, as though she'd caused her death.

"It's okay. I cried a lot about my dad too." Sarah kept squeezing her.

Eventually, Maya ran out of tears and stared, blank-faced, at the water. "What should we do?"

"I dunno. I guess we're both orphans now." She picked up a tiny rock and threw it into the shadows. "Book or Zoe might let us stay with them."

Maya stared down her legs at her toes, mostly hidden in the silt. "You don't know your dad's dead. He's in the hospital."

Sarah grasped Maya's face in both hands, pulled her head up, and touched foreheads, staring eye-to-eye. "You don't know Genna is either."

"I saw her get shot!" screamed Maya. "She dropped her gun. Soldiers don't drop their guns unless they're dead."

Her voice echoed into the distant sewer tunnels. A flurry of scratching in the dark followed.

Maya slapped herself in the chest. "Right here, and she collapsed." She wanted to sob again, but couldn't find the energy.

"They kept saying we couldn't go to the Sanc to visit him." Sarah swallowed hard, fighting back tears. "Every time we asked, they made up an excuse like they knew he died and didn't want me to find out. You know. Stalling. What do you think?"

"Thanks for making me try to feel better."

Sarah threw her arm around Maya and pulled her close. "We could try begging in the Sanc. Maybe I could get some tools an' we could sneak into nice fancy apartments when people are at work and eat their food."

"You're gonna miss everyone. You should go back home. These people are after *me*."

"I'm not leaving you alone here." Sarah's words sounded far more determined than her quivering voice. "If we go back home, we go together. At least if we beg in the Sanc, we don't gotta worry about dosers tryin' to steal our clothes for a fix."

"There's dosers here too." Maya folded her arms atop her knees and bowed her head on top of them. With Genna gone, she didn't much care to move from this spot ever again.

"Yeah, but here, there's a lot better stuff they can steal than clothes from street kids. Kick in a window and take electronics or something. They don't need ta bother us."

Maya sniffled. "We're gonna grow up to be prostitutes, aren't we? *If* we grow up."

"No way. You're too smart for that. You like went to school and stuff."

"Smart's got nothing to do with it. We have nowhere to go and no one to..." Maya broke down crying again.

"Don't be stupid." Sarah jostled her. "Remember that man at the food place? People know you. They'll help us."

Harlowe. Maya sat up straight and wiped her face. Her voice still shaky from crying, she half whispered, "We could go to The Hangar. There's Brigade there. Maybe they'll help."

Sarah quirked an eyebrow. "They won't let a couple of kids walk in there. That's a bar."

"I've been there before. If they recognize me, they'll let me in. Harlowe will let us stay there. Maybe we could be like mascots or something. Can we try that before wandering the streets alone?" She looked up at the black ceiling, lined with hanging strands of unidentifiable gunk that resembled seaweed. "Do you think it's safe to go outside yet?"

"It's never safe." Sarah pulled her feet in close and stood. "But whoever those people were, they've probably given up by now."

"Ascendant security." Maya got up and brushed dirt from her pants.

Sarah glanced back and forth from the ladder behind them to a grating that formed a walkway over three concrete islands, leading to another tunnel on the far side of the cistern. "What's Ascendant after you for? I thought Vanessa didn't want you."

"Umm." Maya tried to think past the cobwebs of loss. "I guess maybe Vanessa knows there's people inside trying to get rid of her. Maybe she wants me for... I dunno."

"Come on. Let's go out a different way in case they're watching the street where they lost us." Sarah took her hand and went for the metal walkway.

Maya tiptoed over the muddy concrete and climbed up after her. The textured grating felt like stepping on a whole bunch of forks pointing upward. "Ow!" She jumped back.

"You could swim?"

The brackish water didn't look any more welcoming than the path of pain. "I dunno how to swim. How deep is it?"

Sarah shrugged. "How should I know?"

Maya whimpered.

"Hey, get on my back."

"You don't have shoes either," said Maya.

"Yeah, but I'm used to being outside. You had nice soft rugs." She grinned.

"I can do it." Maya grabbed Sarah's shoulders and eased herself up on the walkway. She hissed and cringed. "Ooh. Ow."

Inch by painful inch, she followed her friend some twenty feet to the other end. After jumping to more dusty concrete, she picked up one foot then the other, checking her soles for cuts. The idea of being shoeless in a sewer scared her plenty enough without an open wound. Fortunately, the grating hadn't been sharp—only pointy.

Narrow pathways flanked a deeper channel in the passage ahead, the concrete an inch or so under the surface. Murk concealed the depth of the middle, though it *felt* deep. Sarah stepped onto the walkway, into water up to her ankles.

She shivered and scrunched up her shoulders. "It's cold!"

Maya hiked up her pant legs to keep them dry and followed into the frigid water. After the grating, the cold felt good. Slimy moss squished between her toes, occasionally thin enough for the coarse texture of concrete to reach her feet. With two fistfuls of fabric at her thighs, she walked slow, careful not to splash.

Something glided along in the center channel. Maya tracked a vee in the surface as it went by, ahead of a dark, oblong shape. "Eww!" She shivered. "There's a turd!"

If by sheer force of will she could've hovered above the water (and stopped touching it), she would have.

Sarah glanced back over her shoulder. "I don't see anything."

"Go, go!" Maya bumped into her from behind.

"This isn't a sewer. It's a storm drain. Shouldn't be poo down here. Doesn't smell like poo, does it?"

Maya sniffed. Mildew, wetness, dirt. "No."

A few minutes later, they arrived at a rounded hollow in the wall containing a gunk-encrusted metal ladder. Where it met the curve of the ceiling, it entered a tunnel for about six feet to a small chamber that appeared to have daylight in it. Sarah grasped the rungs and pulled herself up. Maya shivered, standing in the icy water, watching her friend climb.

Motion at the right caught her eye, and she focused on another 'turd' gliding along in the current. She stared at it, horrified—and the suspicious object lifted its head to peer back at her. Dark fur. Little pink ears. Beady black eyes.

Not a turd.

Rat.

Maya screamed.

Something tickled her left calf.

She whirled around and gawked at a swarm of rats gathering on the walkway, nosing at her.

Again, she screamed, and jumped on the ladder, no longer caring if the bottoms of her pant legs got wet. Maya scrambled about halfway up the distance from floor to tunnel ceiling when one of the aged bricks in the wall behind the ladder shifted and fell away. A rat stuck its head out, a set of twitching whiskers and a little pink nose close enough for her to kiss. With a shriek, Maya jumped back—and fell into the water.

Panic took her as she went under. Tiny claws seemed to scratch at her from everywhere. Little furry bodies bumped her arms, climbed onto her head, and tried to wriggle under her shirt. Awful water invaded her mouth and nose; she gagged, flailing and kicking. Every time she attempted to scream again, she gulped down a mouthful of horribleness.

A loud splash came from nearby. Something touched her arm; she flailed, trying to get away until she recognized squeezing fingers. Sarah pulled Maya's head up out of the water and held her by the arms.

"Put your feet down! It's not deep!"

Gagging and choking, Maya scrambled to get her legs under her. The murky central channel turned out to be only a few feet deep, coming up to her armpits when she stood. Her feet squishing into a dense layer that felt like snot broke down the last shred of composure keeping her from throwing up.

Sarah held her as she retched up the brackish dirt-tasting water she'd gulped down. When the heaving stopped, she pulled her to the edge. Rats continued to swarm around, climbing them, sitting on their shoulders, and sniffing at the air. Overwhelmed, Maya clung to Sarah and wept.

"Get 'em off me!"

"They're just curious. They want to get out of the water just like us."

"They're gonna bite me and I'm gonna get sick!"

Sarah pushed her up out of the water, a hand on each butt cheek.

Maya shrieked, racing up the ladder. As soon as she climbed onto solid, dry ground in a cube-shaped chamber, she jumped up and down, swatting at herself in a frenetic, whirling dance. Plastic cups and burger cartons crunched and rustled. Sarah's head popped up from a hole in the floor.

"There's no rats on you. Stop."

Maya froze, arms held up like the sprained wings of a chicken. She examined herself as Sarah crawled from the ladder tunnel and got to her feet. Satisfied at not having any passengers, she relaxed and looked around, but couldn't stop shivering.

They'd found another storm drain, a small concrete-walled chamber with a wide opening near the ceiling and a round cover at the top of a short ladder made of iron rods embedded in the wall. Strong daylight leaked in from the street-facing hole, making her squint.

Soaked, the material of Sarah's curtain-dress had turned almost transparent. The waterlogged fabric hung heavy, stretching the spaces between wraps and exposing more safety pins. Fortunately, they'd collected enough dirt from this room to disguise how pitiful a garment it was. Plastic shifting underfoot, Sarah crossed to the ladder and climbed up to the cover. She grunted while pushing at it but gave up with a gasp a moment later.

"It's either locked, something's on top of it, or I'm not strong enough to move it."

Maya shivered. Her once-baggy fatigue pants clung to her legs like a sausage skin, heavy and sopping. She did *not* want to think about what sorts of germs or foulness might be in the water that had gotten everywhere, even drenching her hair to the roots. "What about the hole?"

"Maybe if I stand on your shoulders, I can reach it, then you can climb me."

"I don't think that'll work."

Sarah shrugged. "We could use your pants for a rope. My dress will fall apart."

Maya blushed. "I'd have to take them off." She shrank in on herself. "Not outside."

"Hmm." Sarah looked around at the debris before staring at the drain opening. "We only have to go up a little bit."

"Boost me and I'll see if there's something on the cover."

"'Kay."

Sarah squatted by the wall, bracing her hands against the concrete. Maya gingerly climbed up to stand on her shoulders, also holding onto the wall for balance. When Sarah stood to her full height, the lower edge of the drain came within reach—by an inch.

Maya gripped the rough concrete and struggled to pull herself up, groaning from the effort.

Sarah grabbed her feet and pushed. "Wow, you can't do a pull-up?"

"Lazy rich girl, remember?" Maya got one arm out onto a paved strip and grunted. "And yes, I can do a pull-up, but my arms are tired."

Sarah shoved her upward, propelling her hip-deep in the hole.

She found herself sprawled on the ground at the side of a road that contained more people than cars. Beneath a dark sky, swaths of blue and red neon glowed from the wet blacktop, reflecting the signs on various storefronts, bright enough to make her squint. A moment of looking around made it seem less like a road and more like a wide thoroughfare between two rows of stores. The distant hiss of moving cars came from the right, and headlight glare danced on buildings at the end of the concourse some fifty yards away.

Relieved that she hadn't crawled headfirst into traffic, Maya grabbed the steel shroud around the drain on either side of her waist and pushed herself up and out. Once on her feet, she turned to examine the hatch cover and frowned at a huge blue dumpster parked on top of it. Someone had spray painted 'Burn Ascendant' across the front. Maya walked over and tried to push the dumpster aside but couldn't get it to budge.

"Maya?" yelled Sarah.

She scurried back to the drain and crouched by the opening. "I'm here. There's a dumpster sitting on the lid."

"Ohh."

Maya looked around at the crowd, at all the people in all their nice clothes, walking back and forth while shopping, out on the town, or maybe heading home in a hurry. A time display on one of the stores said 10:08 p.m. Maya scanned the crowd, hunting for someone who looked like they might help Sarah, but everyone she made eye contact with hurried away with a grimace as if looking at her had made them dirty. One woman hiding under a transparent umbrella scowled, likely assuming Maya intended to root around the trash box.

A sharp blast of compressed air went off behind her, making her jump.

She spun, hand over her heart from the surprise of such a loud noise happening so close. Twenty or so feet away in an alley, a man with floppy rubber boots in a drab grey poncho, absent a filter mask, stood by an open metal door. A logo resembling a basket of food on his apron matched the stencil on the door. Fog and mist rolled out into the street behind him from a room that had to be freezing inside. She squatted by the drain opening as if she could hide behind the curb.

The man wheeled a white box out on a hand truck and headed toward the dumpster. A stink like fish surrounded him, leaving Maya confused between hungry or wanting to throw up again. He flipped open the plastic lid and upended the box, dumping reddish liquid and fish parts into the dumpster that kept Sarah trapped.

Maya jumped upright. "Excuse me, sir?"

He glanced at her. "Ain't got no loose change, kid."

"I'm not going to ask you for money. Can you help me please? My friend fell in the drain and she can't get out."

His standoffish air lessened. "Oi what?" After setting the empty box back on the hand truck, two steps put him right in front of her. "You sayin' you got a friend stuck? This ain't some kind of trick, is it? What're ya up to?"

"No, sir." Maya squatted and looked through the opening down at Sarah. "Say something."

"Help!" yelled Sarah.

"Oh, shit," muttered the man. He hurried around and took a knee next to Maya, peering into the gap. "Damn. Uhh... Really is a kid down there."

"Can you move the dumpster? It's blocking the cover." Maya pointed.

"Oh. Yeah. That'd work."

He ambled back to the dumpster and leaned into it. A bit of grunting and shoving later, its wheels gave way and the ponderous trash box rolled clear of the metal disc. Somewhat winded, the man took a few breaths before crouching and lifting the cover. Sarah had been waiting on the ladder right below and darted out into the fresh air as soon as she could.

"Thank you," said Maya.

She went to hug him, but he put a hand on her head to hold her back. "You're welcome, kid. S'awright."

Maya tried not to feel insulted when he wiped his hand off on his poncho.

"Yes, thank you." Sarah smiled at him. Her eyes fluttered and her expression collapsed. She gagged and coughed. "Ugh. What is that smell?"

Chuckling, the man walked off, dragging his hand truck back to the foggy door.

"Fish." Maya took Sarah by the hand, decided on going to the right, and walked. "Come on. I'm not sure exactly where we are, but if we can find an info kiosk, I can get to The Hangar."

"Okay." Sarah pulled her dress up over her nose until they reached the end of the concourse, and the reek of fish no longer tainted the air.

Most people ignored them, but every so often, someone glared or hurried away. A light rain fell, though already being soaked, Maya didn't mind. Rainwater had to be far cleaner than what she'd fallen into. The memory of that water's taste made her gag.

An advertisement on the wall for Ambutin, an Ascendant-made drug, depicted a man leaping out of a wheelchair along with some diagrams showing synthetic stem cells repairing nerve damage. More spray paint scrawled 'die bitch' over it.

Soggy pant legs flapped around her feet as she hurried forward, hoping to find a cross street or something with an information kiosk. She didn't dare ask anyone for directions. Even if a nine-year-old looking to go to a bar didn't get her in trouble, most of the people who noticed her made it clear in their glares or rapid retreats they wanted her to stay as far away as possible.

An electronic poster on the left showed a mother and baby smiling over the logo for Natacil, a nutrient-enhanced breast milk replacement made by Ascendant. A hacker had changed the catchy slogan below the drug name to 'profit pigs.'

"Wow." Maya frowned at it as they passed. "I hope no one recognizes me."

Sarah gripped her hand tighter. "They're pissed."

The long, rectangular courtyard ended at a street with active traffic some forty yards away from where they'd emerged from the underground. Maya again chose a right turn and tugged Sarah by the hand among a crowd of pedestrians. Here, few people bothered to look at them long enough to recognize their filth. Bumps and jostles continued for the length of a block.

"Grr." Maya leaned side to side, trying to peer around all the adults but had a clear view only of grey ponchos, handbags, and the occasional potbelly. "I can't see. Look for a kiosk."

"What's it look like?" asked Sarah "And I'm not that much taller than you."

"Silver. Has lights. A box."

"Like that?" Sarah pointed.

When Maya couldn't spot it, Sarah dragged her ahead to the edge of the curb. Not an information kiosk, but a freestanding sign board with an ad for Xenodril depicting Maya in a glittery blue dress with a huge smile. Someone had bashed in the clear covering over the poster, and spray-painted 'How much is life worth?' over it, along with 'murderer.' 'Burn Ass-endant' decorated the other side.

"No. That's not a kiosk." Maya sighed. "That's either scary as hell or cool."

"What's the difference?"

"Cool if they don't blame me for it."

Sarah shook her head. "You had nothing to do with it."

The whine of fans grew louder. Maya clamped on to Sarah, hiding her face against her friend's shoulder. A standard Authority patrol drone glided by above, ten or so feet over the heads of the crowd. Hats went flying, hair fluttered, and about half of the people raised a middle-finger salute.

Maya peeled her face away from the still-wet fabric of Sarah's curtain-dress to watch the drone glide away. "This is bad. It feels like the Sanc is going to blow up at any minute."

"Yeah." Sarah looked around.

Sniffles and tears came on; the more Maya looked around at so many people, the more alone she felt. She wanted Genna back and couldn't handle the idea of being on her own without a parent. For five years, she'd lived under the care of an AI, an ever-present voice in the ceiling. All the parental authority without any of the affection. In the brief time she had with Genna, she'd come to love the woman a thousand times more than her biological mother. Again, the image of Genna collapsing in a hail of bullets flooded her mind. Sarah held her upright when the strength left her legs, and rocked her again.

"Come on. We gotta find that bar, right? Before someone mugs us and takes our stuff."

Maya pushed aside her grief, wiping her nose on the back of her left arm. "They won't do that in here. There's too many Authority drones, and even in the bad parts, they don't really mess with kids. Unless...."

"What?" Sarah's confidence faltered.

"We find some shithead like Mason."

Sarah's eyes bugged. "Is that—?"

"We keep out in the open and with crowds. Stay together. Scream if anyone touches you."

"'Kay." Sarah nodded and squeezed her hand tighter.

A faint strand of hope struggled inside her. Maya couldn't give up just yet. She had to at least try to find someone who could take Sarah home. It wouldn't be fair for her to get someone else hurt, especially her best friend. Hell, she'd almost already been killed too. *Not like Mr. Needle would've just let her go.* Maya shivered.

"What?"

"Thinking about the guy with that needle. He woulda killed you too." She teared up again. "Thanks for saving my ass."

Sarah grinned. "Did you see his face when I kicked him? I thought he was going to explode from pure anger."

"Yeah." Maya almost smiled.

At the end of the next street, a bright red awning caught Maya's eye over a row of padded stools. Two men in cheap suits sat at a counter, scooping at bowls with chopsticks while slurping up noodles. A short, heavyset Chinese man behind the counter tended a number of steaming pots. Sarah stared at the place with longing in her eyes.

Maya nodded and approached the counter. "Excuse me, sir. Do you have any work we could do for a bowl of soup? We don't have any money."

The proprietor looked at them, eyebrow raised. "You two are far too filthy to work near food. I couldn't even let you clean the bathroom."

"Mmm," said the nearer customer, his mouth full of noodles. He nodded sideways at the girls and put two NuCoin up on the counter.

"Thank you," chimed Maya and Sarah at once.

The cook ladled out a bowl each of basic ramen soup and handed them over with pre-wrapped disposable chopsticks. "G'won over there." He gestured at an alley across the street. "The two of you are in dire need of soap, but the lot what hangs out in that place won't care. Stairs on the left."

Maya's face burned with shame at someone reacting to her the way she'd felt about Farnham. If they stank, she couldn't tell. Nonetheless, she didn't press the issue. After thanking the kind stranger once more, the girls carried their soup across the street. Sarah diverted down a set of concrete steps to an open basement-level door below what appeared to be an electronics store.

The room at the bottom had a number of dingy mattresses scattered about along with copious amounts of random junk and trash. They sat on the least-fetid looking mattress and opened their meals. It took a moment or two for the soup to cool enough to eat in earnest. A pair of older women with wild greying hair wobbled in, both wearing a mismatched collection of random scraps and coats. Neither so much as looked at the girls as they crossed the room to the back corner and sat where a massive collection of old kitsch—mostly cat figurines—gathered around a pair of mattresses pushed close together.

Maya sipped at her soup, testing it while the women pulled out cans of Tuna Blast cat food and forks. Sarah slurped, evidently having a higher tolerance for heat. Gathering a bundle of noodles on her chopstick, Maya stared at the women and raised her fresh, hot noodles to her mouth. *Is that going to be us in fifty years? Still on the street and happy to have cat food?* She looked away from them, gazing into her soup like a fortune-teller reading broth. People feeding them out of pity would last a while yet, at least until they stopped being small. But then what?

Maya ate faster as the soup cooled, and soon they stared at empty bowls. The strong flavor of the broth, like liquefied pork, annihilated the memory of gulping down the water in that sewer.

"My legs hurt," whispered Maya.

"My everything hurts," said Sarah.

Maya looked around. "Is it safe to sleep here?"

"How should I know?" Sarah yawned. "Those women haven't even looked at us, but the place doesn't have a door."

"Hmm." Maya tapped her feet while gazing around, debating. The chase had left her exhausted and her brain had reached a state of such fogginess that not even worry for Genna hit her with any real meaning. "I don't care."

"It should be okay," whispered Sarah. She got up and gathered some old blankets. "We can hide all the way under so no one'll see us.

"Mmm." Maya curled up on her side.

Sarah tucked up at her back, a protective arm over her, and arranged the foul-smelling cloth to cover them. Though Maya's face pressed into bedding that stank like an old man's foot, she fell asleep in seconds.

Maya awoke to Sarah shaking her.

"Hmm?" Maya straightened out, stretching, squinting at the invasion of daylight from the doorway and broken wall.

Men's voices overhead yelled back and forth.

"The guy from the store next door is pissed about a jammer. His phone won't work."

"Oh," said Maya. "No one's gonna get shot?"

Sarah looked up at the floor. "I dunno. They've been yelling for a while and some stuff has slammed. I'm surprised they didn't wake you."

Maya sat up, wiping crumbs from her eyes. Seven other people, all older than forty, snored away on the other mattresses, leaving a handful still empty. A group of cats had gathered around a third can of Tuna Blast the old women set out for their furry friends.

"You okay?" whispered Sarah. "I think a roach bit me."

Maya shivered. "Eww. Where? Nothing bit me."

Sarah blushed. "My butt. There's a little sore spot. Burns like a bug bite, but I didn't see a mark."

"C'mon," whispered Maya with a perplexed shrug. "Let's get out of here before anyone wakes up."

"Good idea."

Maya crawled out from under the ratty blanket, waited for Sarah to stand, and hurried up the stairs to the outside. The bright day offered little sign of rain, and it appeared to be before noon.

She yawned again, ready to go back inside and crawl into bed. "I slept too much. I wanna go back to sleep."

"That doesn't make any sense," said Sarah.

They took turns relieving themselves out of sight behind a dumpster before scurrying out of the alley, holding hands and keeping a wary eye out for anyone trying to grab them.

"So what are we looking for?" asked Sarah.

"An information kiosk." Maya craned her neck around, searching.

An hour or so of walking later, the endless parade of buildings gave way to a section of green on the left where the New Baltimore Nature Preserve occupied a space of about nine city blocks. Mostly trees, grass, and a shitload of pigeons. Gleaming sunlight drew her attention to a shiny silver obelisk bearing a display screen on each of its four faces. It sat at the center of a circle where a red brick walkpath split apart to go around a grove of dogwoods. As soon as she looked at it, she changed her mind about using it. The people coming after her, if they had influence over Ascendant security, might be able to detect her accessing any electronics connected to the AuthNet.

She veered left into the park, adoring the feeling of walking over wet grass. Not far from the edge where the grey city gave way to green, she flopped on a park bench and swung her legs.

"Why'd you stop? Tired?" Sarah perched next to her.

"Yeah. And hungry. I'd kill for a cheese sandwich." Her mood plummeted as guilt over Sarah's father combined with her heartbreak at Genna dying. She pictured the first time she'd ever tasted one of those sandwiches, and her friend's giant, eager smile.

Sarah nodded, despite a quivering lip and a stray tear running down her face. "Yeah."

"I'm going to cry over cheese sandwiches," said Maya.

"Me too."

"I got an idea." Maya teased her toes at the grass. "Why don't we go to the VA hospital and find your dad?"

Sarah looked up at her, bottom lip still quivering, but her tears stopped. "Really? How? Do you know where it is?"

Maya narrowed her eyes at the passing people on the far side of the short grassy stretch. "I don't know. It might be dangerous to use the kiosk, but I'll figure something out."

[19]

MINOR DETAILS

With a renewed sense of purpose, Maya slid from the bench to her feet and headed toward the information kiosk. A search for the VA hospital had to happen so often that it wouldn't stand out. Plus, she could hover a little way off and tell Sarah what buttons to push in case anyone monitored the camera with facial-recognition software.

They crossed a long swath of grass, let go of each other's hands long enough to let a tree pass between them, and continued along the park. A whiff of fried food triggered a growl from her stomach and made her turn.

The kiosk could wait a few minutes.

Maya headed for a pushcart where a man sold some manner of meat-on-a-stick as well as sandwiches. A small line had gathered by it. Maya scampered up a grass-covered hill and trotted over to wait at the end. Her voice echoed from a canyon of buildings on the right, a ghostly whisper encouraging people to buy Gabatin-EX and break free from the chains of depression.

"Umm," whispered Sarah, "what are we doing? Did you find money?"

"No." Maya bit her lip. "I was going to try begging again."

Two people ahead of them got their food and walked away, leaving a man, a couple with a toddler, and a bored older-teenaged boy in a nice suit ahead of her. Maya sized them up, feeling a bit like Vanessa for calculating her best odds at sympathy. One instinct said to go for the mother with a small child, but they might be the least likely, having their own kid to provide for. She eyed the boy in front of her. Maybe eighteen, he looked like an intern, and gave off a laid-back vibe.

Sarah jumped, clamping a hand on her butt and twisting to look. "Ow. Did you poke me?"

"No," said Maya.

"Damn bugs," mumbled Sarah.

"Excuse me," said Maya in a small voice, smiling at the intern.

"What are you doing here?" bellowed a woman from behind them.

The intern glanced back but didn't say anything.

Maya twisted around to peer up at a woman wearing an immaculate white skirt suit, tiny gloss-white handbag dangling from her left arm. She had a pointlessly small hat with a spray of mesh bedecked with pearls and a nose that could've cut armor-grade steel. Something about her triggered instant dislike, and without even thinking about it, Maya gave her Vanessa's head-to-toe glance, smirk, and 'you're not worth my time' face before looking back to the intern. "Sorry to bother you, but—"

"Don't ignore me. You two don't belong here," the woman muttered. "Those Authority fools are too busy with nonsense while vagrants are running about."

"Excuse me," said Maya to the intern. She spun to face the woman. "You're more bothered by a couple of poor kids being in the park than you are at what Ascendant has been doing to everyone for years?"

The woman frowned. "This park is off limits to vagrants. You people belong in the Ash district."

"What's wrong with you?" yelled Maya. "You're whining about the Authority dealing with *real* issues and *real* corruption because they're not here to chase a couple of kids out of your stupid little park?" She trembled with anger. Trying to stare down this woman while having to look up at her left her feeling small, alone, and missing Genna. Angry tears streamed from her eyes as she shouted, "You don't have any idea what's been going on, do you? Or is it that you don't care Ascendant's spraying Fade on people to make them buy drugs? As long as you get your fancy clothes and fancy house, it doesn't matter how many people they kill. You're a sanctimonious, elitist, prissy, chicken-nosed bitch!"

The intern cackled.

Behind him, the husband snickered while his wife gasped.

"That's it. I'll not be talked to like that by the likes of you." The woman pulled out a minicomputer. "I'm calling the Authority."

"Oh, *you're calling the Authority*." Maya held up her hands in mock fright. "Oh no. Whatever shall I do?"

Sarah lunged at the woman, who assumed it an attempt to stop her from calling. She jerked her arm up and away to protect her phone and exposed the real target: her pristine white suit. Sarah smeared black handprints down the front, raspberried the woman, and took off running.

Laughing, Maya darted after her, leaving the snob babbling incoherently, too shocked to form full words. They raced across the grass to the city street and plunged into the crowd, slaloming around slow-moving people while dodging briefcases, coffee carriers, and the occasional stroller.

Maya ran at her side to the end of the block; the traffic signal shifted red within a second of their reaching the edge. She didn't stop, hoping the few seconds it took the cars to get rolling would allow them across.

"Sarah!" yelled a man.

Unable to stop for fear of traffic, Maya sprinted to the far side amid a cacophony of blaring horns. Sarah crashed into her when she halted on the other side, arms wrapped around to cling, her body shaking with breathless laughs.

"Sarah!" yelled the same man.

Maya looked back across four lanes of traffic and down two-ish blocks on the cross street.

Pope shoved his way through the crowd toward them.

"Aaaaaah!" screamed Maya. Her throat closed up. Unable to speak, she bawled like a three-year-old and pointed at him. "Saaaaaah!"

Sarah looked in that direction. "What? I don't see—"

Flashing red and blue lights exploded all around them as three Authority drones swooped in. The sea of drab grey ponchos around them burst apart, people fleeing in random directions. Sarah's curtain-dress whipped in the downblast of fans, which threw Maya's hair in her face.

"Attention, juvenile females. You are hereby detained by order of the Authority. Place yourselves on the ground immediately with your arms and legs apart. You have four seconds for compliance or you will be shot."

Drone Two emitted a mutter barely audible over the fans. "Shot? Really, Jim? They're kids."

Maya looked back toward where she'd seen Pope emerge from the crowd, but he didn't seem to be anywhere. Had he ever been there?

"Two seconds," said Drone One.

"Maya!" screamed Sarah from the ground.

"Okay," yelled Maya. She dove to the sidewalk, arms and legs open in an X.

"Do not attempt to move," crackled the electronic voice overhead. "Authority officers are on their way to collect you. Any attempt to resist or elude will result in lethal force."

Sarah, cheek to the concrete, stared at her, shaking so hard she seemed likely to pass out from terror.

"It'll be okay," said Maya. "We didn't do anything."

"You are not authorized to speak," said the drone.

Maya fumed inside, hoping that bitch in white wasn't close enough to see them. No pedestrians came anywhere near the area, giving the drones a good half-block distance. Fans blasted them with a continuous buffeting of air; Maya closed her eyes to keep sand out of them.

After hugging sidewalk for a minute or two, the crunch of rubber tires rolled to a halt so close she risked lifting her head to look, fearing the car would run her over. The blue-and-white marked Authority patrol vehicle had come to a stop by the curb not too far from her left foot.

The driver's door opened with a hiss and blast of fog. A blueberry climbed out, his attention on his left forearm while he poked at an armor-mounted terminal pad. The three drones stopped leaning forward at the girls and leveled off, their .50 cal machine guns resetting to neutral as they hovered a little higher, lessening the windblast. He walked around the nose end of the car, visor up exposing a thirty-something face with a light brown goatee.

"For f—lying out loud. What the—" He put his hands on his hips. "All right you two, get up."

Maya gathered herself into a squat and eased her way standing, careful not to move too fast. "I think my father is over there..." She again scanned the flow of people across the street, but Pope had vanished. Sarah took a little longer to risk moving, but obeyed. As soon as she got on her feet, she clung to Maya from behind.

"Where?" asked the blueberry, glancing in the same direction.

"Umm. I thought I saw him by that bus stop." She squeezed Sarah's hand. "Did you see him?"

Sarah shook her head.

"He had to be there. I saw him." *I'm not seeing ghosts.*

"Why would your father be there one minute and gone now?" asked the blueberry.

Maya shivered. "I... guess I didn't really see him. Must have been someone who looked like him."

"Do you live nearby?" asked the blueberry.

"No. We're from the Hab." Maya pointed.

"So you're out here alone? No parents?"

"I..." Maya wrapped her arms around herself. "We're alone."

"All right." The blueberry opened the back door of the car. "Get in."

Maya stared at him in disbelief for a few seconds that he hadn't put her in binders. Without a word, she bowed her head and crawled into the patrol car's back seat. Sarah followed, refusing to let go of her hand.

The blueberry shut the door, not quite slamming it, and walked back around the front end, shaking his head. Maya huddled against Sarah, eyeing the heavy-duty steel mesh over the window separating the front from the back. As far as she knew, the Authority had no law banning poor people from any specific area in the Sanc. Granted, if they wanted to be assholes, which often proved to be the case, they could charge Sarah with assaulting that woman. As the drive jostled them about, she weighed the benefits and shortcomings of claiming Sarah just tripped trying to get away from the aggressive snob versus being honest and saying the bitch deserved it.

Sarah looked like a ghost. That she appeared noticeably paler got Maya worried.

"Hey. Don't be scared."

The 'we're so screwed' glare Sarah shot back at her proved she'd lost any hope of seeing tomorrow alive.

Maya alternated from trembling in fear to feeling sick to her stomach as the car drove on. If Pope had really been there, why would he have just left them? Did he fear being spotted by the Authority after talking to the Brigade? Had he really been scouring the Sanc for them? How unlikely could the odds be that they ran across each other like that? Sarah hadn't seen him, and for him to disappear after such an improbable meeting didn't bode well. Maybe he knew where the Authority would take them and planned to be there waiting?

Several minutes later, they arrived at a five-story precinct building. The blueberry pulled down a ramp into an underground parking area bathed in yellow-saturated light. A black security gate closed behind the car at the bottom, dashing any hope of possibly fleeing on foot once they'd been let out of the car. He steered into a parking spot among a row of a dozen other patrol cars, stopping by a white-painted wall. The main entrance stood a short distance away, a pair of sliding doors protected by reinforced armored panels.

After powering down the car, the blueberry got out and opened the driver side rear door.

Maya scooted to the edge of the seat and slid to her feet. Sarah, still shaking, stumbled after her. The blueberry put a hand on her back, guiding her across a section of smooth concrete to the entrance. They walked over a long rubberized strip and into a chilly room with a tall desk. A grey-haired woman in a blue uniform behind it gave the girls a passing look of disinterest before returning to what she'd been reading.

Their blueberry prodded them down a featureless grey corridor and around a corner to another stretch of hall lined with plain, identical blue doors. He steered them to the third room on the left, which contained a steel table and four chairs. The inner wall opposite the door had a huge mirror that showed off every bit of how filthy they'd gotten. Sarah looked grungier since her dress had once been white (albeit yellowed). Maya's black shirt and pants didn't show off the grime as much.

"Have a seat, girls," said the blueberry. He pulled his helmet off and set it on a shelf by the door before ruffling his hand back and forth over his hair. "Unbelievable. Who sicced a pack of drones on a pair of little kids? You two sit still and stay in this room."

Maya walked around the corner of the table and took the farther seat. Sarah sat on the edge of the other chair as if afraid to touch it.

The blueberry walked out, closing the door behind him.

Sarah grabbed Maya's hand in both of hers. "I'm scared."

"This is weird. Isn't it?"

"What?" She bit her lip.

Maya gestured at her. "They didn't put cuffs on us. They haven't shoved us around or hit us. He hasn't even yelled." She looked at the mirror, fully expecting it to be a window for an observation room. They always had one of those in the movies. "He even looked annoyed that someone sent drones after us."

"Umm." Sarah fidgeted, her toes whitening as they tried to grip the floor. "I dunno. I'm too scared to think. I can't believe they haven't recognized you."

"Maybe I'm a non-person now." She folded her hands in her lap and couldn't quite bring herself to care at all what happened to her.

Watching Genna die had done something deep inside she never expected. Now she understood how the woman could've stood at the edge of the wall, staring down fifty stories at certain death and not been afraid. Maya didn't feel inclined to take that jump yet, but the concept of it had gone from ridiculous to almost reasonable. How Maya felt had to be a mere shadow of what Genna had suffered at the loss of Sam. Her mood spiraled downward over a few minutes of silence while Sarah shivered beside her. Once or twice, Sarah almost threw up, but managed to hold it in.

The door opened, and the same blueberry walked in carrying a tray that he slid onto the table in front of them. Maya blinked in disbelief at two plates, each with a sandwich and a little carton of milk. After nudging the door closed again, the blueberry dropped into the chair opposite them.

"Good afternoon, kids. I'm Officer West, but you can call me Mark."

Sarah gave the food a 'yeah right' stare.

"Thank you." Maya picked hers up and sniffed it. Peanut butter and jelly. She took a bite.

"It's fresh," said Mark, a hint of a smile on his lips.

Maya finished chewing, swallowed, and licked the roof of her mouth. "I wanted to know what it was so I didn't expect cheese and get sweet."

He chuckled and nudged the plate closer to Sarah. "Go on, eat. It's okay."

She took the sandwich and nibbled at the crust.

"Some bad people dressed up like Authority officers abused her. She's afraid." The two bites Maya ate reawakened her hunger, and she chomped a huge mouthful.

"People impersonated the law?" Mark raised an eyebrow.

Maya held up a finger while she hurried to chew the sticky peanut butter. Glugging a mouthful of milk gave her back the ability to talk. "The ones Ascendant bought."

"Oh..." He shook his head. "Well, you two aren't in trouble just yet. Why don't you go on and tell me how you wound up out there all alone."

"I thought you arrested us because of that awful woman." Maya bit her lip, hoping truth would work in her favor.

"Well, we did receive a report of vandalism, involving suspects fitting your descriptions. Another unit responded but couldn't locate any evidence of vandalism. A few witnesses said this woman tried to grab your friend here and drag you out of the park. Got her outfit all smudged up."

Sarah's head snapped up, eyes huge. "Umm... what?"

"I had a feeling." Mark shook his head, then chuckled. "Don't worry about it. Ed fined her for filing a false report. Even if you didn't, uhh, decorate her jacket, it's not a violation for the non-wealthy to be in the park."

Sarah took a real bite.

"We live in the Habitation District, Block 13. Some men dressed as workers kidnapped us and brought us to... a hotel I think. A man was going to kill me with a needle. My mom found us and tried to save me, but—" Maya choked up.

"You're safe now." Officer West tapped at the screen of a data pad. "No one's going to hurt you. It's okay if you don't want to talk about it just yet."

She put a hand over her mouth to help fight back tears, breathing through her nose. Sarah's expression had hardened to a distrustful glower as soon as he said 'no one's going to hurt you.' She remained defiant, though continued to tremble.

"I can talk about it." Maya closed her eyes and tried to tell herself this blueberry actually cared.

"All right. You said a man with a needle tried to kill you?"

"Yes." Maya, in a quiet monotone, explained everything from the workers barging into the apartment to their waking up in a strange hotel room. She left out Ruiz scanning her to make sure she wasn't an android.

"This man. What did he look like?" A small blue light from the data pad screen glimmered on the contours of his armor, wavering in time with his voice as if reacting to the sound.

Maya bit her lip. "Does it matter if he's dead? You don't have to arrest him."

"You think he's dead?" asked West.

"Yes. I saw him get shot. He almost fell on me."

West raised an eyebrow. "Who shot him?"

"I'm not sure exactly. They fired through the windows from outside. More men in armor. It looked like Ascendant security, but I don't know why they'd care about me. My mom was right outside trying to save us, but the other men kidnapped me again... and they shot her." She leaned forward, gripping the table. Wide, pleading eyes leaked tears down her face. "Please, did you find her? Is she okay?"

"I'm sorry. I do see a few incidents in the system at hotels recently involving gunfire. But I wasn't on the scene. It looks like the Authority recovered a number of bodies at two of them, but I'll need to check with whoever got the dispatch for any specific identification."

Sarah finished off her sandwich, then glugged down her milk in one pass.

"What are you going to do with us?" asked Maya. "I'm sorry for yelling at that woman, but she was being *so* mean to us."

"Probably drive us back to the Hab and leave us in the street," muttered Sarah.

Maya hung her head. "That's okay. Maybe Zoe an' Doc will take us in."

"Do you have any other family?" asked Officer West.

"Her father's in the VA hospital... Umm, Bill?" Maya glanced at Sarah, hand grasping the air as if trying to pluck a word from a tree.

"Sergeant William Hawthorne," said Sarah, her voice wavering. "He's got a prosthetic right arm, a cheap one. He's in the VA hospital now. I think. Unless they lied to us and he's dead."

Maya put an arm around Sarah's back and squeezed her.

Officer West nodded, tapping at the data pad screen again. "That it?"

"My mother's name is Genna." Maya wiped at her face. "Maybe was."

"What's your last name?" West glanced between them. "Sarah Hawthorne, and you are?"

Sarah's eyes bulged.

"Maya. We don't use last names. Just Genna and Maya."

"Why do you think that man wanted to hurt you?" Officer West sounded sympathetic but also skeptical.

"I'm sorry. You're asking a nine-year-old why some creep in a Mario Scarpani suit wanted to kidnap and kill her." Maya fidgeted.

Officer West reached over and gave her shoulder a pat. "I think I'm speaking with a very mature and intelligent little girl who's not *quite* showing her whole hand. How many nine-year-olds would recognize a Scarpani?"

I am a shitty liar. "I guess you know who I am."

"Well, your face was on every TV screen in Baltimore not too long ago." He chuckled. "You're even wearing the same outfit."

Maya stared into her lap. "I only *have* one outfit."

"Why do you think they tried to hurt you?" asked Officer West.

"The men who abducted me thought they can take over Ascendant if they kill Vanessa, but I'm still somehow in the way. He said they have to kill me first because of her will. Those men are dead, but they were only hired thugs."

He nodded. "All right. I need to go file this report. You two still hungry? Want more food?"

"Yes, please," said Maya.

Sarah nodded.

"All right. Be back in a little bit." Officer West walked out, carrying his data pad.

As soon as the door shut, Sarah pulled her feet up on the chair, wrapped her arms around her legs, and cried.

Maya leaned close. "I don't think he's trying to trick us. If they were going to be mean, they wouldn't be letting us eat."

Still shaking, she lifted her head from her knees and met Maya's stare. "This is *so* weird. Why aren't they being assholes?"

"I dunno." Maya plucked at Sarah's curtain-dress. A safety pin fell to the floor with a soft *click*. "Maybe because you look sad and forlorn, and I'm just that cute."

Sarah gave her a raspberry.

A giggle fit lasted only a few seconds. Maya held her friend's hand and gazed at the door, wondering how long they'd be stuck in a locked room.

THREE OPTIONS

Maya sat in silence, swishing her legs back and forth while frowning at her bare feet. Before true anger took hold, she sighed at Sarah. Her best friend had never owned shoes at all. Being angry at the *inconvenience* of leaving hers behind at the apartment made her feel snobbish and spoiled, like the woman who'd caused trouble at the park.

Faint gurgling emanated from Sarah's stomach, alarmingly loud in the stillness.

When it happened again a few seconds later, Maya snickered. Her stomach emitted a similar noise. Sarah managed a flimsy smile but no laugh could break past her terror.

"I don't think they're going to hurt us," whispered Maya.

Sarah opened her mouth to speak, but clamped it shut at the approach of footsteps outside.

A woman in a blue uniform rather than armor entered. She introduced herself as Officer Harris while giving them each another PBJ and a small milk carton. Once the girls started eating, she asked a few of the same questions all over again: where they lived, names, ages, relatives, and eventually if they'd been injured, touched inappropriately, or made to do anything they didn't want to.

"No." Maya shook her head and re-told everything from the fake workers knocking them out with chloroform-soaked rags to being chased down by armed drones.

Officer Harris took notes while Maya spoke. Upon finishing her questions, the woman gave them a warm smile and left.

Maya looked around at the featureless white walls. She spent a while staring at the mirror, wondering if someone watched them in hopes of catching them saying something that would get them in trouble when they thought no one could hear. Maybe they suspected Maya knew about the Brigade, and that's why Pope disappeared. But that didn't make too much sense either. He'd only just met with them; the Authority couldn't possibly have known of his association.

"We've been in here forever." Sarah lowered her feet to the floor and stood. "Ugh. I need a new curtain. It's all crusty and stiff. That sewer water had so much crud in it. This is exactly why I didn't wanna wash it." She fussed at her dress.

"I thought you said it wasn't a sewer." Whatever had been in the water had left Maya's shirt and pants with the same uncomfortable rigidity after drying.

"Whatever... *drain* water." Sarah paced around the table. On her third orbit, she tested the door. "Yeah. They locked us in. I knew it. We're arrested."

Even expecting it, hearing proof pulled the rug out from under Maya's calm and got her hands shaking. "M-maybe they just do that automatically. You know, like they don't want two little kids wandering off on their own and getting hurt?"

"Not funny." Sarah folded her arms. The lowest wrap of her curtain-dress came loose in back and dangled down. "The Authority doesn't think we're people."

"That's what we're trying to change." She sighed. "People fear and hate the Authority because everyone knows Ascendant bought them. They weren't keepers of the law before, just company thugs. And that bitch doesn't care about anyone who doesn't have money. They've been nice to us. It's already changing. A lot of Authority are veterans like your dad."

Sarah abandoned the door and paced around the table again. The hanging scrap of fabric sagged longer, dragging on the floor. The lowest part still pinned together across her backside drooped, threatening to rip loose and fall. Maya stared at it as another safety pin pulled free from the material.

"Uhh..." said Maya.

"They're probably trying to figure out what to do with us. We're too little to kill. Maybe we're too little to put in jail." She rubbed her forehead, sighing.

Another pin tore away, and the brittle fabric slid down, exposing her butt. Gaps between where she had wrapped the curtain around her body stretched at the safety pins, widening, exposing more skin.

"Umm, Sarah?" asked Maya.

"What?" Sarah stomped, hands balled to fists at her sides, and the rest of the garment broke free of her shoulders. She clamped her arms tight, catching the falling material and barely managing to keep her crotch covered as safety pins rained to the floor around her. Rigid, wide eyed, and red-faced, she shivered in place. The mirror behind her reflected her paleness, skin tiger-striped with dirt wherever the dress hadn't covered. "Crap."

Maya shifted forward in her chair and started pulling her arms into her sleeves. "Take my shirt."

"Keep it. It's not long enough." Sarah shuffled back to her chair, holding the clump of disintegrating fabric to cover her crotch. "As if being arrested couldn't get any scarier."

Maya looked at the dead garment. "Guess that curtain was pretty old."

"Guess." Sarah sniffled. Her face darkened to match her hair color.

"My shirt is long enough to cover me. Take my pants."

Sarah looked at her, guilty, but pleading. "Are you sure?"

"Yes," said Maya without hesitation. "They're way loose on me, so you should fit."

"'Kay."

Maya stood and undid the button at her waist. Before she could shove her pants down, the door opened.

Sarah screamed, curling up in a ball on the chair.

Officer Harris peeked around the edge. "Sarah, is it? Here..." The woman hurried over, set a fat plastic-wrapped pouch containing grey fabric on the table, and promptly backed out, closing the door.

Sarah stared at it.

"What's wrong?" Maya blinked.

"I don't wanna wear a prison suit." She shivered. "I'd rather be naked."

"It's not a prison suit." Maya pointed at it. "Looks like sweat pants. They don't make prison suits outta that stuff. Prison suits are like bright orange or yellow."

Sarah tore the packet open, discovering a plain grey sweatshirt, sweat pants, and pink flip-flops. She tossed the mangled curtain aside, dressed in haste, and sat once more, arms crossed over her chest. The clothes appeared sized for a tiny woman and fit her with plenty of room to spare. "Wow, it's so soft."

"See?" Maya grinned. "They're being nice to us."

"What are they going to do with us? How long are they going to keep us locked in here?"

"I dunno." Maya swung her feet back and forth, mildly jealous of Sarah's new flip-flops. Of course, she loved her sneakers more, but damn kidnappers and their horrible timing. "Before the war, they had this social services thing that used to help kids like us, but I don't know if they still have it."

"Are they going to separate us?" Sarah grabbed her arm.

"No. I'll completely lose my shit if they try." Maya put a hand over Sarah's. Four seconds later, dread that the Authority *might* separate them made her break out in sobs. After losing Genna, being taken away from Sarah would break her. She'd do something drastic.

"I won't let them split us up." Sarah pulled Maya into a standing hug. "No way."

Maya's bawling leveled off to quiet sniffles as she clung.

Heavy footsteps coming down the hallway outside a few minutes later gave Maya back some confidence, or at least enough presence of mind to hide her emotions. The door opened, revealing Officer West and another man in Authority armor. Neither had helmets, and both appeared warm and cheerful.

The newcomer handed Maya a smaller set of pink flip-flops.

She put them on one after the next and peered up at them. "Please don't split us apart."

Sarah leaned in front of her protectively.

"No plans for that, Maya." Officer West gestured at the door. "Come on. We've found your mother and are going to bring you home now."

Genna's alive! Maya squealed with delight; elation got her trembling. "Thank you!"

Officer West took her hand and led her out into the hallway. The other blueberry escorted Sarah the same way. They turned left, going deeper into the corridor rather than back the way they'd entered from. Maya didn't pay it any mind, assuming the building had more than one entrance and they weren't going back to the garage full of patrol cars.

Two hallways and three turns later, West approached an elevator flanked by vending machines and poked the call button. A double-width corridor ran perpendicular to the elevator bank, with glass-windowed offices on both sides and a huge room full of cubicles and desks about forty feet away. A few people close enough to notice them waved at her and smiled.

West guided her into the elevator, the other man and Sarah following.

"Is she hurt? I watched her get shot," said Maya, bouncing on her toes.

"Didn't look hurt to me." The other blueberry shrugged.

Maya's mind raced for an explanation of what she'd seen. Maybe the bullets had hit the car and bounced over Genna, scaring her so bad she fainted? Maybe they shot her rifle and somehow didn't hit her, or they bounced off a button on her shirt or something and... She bit her lip. *I don't care how. She's alive!*

Lights on the panel by the door lit up as the elevator climbed past the second-through-sixth floors, stopping by 'H.'

Maya furrowed her eyebrows at it. "Why are we going—?"

The doors parted, revealing the roof, as well as a small white helicopter with an Ascendant logo on the side. A young blonde woman in a dark jumpsuit sat at the controls, and a middle-aged hulk of a man in an expensive black suit stood by the open side door. The rotors glided in a lazy spin, adrift in the wind.

Her jaw dropped. "No... no! That woman's not my mother!" She backed up. "I don't wanna go there! I want my real mommy!"

Officer West scooped her off her feet and carried her into a stiff breeze.

"No! Please! No!" Maya squirmed, losing her flip-flops as she kicked and struggled.

West handed her off to the big man, who pinned her wrists together in one hand and held her under his arm like an angry football. Sarah let the other blueberry lead her to the helicopter without a peep or sign of protest, though she did stoop to collect Maya's flops on the way.

After Sarah climbed into the mini-heli, the big man shook West's hand and boarded, pulling the door shut. He sat in a rear-facing seat with Maya in his lap, his giant arm pinning her against his chest.

"Help!" Maya stared out the window at West. She squirmed more out of protest at being held than a serious attempt to overpower such a big man. "Vanessa's gonna kill me! She doesn't want me!"

"Calm down, kid," said the big guy. "Your mother's been worried sick about you. She's not going to hurt you."

Maya kept wriggling and fighting. "Get offa me!"

"Look kid, you got three choices: duct tape, a shot of night-night juice, or behaving yourself."

"Grr!" Maya glared at him.

He held up a little black case. "Night-night?"

Sarah's eyes widened into a terrified, pleading stare.

"Fine." Maya sagged limp. "No needles."

"You okay back there?" asked the pilot, who sounded like a teenage girl.

"Yeah," said the man. "Let's go."

Sarah folded her hands in her lap, staring guiltily at the floor.

The whole cabin vibrated with the engines winding up, and within a moment, the roof of the Authority station seemed to fall away while they stood still. A moment or so after liftoff, the big guy picked Maya up, spun her around to face him, and set her in the seat next to Sarah.

"Now I know you're not dumb enough to jump."

Maya trembled at the thought of being taken *to* the woman who said 'go ahead kill her. I'll make another one.' She couldn't imagine anything happening other than Vanessa having her killed as revenge for that video. "I'm gonna throw up."

"Hey, kiddo, don't be scared," said the pilot via a speaker in the ceiling. "This is safer than a car."

"I'm not afraid of crashing." Maya put a hand on her belly, which gurgled. The essence of peanut butter and jelly flooded her throat. "Vanessa's going to kill me. And I don't mean like a kid says, 'oh, Mom's gonna kill me.' I mean literally end my life. Please fly us to the Hab and let us go."

"Aww, you poor thing," cooed the pilot. "Whatever those awful people who kidnapped told you, it's a lie. You're so lucky to get out of that filthy place in one piece."

"That *filthy place* is my home," mumbled Maya.

The big guy pulled out a minicomputer and began reading.

Sarah rubbed her hands down her thighs over and over again, though her expression gave no clue as to whether she adored her new clothes or did it out of nerves. Maya leaned against her, clinging to her arm. She'd only ever seen her friend wearing that toga-like curtain. The clean sweat suit made her look like a Citizen.

They were watching us. That woman brought her clothes too fast. She tapped her foot on air. Maybe the Authority had seen the crummy improvised dress as soon as they'd been brought in and decided to replace it right away, not as a reaction to it falling to pieces. Maya fidgeted at her pants, hoping they wouldn't meet a similar fate. Sarah's dress had been brittle even before she found it. Those curtains were likely older than her and had been exposed to the elements for years before Sarah ever touched them.

Out of nowhere, Maya got angry at The Dad for not taking care of his daughter.

The Sanctuary Zone gave way to the scattered debris of Dead Space. Maya leaned closer, peering past Sarah at the left side windows.

"Uhh, where are you taking us? You're leaving the Sanc." Maya looked at the man. "Are you going to kill us?"

The man looked up from his device and sighed. "You're obsessed with being killed, kid. What did those Brigade morons do to you?"

Maya folded her arms. "Well, at first, they kidnapped me trying to get Xenodril. I figured out pretty quick that Vanessa decided it cheaper to just let them have me than try and send someone to help, so I had to save myself. I knew I was in deep shit when they vidcalled her for a ransom. Vanessa looked me in the eye and told them to kill me. She said she'd even watch if it got them to stop bothering her."

"You don't believe she really meant that, do you?" asked the pilot, sounding shocked.

"Uhh, yeah. I do. If you saw the look on her face, you would too." Maya scowled at the floor. "I found a real mother, someone who actually cares about me." *And she's dead.* Her composure cracked, a crumbling dam about to yield to the fury of a penned-in ocean. She pushed it aside with anger. "I'm surprised she paid for the fuel for you to come get me. Maybe you should use that duct tape. I prefer to be tied up when I'm being kidnapped against my will."

Sarah shot her an 'are you nuts?' stare.

"Against your will? Is there such a thing as being kidnapped willingly?" asked the big guy.

"Hah!" The pilot laughed. "Don't do that to Bruno. His brain can't take it."

Maya blinked. "Really? His name is Bruno?"

He shook his head. "No. It's Benson."

"He looks like a Bruno though, doesn't he?" asked the pilot.

Benson sighed.

"She's far too happy," muttered Sarah.

"Okay, you seem like nice people." Maya grabbed the seat on either side of her legs. "Will you please take us back to the Hab? Don't let her kill me."

"Relax, kid." Benson lowered his microcomputer again with a trace of a sigh. "She is not going to hurt you."

Maya curled up in the seat, clinging to Sarah. Faced with two options, going out the door of a helicopter in midair or being brought to Vanessa, she found herself struggling to make a choice. Benson continued reading. Aside from the pilot's occasionally cheery humming, no one spoke for about fifteen minutes.

Light along the ground made Maya look at the door, where a narrow window by the floor offered a view of a small pocket of modernity, a tiny Sanctuary Zone. She stretched tall, up on her knees in the seat to peer out the side window. A long strip of glow cut across the bleak darkness toward the glimmering castle-like sprawl of the Baltimore Sanctuary Zone, a connecting road.

That has to be the Dublin Protected District. Maya's brain leapt into gear, remembering old AuthNet sessions and e-learns. About thirty miles northeast of Baltimore, the DPD held mostly residence buildings, parks, and a couple malls for the well-to-do Citizens. Fair bet the Authority there would be still on Vanessa's payroll. Being taken here wouldn't have been as terrifying if she at least had some hope Genna might be out there still.

Defeat sank its teeth into her heart, and she wept in silence upon Sarah's shoulder.

The mini-helicopter entered a slow, descending left turn, heading for a small pad notched from the side of a tall, white-and-mirror skyscraper. A taper narrowed the upper quarter of the building. Six stories continued over the small patio-like landing area that held a raised hexagonal pad, a walkway, and a door, along with an array of lights.

The helicopter alighted on the metal hexagon with a barely noticeable tap.

Benson stared at Maya, his expression beleaguered. "Are you going to flip out again?"

"How likely is it for crying, begging, and pleading to change your mind?" asked Maya.

Sarah glanced at her. "It's not going to help."

"Listen to your friend, kiddo." Benson gestured at her.

"Fine." Maya frowned. "I hope you'll be able to sleep at night when I mysteriously vanish."

Benson disembarked and helped Sarah out of the helicopter. Downdraft from the rotors whipped her hair into a fury. She tried her best to hold it down and backed toward the stairway leading to the roof from the helipad. He grasped Maya under the armpits and lifted her out, setting her on her feet before taking her by the wrist in a gentle but firm hold.

Flip-flops snapping against her heels, Maya trudged reluctantly down three steps and along a path defined from the roof by reflective yellow paint. At the far end, a silver double door opened, revealing an elevator. Benson tapped the button for the 88th floor, two below the landing pad.

Doors on the opposite side of the elevator opened when it came to a stop, exposing a short corridor with old-looking paintings of landscapes on either wall between fake plants. Benson entered first, the pale carpet muting his footsteps on the way to a burnished steel door with an electronic access panel. Maya stumbled behind him, futilely trying to resist being dragged by the arm. The air smelled too clean, laced with the fragrance of flowers and wood polish.

Benson swiped his hand at the panel. A few seconds later, it beeped and the door opened.

In the middle of a fancy, penthouse apartment stood Vanessa Oman, dark brown skin striking in contrast to her peach-colored skirt suit and matching shoes; a spray of tiny blue flowers erupted from her breast pocket.

"Maya, dear." Vanessa smiled. "I'm so glad you're all right."

The convulsion hit her before she could think; Maya lurched forward and threw up all over Benson's shoes.

[21]

ON TOP OF THE WORLD

B enson jumped back as Maya erupted with a fountain of puke. She collapsed on all fours in the little hallway, heaving, choking up half-digested PBJ and milk.. Sarah squatted behind her, patting her on the back and fighting to hold back tears.

"Uhh," said Benson. "Guess she got airsick."

Sarah kept patting until Maya stopped heaving.

"Go clean yourself up then. And try not to track it on the carpet." Vanessa dismissed Benson with a wave.

"Right away, ma'am." He slipped off his shoes and hurried deeper into the apartment.

"I had no idea you had issues with flying," said Vanessa. "Or I'd have sent a car."

Maya wiped her mouth on the back of her hand, glaring at her. "You barely know anything about me at all."

"Come inside already." Vanessa shook her head.

Sarah helped her stand, whispering by her ear, "I don't trust her."

"Yeah." Maya stepped over the puke and crept into the apartment; the smell of PBJ made her gag again.

A brush of air-conditioning pushed the hair off her cheeks. The place looked about double the size of the apartment Genna's crew grabbed her from. Maya's heart sank like a stone in her chest. She'd give anything to be duct-taped in that bag again.

"Ahh, well. It's good to see you survived that horrible ordeal in one piece." Vanessa smiled.

"Are you surprised they didn't kill me? I mean, you *told* them to." Maya tried to glare at her but something—guilt, the years she'd spent thinking of that woman as a parent, fear for her life—made her flinch and stare downward. "You looked right at me and said it."

Vanessa sighed. "I would have thought you learned better than that, my dear. I knew they wouldn't. You were all they had. The only advantage. If they did anything to you, they walked away with nothing. I knew they wouldn't do it."

"Maybe you believe that, but I think you really didn't care either way." Maya scratched at her stomach, still staring at the carpet. "You know what real mothers do? Real mothers pick their missing kids up in person at the Authority precinct. Real mothers, I dunno, *touch* their kids instead of cringing away. Maybe a pat on the head, or, *gasp*, a hug?"

"I can smell the sewer on you from here."

Right. "I guess I should be happy you took time out of your schedule to be in the same room when there isn't a commercial to be made."

"I'm glad you appreciate the sacrifices I make for you." Vanessa walked around a huge white sectional and stopped only a few feet away. "My, my. You do need a bath. Well. You may not believe me, but I *am* happy you are in one piece."

"Cheaper than buying a new fertilized embryo?" Maya tapped her foot. "Oh, you know what else real mothers do? They *meet* their children before they're out of diapers."

"You really should work on your tact, young miss." Vanessa circled to the left, eyeing Sarah. "And this would be your friend."

Sarah stared at her, somewhere between petrified and furious.

"I have some unfortunate news, I'm afraid. Regretfully, your father passed away earlier this morning." Her lips twitched, the same way they always did whenever she won. The bitch enjoyed that.

"What?" Sarah gasped. "No!" She fell to her knees, shaking.

Maya scowled at Vanessa and knelt to embrace Sarah. "Leave her alone."

"You're lying," mumbled Sarah between sobs.

"I know it's difficult to accept. The man's weakened condition allowed his cancer to advance rapidly to the point of being untreatable." She paced side to side as if in a boardroom meeting. "It pains me whenever a veteran loses that last battle. Had he sought treatment months ago, we could've restored him fully."

Sarah fell sideways, all strength gone from her muscles. Maya held her as she cried so hard she couldn't breathe.

"Why are you doing this to her?" asked Maya. Hearing Sarah wail brought back all the pain of losing Genna.

Vanessa put on her compassionate face. Maya trusted it about as much as she'd trust DeeDee. Well, perhaps a *little* more. Whatever lay in store for her here would certainly not include being molested. At least she'd give her biological mother that much. Granted, both amounted to prostitution, though Vanessa's form of making Maya sell her body didn't involve sex. "This isn't going to be easy to hear, but you are much better off without him."

Sarah lifted her head. "What? How can you even say something like that? Go to hell. What is *wrong* with you?"

"You surely can't see it." Vanessa sighed. "Poor thing. That man expected a little girl to take care of him like a wife. You cooked, cleaned, and waited on him, didn't you? You fed him like a toddler when he became too sick to eat on his own. What did he do? Certainly not be your father, spending his pension on booze instead of seeing to your needs. It's kinder for you that he's gone. You will be much happier here."

"I loved him," whispered Sarah. "He's my dad. That's all that mattered. He was sick. He didn't know any better." She sniveled. "He died trying to stop *you* from taking Maya."

Maya huffed in and out her nose, giving fury a few seconds to tamp down her sorrow. "That's not even funny. *You* calling someone a bad parent. You couldn't even *call* me to say goodnight."

"You are mistaken, girls." Vanessa wagged her finger. "The miscreants who are responsible for your father's death are the same ones who abducted you yesterday. They are *not* working for me. Quite the contrary, I would very much like to see them all put down like the skulking rats they are. I have not yet identified the head of the serpent, but when I do...."

Sarah blinked and snapped her head up. "How do you know so much about us?"

"The poor man was rather talkative in his last moments."

"*You* killed him!" Maya shouted, jumping to her feet.

Vanessa pinched the bridge of her nose and sighed. "No, Maya. He died to cancer. A rather unexpected sudden surge and metastasis. I had hoped he could prove useful in finding you."

"You don't want me." Maya took a step back. "You never wanted me from the day you realized I wasn't cruel like you. Once you knew I could never kill people for profit, I became 'flawed.' Just let us go. You never even *liked* me."

Vanessa's expression sharpened. Heads of companies often withered from that glare. "I suggest you behave yourself, unless you fancy something rather unfortunate happening to that hermit you've attached yourself to."

"Pope? He's alive?" Maya blinked.

"For now." Vanessa glanced at her minicomputer.

Benson emerged from the interior hallway, carrying his shoes. His pants bore no trace of vomit and a faint cologne scent hovered around him.

"Wait outside for me, would you, Benson?" Vanessa smiled at him.

"Yes, ma'am." He gave the girls a brief nod before walking out.

As soon as the door closed, Vanessa's fake smile vanished. "This is your home, Maya. I imagine those dust rats have filled your head with all manner of nonsense. Even that little presentation they made you put on won't matter."

"Oh? I think it's already mattered. Besides, you told the whole Eastern Seaboard that I never existed. What are you going to say now?"

Vanessa laughed, covering her mouth with a dainty hand. "For such an intelligent person, you are so naïve. I merely have to explain that it was a necessary ruse to lure out the Brigade terrorists who had kidnapped you. And then go on to express how happy I am that you have returned safe."

Maya wrapped her arms around Sarah, nestling her friend's head to her chest as she wept. "The Authority won't believe you."

"Oh, I think they will after we make a happy reunion video. Also, prepare yourself mentally to record some additional advertisements. We're about to launch a new skin de-aging cream."

"How about, eat a dick?" asked Maya.

Sarah's sobbing barked with an unexpected laugh.

"My word." Vanessa gawked. "You *have* been associating with some rather questionable people. That is truly unfortunate. Maya, you should take some time and consider your position carefully. The residents of a certain little rathole might have an unfortunate day ahead of them. That little half-Chinese girl *is* rather adorable. It might actually sadden me if something were to happen to her. Or that scrawny ragamuffin boy with a pronounced allergy to shirts. He is painfully cute."

"No!" shouted Maya. "You wouldn't! Leave them alone!"

Sarah scowled at Vanessa.

"You accuse me of willfully distributing the Fade virus for no reason other than profit, claiming thousands of innocent lives, and you think I'd bat an eyelash at a handful of Frags caught in an unfortunate building collapse? I hear those old structures are rather prone to it."

Maya shivered. "Please don't hurt them."

Vanessa took a step for the door. "Would your delicate, overdeveloped conscience feel better if I were to allow your friend here to go back there? Even if she's an orphan now?"

"No." Maya shook her head. "I want her to stay here."

Sarah gave her an odd look.

"Very well. Both of you go clean yourselves up right away. You're absolutely filthy. You'll find things in the closet to wear, her as well. Don't bother trying your old trick. The AI won't allow you to leave unless you are escorted by one of my staff."

"Why do you even want her?" Sarah coughed and wiped her nose. "It doesn't make any sense at all."

"The will," said Maya. "She needs me alive to protect herself."

"Very good." Vanessa slow-clapped. "In a somewhat twisted turn of events, you simultaneously made my life exceedingly difficult, but also protected it."

"Huh?" Sarah looked back and forth from Maya to Vanessa. "You should be in jail for using Fade on everyone."

"I thought you disowned me," said Maya.

"Oh, after that little exchange at the prison, I had planned to."

Vanessa frowned. "The ads weren't meeting rating goals anyway. Your disappearance might've been a cost-saving proposition: security, food, clothes, and so on. But the timing of your adorable attempt at being inspiring wound up being good for me. With those Authority nitwits initiating an investigation into your accusations, it put a freeze on my ability to change legal documents related to the company. I *couldn't* remove you as my heir." She scoffed. "I should've done it once I realized you didn't have what it takes to run a company as prestigious as Ascendant."

Maya gave her the finger. "You should go back to school. Prestigious isn't the word you're looking for."

Sarah blinked.

"And, 'cause I'm stuck in the will, if those people kill you, I get control of the company by some trustee they won't be able to touch. So by keeping me here, where someone would need another nuke to get to me...."

"It's about time you showed some evidence of all the money I spent on your genes." Vanessa clucked her tongue.

"I *am* smart. I'm just not heartless." Maya folded her arms. "You forgot to select that option when you ordered me."

"Well, I suppose we will need to adjust that bleeding heart of yours. Pity those amateurs got in the way. I was rather looking forward to having that wretched woman you've become so enamored with executed for treason and kidnapping. She got lucky. A bullet was *much* faster. Don't worry dear. By the time you're an adult, we shall have corrected your unfortunate sense of empathy."

Maya draped herself against Sarah, lacking the strength to even sit up under her own power. Sprawled on their knees, the girls clung to each other.

"Ta. Back soon." Vanessa waved at them moving only her fingers, her large smile showing perfect, super-white teeth. She strode out into the hall, the door sliding closed behind her with a soft pneumatic *hiss.*

Benson's murmuring echoed briefly outside before fading to silence.

"What the hell?" asked Sarah. "You told her to keep me here?"

Maya squeezed her tighter. "You know where I am. She wouldn't have let you go. They would've killed you."

She squeaked and shivered. "You think so?"

"It's Vanessa. She gives Fade to four-year-olds to make money. She doesn't want anyone finding me." Maya sniffled into her shoulder. "I know she would."

The lavish penthouse at the top of the world—or what remained of the world—hung in dreadful silence, save for the soft weeping of two girls with broken hearts.

FIVE-STAR PRISON

Maya lay upon a cloud-soft mattress beneath silk sheets, staring at a plain grey ceiling.

Essence of honey-lemon chicken swirled at the back of her throat from the Hydra meal she'd eaten hours before. The bedroom's enormous walk-in closet held a vast array of Maya's fancy dresses. A little section at the back held much less fancy clothes for Sarah. All but one pair of shoes were Maya's size, but even the least extreme—shiny white kitten heels—looked woefully uncomfortable. Another set of kitten heels, but not a designer brand, sat beneath Sarah's clothes. She wondered if Vanessa had planned to keep Sarah in tow when dragging Maya around to company functions, an ever-present 'piss me off and you know what happens to her' threat.

Her friend curled up beside her, also in a pink silk nightie. Sarah hadn't stopped crying from the moment Vanessa left, including the whole time Maya showed her how to use the electronic bathtub. Sarah didn't even ask about the hole at the back end of the tub that contained the hair machine. More out of routine than desire, Maya had brushed her teeth (because a brush and toothpaste existed here) and then taught Sarah how to do the same. The older girl continued weeping, though as an intermittent sniffle or soft whimper.

I wonder what Pope is doing. She teared up again, thinking of him getting cute with Genna. Despite Vanessa's assurance that he remained alive, Maya figured she'd imagined him showing up on the street right before they got picked up by the Authority. He hadn't looked angry or devastated by Genna's death. Would he try to find her? Should she even go with him if he did? It didn't seem likely. A man like that would probably welcome the chance to go back to his quiet solitude.

Everyone will be safer if I stay here.

At Sarah going quiet, Maya opened her eyes and rolled her head to the side, coming nose-to-nose with her.

"Hey," whispered Sarah, wide awake. "Guess you can't sleep either."

"No. I don't think anyone sleeps their first night in jail."

Sarah emitted a combination sob-giggle. "I didn't think jail had such nice beds. This is too soft."

"We can't leave. It might be comfortable, but we're still prisoners."

"Yeah."

Maya blinked a tear from her eye. "I'm sorry they took you too. Are you angry because I'm glad you're with me?"

"Maybe a little but... if my dad is really dead, I don't have anywhere to go." She managed a weak smile and grasped Maya's hand. "I'm glad we're together too."

"I'm sorry you're in danger. She's going to hurt you if I do anything wrong. I won't. I'll do whatever she wants."

Sarah shivered and scooted closer. "I'm scared."

"I am too, but I won't do anything to make her hurt you."

"Do you think she was lying about my dad?"

Maya broke eye contact.

"You believed her." Sarah let out a shuddering sigh.

"Sorry. She's got this little thing with her lips whenever she does something she thinks is a total win. Vanessa loves it when she makes a checkmate move at a negotiation and sits there watching the other person squirm with no way out. She loves it even more if she hurts them doing it." Maya swallowed a lump in her throat. "I'm sorry. If I wasn't in your apartment, they—"

"Stop." Sarah rolled flat on her back and took a huge breath before wiping her face. "If you'd been with Doc and Zoe, they'd be dead now. Or Arlene and Brian."

"I would *not* stay with Brian." Maya grumbled.

"You know what I mean. It wouldn't matter. It's not *your* fault." She sighed. "I guess I should stop crying so much over my dad. And Brian wouldn't have tried to protect you. He'd have let them have you."

"Yeah." Maya looked at her again. "Why wouldn't you be upset over your father?"

"Dad was nuts. He barely did anything. He loved me, but didn't take care of me like a dad should. It's not his fault. The things he saw during the war broke him. I hate her, but Vanessa isn't wrong. Even Genna kinda said the same thing, but not quite so mean."

"Sarah." Maya rolled on her side, facing her. "Your dad really did love you. I could see it whenever he looked at you."

She sniffled, tears welling in her eyes. "Sometimes it was like he'd go back to how he must have been before the war. But most of the time, he was someone else." She picked at the bed for a few seconds in awkward silence. "Should we try and escape?"

"Not worth it. There's only one door and a fire exit. Both computer controlled. Even if we *could* get out, she'll hurt everyone in our building."

Sarah sat up, elbows on her knees and her face in both hands. "She killed him. You're right. But why?"

"She knows we're like sisters and wanted to use you to control me." Maya propped herself up on her elbows. "When I first met you, I was scared. I'd never been around any other kids."

"That's sad." Sarah wiped her face and nose. "What time is it?"

Maya glanced at the nightstand clock. "Almost two in the morning."

"Ugh." Sarah flopped back down. "I can't sleep."

"Me neither."

Maya closed her eyes and put an arm across Sarah. Perhaps if she stopped *trying* to sleep to get away from all the pain and guilt swimming around in her head, she might drift off. Eventually, Sarah rolled toward her and grabbed her like a giant, living teddy bear. No matter how hard Maya tried to think of anything else, the image of Genna collapsing behind the car played over and over in her mind.

A heavy stone burdened her chest where her heart should've been. Maya stared at the ceiling, trying to think of any possible way to escape.

SLEEP SNUCK IN LIKE A THIEF UNDER COVER OF DARKNESS. MAYA moaned and sat up, head wobbling about for a moment or so until the fog cleared from her mind. Half-closed eyes focused on the blur of cyan light at her left, which sharpened to 10:17. Sarah had flopped on her back and lay sprawled with her arms and legs askew.

After a yawn and a stretch, Maya slipped out of the bed and hit the bathroom before wandering back and standing in the middle of the room, swaying on her feet. She scratched at her stomach and stretched again. A peek in the closet at all the expensive dresses, plush sweaters, and fanciness made her frown—and feel guilty. Kids in the Hab were lucky to own a complete outfit of actual clothes, and if they had to wear curtains, carpets, or plastic bags, they at least felt grateful to have that. People living on the edges between the Hab and the Dead Space made do with even less.

Here, she gazed upon upwards of forty different ensembles and didn't want any of them. All the sheer, narrow dresses barely let her walk at a full stride. Wearing any of them out in the real world would be dangerous: she couldn't run. Not to mention, none of them offered much protection against the cold. Summer only had another month left; she wondered if the heat in her real home worked. The thought that she'd never be there again to find out got her lip quivering.

Maya looked down at her bare feet. *Maybe if I stay in my nightdress, I'll get kidnapped again.*

She retreated from the closet and took a seat on the foot of the bed, waiting for Sarah to wake. Like her old room, this one contained no toys, dolls, or anything intended to be decorative or warm the space. Pale grey walls, two windows covered in electronic blinds, and a closet with louvered doors.

Prison, first class.

The dark thought that Vanessa had finally given her a doll—Sarah—to keep her company made her cringe.

Eventually Sarah stirred, sucking a deep breath in through her nose before opening her eyes. "Hey."

"Hey."

Sarah crawled off the bed and trudged out of the bedroom. Maya followed her until halfway down the hall where they split up—Sarah ducking into the bathroom while Maya continued to the kitchenette. She pulled a chair over and climbed up to kneel on the counter. Two cabinets above the Hydra held four large boxes of meal trays. She spent a few minutes perusing the breakfast options. The waffle made her cry a little, thinking of Genna and her cereal, so she took an omelet.

"Careful, you're going to fall." Sarah walked up and put a hand on her back.

"What do you want to eat?"

Sarah shrugged. "I don't care."

Maya held up her tray, showing a picture of an omelet and home fries on the foil cover.

"Sure."

With two omelets in hand, Maya climbed down and put one in the Hydra. Sarah studied the machine, enthralled. At the push of a button, it began the process of warming and rehydrating the contents of the octagonal black plastic tray. Forty seconds later, the foil cover swelled, emitting steam.

"That's kinda cool," muttered Sarah. "Never saw one of these working before."

"Foz has one, but he's never going to sell it for what he's asking. No one out there has that much money."

"Are they really that expensive?"

Maya shook her head. "No. Not here anyway." She opened the door and pulled the tray out by pinching the thin edges. "Here. Take this one. It's hot. Don't touch anything but the lip around the outside."

"Okay."

Once her breakfast finished in the machine, Maya joined her at the table and peeled the covering off. The spongy yellow egg-like substance didn't hold a candle to Naida's handmade omelet, but she couldn't say it tasted bad.

After eating, Sarah wandered out into the living room. When she got close to the front door, an electronic male voice broke the silence.

"I'm sorry. You are not authorized to operate this door."

Sarah gave the ceiling the middle finger and kept walking to the windows. She parted the vertical blinds and stuck her head up to the glass. She shivered. "Holy crap. We're so high up."

"Yeah."

Blinds fluttered, clattering against the glass as Sarah moved away, heading for the giant flat panel television. "So what's this do?"

"It's a TV. Watch shows, surf the AuthNet, movies... video games."

"Oh. I didn't think TVs got this big."

Sarah headed down the hall, exploring, with Maya in tow. This apartment didn't have a large patio off the living room where a helicopter could land like the penthouse she'd spent five years in, only normal-sized windows. The exits consisted of the front door and one silver metal hatch labeled 'FIRE,' which wouldn't unlock unless the building's alarm system detected an actual fire.

Maya examined the windows, noting not one of them could open, and followed her friend's wandering until they stopped at the bathroom door. Sarah whistled at the electronic tub, digital control panel for a toilet, powered soap dispensers on the sink, and all. She pointed at a bank of buttons on the wall above the tub. "What's that do?"

"I showed you last night."

Sarah traced a finger over the controls. "I wasn't really listening."

"It's for the bath." Maya climbed over to stand in the tub, and indicated the top row. "These buttons add suds. This one sets the fragrance." She gestured at the next row of buttons. "This is the control for the water jets, and the last set is like bath bombs."

"Wow..." Sarah blinked. "Uhh, what's a bath bomb? Do they explode?"

Maya couldn't quite find the mood to laugh, but did smile as she explained them.

"People spend money on that?" asked Sarah. "What's that hole?"

"It washes your hair..." Maya glanced at her friend's past-butt-length red squiggles. "You might have too much for it, but *please* don't cut it. It's so pretty."

Sarah almost smiled.

"Like this." Still dressed, Maya reclined as if taking a bath. After using some buttons to adjust the elevation of the unit, she leaned her head back into the opening and pretended to soak in a luxurious mass of suds. "You soak and the machine in the wall washes and fixes your hair."

"Fixes?"

"Like combing and brushing as well as washing. I think it can even do straightening."

Sarah folded her arms. "If that machine tried to straighten my hair, it would probably burn itself out."

Maya laughed, picturing the machine overloading.

"So, what's that?" asked Sarah, turning her attention to the control panel on the toilet. "What's all this stuff? I've never seen a toilet with blinking lights and buttons before."

"Most of that is the self-cleaning electronics." Maya stepped out of the tub. "No one ever visits. There's not even a cleaning person or anything. I mean, the last place had these little round robots that did the floors. This place is bigger; maybe they'll have someone show up."

"I guess Vanessa figured out she messed up, huh?" Sarah put an arm around her shoulders.

"Huh?"

"She didn't leave you alone this time."

Maya clamped on and cried. Once she regained her composure, she managed a sad giggle. "You're still trying to take care of me."

"I'm the oldest and we don't have parents."

Maya hung her head, thinking of Genna.

"I can't believe you didn't want to be here." Sarah led her out into the hall and into the never-used master bedroom. A few vases perched on narrow tables and an abstract sculpture of black glass as tall as Maya that could've been a dancer or an avalanche stood in the back corner. "It's like a palace."

"I was so lonely." She tugged Sarah back out into the hall and pointed at the video phone in the wall. "I'd call Vanessa every night, hoping she would come home and spend time with me, but she didn't care. She wouldn't even answer to say good night."

"Sorry."

Maya looked her in the eye. "I'd rather live in a plastiboard box in an alley with you and Genna and all the others than be here."

Sarah hugged her.

"Even if dosers steal everything we have."

Sarah laughed. "I'm laughing so I don't start crying again."

Reality fell upon her shoulders with the weight of a collapsing high-rise building. Vanessa had won. Nothing Maya did now would change that her brief taste of having a *real* mother had ended. A feeble itch to escape reared its head and withered. Why bother running? Genna was dead; she had nowhere to go, certainly nowhere worth risking the lives of her friends. Strength fled from her legs, dumping Maya to the carpet in the hallway. Quiet tears ran from a glassy stare into nowhere. Sarah said a few things, but her voice had lost any meaning, a mere warble from above.

Thin arms encircled her. Sarah grabbed her own wrist in front of Maya's chest and hauled her upright. When she refused to stand by herself, Sarah backed toward the living room, grunting while dragging her along. After depositing her on the sofa, she wrapped Maya with a nearby blanket, and sat beside her.

The image of Genna taking a bullet in the chest and collapsing behind the parked car replayed over and over in Maya's mind while Vanessa's laughter echoed overhead. Hugging her legs, she cried onto her knees without making much noise. Sarah sat beside her, sniffling as well while murmuring comforting things. After a while, she emitted a discontented grunt and leapt to her feet, causing Maya to wobble on the cushions. She didn't pay much attention to the blur of red hair moving off to the right. Before long, a harsh buzz came from the front door. Sarah crossed the room to the kitchenette, and the sounds of rummaging filled in the silence. Again, the blur of red crossed Maya's periphery.

An indistinct haze of minutes later, a *bang* made Maya jump.

She wiped at her eyes and peered over the back of the couch.

Sarah lay flat on her back by the door, a wisp of smoke trailing up from the access panel and a common table knife in the girl's hand. Her hair fluffed up, far too long to stand fully on end.

"Are you okay?" whispered Maya.

"I would not recommend doing that again," said the house AI.

Sarah raised her left arm and extended a middle finger to the ceiling. "Hit something I shouldn't have. I'm okay. I don't think I'm gonna pick this lock with a knife."

"I would not recommend attempting that again," said the house AI.

After waving the middle finger back and forth a few times, Sarah groaned and stood up.

"Don't hurt yourself." Maya curled up against the sofa back, her body wracked with silent sobs as her sorrow over Genna's death grew painful.

"Hmm." Sarah returned to the kitchenette.

A faint *clank* of a knife being returned to a drawer full of silverware preceded her padding out and approaching the living room window. She crawled in between the vertical blinds and felt around the sides. Soft knocks and thumps accompanied muted grunts. Before long, she went down the hall. Maya remained on the couch, wondering if she could say something bad enough to Vanessa to make the woman kill her.

Mom would be pissed at me for thinking that.

She pictured Genna angry, pointing, upset for her teasing at the idea of suicide. Worse, if she made Vanessa mad enough to kill her, she'd certainly hurt Sarah too. Maya grabbed one of the small green throw pillows, into which she bawled for several minutes. Sarah tromped back in grumbling. At the sight of Maya lost to uncontrollable grief, she hurried over, climbed up onto the couch, and pulled her into her lap.

"I'm here. You're not alone."

Maya sniffled. "I know."

"I can't find a way to get out of here, but I'm not done looking."

"Why?" Maya wiped her face on her arm. "Don't bother. We can't get out. Even if we did, Vanessa will kill everyone."

Sarah rested her chin on Maya's shoulder and rocked her side to side. "We'll figure something out. You're smart, right?"

"It's no use. Where would we even go?" Maya fought the urge to break down again, grief clear in her voice. "I don't want my mom to be dead. I want my mom."

Sarah squeezed her. "I miss my dad too."

"Maya," said the house AI. "Your mother is very much alive."

An explosion of hope warmed Maya's chest. She sat upright, staring at the ceiling wide-eyed. "Really? That man didn't kill her? Where is she?"

"Presently, your mother is in her office attending to a conference call."

Maya crumpled, clutching her gut as if Moth had punched her.

"Wow," whispered Sarah. "Whoever that is, is a *real* asshole. Don't listen to him."

"No!" Maya flailed away from Sarah and jumped to her feet. "That bitch is *not* my mother!" Overcome by pure rage, she looked around for something to smash and zeroed in on a two-foot-tall square silver vase sitting on a tiny table by the wall near the front door holding four imitation pussy willow strands and a bunch of glass beads.

As soon as she grabbed it, the AI said, "Feel free to break whatever you do not mind your friend being punished for."

"Uhh..." Sarah gave the finger to the ceiling again.

Maya froze with the vase over her head in both hands. Anger melted to dread. Before her arms shook to the point of dropping it by accident, she eased it back onto the table and ran to the sofa.

"Your mother does not want you hurt, Maya." The AI simulated a sigh. "She is merely disappointed in you. If you only lived up to her expectations, your mother would warm up."

Maya fell heavy on the couch, arms folded across her legs, staring down at her toes. "My *mother* is dead."

"I hate that guy already," said Sarah, leaning close and rubbing Maya's back.

"It's not a guy. It's an AI. Artificial intelligence. Basically a robot babysitter because Vanessa can't be bothered to even talk to me when it doesn't make money. She wouldn't even hire a real person to watch me."

"I do not get sick. I do not sleep. I do not require vacation time, food, or lodging," said the AI. "It is quite a logical choice."

Maya flopped back on the couch. "He's totally got the emotional support thing down."

Sarah's face did something between a grimace and wanting to laugh.

"Hmm." Maya narrowed her eyes at the entertainment center. She pushed off the sofa and plopped down in front of the TV, opened the glass-doored cabinet, and pulled out a keyboard. "Since we're stuck here, wanna play a game?"

Sarah trailed over and sat beside her. "What kind of game?"

"Got a bunch." Maya booted the terminal system.

A user login 'M_OMAN' flashed by too fast to react to, and the 110-inch TV flooded with a desktop loaded with icons. *Damn. Guess I'm on lockdown. I wonder if the Hangar has a 'net site? Maybe I can make contact.* She opened an AuthNet browser. It showed an 'access denied' page, even to the primary search engine.

"What the... is the net down?" She grumbled.

"You don't have access to the AuthNet," said the house AI. "Vanessa has instructed me to block all outside connections until further notice."

"What about e-learns or research for school assignments?" Maya glared at the ceiling.

"You have already completed coursework equivalent to high-school graduation. I believe Vanessa feels you are too immature for more advanced courses yet."

"Bullshit. She thinks I'm going to do something."

"Well," said the AI. "Wouldn't you? I may lack any sense of human emotion, but I am capable of understanding the dynamic between you and your mother has changed. You have misbehaved and are... I believe the term is 'grounded.' It would be best for you if you accepted your position and stopped trying to make life difficult for your mother."

Almost in tears from anger, she checked her games folder. All but two remained. The missing ones required 'net access for multiplayer. She didn't feel much like playing at the moment but opened a racing game where players controlled flying vehicles shaped somewhat like motorcycles without wheels. After rummaging the cabinet, she handed Sarah a controller. As much as she wanted to escape, she didn't really have anywhere to go and didn't want to test Vanessa's threat to kill everyone. If the woman made good on knocking down the whole building, more than the people living in it would be hurt.

"You can play. I'm too angry right now."

Sarah took the controller with some reluctance, and after a little coaching, started playing. Her eager, awestruck reaction to a game with modern graphics compared to the ancient machines in the basement back home lifted Maya's spirits. After watching her friend twisting her body with each turn, roaring whenever she had to shoot an obstacle out of her way, and cheering each time she reached a checkpoint to add a little more time to the clock, Maya caved in and joined as a second player.

If she had to accept being locked up to keep her friends alive, so be it. At least the video game appeared to take Sarah's mind off her father's death for a little while. Unfortunately, every time the girl squeaked, cheered, or grumbled in response to the screen, Maya dreaded what might happen to her if Vanessa got angry.

[23]

THE IRONY OF LIES

Hours passed careening down virtual racetracks, from tubes to half tunnels to courses defined by floating rings. Maya had played these games to death, but she'd never had a friend to share them with before. Two-player was *way* more fun than she remembered these games being alone. Maybe she could tolerate being kept here. Perhaps she might even manage to convince Vanessa to stop using Fade on people.

Maybe she'd sprout wings.

The game paused.

"Hey," said Sarah. "Why'd you stop it?"

"I thought you did." Maya blinked.

"Maya, it is time for dinner," said the AI.

"What are you making, *Dad*?" asked Maya.

The computer didn't reply, nor did the game respond to the unpause command.

With a heavy sigh and an eye roll, Maya set the controller down and stood. Sarah followed her to the kitchenette.

"I know why you stay in your nightgown all the time." Sarah slid into a chair.

"Why?" Maya climbed up onto the counter and grabbed two Hydra trays without looking.

Sarah stretched forward over the table, resting her head on her extended arm. "Because your closet is full of tight, shiny dresses. They look *so* uncomfortable."

"They are. Half of them I can't breathe in, the rest I can't walk in." Maya mimed taking tiny, rapid steps. "Add heels, and I keep falling over."

"Ugh. Sorry." Sarah leaned on the counter, arms crossed.

"Yeah. I'd like to have some actual pajamas though. Soft pants with floppy, warm feet." She popped a Hydra tray in and tugged at her nightdress. "Vanessa always gets me these super-thin silk things."

"Well, they are comfortable."

Maya shrugged. "As long as it's not cold. And she's too cheap to turn the heat up, so...."

The house AI simulated a sigh. "Adjusting ambient temperature to seventy degrees."

Beep.

"Wow, she's splurging." Maya looked at the un-hydrated tray and the one in the machine. "Do you want stir fry shrimp or Salisbury steak?"

"What's that? Sals berry?" Sarah pushed herself up off the table. "They put fruit on steak?"

"It's a fancy way to say 'hamburger without a bun.'" Maya pulled the shrimp out of the Hydra and set it on the table.

"I don't care. I'll have the burger if you don't like it."

"It's not bad. Just plain." She popped the tray in and hit the button. Two minutes later, she pinched the tray and carried it over to the table. "Food's food." After a few seconds of staring, she frowned. "I miss Book's burritos."

"Yeah. Me too." Sarah tugged the shrimp closer and sniffed. "I never had shrimp. I might not like it."

After a nibble, she cringed and pushed it toward Maya. "It's sweet. Fish shouldn't be sweet."

Tears welled in Maya's eyes. "I wish we could have cheese sandwiches."

Sarah swallowed hard. After opening and closing her mouth a few times, she nodded.

They ate for a little while without talking, both dabbing at their eyes.

Maya swung her feet back and forth while Sarah slumped over the table, head resting on her arm, staring sideways at her dinner. Wisps of steam from the meal tray floated up past her face.

"I guess this isn't so bad. I mean, sure, we're kidnapped, but it's kinda nice being clean and having real food."

Maya pushed shrimp, veggies, and rice around. "I don't trust Vanessa."

"You think she'll hurt us?"

"I don't know. Right now, she's protecting me because if I die, those people can try to kill her and take over Ascendant. As long as I'm alive, they don't get easy control." She mulled while pushing an impaled shrimp like a plow through orange sauce and rice. "I don't think she's going to kill me. She knows keeping me here is more painful. But I think she could if she wanted to. She'd do anything to hold on to her power. I hate it here, but I'm scared of what she'll do if I try to run away again."

Sarah looked around. "You really hate it here? It's like we're not even on the same planet anymore."

"I hate it less since I'm not alone." Maya reached across the table.

Sarah took her hand.

"Sorry for getting you stuck here too." She lowered her voice to a whisper. "She'll hurt you if I mess up. I don't think we're really safe here no matter how nice it is. I want to get out of here, but I don't want people to get hurt." Maya bowed her head, seasoning her dinner with a few tears. "I'm gonna stay and do whatever that bitch tells me to do. Maybe she'll at least not kill *you* when she doesn't need me anymore."

"How can you give up after all that stuff you said to the world? That was like *so* inspiring you made me cry. I heard you even made some blueberries cry."

Maya's voice shook with fear. "You heard that woman! She's going to kill everyone we know. It's not worth it. I'm stuck. What's the point?" She slouched, energy fading from her words. "I hoped that message would make more of a difference. Maybe I *am* just a little kid who thought I could make a wish and it would come true. But it didn't come true; it died. I thought when people saw proof that Vanessa was the reason Fade made them sick, they'd arrest her and the Authority would stop being jerks and everything would change, but she lies. Vanessa lies and people believe her. Why?" Maya cried in earnest. "How can people listen to all her bullshit and not even question her? What can I do anyway? I may be smart, but I'm still only a little girl. I'm not strong. I can't fight. I don't have any weapons or training. If I don't do what she wants, she could kill all our friends, everyone I care about. Even you. I don't have a choice."

"Don't give up. Please. When we got arrested, I thought they were gonna hurt us and treat us like trash like they did whenever they called a lockdown. When that blueberry made us get in the car, I thought we were being taken off to die." Sarah shuddered. "I was wrong. I'm not even sure we got arrested anymore. It almost was like he wanted to help us. You did start change. That little drone thing? When they raided the building, they didn't leave us all tied up again."

Maya shrugged. "I guess."

"Vanessa wouldn't keep us here if she wasn't scared. She's like an end boss. You can't beat her in one hit."

Maya giggled.

They finished eating, tossed the trays in the bin, and relocated to the living room. Maya held up the blanket, and the girls cocooned themselves together on the sofa, watching cartoons. One episode ran into the next, and the warmth lulled her into a sense of contentment. She pondered the finer differences between being a child subject to parental rules compared to being in captivity.

This is captivity. A parent would care.

"MAYA," SAID THE AI.

She awoke, still burritoed in a blanket on the couch, her face mushed against Sarah's shoulder. The TV screen showed black. Brighter sunlight than ought to be out at the hour she expected poured in the windows.

"Mmm..." She squirmed.

"Maya. Wake up," said the AI. "You need to clean yourself up immediately. An aesthetic technician is on the way up to prepare you for the recording session."

A momentary urge to tell the AI what it could do with itself died at the tip of her brain as Sarah's breathing tightened and relaxed the blanket wrapped around them. Defiance would only get people hurt, starting with her best friend. "Okay."

She extricated herself from the sofa and trudged down the hall to the bathroom to pee. As if on autopilot, she tapped the console to fill the bath, shirked off her nightdress, and reclined in the warm, soapy water. Maya lay for a little while, staring at the immaculate white drop ceiling, but couldn't concoct a functional escape plan in a few minutes. With a resigned sigh, she scooted back and leaned her head into the hollow in the wall, where a mass of tiny articulated metal arms set to the task of washing her hair while she attended the rest of her body with a cloth. She finished cleaning herself, then relaxed and let the machine work, fighting the temptation to enjoy the massaging on her scalp while soaking in warm suds.

The sudden start of the hot air dryer behind her startled her out of a catnap. Once the hair machine shut down, she reached a leg up and poked the drain button with a toe, allowing the tub to empty. When the last of the water vanished with a slurp, Maya climbed out of the tub, dried herself with a towel, and padded back to the bedroom. She pulled on a clean pair of underpants, frowning at them, remembering how the immaculate white cloth had once made her feel darker, as if that would make Vanessa like her more.

Maya sat on the edge of the bed in only her underpants, swinging her feet. Minutes passed. The floral scent the machine put in her hair suffused the entire room. Her eyes half closed, she swayed, fighting the urge to flop backwards and pass out. A short while later, the front door opened and the AI voice spoke in the distance, too soft to make out what it said.

"Maya?" asked a woman. "Hello? Oh, hi. You're not Maya. Who are you?"

A tiny murmur replied.

"Hello, Sarah. Do you know where Maya is?"

"She is in her room," said the AI.

"Down here?" The woman's voice got louder. "Maya?"

"Here," said Maya.

A thin, younger woman with long black hair and striking blue eyes peered around the doorway, smiled, and walked in. Skin even paler than Sarah's, without a trace of freckle, glowed in the sunlight. The woman didn't even look human, as white as a sheet of new paper. "Well hello, sweetie." She hurried over. "I'm Amy."

"Hi." Maya kept swinging her feet, her brain grinding on if everyone would be safer if she died.

"I'll be helping get you ready for the shoot today," said Amy in an annoyingly cheerful tone.

"Yes. I know what an aesthetic technician does. You look young. I've probably done this more than you have. Is this your first or second assignment?" She slid off the bed and stood, arms out. *I'm a paper doll.*

"Aww. You're adorable." Amy smooched at the air by Maya's cheek and headed to the closet. "Let's see what we have to work with."

Maya rolled her eyes and huffed.

"Morning," mumbled Sarah as she walked in. She crossed the rug and sat on the bed.

"Hey," muttered Maya. "That woman makes you look tan."

Sarah managed a feeble smile. Not the laugh Maya had hoped for.

A few minutes later, the continuous pleasant humming in the closet ceased. Amy emerged holding a bright purple dress with a metallic sheen. She held it against Maya's front, appraising it. The design bared her left shoulder and hung past the right knee while staying short on the left.

"Is that a pincher or a 'can't walk' dress?" whispered Sarah.

"I don't remember wearing that one before but it looks like a pincher," whispered Maya.

"This should be perfect," said Amy. "Your mother is going to be wearing blue."

She's not my mother. "I hate high heels."

Amy blinked. "High heels? At your size? That's cruel. Who'd put a girl your age in high heels?"

Maya's contempt for the young woman lessened somewhat. "Uhh, yeah. They always make me wear heels. Once, at a quarterly review presentation, they had me walking back and forth on the boardroom table holding up posters. You were just in the closet; didn't you look down? *All* the shoes in there are high heels."

"Oh, that's awful. Who approved that?" Amy shook her head. "You could've slipped and broken your neck. I'm not going to put you in heels." She pulled a data pad out of her purse and read over something.

"Perfect. We're not doing any wide angles today, so it doesn't matter what's on your feet. No one will see below your waist. You could wear bunny slippers if you wanted to."

Maya's expression remained a flat, blank stare. She twisted to look at Sarah. "This woman is more concerned about me than Vanessa."

"Aww. Your mother is a very busy woman. Sometimes parents in her position don't have as much time to spend with their children as they'd like. You know, in the past, the rich and powerful always hired caretakers to look after their children and rarely spent time with them in person."

Maya frowned, glancing sideways at Sarah. *And they had whipping boys—or girls. I mess up, she gets punished.* She put on a Vanessa-esque false smile. "Looks pretty."

Amy pulled the gown over Maya's head, adjusted it, spun her around, zipped up the back, spun her to face forward again, and adjusted it some more. "There. Now, for the rest."

Maya sighed, fidgeting at her left armpit. "Pincher."

Earrings, purple lip gloss, a little violet-glitter eye shadow, and a half hour of fussing with hair later, Amy grinned. "You are so pretty. I'm *so* jealous of your skin. You've got the *perfect* complexion for television. Not too dark, not too light. Me? I'm so pale I practically burn out display screens, and it's murder finding good cosmetics. I hope you don't mind."

"Thanks," droned Maya.

Amy squatted to eye level and fussed at her bangs. "Let me see what sort of shoes you've got to work with."

"Can I skip shoes? Maybe if I don't wear any, someone will kidnap me again and get me out of here."

Sarah stifled a laugh.

"Oh, Maya." Amy offered a sad sigh. "You have so much to be thankful for. There's so many kids your age out there who have nothing."

Maya thought of the children living in plastiboard cartons with bits of carpet, plastic bags, or curtains for clothes, some without even that. When she'd run off to find Genna, one woman had fed her without hesitation, a strange child she'd never laid eyes on before. As soon as she remembered that family of Frags, she felt jealous of them despite their poverty. A scrap of carpet tied on as a loincloth with a power cable would be more comfortable than her present gown.

She fidgeted at her left armpit but couldn't get the fabric to stop digging in.

"I'm forgetting something." Amy glanced around in thought for a few seconds before a look of enlightenment hit her. She pulled a transparent tablet from her purse and handed it to Maya. "Here's your script. They tell me that you're an old pro at this, right? Hmm. I wonder if there's anything we can accessorize you with." She wandered into the closet.

Maya looked down at glowing green letters floating within the plastic. The speechwriter wanted her to ramble about how the Brigade had abducted her and forced her to lie to make Vanessa and Ascendant look bad, while acting happy that she'd finally been rescued and brought home to her loving mother. "Oh. That's why the AI didn't wake me up in time to eat breakfast. It knew I'd throw up having to say this."

Sarah bit her lip.

"Ironic," muttered Maya.

"What?" asked Amy, from the closet. "Did you say 'ironic?'"

Maya skimmed the bullshit again. "Yeah. Ugh."

"There's nothing in there but tiny high heels and one pair of slippers," called Amy.

"I told you," muttered Maya in a singsong tone.

Amy emerged from the closet, one hand to her forehead in disbelief. "I didn't think they even made stilettos that small. What is *wrong* with people?"

"Told you," said Maya.

"What did you mean by ironic?" asked Amy, smiling.

Is that word too complicated for you? Maya waved the tablet at her. "Oh, this whole script. It's ironic because I've been kidnapped and I'm being forced to lie and say I was kidnapped and forced to lie."

"I'd laugh, but that's awful," muttered Sarah.

"If I don't say this stuff, Vanessa's going to hurt you." She frowned. "If I do say this, it could hurt a lot of people."

Sarah leaned forward and put a shaking hand on her arm. "I don't wanna die, but if you think a lot of people are going to get hurt, i-it's okay. M-maybe she'll just do something cruel to me instead of killing me. I won't be mad at you if you do what you think is right."

Amy hummed merrily to herself, smiling as she made a few touch-ups to Maya's cosmetics. Maya shivered, feeling sicker and sicker. Her first and best friend had given her the okay to risk her life to spare the guilt of helping Vanessa go back to condemning the poor to a horrible death in the name of profit. The floating letters blurred into an indistinct patch of meaningless green luminescence.

She sniffled, blinked away the urge to cry, and focused on the words. "I can't put you in danger. If she's going to hurt you in front of me, I'm going to cave in."

"You have to. Don't let her win. I'm not more important than all those people." Sarah slid off the bed, whispering at Maya's ear, "Do it for Sam."

A pang like an icepick in the gut stalled her mind. Invoking Genna's dead son filled her with a raging storm of regret, grief, and anger. So many people had died to defy Ascendant. She couldn't give up on every-one. The half-grey face of five-year-old Ashley came to mind. Because of the Brigade, that girl's death sentence had been revoked. Because of her video, the Authority had changed. But, Sarah was her best friend—no, more than best friend. They'd become family. Could she really put the lives of thousands of people she'd never seen over one person she loved like a sister?

Before the explosion of tears could start, she thought about how much she hated Vanessa. If she cried now, her makeup would run and probably dribble on her dress. She'd get in trouble, and that would likely hurt Sarah.

Standing up for Sam and all the people Vanessa had killed with Fade would hurt Sarah too, but at least it would mean something. She turned, grasped Sarah's shoulder, and bowed her head.

"Okay. For Sam."

[24]

A GAME OF DRESS-UP

Sitting once more on the living room sofa, Maya memorized only the opening few lines, having abandoned the idea of going off-script and saying the truth. After the damage she'd already caused to Ascendant with a video message, Vanessa would never approve a live feed. Though the woman had not been a product of custom genetic selection like Maya, she wasn't an idiot. Any blurting would never make it to the broadcast. In fact, she probably expected Maya to try something like that.

Anything she said that Vanessa didn't approve of would stay in the room and result only in some manner of punishment. How loud would that witch make Sarah scream before Maya couldn't take it anymore and she gave up? Faced with the horrible choice of putting Sarah at risk or throwing away everything the Brigade had accomplished, she could come up with only one good idea: act like she tried to give the speech and keep falling to pieces. Of course, they could have one of the android decoys recite those lines, or fake it with computer graphics—but the woman wanted to hurt Maya.

Maybe if she kept crying, Vanessa would get frustrated and call it off to 'give her time.'

Or she could pull out a gun and put it to Sarah's head.

No, she might be a bitch, but she's not stupid. She knows I'm only a little kid. Even she wouldn't expect me to be able to smile and act happy with a gun pointed at my best friend's face.

Sarah, still in her pink nightdress, sat on the sofa beside her, shuffling her feet back and forth over the rug. Her slouched posture, downcast eyes, and shaking hands—as if she awaited severe punishment—reinforced Maya's wimp-out decision to try stalling.

The little girl having a meltdown angle would have to work. She'd pretend to obey but be unable to. She *was* only nine years old. They couldn't expect a kid her age to smoothly lie to the world like that with a straight face. Maya clutched the tablet in guilty rage. She *had* lied to the camera for years, but all those lies she'd told about Ascendant's drugs had been abstract things, distortions of facts from dry scientific papers. Back then, she'd never looked into the eyes of a Fade victim. Even a child like her could read a script about overstated medical benefits or omit any mention of side effects. Did it count as lying if she didn't know about the side effects until *after* she recorded an ad? But to lie about the Brigade? About people she'd met? About people she'd watched die fighting for a better life? Thinking of Binks' cremation, a man who'd been killed trying to protect her, Maya gripped the rug with her toes, trembling from anxiety. Sarah gave her the okay to defy Vanessa no matter what happened to her. Intellectually, it made sense. One girl's life for all of society—but with each second passing, betraying her became a greater crime.

Paralyzed with indecision, Maya caught herself about to cry and thought of how angry she'd been with Brian to stop herself before her makeup ran.

"Aww, honey," said Amy in a sweet tone. "I thought you were an old pro?"

"I am. It's not the camera I'm afraid of," muttered Maya. "They don't want me to sell drugs this time. They want me to kill people."

"Oh, sweetie. You're taking it a bit too far. This is only a happy announcement that you've been found and brought home."

Maya shot her a flat look, holding up the tablet. "You didn't actually read this, did you?"

Amy fussed at Maya's hair. "You are so pretty."

"All the toppings," mumbled Maya.

Amy tilted her head. "What?"

"I'm a genetic pizza," deadpanned Maya.

An electronic *bong* emanated from the elevator, which meant the production people and Vanessa had entered the little hallway outside. She didn't bother trying to calm down or think distant thoughts. Maya wanted to be emotional, unfocused, unusable for a PR video.

She shivered at the *pssh* of the front door opening. Via the reflection in the blank television screen, she watched Vanessa walk in, followed by two blueberries, a man and a woman, in armor. Behind them, Benson and two other not-quite-as-big men in black suits entered, then a handful of people carrying equipment boxes, cameras, lights, microphones, and such.

She stared at the two Authority officers. "Blueberries? Really?" muttered Maya. "What does she think I'm going to do, pull a gun out of my butt and shoot her?"

Sarah got a case of the giggles and failed at hiding it.

The female blueberry turned her gaze toward Maya, the blank-faced blue-and-silver helmet accusing. A nameplate over the left breast read: 'OFC Davies, M.' Maya fidgeted, but the woman didn't stop staring at her. What had Vanessa told them about her? These two probably remained loyal to her, mere corporate thugs without a scrap of actual care for the law. A sick whirlwind started in Maya's stomach at the idea they'd been brought here for Sarah. Of course, Vanessa wouldn't get her hands dirty. She wanted to run over and hug her as-good-as-sister, but the weight of the female blueberry's stare pinned her to the cushion.

Maya cringed. Everything about that woman's body language said she couldn't wait to hurt someone.

Two skinny men with frizzy black hair ran about the living room searching for 'the best' place to set up a background screen while eyeing the ceiling lights and complaining to each other.

Benson and his two associates headed to the kitchen.

The production crew ran about opening their boxes and running cables around. Vanessa spent a few minutes having Amy check her makeup and royal-blue gown before approaching the sofa. She gave Sarah a glance of mild disdain, which slapped the mirth right out of her.

"You," snapped Vanessa, "stay out of the way and be quiet."

Sarah scrambled to her feet and ran toward the bedroom.

Vanessa turned toward Maya with a smile more plastic than a Hydra tray. "Now, this will be just like you're used to."

"'Kay." Maya stared down, flicking her thumbnail at the edge of the clear tablet.

"You *are* worried about your friends, aren't you?"

Maya raised her arms off her lap, showing off her shaking hands. "Just a little."

The female Authority officer took a position by the left end of the couch, her attention still locked on Maya, as if expecting the tiny girl to attack Vanessa at any second.

Maya sighed. "Why aren't you just using fake video of me like you did before?"

"That wasn't false video. We used one of the androids. Computer animations are not perfect, and they cannot project the same authenticity in their emotions."

CG has more emotion than you do. Maya gave Vanessa a scathing glare but shrank away as Officer Davies loomed closer.

Sarah returned in a pink angora sweater and white pleated skirt. She eyed the production crew with narrowed eyes, the same way she always looked at locks she meant to attack. Alas, between Vanessa and a blueberry so close, she gave the sofa a wide berth and took a seat on a chair by the far wall. Having her friend perch so far away rather than next to her ramped Maya's fear up from shaking hands to full-body trembles.

What's she going to do to Sarah if I mess up?

Finally locating a place where the 'light contamination' didn't bother them as much, the frizz-haired men extended aluminum poles and unrolled a green-screen background.

A woman and three others set up recording equipment and ran even more wires among them while the AI directed them to the nearest wall outlets for power.

"I trust you've studied your lines?" asked Vanessa.

"Yeah. Do we have to do this today? I'm still upset over watching my *real* mother die—and being kidnapped twice. I don't know if I can say all this stuff without crying."

Vanessa gestured dismissively at Sarah. "You'll just have to rely on your acting coach."

Maya glared at Vanessa, which caused Officer Davies to edge closer.

She shot the armored woman a 'go to hell' look and muttered, "Like I'm going to do something."

"Testing one," said a man, his voice thundering across the apartment at the head of a wave of feedback squeal.

"Fuck!" shouted an Asian guy kneeling in front of the bank of electronics as he tore off his headphones. "Gain! Down on the gain!"

Vanessa scowled. "You people *have* done this before, have you not? I hope this won't take all day. I've an important meeting in two hours that I will not be late for."

Maya grinned mentally. *She's gonna storm out after two bad takes.*

"You look quite pretty today." Vanessa fussed with her hair while gazing into a hand mirror. "Make sure and put on a nice big smile. I don't foresee much reason to involve you with too many more media presentations. Marketing is already working on a new mascot, a cartoon character of some sort, I believe. One of those nauseatingly high-pitched ones with the big eyes. Japanese something-or-other. Much easier to manage an advertising face that can't think for itself or develop crises of conscience. For now, I still need you to help restore the Citizens' faith in Ascendant. Once they see how happy I am to have my beloved daughter back, things will return to normal."

Maya looked away and gagged.

Officer Davies scoffed.

Vanessa blinked as if slapped. After a momentary glare, she stepped up and got in the woman's face. "I'm sorry, did you say something? Are you forgetting your place, officer? Do you have some kind of problem here?"

Benson and the other two bodyguards drifted out of the kitchen, observing the exchange.

Despite the woman's apparent hostility, Maya felt sick having to watch an Authority officer kowtow to her ex-mother.

The officer bowed her helmet. Vanessa started to turn back to Maya with that smug smirk of sanctimonious victory, but the officer lunged forward and drove her fist into Vanessa's jaw. The tall, reedy woman slammed into the floor in the blink of an eye and slid halfway across the living room before taking out one of the poles holding up the green-screen background.

"You're damn right I have a problem," said a digitized, crackling woman's voice over tiny speakers. The blueberry took a step closer to Maya. She reached up and removed her helmet, letting long dreads bedecked with wooden beads unfurl down her back. "You took my daughter."

Genna's hard expression softened to concern.

Maya dropped the transparent tablet, staring open-mouthed. Her brain jammed, unable to believe what her eyes tried to tell it. Tightness gripped her middle. It took her four seconds to draw a breath.

"Oh, shit," whispered Sarah.

"Mommy!" screamed Maya. Her muscles refused to move. She clutched her hands at her chin, shaking from a tidal wave of emotion too titanic to fit into her small body. Unable to process anything, she burst into tears.

[25]

RIGHTFUL PLACE

The production crew all froze, their expressions a mixture of shock, horror, and awe. Amy screamed. Benson ran to the semiconscious Vanessa, while his two pals stared at Genna.

"That bitch ain't a real officer," said the bodyguard on the left.

Both men charged.

"Mommy!" Maya started to leap off the couch, but Amy grabbed her from behind and pulled her back. Her chest ached from sobbing so hard. The rapid torrent of emotion from the depths of fear and surrender to shock and elation had left her too weak and uncoordinated to wriggle free.

Genna rolled under the left man's incoming fist, trapping his arm into a jujitsu toss. She flung him to the rug and sprang upward out of the maneuver, driving her hand into the second man's throat. His feet shot out from under him, and he landed on his back. The first man got to his feet and grabbed for Genna. She spun with a rapid double-punch, one to the gut, the second to the base of the neck, leaving him gurgling and convulsing before grabbing his right arm and flipping him to the ground again. As soon as he landed on his chest, she twisted the limb up and braced the elbow against her knee.

Benson dove at her; Genna abandoned her intent to break the arm and dropped in place, rolling to the side as the big guy careened overhead and landed on the rug.

Four of the production crew sprinted to the kitchen while two ran for the front door. Vanessa hadn't moved since she'd slid to a stop. Maya reached one arm toward Genna but couldn't find the strength to put up a real effort to get away from the frantic, clinging Amy, who had dragged her around to put the couch between them and the brawl. As the reality of seeing her mother alive sank in deeper, her legs turned to jelly.

Genna traded punches with one of the men, showing little effect from his strikes, but knocking the wind out of him. Benson pushed himself up, growled, and jumped upright. Three men surrounded her, hands twitching like cowboys from a movie.

If not for Amy holding Maya up, she would've fallen to the floor. She kept reaching for Genna, wanting to touch her to make sure she really existed.

Sarah ran over and clung to her side, grinning.

"Ugh." Vanessa moaned. "What happened? Why am I on the floor?"

The bodyguards and Genna blurred into motion. She elbowed Benson in the gut with her right arm before spinning into a knife-hand strike to one of the smaller men's throats that pummeled him to the floor and left him gagging. The third man punched her in the back and grabbed her arm, but she reversed and dragged him around in front of her to absorb a roundhouse kick from Benson that knocked him senseless. She tossed the semiconscious man to the side.

Benson snarled and tried to knock her head off with his huge fist. Genna caught his arm, taking a single rearward step. Her eyes flared wide in shock at a woman pushing him back. His face reddened, veins rising in his forehead. "Y-you're just s-standing there?" He gurgled at the other blueberry, who looked bored. When the man didn't react, he glowered at Genna. "The fuck are you so strong for a bitch?"

"494th Night Terrors," said Genna in an eerie, calm tone. "Special Operations. I've had a little work done."

She switched from pushing to pulling, dragging a startled Benson into a chokehold that forced him to his knees. Bodyguard Two sat up; she kicked him in the face, knocking him flat. "You damn lucky I know your asses is hired help."

"Benson was kinda nice," blurted Maya. "Please don't kill him."

Genna grunted and squeezed until the tall man passed out.

"Holy shit," said Amy. "She just... she just beat up three men."

Maya pulled away from the shocked woman and ran to Genna. "Mom!"

"Baby girl." Genna scooped her up.

"Mom!" Another wave of joyful sobs came on, leaving her babbling and clinging. "You're not dead. I saw you get shot!"

Genna whispered, "Had a vest on. Knocked the shit outta me, but I'm okay."

Vanessa, dazed and flat on her back, shoved the green-screen post away and stared up at them. "That's not your mother." She shook her head before rolling around onto her knees and standing. "That woman abducted you for a ransom. You endeared yourself to her as a survival mechanism, but that's all. This is your home."

"At first." Maya pressed herself against Genna, shying away from the approaching Vanessa. "Since you weren't going to help me, I had to do something. But she wasn't like the others. She wouldn't let them hurt me. *You* told them to kill me and didn't even flinch. You'll just make another one, right? No mother would ever say that. You're *not* my mother!"

"What?" Vanessa blinked. "I thought you were smarter than that. This criminal couldn't possibly offer you even a quarter of the life you could lead here, the life you deserve. Y-you'd prefer to live in filth with those cockroaches than take your rightful place at the top of my society? I am bringing our country back into a new age of prosperity. A country you will eventually inherit. Do you honestly expect me to believe you don't want that?"

"Yes," said Maya.

The instantaneous response seemed to stun Vanessa silent. Two thin trails of blood leaked from her nose, dripping from her chin.

"This is my mother. She could've run for her life, but she got in front of a soldier with cyborg arms to protect me. When you took me far away and put me up in this tower, she could've given up, like I did, and walked away, but she came for me. My mother actually cares about me, not about how much I'm worth to the company."

Vanessa narrowed her eyes at the still-placid male officer. "You don't understand anything. You're a spoiled child who doesn't realize the full depth of the position she's in."

"No. I understand perfectly what position I'm in. I'm a prisoner. If I don't do what you want, you're going to hurt people I care about. As soon as I'm no longer useful, you'll probably kill me too."

Genna snarled at Vanessa.

"You are right about one thing. I don't understand how a mother could be like you." Maya glared. "Thirty-seven percent of my DNA might be from you, but you're not my mother. You didn't even want me around until I was old enough to walk. I saw those emails."

"This." Vanessa gestured at the TV and game system, then the rest of the penthouse. "You are serious? Here, you have everything. You want for nothing. You have comfort, security; you never have to wonder where your next meal is coming from."

Genna tried to set Maya down behind her, but she refused to let go.

"Security?" Maya blinked in disbelief. "Really? As soon as you get tired of having me around, we die. If I say the wrong thing, you hurt Sarah. If I try to escape, you said you'd kill the kids in our building. That's not security. And I don't have everything here. If you put a flower in the most expensive flowerpot in the world, give it the most expensive dirt in the world, and water it with the most expensive water in the world, it will still wither away without sunlight." She looked down.

A brief sign of impressed surprise flickered from under Genna's glower. She clenched her fist and leaned closer.

Vanessa took a step back, her expression more blank than Maya could ever remember seeing it. "All right then. Fine. If that's what you want. Take the ungrateful little thing and get out of my sight. Stupid child. Only a fool would walk away from what I can provide to go live in a rat's nest. Those snakes trying to wrest control of Ascendant away from me aren't going to stop until they kill you. If you'd rather take your chances out there without my protection, then go."

The blueberry's helmet turned toward Genna.

"Well. Go on, leave if it's what you want." Vanessa waved dismissively and started to walk toward the bathroom.

"You're forgetting something," said Genna.

Vanessa stopped and glanced back.

"She's scared," said Maya a hair over a whisper. "She's not giving up too easy. She knows you can kill her and doesn't want to die, but she can't admit it so she's gotta act like it's her idea." Her voice rose to normal volume. "I don't think I'm worth enough to waste money on revenge. She'd have had to have loved me once to hate me, but she only thought of me as a company asset. All she loves is power."

Vanessa narrowed her eyes.

"Ouch," said the blueberry.

"Why are you just standing there like a useless tit, watching this woman attempt to abduct my daughter?" snapped Vanessa. "I should have you dismissed. Dismissed and charged as an accessory."

"Sorry, ma'am. You're not my boss." A man's voice answered, clipped short by the static pop of helmet-mounted speakers. "You're a Citizen like anyone else." He tilted his head side to side, stretching his neck. "Not sure if you got the memo, but Ascendant doesn't own the Authority."

"So you think." Vanessa scowled.

"Nah." Genna shifted Maya to her left side and approached Vanessa. "That ain't it. Your forgettin' got nothin' ta do with this girl. You forgettin' that *shit* you set loose killed my son."

"Oh, crap," muttered Sarah.

Vanessa stiffened. "We have programs to provide low-cost options for minors."

"Yeah well. That must be new." Genna glanced down, rage clear in her expression and the subtle shaking of her body. "I did everything I could for him, and yo' goddamned Authority dragged us out inta the street. Asked me who they should kill first. Did I wanna watch him die, or did I wanna make him see me die. 'Less your 'low-cost option' is a motherfuckin' bullet, you full of shit."

Genna's fist flew like a lightning strike.

Vanessa spun from the hit, her chin leading the way around in a spiral dance. She pirouetted twice and fell into a stack of video recording equipment, taking it down as she crashed to the floor on her chest.

"That was for me," said Genna.

Maya gave her a quizzical look. "Wasn't that for—?"

Genna grasped the Authority assault rifle hanging across her chest. "*This* is for Sam."

"Whoa!" yelled the blueberry. He raced from his position by the sofa and grabbed Genna's arm, pushing her aim off Vanessa. "We came here to get your daughter back. Not assassinate anyone. And not in front of the kids. You think Maya wants to watch her die?"

Vanessa moaned and pushed herself up a little, rolling to sit.

"Killing her won't bring Sam back. I don't want to watch that. Please don't." Maya looked at Vanessa. They locked stares for a moment; the woman seemed surprised. "She may be heartless, but it feels wrong to kill her. I don't want her to die."

Genna shoved the blueberry off her arm, staring at him. "You know how long I spent dreamin' of finally gettin' this chance?" She raised her rifle at Vanessa.

"Mom. Please don't," said Maya, cringing away.

"Wait," yelled the blueberry.

A loud buzz came from the ceiling, followed by hissing as plumes of mist sprayed down in a grid pattern. In under a second, shin-deep fog covered the floor. The cloud rose at an alarming pace, the gaps between falling columns shrank, stealing visibility.

Amy ran for the front door but tripped over something, probably Benson.

"Try and kill me if you want, but you don't have much time. Small lungs won't handle this toxin for more than a few seconds," said Vanessa, sounding weary.

Growling obscenities, Genna scooped Maya up in her arms and whirled in place. "Sarah?"

"Here. I'm—" Sarah's voice cut off to choking.

Maya's eyes burned from caustic fumes that stole the breath from her throat. She put a hand over her mouth, coughing and gagging.

"I got her," yelled the blueberry.

"Now! Need that ride," shouted Genna before looking around and muttering, "Damn that bitch. Lost her."

"Forget her," said a male voice from something electronic near Maya's head. "Get the girls out of there."

Maya gagged on mucus, barely able to see anything but blur. Head spinning, she held on, choking and sputtering. Snot streamed from her nose, making it even harder to breathe.

A sudden gunshot made her jump. Genna leaned back and kicked at something. The crunch of boot on broken glass sounded over and over. Maya grabbed at her neck, fighting for air, half aware of a warm breeze washing over her. Her throat closed up, refusing to let her inhale.

Genna grunted. The pale blurry mass of fog-covered carpet shifted to a long, sparkly stretch of mirrored windows going downward. Weightlessness. Swinging.

"Hang on, baby girl," yelled Genna.

A rush of sound came on as if someone had turned the volume of the world back up. The roar of a mini-copter's rotors thundered overhead. What had been a gentle breeze grew to a punishing downblast. She rasped, gulping air, hoarse croaking noises vibrating in her head with each breath. Blurry vision came into focus; a long streamer of gooey snot trailed from her nose, falling away into the oblivion of an eighty-story drop.

Genna pulled her up and over the landing skid, pushing her onto the hard metal floor before crawling in behind her. Lying on her side, Maya convulsed, clutching her gut. Genna plucked her up and belted her into a padded seat. The blueberry appeared, rising into the open doorway on a winch line. Sarah clung to him, her hair a wild thrashing mass of red. Genna helped them in, easing Sarah's semiconscious body from his arms and laying her in the seat next to Maya. Snot bubbled at her nose. A few seconds later, she erupted in a coughing, gagging fit. Slime exuded from her face in a stream.

The blueberry scrambled in and pulled the side door shut with a loud *thump*. "Damn. That wasn't exactly clean but, we're out."

As soon as the door shut, the mini-copter tilted hard forward, accelerating.

Maya coughed and spat to the side, an endless flow of goo dangling from her nose. Her eyes and throat burned so bad she wanted to scream, but she had no air for it. Every time she tried to suck in a breath, she wound up choking on mucus.

Genna collapsed in the rear-facing seat to the right of the cockpit access. The blueberry took the other side and removed his helmet, revealing a thirty-something man with light brown brush cut and a big grin.

Barnes.

Maya reached for Genna; trapped by the seatbelt, she couldn't get up. "Mom!" Speaking offended her stomach. She bent forward and hurled all over the floor.

Within seconds, Sarah snapped out of her stupor and followed suit, spitting up bile and phlegm while wailing, "It burns!"

"I know it's been a couple years," shouted Pope from up front, "but I don't think my flying's that bad."

Maya held her head. Despite being woozy, sick to vomiting, and suffering a punishing headache, she shivered with joy.

[26]

FIGHT OR FLIGHT

Once the helicopter stopped climbing, Genna unbuckled herself. She perched half a butt cheek on the edge of Maya's seat and took her hand, patting her back while she coughed up the last of the bile and phlegm. Genna swiped a three-foot-long tendril of snot away from Maya's nose and tossed it to the floor.

Sarah moaned, "Make it thoph," a few times while hacking up trails of slime. Her nose looked like a raw egg-white dispenser stuck on full blast.

"What'd they hit you with?" yelled Pope over the engine.

"Smelled like CS. Feels like they mixed it with a knockout agent too. Bitch is a piece of work, but she ain't stupid 'nuff to use anything lethal inside her own house. Shit. Dammit. She faked me out." Genna's eyes had reddened from the pacification gas but grew darker still with fury.

Maya held up her bare feet. "It worked."

"What worked, baby?"

She laughed, despite crying. "You kidnapped me again."

Genna looked at Barnes.

"No idea." He shrugged.

Sarah grinned.

"Shit, hold on," said Pope.

"What?" Genna's smile died.

"Ascendant drones coming on fast. This Skysprite can't outrun them."

"I got it." Genna grabbed the Authority rifle. "Barnes, cover your side."

"Those R-11s won't work." Barnes nodded at her rifle. "Those drones have Gen-4 carbon fiber Kevlar weave. You'll burn a whole damn mag taking one out and there's at least six of them. Need a lot bigger than 4.7mm."

"I could always flip them off." Genna slid the right-side door open. Mirror-windowed skyscrapers hurtled by outside, the reflection of their little helicopter seeming to hang still against a shimmery chrome backdrop. "You got a better idea?"

"Yeah. I got an idea. Take the stick," yelled Pope.

She aimed her rifle out the door for an instant before growling and rushing to the cockpit. The copter bobbed and swerved. Seconds later, Pope crawled into the back with his sniper rifle.

Barnes' eyebrows went up. "Okay, that'll make a hole."

"Why are—?" Sarah screamed when machine gun fire erupted outside.

Gravity upended as the copter plummeted in a sudden, sharp dip. Maya gurgled, her headache throbbing. More gunfire went off behind them; orange streaks flashed in the air outside the door, gleaming on the silvery windows.

Pope sat on the floor, one boot braced against the doorframe. He perched his rifle in the crook of his left arm and put his eye to the scope before yelling, "Ready."

The copter rotated a quarter turn to the right, angling his door to the rear as it glided sideways between two rows of skyscrapers. Maya's jaw dropped open at the cloud of three-fanned Ascendant drones chasing them.

Crack.

Pope's body jerked back as a long shell casing came flying out of his rifle and clattered to the floor.

One of the drones twisted side to side before it fell into an ass-over-nose tumble toward the road.

Crack.

Another drone went into freefall.

Barnes aimed out the door as well.

Maya clamped her hands over her ears, as did Sarah.

The assault rifle chattered, rapid fire from the much smaller caseless bullets more like a growling bear than a gun going off. Sparks danced around the drones. One developed a smoke trail but kept flying. Tracer streams flew past the helicopter from multiple .50 cal machine guns. Genna evaded with a sudden two-story drop. Gravity seemed to cease existing for an instant. Most of the incoming fire went high, but a *clank* or two came from overhead and something started buzzing a warning tone in front. Maya grunted as a stiff climb crushed her into the seat. Another barrage of fire went below them.

"Shit!" shouted Genna. "Hang on."

The helicopter rotated to face forward. One more *crack* from Pope's rifle triggered a distant *boom* and a flash of bright white.

"Hah," yelled Pope. "Hit the battery. Those *Gungsu* drones used to go off like a fireworks display if you hit 'em in the right spot."

Barnes laughed. "Yeah, but those fuckers usually didn't swoop in low enough to shoot."

"Not with a tiny little rifle like that." Pope winked at him.

Genna pitched the copter into a hard left dive, skimming down an alley so narrow Maya screamed, expecting the rotors to clip the walls. The high-pitched whirr of drone fans rose to a peak and fell off as their pursuers failed to negotiate the turn. Seconds later, the buildings vanished, revealing an endless wasteland of broken houses, old suburbs reclaimed by nature.

Another barrage of gunfire went off outside.

An explosion of white fluff flew from the seatback between Maya and Sarah, and angry buzzing/beeping erupted in the cockpit. Sarah screamed and lapsed into coughing again. Scared mute and rigid, Maya stared at the hole behind the padded seatback, where a .50 cal round had warped the metal forward. She turned her head to the right and blinked at the sparking, smoking hole in the console up front.

Genna pivoted the copter sideways again. Pope fired twice in two seconds, and Barnes offloaded another long burst. The middle drone dropped like a rock, and the one on the right side of the formation entered a wild corkscrew spin, careening into the ground like a missile five seconds later. The last drone kept flying but glided in a pin-straight line, no longer following them.

"Nice shot," said Pope, eyeing the spinner.

"Thanks. Fans don't have much armor." Barnes winked. "Looks like you blew out the antenna on the last one."

"Yeah." Pope sighted on it. "No sense leavin' a job half finished."

Crack.

A distant *plink* echoed back.

The final drone burst into a smoking, sparking mass, and tumbled out of the sky.

"Hey Gen, we're kinda low," yelled Pope.

"I know," shouted Genna. "That's because we're crashing."

"Oh." Pope sprang from his firing position to a seat and strapped in.

Maya screamed and shut her eyes.

Sarah fumbled to grab her hand.

A few long seconds later, hard deceleration pulled Maya forward. Only the seatbelt across her hips kept her from flying into Pope. The engine shuddered, shaking everything with such fury it seemed the little craft would break apart. Metal ground against metal overhead along with the whining, labored protests of the engine. Snaps and clanks came from everywhere. Broken branches and leaves flew in the open door.

The small helicopter jammed to a hard stop and dropped a few feet to the earth with a splintery *crunch*. Maya flew forward as the crash tried to catapult her out of her seat, but the seatbelt caught her. Rebound whacked her head into the padded seat hard enough to leave her seeing stars. On top of the headache from the gas, the impact made her heave a few times, but she had nothing in her belly to throw up. She floated through a few seconds of pain and nausea before she regained the ability to see more than a blur.

Engine noise cut out to the faint growling of gears overhead, which quieted after a moment. Only the buzzing and bleeping alarms from the cockpit broke the stillness. A wall of leafy green blocked the right side door. Maya peered past Sarah out the left window, down a street full of debris and broken telephone poles, lined on both sides with battered houses.

"Not bad," said Pope.

"Ehh. Could've been smoother." Genna grunted. "Had a choice between house or tree."

"Always choose the tree," said Pope.

"Yeah." Genna chuckled. "Tree kinda objected though. Got a knife on you?"

Pope moved to the cockpit. Maya stared at a crumbling house overgrown with bushes and ivy, wondering what it must've been like to live in this place before war ruined the whole world. A handful of decades-old cars sat on either side of a street crisscrossed with mossy cracks.

"Aww, shit," Pope grumbled.

"It looks worse than it is. Armor took most of it. Hope they don't keep the rental deposit on this bird." Genna chuckled.

Maya pulled open her seatbelt, leapt over the slick of vomit, and scrambled to the cockpit, where Pope sawed at a broken tree branch that had pierced the front canopy and impaled Genna's left shoulder. A larger branch speared the wall next to her head hard enough to dent the metal. The nose of the copter rested against the trunk. Cracks spiderwebbed the canopy, but the reinforced plastic hadn't disintegrated.

"Least I took care of camo-ing the heli." Genna gritted her teeth as Pope snapped the wood and pulled it loose. An inch or so at the tip had turned red.

"I hate splinters," said Pope, tossing it.

"Heh." Genna pulled herself out of the pilot's chair and plucked Maya off her feet, carrying her to the side door. After a quick look around, she jumped down to the road. "You okay, baby?"

"Yeah." Having Genna back overwhelmed her all over again, and she clung, unable to do much but cry happy tears.

Barnes carried Sarah from the copter and set her on her feet outside. "They're probably not going to be happy about us losing the heli."

"It ain't totaled," said Genna. "They can fix it."

Pope took a knee by Sarah, giving her a once-over. "You awright?"

"Little sick. It hurts to breathe." She patted herself on the chest. "My lungs are on fire."

"Me too," muttered Maya.

"Take big, slow, deep breaths," said Pope. "Let clean air in and bad air out."

Maya spent a moment breathing as instructed, looking around at what had to be Dead Space. At least the cannibals, dosers, or whoever else lived out here wouldn't be so scary with three adults watching over her. Especially three adults with big guns. She frowned at her shiny, purple dress. "I should take this off. It stands out too much here, and I can't run in it."

"Naw, don't you worry, baby. We got you covered." Genna patted her back.

Barnes took point, heading south. Pope picked Sarah up and carried her, walking alongside Genna.

For a while, Maya held on. A mixture of adrenaline from the helicopter chase and joy at having her mother back kept her shivering. Long-abandoned houses, all overgrown, surrounded them. Bushes and tall grass had taken over once-nice lawns. Every so often, a rusting swing set or a collapsed deck hinted at the world as it had been before the war. More often, charred barrels, tents, and barricades made of old cars reminded her of the world as it had become.

In the distance, a pale boy of about eleven climbed up to stand on a fallen chunk of concrete wall, watching them. Shaggy brown hair hung halfway down his chest, his only clothing a scrap of bath towel serving as a loincloth. Behind him, a man in a skirt made of hubcaps, license plates, and tattered denim leaned on a spear. They seemed more curious than hostile, no doubt attracted by the crash. A hint of burned rubber and wood smoke tinged with charred meat wafted by on the wind.

"Was that really you?" Maya lifted her head from Genna's shoulder to look at Pope. "Right before the drones got us, I thought I saw you."

"You did," Pope mumbled. "Didn't want to risk a pissing contest with the Authority in the middle of the Sanc. Especially with machine guns floating over you two."

"How'd you find us?" Maya blinked.

Pope grinned and patted Sarah on the backside. "Her butt did most of the work."

Sarah's head popped up, eyebrows furrowed. "What?"

Maya gasped. *She's got a chip!*

"Vet's kid. You got a locator chip." Pope chuckled. "Didn't take but about ten minutes for that Zeroice guy to get into the system and give us a fix on where you were."

Sarah stuck a hand inside her skirt and grabbed her rear end, looking confused. "Why's it in my butt and not my hand? Don't they put chips in the back of your hand so you can like wave them at stuff to pay or open doors?"'

Pope cringed. "Umm. Well, you got it as a toddler most likely. Small hands and—"

"So no one cuts your hand off and uses it to fake being a Citizen," said Maya.

Sarah let out an "Eep" and shivered.

Maya giggled. "Guess you gotta wave your butt to buy stuff."

The joke made Sarah crack a tiny smile, though she remained mostly terrified.

"Lost you for a day or so there," said Genna. "You had me so scared. Don' mean that as you did nothin' wrong."

"We were underground. A cistern," said Maya, shaking. "Full of rats!" She thought back to the room of mattresses. "And that place was jamming... The roach bite!"

"Oh!" Sarah looked at Pope. "Does the chip get hot? I think I felt it a couple times."

"The jammer," muttered Maya. "That probably made it overheat."

"Zero made it vibrate in case you knew you had it, trying to send you a message we were coming."

"I didn't know I had it." Sarah sighed. "How'd you get blueberry armor?"

Barnes looked back over his shoulder. "We have some people inside. There's a lot o' ex-military in the Authority. Those friendships don't die."

"Oh. I thought they were changing. They seemed nicer." Maya wiped her nose, still running from the stuff Vanessa hit them with. "They were friendly to us. Even gave Sarah clothes."

Genna squeezed her tight. "Maybe some of 'em are, but a lot still look down on Nons. Can't say it wasn't worse before the investigation. The ones inside the Sanc are usually more laid back on account o' their havin' better surroundings and more fluff shit to deal with."

"Like being called on poor people for de-beautifying the park," muttered Pope.

Sarah spat to the side. "Bitch."

"That was awesome when you got her!" said Maya, miming raking her hands down the woman's shirt. "The look on her face was perfect."

Sarah giggled.

"Ones who always go out to the Hab are the pricks." Genna kicked a rock, sending it into the window of a decrepit house.

Maya peered over Genna's shoulder, back at the distant glow of the Dublin Protected District. Vanessa had looked dumbfounded at Maya's choice. Sure, she'd miss her modern games and the huge TV—the only real loss. Playing *Ultimaglide* with Sarah had been fun, the most fun she'd ever had in that world, but she'd trade a million sweet video game systems to have her mother back, let alone have a mother at all. And the comfortable apartment was in no way worth the constant worry Sarah would be hurt or killed for a screw up.

Worry followed close behind. Maya watched the shadows in every space between buildings or every missing car door. A pack of cats nesting on the front seat of a rusted-out pickup truck stared at them.

Vanessa had looked surprised when Maya asked Genna not to kill her. The woman didn't have to know the primary reason for her request—she didn't want Genna to go to jail for murder. Though a small part of her, perhaps that thirty-seven percent DNA, couldn't quite summon the desire to see Vanessa Oman shot in front of her, even after she'd basically admitted to killing The Dad, or at the memory of little Ashley who'd almost died to Fade. That girl's mother *had* died to it, as had countless others, especially Genna's son. Lives cut short or ruined forever by greed. And, well, Vanessa had been right about one thing. Maya *did* have an overdeveloped sense of compassion. She didn't really want *anyone* to die.

Killing her is too fast. Her ego wouldn't last long in jail.

A few hours later, with the late afternoon sun blending into the western horizon, the main part of the Baltimore Sanctuary Zone finally came into view up ahead. The huge white wall glowed in the radiance of a hundred lights, all scanning the ground for vandals, terrorists, or miscreants. Drones glided back and forth in a constant barrage of noise, spotlights, and machine guns.

Maya tensed.

"It's all right, baby." Genna hefted her to sit a little higher on her hip. "Authority ain't gonna give us a problem."

"Okay." She eyed the men and women staffing the checkpoint by the gate.

Barnes jogged ahead of the group, hand raised in greeting. He chatted with some of the blueberries for a little while before gesturing for everyone to follow. Genna offered quick nods of acknowledgement to the officers as she hurried by. One of them muttered to Barnes about wishing he could've seen the look on Vanessa's face when Genna'd slugged her. A female officer doubted anyone had the nerve to hit that woman.

Mom almost shot *her.* Maya rested her head on Genna's shoulder, hoping the obvious display of affection would help convince the blueberries to let them pass without a problem. Barnes lingered in conversation with the gate staff, jogging to catch up soon after. Pope led the way as they walked into the Sanc. People kept their distance, likely due to the borrowed Authority armor. Feeling safe in her mother's arms, Maya's sense of safety increased; she passed out from the aftershock of adrenaline.

MAYA AWOKE WHEN GENNA EASED HER ONTO THE MIDDLE SEAT OF an e-van. She yawned and pulled herself in. Sarah climbed up and plopped down beside her. Genna removed the armor chest piece, wincing as the shoulder plate peeled away from the wound she'd suffered at the crash landing. Her white tank top had turned dark red all along the left side to her belt. The peeling scab reopened, sending a rivulet of blood down her arm.

Pope took a first-aid kit out from under the driver's seat, from which he removed a roll of gauze, some wipes, and tweezers. Genna sat on the running board while he cleaned a few stray splinters, dabbed at the spot with alcohol pads, and bandaged it.

"Shit, that burned," said Genna in a deadpan voice. "That should hold me 'til Doc can look at it."

"You're pretty when you're bleeding." Pope grinned.

"Oh, something I should know?" asked Barnes, grinning.

"Shut up and take my armor." Genna smiled and threw the Authority belt to Barnes, who caught it, laughing. "Jackass."

Genna removed the leg plates and stuffed the armor piece by piece into a black duffel before unloading the compact rifle and adding it to the bag, which she handed to Barnes.

"Be careful," said Barnes.

"You know me." Genna winked.

He held up the duffel as if offering a toast. "That's why I said be careful."

She grabbed the bag as he started to walk off, pulling him back a step. "Barnes. Thanks."

"I like the kid too." He winked. "See you soon. How long you think it'll take?"

"Depends on what Zeroice finds."

Barnes walked away backward. "Right. Let us know." He spun on his heel and hurried off.

Genna climbed in to sit with the girls while Pope took the driver's seat.

"Why did the Authority let you carry guns into the Sanc?" Maya leaned against her.

Pope pulled out into traffic, driving in no great hurry.

"Veterans, right?" asked Sarah.

"Well, there's some inside the Authority who think like you do. That Vanessa oughta be kicked down off that high perch of hers," said Pope.

Genna closed her eyes, mumbling.

Too tired to want to talk about what her mother may or may not want to do to Vanessa, Maya contented herself to lean against her, thrilled beyond measure to have her back. A minute into the ride, noticing Sarah sat conspicuously apart, she reached over, grabbed a fistful of pink angora sweater, and pulled her close.

Sarah raised a fearful glance up at Genna.

"We heard, baby. I'm sorry." She grunted, raising her left arm around both girls. "I thought it was safe. Two weeks an' no sign of anything. What happened to your father's on me as much as it on the fu—bastards who shot him. We ain't gonna leave you out on no street."

Sarah bowed her head against Maya and blubbed "Thank you" before lapsing into a few minutes' worth of crying. After, she sniffled and wiped her face. "You didn't know. And Vanessa killed him. She basically said she did, while he was in the hospital."

Genna's expression turned somber. Eyes downcast, she spoke in such a quiet tone, Maya had to strain to hear her over the electric motors. "After we lost the tracking signal, we figured you might try to go to the VA, so we went there. Jack told the desk nurse they were buddies from the war, but they said he'd passed earlier that morning. The doctors seemed bewildered. One told us they thought they'd gotten him stabilized; the cancer had reduced. They expected it to be gone in a month. Somehow, it exploded overnight and got into his brain. By the time they noticed, they couldn't do anything."

"Vanessa killed him." Sarah sniffled. "She did that to him somehow."

"Sorry." Maya covered her face with her hands, holding back tears of guilt.

"Don't cry. It's not your fault." Sarah nudged her in the side. "I'm really happy you're not an orphan anymore."

Maya lifted her head with a mournful stare. Sarah hadn't meant to make her guilt heavier, but she had.

"Neither are you." Genna grimaced as she gave them both a squeeze.

Sarah's expression couldn't seem to make up its mind between smiling or crying.

"Careful with your arm." Maya squirmed around to look at the bandage. A dot of blood marred the surface of the gauze.

"Quick stop." Pope slowed and pulled over.

Genna opened the sliding door, revealing a sidewalk packed with people in drab clothes, most of them grey ponchos and air-filter masks. One man with a lime green sphere of afro and silver wing-shaped sunglasses waved small tins at passersby trying to sell 'clean rations' to the Nons who'd come into the Sanc to work for the day. Beyond the steady shuffle of bodies sat a storefront with mannequins in the windows. On the left, a male figure wore a plain blue-grey shirt and white pants. On the right, a female had a pale green blouse, teal microskirt, and black leggings.

Eager to escape her gaudy dress, Maya scooted across the seat to the edge and jumped to the sidewalk. Sarah climbed out and pulled the door closed as Pope came around the front end. They weaved past the pedestrians to the store, triggering a series of soft electronic chimes when they entered. Clothing on shelves and racks appeared clean, but the air tasted of dust and caramel.

A heavyset elderly woman with an enormous vape inhaler emerged from a curtain at the back. Head stooped, face hidden behind a curtain of whitish-grey hair, she shuffled closer, flanked by a pair of twin teenage girls in identical plum dresses. The girls moved with an eerie similarity that made Maya wonder if they might be androids. Though, aside from anti-kidnap decoys or wartime bombs, she didn't think any companies manufactured child robots. Since they appeared about fifteen, she figured them for real people, albeit strange.

The old one raised her head, revealing her face. The woman's right eye appeared three inches wide, ringed with metal. Maya clamped her hands over her mouth to keep from making a rude noise. Tiny blinking green lights around the eye revealed a thick electronic monocle, a cybernetic graft, which whirred to focus.

"Hello," said the elder. "Can we help you?"

"Hi," chimed the twins in unison. They smiled the same smile, and leaned the same way to the left while waving.

"I'm May," said the one on the right.

"June," said the other.

Pope and Genna exchanged a glance.

The girls approached Maya, circling and studying her dress.

"It's so pretty," said May. "Is that a Valisa?"

Maya offered a weak shrug. "I think so."

"Looks like a Dori Kavan to me," said the old woman.

June brushed her fingers over Maya's side, testing the material. "Ooh, I think you're right, grandma."

"You're adorable, but your makeup has run all over." May grabbed a swatch of scrap fabric from the sales counter and dabbed at Maya's face.

"Hi." Genna nodded at the elder. "Need some everyday clothes for the girls. Do you have shoes their size too? Preferably sneakers or boots, something that won't fall apart."

"Of course." The old one gestured at the back left corner of the store. Her monocle whirred again, making that eye shrink. "Do you mind if I ask why you're bringing a girl with such an expensive garment here to purchase ordinary things?"

"Grandma," whispered June. "That's *her*."

"Eh?" asked the old one, twisting to peer at May.

May pointed at June.

The old one pivoted. "Eh?"

"The girl from the video," said June. "That's Maya. She's awakened the people."

"Oh!" The elder clapped. "Forgive my eyesight. This way, please."

Over the next half hour, the twins helped Maya and Sarah try on a few things. The elder's monocle evidently allowed her to 'measure' customers' sizes at a momentary glance. She must've had another implant with an inventory database, as she recited numbers without delay that guided her granddaughters to various items, which they retrieved from shelves to show.

Genna bought them both dark fatigue-style pants similar to the ones left behind at the penthouse, as well as a pair of jeans apiece. Sarah kept examining dresses, but life out in the Hab didn't lend itself to such garments. They got sneakers, as well as black rubber/nylon sandals the old one threw in for free since she'd been unable to sell them. At Maya's suggestion of a nightdress or pajamas, Genna tossed in a couple of mens' T-shirts. The store had some nighties, but they appeared to be actual silk and one cost more than the rest of the stuff combined. Maya leapt into the black fatigue pants and a dark blue T-shirt, the only one in the entire store she didn't swim in. May lifted her up to stand on a cube-shaped table, and did a quick hem on the pant legs while June did the same for Sarah.

All told, everything came out to $305. Genna counted out 79 NuCoin and $1.

"Can we trade the dress?" asked Maya, holding up the metallic purple silk.

Genna looked at the old woman. Sarah bundled up her pink angora sweater and white skirt and stuffed them in the bag.

"It's a lovely piece," said the elder, "but there's maybe twenty people in this part of the world who could afford it, and I don't think they have a daughter the right age. It would never sell. Garments like that are always custom ordered. I really never did understand why anyone would buy such expensive clothes their child would only be able to wear a few times before outgrowing."

"Okay." Disappointed, Maya bundled it to keep.

Clutching her bag of clothes, Sarah looked up at Genna and Pope with teary-eyed gratitude.

The old one collected the money and her gargantuan eye winked at Maya. "Keep up the good fight, child. Don't let them win."

May and June stood close by, hands folded in front of them. "Fade took away our parents."

Genna bowed her head.

Maya put an arm around her mother. "I'm going to do everything I can, but I can't do it alone. It's people like you who'll make the Authority remember what they promised to do. I won't give up."

"'Mon," muttered Pope, tugging on Genna. "Need to get that arm looked at."

The elder nodded, smiling, and took a long pull from her vaporizer, exhaling caramel apple fog. Maya held her breath, wary of winding up addicted to nicotine, and waved farewell. Pope led them out to the van. The girls climbed in back, though Genna sat in the passenger seat this time.

Sarah rubbed her hands up and down her legs, grinning. "These are the exact same style as the ones the dosers stole, only black instead of camo. Thank you! It's like I got my pants back."

"You're welcome," said Genna, grinning.

"Have the location?" asked Pope.

"Yeah." Genna pointed left. "Take that corner, go six blocks down, and hang another left."

"Where are we going?" asked Maya. "Not home?"

Genna leaned around between the front seats and smiled at her. "Soon. We ain't quite done here yet."

FADING HOPE

Maya gazed out the window at shops, people, steam-shrouded noodle stands, and a slow-drifting Authority drone hanging around the second-story level. A softball-sized orb at the nose end panned back and forth, glint flashing off the lens on the front.

They're always watching everyone.

She looked down. Even if the Brigade could dethrone Vanessa, the Authority would remain. Someone would eventually fill in the void. Pope mentioned the Eastern Seaboard Commonwealth still had a president or 'provisional governor,' and some kind of government. But if so, how did Vanessa get so much power over Baltimore?

It couldn't all be Xenodril. Ascendant manufactured at least thirty other critical medical products no other company made. That didn't matter *too* much, as the war had essentially destroyed international trade. People had access to only things made nearby. Of course, much of their money came from cosmetic drugs.

Ascendant had established its importance in reviving a civilization that didn't need to pick through rubble to survive. But Xenodril had been their ticket to prestige. In the waning days of the last war, they had developed it—or so they claimed—and gave it away to anyone who needed it. Maya hadn't been born yet, but the AuthNet archives were full of stories about how the company 'saved the free world' from the unknown threat. Fade had affected every nation involved in the Final War. Ascendant had even sent Xenodril to Korea and China, despite all sides believing the disease had originated from the enemy. The company had done nothing to settle rumors of hostile aliens or an asteroid mining accident releasing deadly bacteria from another world.

A scowl warped her reflection in the window. *Ascendant invented Fade. They had to. No other company had even been close to trial drugs. They couldn't have made Xenodril unless they knew exactly how Fade worked.* She fumed. Of course, at that point in the war, the number of intact pharma companies could've been counted on one hand. Ascendant winning the development race might have been due to their being best funded and best equipped, but it made so much more sense that they were able to invent Xenodril so fast because they'd come up with Fade in the first place. Probably at the request of the government for a weapon.

But why do that and then give the cure to *both* enemies?

They didn't have time for field trials. They couldn't test Fade before they used it, and it got away from them. Too contagious. It hit everyone so fast no one knew which side set it loose. Ascendant thought it would kill everyone. They gave away the cure for PR and came up with the alien crap to keep people from finding out where it really came from.

"Maya?" asked Sarah. "Are you okay? You look like you want to kill someone."

She relaxed with a sigh and explained her theory about Fade while Pope drove them into an underground parking area below a dingy apartment building on the high end of low.

"Never thought about that before, but I can see it happening. That shit came out of nowhere," said Pope. "I mean, my unit was ready for NBC, and we were small enough to avoid the worst of it, but we saw some awful things before the Xeno showed up."

Genna grumbled. "When they started sendin' out the vac shots and the Xeno to us, no one was fightin' for a country anymore. Wasn't enough of one left. We all just tried to survive. Even the Koreans. Sometimes we'd trade ammo, but we had these former officers get the emperor complex and make little kingdoms. Koreans would be at war with other Koreans. Our guys sparred with our guys over territory. Ascendant probably gave away the Xeno as a middle finger to the government for not paying them. Or maybe they figured out they'd killed everyone."

Pope pulled into a parking space by a thick square column. A fist-sized gouge in the concrete under '04' in flaking blue paint still held the bullet that had made it. The console shut down, darkening the van.

"Are we going to live here now?" asked Sarah, her voice small.

"No." Pope opened his door. "Just meeting some people. Maybe stay here a night or two depending on how it goes."

"'Kay."

Maya pulled the side door open and jumped down, reaching back in for her bag of clothes.

"You can leave them in the van. We won't be here that long." Genna patted her on the head.

Sarah climbed out.

"Okay." Maya pushed the door shut.

She followed behind Genna and Pope, with Sarah at her side, across the parking area. Sarah glided off to the left to avoid walking in a shallow black puddle. When she rounded the other side and got close again, Maya laughed.

"What?" Sarah gave her a look.

"You have shoes on now and you walked around the puddle. If you didn't, you'd have gone through it."

"I don't wanna get them dirty. I *just* got them." She poked Maya in the side. "They feel *so* weird."

Maya faked exasperation. "That's the entire point of shoes, so you don't have to worry about stepping on bad stuff."

A dark-skinned man in a grey jumpsuit dragged a wheeled dumpster out of a cinder-block-walled corridor and passed between them and the elevator. He offered a brief smile before continuing left to the ramp. Pope returned a quick wave. The elevator opened as soon as he touched the call button. After everyone got in, Genna selected the thirty-first floor. Soon, the doors opened again to reveal a corridor with pale blue-green carpet and neat but plain walls. A few spots of plaster patch peeked out from behind small art prints hung at strange heights, halfway down the wall or even close to the floor. An aroma similar to bread left a little too long in the oven lingered in the air. Tall, rectangular silver panels lined both sides, metal doors without knobs. Each had a small control panel in the wall to the right with a few buttons and a tiny screen.

"Zero's picked a five-star place." Pope swiped his finger at a low-hanging picture as he passed.

"Beats his old haunt," said Genna. "I need a disinfectant wipe just from thinking about it."

"Five-star apartments are overrated," muttered Maya.

Pope stopped a few doors past the middle of the hall and knocked. A moment later, a tiny light winked on at eye level. It went out, and the door slid sideways into the wall with a soft scrape, revealing Zeroice, his neon-blue hair hanging loose around his bare chest. A tattoo on his left pectoral depicted a stick-figure man at a desk with a wire going into the side of his head, a skull surrounded by a jagged star. Cartoon electrification.

"Hey. 'Mon in." Blue silk pajama pants swooshed with each step he took back into the apartment.

"At least you're wearing pants this time," said Genna.

"I was wearing pants last time too."

The door closed behind them.

"You were?" Genna put her right hand on her hip, leaving her left arm hanging. "Where's Doc?"

"So? They were short." Zeroice flopped at his desk and swung his chair around to face the room. "He's on the way. Authority detained him near the gate."

Maya glanced at a queen-sized bed covered in boxes of electronics, bundles of wire, and men's clothes.

"Shit, what now?" asked Genna.

"Nothing like that. Sounded like a bunch of people got fucked up by a drone crash and he scanned as a doctor."

"Oops," said Pope.

"Nah." Zeroice laughed, pulling his hair out of his face and tucking it behind his shoulders. "South end. Not your fireworks show in Dublin. He oughta be here soon."

Sarah nudged Maya and flared her eyebrows.

"I dunno," muttered Maya on the way to the sofa where she took a seat. When Sarah hopped up next to her, she shrugged. "Guess we just sit and wait."

"So where do we stand?" asked Pope. "Any luck?"

"Well, you know the routine. Good news and bad. I worked out a way into the Ascendant network. There's a decent chance it'll give me access to the data we need, but"—he looked at Genna—"you aren't going to like it. Not even a little bit."

"I already don't like the sound of that." She tried to fold her arms but cringed and decided against it.

Zeroice held his hands up, shrugging with a cheesy smile. "Ascendant has a dark fiber line that connects their two main buildings in the Sanc, plus runs out to a facility they have in Aberdeen. That fiber isn't accessible to any outside networks. It's their internal private system. There's no physical route between it and the AuthNet, so the only way onto that segment is to either get into their building or tap the fiber line."

"Okay. What about that is supposed to piss me off?" Genna raised an eyebrow.

"Unless your Brigade friends have access to heavy digging equipment, or you feel like getting into a firefight, there's only one spot with feasible access to the line."

Maya sat up tall. "He wants me to do something."

Genna spun around to look at her. "What?"

"Why else wouldn't you like it?" Maya thought of the old woman from the clothing shop, her granddaughters orphaned by Fade. "What do I have to do?"

Two rapid knocks came from the door.

"I got it." Pope pulled a knife and crossed the room.

"Well." Zeroice sighed and gave Genna a 'please don't hit me' smile. "The fiber line runs underground. I found a spot where it shares an AuthNet backbone conduit located in a pipe tended only by bots. There's a repeater unit there we can use, so we wouldn't even need to tap the fiber."

"House call." Doc Chang strolled in carrying a metal case. "Took one to the arm? Didn't I tell you to rest after that broken rib?"

Genna sat on the foot of the bed, glaring at Zeroice. "Just a little splinter in my shoulder. Damn tree got in the way of our helicopter."

"Pipe's too small for an adult, right?" asked Maya.

Zeroice nodded. "Yeah. That's why it's only bots. Used to be a water line, but they repurposed it during the rebuild. A nice clear shot across the Sanc with two-inch thick steel walls. You're so damn small, you could get in there and add a couple components to the box, give me a wide open door."

Maya nodded. "Okay."

"There's got to be something else." Genna grunted as Doc unwound the bandage. "We just got her back. I ain't riskin' her. We need another plan."

"I can do it," said Maya.

Zeroice tapped his finger to his lips in thought. "Well, I figured you'd say that so I have an alternate."

"Good." Genna's eyes flared wide; she grabbed the mattress and squeezed. "Shit. Doc."

"Sorry." He held up the conical wad of gauze on tweezers that Pope had packed into the wound. Blood running down her arm stopped on the pad he held against her skin to catch it. "Can't leave this in there."

"Alternate plan: A team infiltrates the basement level of Ascendant Tower, sneaks past an initial security checkpoint and overrides the elevator to the sixth floor. There's a forty-five-meter-long corridor with motion tracking sentry guns that leads to another security checkpoint with four to six guards. From there, an access controlled door leads to the primary network center. If you go in hard, you'd have two-ish minutes to find the right component cabinet, install the tap, and get out before the place is covered in blueberry syrup."

Genna's glare hardened. "That ain't no alternate plan, that a bunch of horseshit to justify makin' a little girl do somethin' stupid."

"How dangerous is it?" asked Maya.

"No," said Genna.

Maya slid from the couch and walked over, standing halfway between Zeroice and Genna. "If they didn't think anyone could fit down there, they wouldn't put anything in it that could hurt me."

"He said robots." Genna winced as Doc cleaned the wound. Sweat covered her face and forehead in beads.

Zeroice drummed his fingers on his knees. "They're designed to scan the cable for damage and deal with rats. There's three possible dangers to the kid going down the passage. One, she gets physically stuck. Two, a robot senses her and sets off an alarm. Three, someone notices you"—he nodded at Genna—"loitering around the opening, and calls the Authority."

"Just don't look poor," muttered Sarah.

"There's—ahh shit!" Genna clamped her jaw shut, shaking as Doc injected a silvery-white substance into the hole in her shoulder. She shuddered, fighting past the pain to gasp, "No countermeasures down there?"

"Nothing that should be deadly to a person, even one her size." Zeroice leaned back in his chair, steepled fingertips together at his chin like a mad scientist. "They didn't install many defenses because they didn't think anyone would ever get down there." Zeroice held up a plastic box with a circuit board and dangling wires about the size of a pack of cards. "Anyone small enough to get in there would be more likely to chew on this than know what to do with it."

"Can't you hack one of those bots to do what you need?" asked Pope.

"The pipe is too deep and thick for wireless. I can't get to the bots. I'd have to hack into the primary AuthNet Admin channel to access the control routines for the whole Sanc, and that's a whole lot harder for something basically a child can do."

"If wireless signals don't work down there, how are you going to get in with that box?" asked Maya.

"Alternate cable run. On your way out, you'll unspool a wire to a transmitter Genna sets up by the pipe opening. It won't matter if anyone finds it in an hour. Not like we're trying to leave a permanent stealth access point. We only need that one bit of data."

"I'll go." Maya took a step toward Zeroice. "What do I have to do?"

Genna stifled a growl at whatever Doc did to her arm. "Baby...."

"Are you sure?" asked Sarah, walking up behind her. "There might be rats in there. I could go."

Zeroice looked at the girls. "Uhh. I don't think you'd fit. It's going to be a little tight for her, and there's nothin' to her."

Sarah lifted her shirt to show off her stomach and ribs. "I'm skinny, too."

Pope patted Maya on the shoulder. "She's got some experience crawling through pipes. I can rig a harness to pull her back if she gets wedged. What's the distance from entry point to objective?"

"Motherf–" Genna looked down. "If something happens to her...."

"I'm moving to Panama before you find me." Zeroice chuckled. "About fifty meters. The entry point is a maintenance hatch for manual insertion of robots. It probably hasn't been opened in years."

Pope nodded. "Doable."

"The hell," muttered Genna. "Are you sure?"

"All set." Doc patted the replaced bandage. "The gel will evolve into replacement tissue in about eight hours. The more you use the arm, the longer it takes."

"I'm ready," said Maya.

"Doc, can you check the girls? We got hit with CS. Probably some custom cocktail. I think it had a sedative in it."

He nodded and headed over to Sarah.

"Cool." Zeroice stood and gathered some supplies. "Got two BMA uniforms so you can act like workers." He held up a blue jumpsuit with 'Baltimore Municipal Authority' stenciled across the back. "Should keep most people from buggin' you while you're waiting by the opening." He tapped a lunchbox-sized device. "This is the transmitter you'll hook the line up to once it's active. As long as it's outside the pipe, it should be good." He handed the smaller device to Maya. "This is the trickiest part."

She looked at it. A shroud of off-white plastic wrapped around the electronics, covering it except for the underside of the circuit board and a flange along the narrow end with hundreds of contacts, like a cartridge to be plugged in. Three wires dangled from the opposite end, one with a Cat-5 socket, one with a fiber connector, and one with a five-pin metal prong.

"C'mere." Zeroice slid his chair to the side so she could get closer to his monitor. He pointed at a diagram of a box. When he tapped a key, the front face animated opening. "You'll pull the shroud up like this to get at the insides."

"Okay. Is that the tricky part?"

"Wiseass." He smiled and pointed at a row of four rectangular sockets along the left side under the hatch. "Plug it in the third one down from the top, with the circuit side facing to the right and the wires toward you."

"I can still smell it in her hair, and her eyes are red." Doc patted Sarah on the shoulder. "She should hop in a shower. Keep the water cool. If it's too hot, her pores will dilate and the agent will irritate her skin. And you should wash any clothes that got exposed—twice." He tapped on Sarah's chest while she breathed, his ear by her mouth. "Sounds like there may be some inflammation of her lungs, but it's not enough to be alarming."

Genna nodded.

Maya turned the cartridge over to match his description. "Okay. I'm not *that* stupid. I know the edge with the contacts needs to go into the connector inside."

"The Cat-5 goes to the wire you run back outside. Ignore the fiber; we don't need it here." He pinched the odd plug. "This one is for power. It goes to the AUX port here." He tapped the diagram.

Maya glanced up at him. "You said this was tricky."

"Heh. Sorry. Not used to kids your size having the attention span to absorb this sorta stuff."

She tucked the device into the thigh pocket of her fatigue pants. "Let's do it."

Doc Chang beckoned Maya over. She approached and pulled her shirt up so he could listen to her breathing. He examined her for a while, then patted her on the head. "Her breathing's a little rougher. Smaller lungs. Again, nothing to be overly alarmed about as long as they keep getting fresh air. Should get both of them rinsed off ASAP."

"Hey, mind if I ask who you're sellin' the Xeno formula to?" Zeroice closed the diagram and opened another window where white text scrolled over black.

"We're not selling it." Maya shook her head, arms folded, and held her head high. "We're going to send it to every pharma corp capable of producing it."

"What?" Zeroice blinked. "You know how much this is worth?"

Maya glared. "Yes. And that's exactly why we have to give it away. There's no use for Xenodril anymore aside from Ascendant releasing Fade to kill people for profit. If they can't make money on it, they won't bother."

"Hope you know what you're doing, kid," said Zeroice.

"I do." Maya offered a resolute nod. "This is for Sam."

Genna's eyes welled with tears. When she raised her arm, Maya ran into a hug.

[28]

THE CONDUIT

Genna decided to lay low for the rest of the day, keeping Maya and Sarah with her at Zeroice's new apartment. Genna dragged them into the bathroom, sharing an irritating chilly shower to clear the remnants of the CS agent. She rinsed out the girls' eyes and made sure they cleared any possible traces of chemical contamination from their bodies before sticking her face into the stream.

They all wore towels for an hour or two while Genna washed and dried their clothes. Even though they'd gotten new things from the store, any chemicals on their skin had absorbed into the fabric.

Genna and Pope decided to make their move the next day, after Pope had a chance to recon the area and get whatever tools necessary to open the hatch. The comment about 'doing this for Sam' made Genna clingy, not that Maya minded. Zeroice set them up with some video games, a system far better than the arcade games in the basement at home and almost as good as the one at Vanessa's.

Still, co-op with Sarah made the time fly.

Pope returned in a few hours with Chinese take-out for everyone and a big wrench.

"Planning on doing some heavy construction, or is that for breaking skulls?" asked Zeroice.

"Heh." Pope tossed the enormous tool up and caught it by the handle. "Multipurpose."

He'd also picked up a nylon climbing harness that Maya tried on. A rope clamped to the center of her chest would provide an emergency escape if she became wedged and couldn't move on her own. That night, the girls slept between Genna and Pope on the bed, while Zeroice couch-surfed. Maya couldn't remember ever having felt so safe.

THE VAN GLIDED DOWN THE STREET IN THE POST-COMMUTER SURGE hour. They stopped to pick up a light breakfast of fast-food egg sandwiches and ate on the ride. At 10:44 a.m., Pope pulled over by a metal railing where a stairwell led down to a sunken concrete trench full of industrial machinery, fat grey-painted pipes, and windblown trash.

Genna and Pope changed into the BPA workers' uniforms before getting out. He walked around to the back doors, grabbed a toolbox, and jogged down the steps. Maya followed, anxious but not frightened, more wanting to get it over with and go home than being scared to do it. Sarah hovered close behind.

One story below street level, the walls radiated the stench of piss and mildew. Scraps of fabric and char marks gave away where vagrants had camped or cooked. Several dubious stains caused Maya to look away before she tried to figure out if someone died there or merely threw up. A minute's walk from the stairs, they reached a forest of intertwined pipes that ranged from two-inches in diameter to big enough for Pope to crawl into. He approached a spur leading off from a longer pipe with a smooth, curved endcap labeled 'SEWER.' Though it had a bolt fitting every three inches around the outside, only five had nuts securing them.

Pope hesitated, walked past it surveying the other pipes in the area, and backed up once more to stare at it. He leaned past the end cap to study the pipe itself, then checked and rechecked his minicomputer. "This has got to be the one. It looks larger than he described it."

"Still ain't that big." Genna walked back and forth around it, shaking her head.

Maya ducked under the pipe end and traced her fingers over

lettering raised out of the metal that repeated 'water main' every three feet along the length. "Hey... it says water main on the pipe."

"Hope 'sewer' is a dissuasion tactic, or this is about to get stinky." Pope set down the toolbox and took the giant 'beat a guy to death' wrench from it.

While he attacked the pipe cap, Genna helped Maya into the harness, fitting it around her chest, waist, and thighs. "How's that feel?"

"Annoying." She smiled.

"Yeah, well." Genna grasped the harness and lifted her off her feet. "It'll support you."

"You know our first jump in training, this guy Private Randall screwed up his harness." Pope almost lifted himself off the ground by pulling on the wrench. "Come on, bastard. Crack. Anyway, when his 'chute deployed, all his weight came down on his balls."

"Ugh." Genna cringed. "If I had a NuCoin for every time I heard that story."

"Heh. Ain't a story, I was there." Pope winked.

"Nah, I mean there's a lot of dumbasses." She chuckled. "My group had one too."

"Randall was a piece of work." The wrench screamed as the nut gave and the motor spun to full speed. "Poor bastard's name was Randall Randall. Bet his parents thought that was cute. We called him R2."

Maya rolled her eyes.

Sarah kept her back to the wall of pipes, watching the top of the other side. Her hair and skirt fluttered in a light breeze.

A few minutes later, Pope finished fighting with the last nut and dropped the wrench back in the toolbox. "Well, that's a good sign. Cap didn't blast off in a torrent of horror."

Genna grabbed handles on one side, Pope the other, and they pulled the endcap free of the pipe and eased it to the ground. When no foul smells emerged, Maya stepped up and stood on tiptoe to peer over the bottom. A six-foot length extended downward at an angle to the main pipe underground, which had an inch-thick blue cable run along the bottom.

"This is it," said Maya. "Boost please."

"Wait." Sarah bounced. "That's big enough for me. I'm going with her." She picked at her fluffy sweater. "Lemme change."

"Hurry up," said Pope.

Sarah ran across the drainage channel and up the stairs.

"Pink angora is so out of style for crawling through old pipes," said Maya.

Pope clipped a carabiner to the harness, connecting her to a coil of rope in the toolbox.

Genna gathered Maya's hair into a scrunchie before putting a headband on her that held a small flashlight. "You sure you wanna do this, baby?"

"Yes. We're here already anyway. If Vanessa won't make money on Fade, she won't bother." She looked up at Pope. "Give me a boost? I wanna get this done and go home as fast as possible."

"Don't forget these. I don't want you cuttin' your hand on any of that nastiness in there." Genna handed her a pair of military gloves with rigid panels on the palms and knuckles, the smallest women's pair Pope could find on his preparatory run. Maya pulled them on despite feeling ridiculous with such oversized mitts. She grabbed the spool of Cat-5 cable and hung it around her neck on a string.

He chuckled, but hoisted her up into the spur.

Maya crawled ahead while adjusting her flashlight so the beam pointed where she looked. The offshoot held a minimal amount of gunk, but the older pipe it intersected had a crusty layer of rust flakes, corrosion, and sediment along the bottom. Thankful for the gloves, she set a tentative hand forward. The layer crunched but didn't hurt her knees. Maya advanced into the main pipe, her shoulders and butt brushing the top. She couldn't quite crawl at full height, but at least she didn't have to drag herself like a worm. Within a minute, the taste of metal settled on her tongue with each breath, and the dark, tight confines got under her skin. The little light on her headband gave her a view only twenty or so feet ahead, before the feeble glow drowned in the darkness.

Crawling fifty meters deep into a pipe too small to turn around in didn't seem like such an awesome idea anymore. She halted, staring down at the blue cable as thick as her wrist. *I gotta do this.* Crunching filled the silence, despite Maya not moving.

"Hey!" Sarah's voice echoed past her, frighteningly loud despite not being a shout.

Maya bowed her head and peered between her legs to the rear.

"Ack!" A short distance behind her, Sarah raised an arm to shield her eyes from the forehead-mounted flashlight. She'd changed to her black tee and probably her BDU pants, not that Maya could see her legs. Sarah crawled ahead on her elbows, her hands wrapped with fabric scraps for protection—most likely Pope's doing. The pipe didn't have enough room for her to get up on her hands and knees. "That's bright."

"You can wait outside," said Maya.

"Uhh, how about no." Sarah stopped right behind her. "Come on. This place sucks."

Maya grinned and lifted her head to face forward. Not being alone made the dark tube stretching in front of her much less frightening. She made her way forward, the crunch of debris underneath and Sarah's soft grunts and gasps filling the quiet.

"I can't believe we're letting them do this," said Genna, her voice carrying down the pipe.

Pope muttered something too low to make out.

Confident the plated gloves would protect her hands, Maya crawled as fast as she could, straddling the blue cable. Every so often, a flake of corrosion above snagged on her harness and broke off.

"It smells better in here than it did outside," whispered Sarah.

"Yeah."

Minutes later, the rope attached to her harness stopped short, almost making her kiss the pipe.

"Oof."

"Sorry," whispered Sarah. "My fault. Put my arm on it."

Maya pushed herself up. "'Kay."

"Are you scared?"

"A little, but only of getting caught." Maya resumed crawling. Determined grunts and the occasional crunch of rust flakes breaking away from the pipe echoed for several minutes. Eventually, a flash of white up ahead caught her eye. "I think I see it!"

"Good. I can't wait to get out of here."

Maya laughed. "It was your idea to come along."

"I saw the way you looked at the pipe. You were gonna chicken out."

"Was not."

Sarah poked her in the butt. "Were too."

"Yeah... Okay. Maybe I would have."

As she drew nearer, the spot grew into the front face of an electronic component in a space where the pipe expanded to a small chamber. Fittings on the top and bottom suggested a pump used to be here, but the turbine had been removed when they repurposed this pipe for a network conduit. Maya scooted up to the component and rolled on her side, the spindle of Cat-5 wire around her neck almost in her lap. The fat blue cable she'd been following went into the left side of the repeater unit and came out the other, continuing ahead into the dark. A row of status lights on the top right corner of the box fluttered with network activity on twenty channels, offering a feeble amount of visibility.

Sarah dragged herself out of the pipe into the wider section, but didn't have enough room to get her legs all the way out of the pipe, so she propped herself up on her hands like a landed mermaid.

Maya removed the gloves, set them aside, and pulled at the hatch, but it wouldn't open. "Uh oh." She tugged at it again. "Damn."

"What?"

"It won't open."

Sarah pressed closer. "Let me see."

"'Kay." Maya leaned to her right.

"It's locked." Sarah pointed at a silver keyhole at the center of the bottom.

"Can you pick it?" asked Maya.

"My bag's back home, and I lost the spare when my dress fell apart." She grumbled. "This can't be a complicated lock. I should be able to rake it."

Maya closed her eyes and thought bad words.

After a minute or three of hunting around, Sarah picked up a thick metal flake. She wedged it in a ventilation slat on the box and snapped off a thin, toothpick-sized fragment. After making a second thicker one, she dropped the remainder. She scooted deeper into the chamber and rolled on her side, head in Maya's lap. After a bit of squirming to adjust her angle, she inserted both improvised tools in the keyhole, using the thicker spur to tension the lock while raking the thinner one back and forth.

"Is that going to work?" whispered Maya.

"I don't know. I gotta be careful. These picks are brittle. If they break off inside the lock, we're going to be stuck."

Maya nodded. The scratch of metal scraping made her squirm, like an itch somewhere deep inside her body she couldn't reach.

"Crap!" whispered Sarah. She dropped one scrap and pinched a broken end between two fingernails, managing to wiggle it out of the lock. "Whew."

She made a replacement sliver, and tried again.

Maya held her breath.

"I'm getting some of the pins." Sarah's extreme concentration forged a stone-faced glower. She let a hint of a whine out her nose. Maya stared wide-eyed, not even breathing in case that faint sound would distract her. As if body language could somehow speak to the lock, Sarah twisted her entire body along with her effort to turn the picks.

The lock rotated with her, and she pulled the hatch open.

"Awesome!" Maya held her fists up.

"Okay. All you. We're lucky that was a super-crappy lock. Like an old vending machine." Sarah wriggled backward into the pipe they'd come out of, clapping rust off her hands.

"We're almost done." Maya pulled the cartridge from her thigh pocket, held it up with the circuit-board side facing to the right, and socketed it in the third port down from the top. She leaned close, squinting at tiny plastic letters in the dim light to figure out which port had the 'AUX' label.

Sarah pulled the Cat-5 cable, unwinding a little and connecting it to the dangling cord protruding from the back end of the add-on module.

"Got it." Maya plugged in the AUX cable, and a bunch of flashing green lights lit up on the cartridge.

Sarah rolled flat and pushed herself backward into the pipe. Maya, small enough to turn around in the pump housing, put her gloves back on and crawled after her, face to face. The spindle hanging from her neck rotated as they progressed, network cable unwinding and trailing off between her legs. Sarah's eagerness to get out of the pipe showed clear on her face and in her rapid backward shuffle.

The pipe shook with a sudden, loud *clank*.

"Eep!" yelled Sarah, stopping short. She tried to look behind her. "Crap! I think I kicked something."

Maya leaned forward, peering over her. Light glinted from a barred grate a few inches past Sarah's sneakers that must've snapped down like a guillotine. Fortunately, it jammed three-quarters of the way closed, tilted at an angle, higher up on the left. "Bars behind you."

"What was that noise?" yelled a distant Genna.

"A grate shut on us," shouted Maya. "We're stuck!"

A flurry of chickpea-sized pellets fell from above, bouncing off Maya's head before collecting on the bottom of the pipe.

Sarah picked one up and held it into the beam of the flashlight strapped to Maya's forehead. "Rat poison. It thinks we're big rats."

"What thinks we're big rats?"

Sarah shrugged. "Whatever I just stepped on."

"Rat gate," shouted Maya. "How long do they stay down?"

"Shit!" yelled Genna. "I knew this was a god damned stupid idea."

"I don't think it's gonna open," whispered Maya. "It looks broken."

"I'm sorry." Sarah shivered. "I should have waited outside."

"You got the lock, and I wouldn't have been brave enough to keep crawling if you weren't here."

Sarah managed a worried grin.

After a nervous delay, Genna yelled, "Zero said a couple hours."

"Crap," yelled Maya. "We're going the other way. I don't wanna sit here for hours."

Silence hung in the pipe for a moment before Genna replied, sounding worried. "Nearest cap is two miles."

"Should we wait for the rat-killer robot?" shouted Maya. "And I think the grate is broken. It's tilted and didn't close all the way. It might not open again."

"Shit!" yelled Genna. "Okay. Go. We'll meet you on the other end."

"Wait!" Maya unhooked the carabiner from her chest and looped it through the lanyard holding the Cat-5 spindle before clipping it around the rope. "Pull the rope out. The wire's on it. The box is turned on."

"Don't disconnect your safety line," shouted Genna.

Sarah covered her ears.

"Do you have two miles of rope?" yelled Maya.

Pope's laughter echoed back.

The rope went taut, and gently tugged the spindle over Sarah. She shifted to the side so it could roll along the pipe instead. It became stuck at the grate, but she kicked it through the higher side.

"We're so lucky that thing jammed." Sarah whistled.

"I don't think you understand what lucky means."

"If it came down all the way, we wouldn't have been able to get the wire out. That spool's bigger than a rat."

"It would've been annoying, but we could've done it." Maya waved her hand around. "Unwind it all, tie the wire to the rope and leave the spool behind."

"Oh." Sarah scratched at her head. "Does it hurt?"

Maya crawled backward to the pump chamber and turned to face the other way. "Does what hurt?"

"Being smart."

"Hah."

Maya crawled backward for a few meters until they reached the pump area, where she turned around to face forward. Seams on the opposite side from the network box suggested a hatch that likely led to the outside, though couldn't be opened from the inside—at least not without a plasma cutter. That left only the pipe as an option.

Her fear grew, not knowing what waited for them deeper in. Rat-killing robots, rats, electronic sensors, another rat-grate that worked and would trap them for real, or something worse. *Sitting here won't get us out.* Maya crawled forward. At least having Sarah with her kept worry at a manageable level. She rambled about random, happy things like video games, or Emily talking to the faeries that lived in their building.

"I bet Marcus is worried about you," said Sarah.

"Shut up." Maya grinned. "Eww."

"He really likes you."

"Eww." Maya rolled her eyes. "Eww. Eww. Eww."

"You don't like him?"

She huffed. "He's okay. But eww. I'm not kissing a boy."

Sarah giggled.

After a few silent minutes of crawling, Maya blurted, "Maybe when we're older."

"So you *do* like him."

"Eww."

Sarah's laugh echoed for seeming ever.

More crawling.

"How many meters is two miles?" asked Sarah. "Is this going to take long?"

"A mile is 5280 feet, meter's about 3.2 feet ... about 1600 meters. Two times."

"That's a lot."

"Yeah. I think it'll take us about two or three hours. Feels like we're going about one meter per second."

"Speak for yourself," said Sarah. "The pipe keeps trying to pull my pants down."

"Are you claustrophobic?"

Sarah hesitated for a few seconds. "Was that a real word?"

"Yeah. Means afraid of tight places."

"Is there a word for being sick of tight places but not scared?"

Maya pondered. "I don't think so."

"Well, whatever that is, I am." Sarah grunted. "Watch out for anything sticking up that could be another rat trap. My foot hit something."

"Okay."

Maya slowed a little, sweeping her head-mounted flashlight around to study the pipe for any signs of traps or grates.

"I hope they don't turn the water back on," said Sarah, a long while later.

Maya shivered. A spike of fear made it momentarily hard to breathe from the mere idea of being stuck in a pipe while it filled with water. "Don't say that...."

"Are you afraid of drowning?"

"Uhh, yeah." Maya scoffed. "What kind of question is that? It's a horrible way to die."

"Sorry. I'm getting scared now. Saying stupid things."

"No, talking about Marcus is stupid things. Talking about drowning is morbid things."

"Whatever." Sarah giggled.

Maya closed her eyes for the span of a few breaths. "This pipe hasn't had water in it for forty years."

"I believe you."

Minutes later, a dark patch on the pipe stood out from the pervasive rusty brown.

"I see something."

"The end?"

"No. We're not even halfway yet."

"Ugh."

Maya crept up to the black smear. At a few feet away, what had appeared to be a dark stain became obvious as a missing section of pipe wall. She stopped short; Sarah's head bumped into her rear end.

"Oof," mumbled Sarah.

"Sorry. There's a hole in the pipe."

"What?" Sarah sounded excited. "Can we get out?"

"The pipe broke." Maya bit her lip. "You know, this was a really stupid idea. Mom was right. What am I doing down here?"

"Saving the free world, or what's left of it, from an evil bitch."

Maya giggled.

"Can we get past the hole?"

"I dunno. It's big, but it's mostly on the side."

She edged forward and peered into blackness. Her flashlight glinted from parallel metal rails on the ground far enough below to make the idea of jumping scary, but right under the hole in the pipe, a mound of dirt came up about halfway, leaving a drop of about six or seven feet. It looked as though the ceiling had collapsed. Metal beneath her creaked. The egg sandwich she'd eaten before did a full-on ballet production in her gut.

"Umm. What do you think?" Maya flattened herself against the left side, away from the hole, and peered down past her body at Sarah's pale face and saucer-wide blue eyes. "Keep going down the pipe and hope they can find another cap, or try an old tunnel that might cave in if we fart too loud?"

"It's that bad?" asked Sarah.

Maya looked out the hole again. Aside from the area below the pipe, the glint of metal rails in her flashlight beam appeared uninterrupted. "Maybe not."

"I think I'd rather walk than crawl."

"What if it's a dead end? There might be a cave in later on, and once we go down, we won't be able to climb back up here."

"Oh. Okay." Sarah sighed. "Keep going then."

Maya shifted to all fours and crept past the opening. The third time she put her hand down, the rusted metal gave way. She let out a shrill scream and rode a four-foot long slab of rusting metal down to the dirt pile. The pipe shard stopped dead on impact, but she kept sliding, rolling over twice, before coming to a halt on her back between the train tracks.

"Ow," said Maya, more out of surprise than pain.

"Maya!" yelled Sarah from above. "Are you okay?"

She spat out dirt and sat up. "Yeah. Guess we go this way."

Grunting from above let her zone in on Sarah. She pointed her head (and flashlight) up, so her friend could see. Sarah lowered herself out of the pipe, hung by her hands for a second, and let go. She landed feet-first on the dirt mound and fell into a backward somersault, skidding to a halt half on top of her.

Maya grabbed on. "Are you hurt?"

"No." Sarah clambered upright, pulled Maya to her feet, then dusted herself off. "So, umm, which way do we go?"

Maya looked up. The pipe ran perpendicular to the subway tunnel, so neither option would take them closer to where Genna/Pope waited. "I don't know. Hang on. Be quiet."

Sarah nodded.

Eyes closed, Maya concentrated on listening. Amid the sound of her rapid heartbeat and the rush of air in her nostrils, a faint car horn blared. Evidence of civilization offered hope. She rotated a half turn and kept listening. A shout and the whirr of a passing drone fan seemed to be on her left side. Again she turned. Seconds of silence passed. The *thump* of a distant car door slamming came from the right.

"That way." Maya pointed to the right.

"It's creepy down here. This is way scarier than the pipe."

Maya looked down at a sunken channel holding the train tracks. Narrow flat sections ran parallel to the track, but it didn't look like people belonged down here on foot. With little other options, she started walking, trying to step on the metal blocks holding the rails in place. "We can actually breathe in here. How is it scarier?"

"It kinda looks like a place where zombies are gonna get up and come after us."

Maya gasped and whirled to stare at her. "Don't even say that!" She jabbed a finger at her a few times before her brain woke up. "Zombies aren't real."

"I know, but this looks like the—"

"Stop!" Maya tried to plug her ears, but the oversized gloves made it impossible. Instead, she clamped her hands over them. "La la la la la."

Sarah laughed and pounced, fake-zombie clawing at her while making growls and 'rawr' noises.

"Eeep!" Maya flailed, giggling. "Stop! Really. We don't know what's down here, and you don't have a Hornet."

Sarah covered her mouth; her expression said 'oops.'

Maya took the gloves off and stuffed them in her thigh pockets. Every ten steps, she looked down to watch for holes, traps, rats, or anything that might make her fall and hurt herself, but by some miracle, the tracks remained clear almost as if the subway line still ran. Except for a few buses, no form of public transportation existed after the nuclear bombardment, making the cleanliness eerie. Boats still made the trip to Europe, and the Authority had helicopters, but subways?

She picked up to a light jog.

"What's up?" asked Sarah, unwrapping her hands and pocketing the cloth strips.

"The tracks are too clean."

"So?"

"So, I don't wanna get hit by a train."

Sarah laughed. "There's no trains."

"I know that's what they *say*, but they also said Fade came from aliens." Maya glanced at her for a second before watching where she stepped again. "Why else are the tracks clean?"

"Maybe the zombies ate all the junk."

"Shut up." She grinned.

"Or took it home to their zombie houses."

Maya swatted at her, and they both wound up laughing despite being scared. For a while, she tried to balance walk on one of the rails, waving her arms about. Sarah hopped up on a rail too, but made it look easy.

Ambient noise of the outside world grew louder with each step, eventually overtaking the scuff of their sneakers on the ground. For what felt like an hour, they traded nervous conversation about Book's most recent story or hoped that Genna and Pope wouldn't be too upset with them for changing course.

Weak light gleamed on white bricks up ahead on the left where the passage curved to the right. Hopeful that meant an exit, Maya hustled up to a jog. The eerie remains of an old station platform came into view on the inside of the turn.

A scattering of LED bulbs around the walls and ceiling flashed and fluttered, casting the open area of benches and red tiles in an eerie, otherworldly presence. Small black blurs zipped around in the shadows, one knocking a beer can rolling. Benches, empty for decades, held the withered remains of magazines. The wide-open area extended about thirty feet in from the tracks, ending at a partition covered in ads for movies made before Maya had been born. An archway at the center offered a view of a similar sized space behind it, the farthest wall a glass-encased ticket counter covered in dust. The echo of traffic, people, and drones carried across the abandoned train station.

"Whoa," whispered Sarah. She crept up to the platform edge, as tall as her chest, and leaned forward.

"There's rats," said Maya.

"How many?"

"More than I'm comfortable with."

Sarah glanced at her. "So, one?"

Maya poked her in the side. "Not funny."

Air shifted in a quick breeze, dispelling the stagnant tunnel atmosphere with the crispness of outdoors. A second later, it turned foul.

"Ugh." Maya coughed. "Sewer?"

Sarah lifted her shirt up to cover her face and shrugged.

"I hear people. There's gotta be a way out." Maya pulled herself up out of the track, stood, and clapped dust from her hands.

Sarah climbed up behind her. "It's so creepy."

"Stop trying to scare me." Maya walked around an aluminum bench, heading for the archway, as the area by the track had no other way to go.

A shadow zipped across the tiles at her left, making her jump and squeal. The rat disappeared into a mound of trash. She stood frozen, hands clutched at her chin, shivering and staring at the spot until Sarah put a hand on her shoulder.

"Just rats. They won't bother us. They'll also bother us less if we don't stay here."

Maya nodded and hurried for the archway, ignoring all the moving shadows at the corners of her vision. The smell got worse with each step she took, becoming eye-watering by the time she reached the opening in the wall that divided the boarding platform from the inner station. Dark blood smeared a tile column near the ticket booths, and dirty cloth strips piled here and there, as if an entire empire worth of mummies had exploded.

"Wow, this—"

Sarah screamed.

Maya whirled to the left. Dozens of bodies wrapped in the bandage-shrouds of Fade victims lay in a heap at the far end of the room, covered in rats. She whipped her head to the right, spotting another large group of dead people stacked against the wall on that side as well. Sarah's talk of zombies kicked her imagination to overdrive; she expected them all to get up and blame her for their deaths.

A huge, ink-black rodent on a man's chest stopped chewing on him. It perched up on its hind legs and stared her straight in the eye, bloody whiskers twitching.

Maya shrieked. She leapt at Sarah, grabbing her, and screamed again.

"Oh, shit," gasped Sarah between gagging. "It stinks so bad."

"N-not. N-not z-zombies," muttered Maya.

The big rat kept staring at her. She turned in place, whimpering, terrified the dead would demand revenge. Her gaze shifted from body to body, watching. To the far right of the glass-encased ticket stations, an opening led to a corridor with brighter light, and more bodies. The sounds of the outside world emanated from a ninety-degree corner at the end.

"No..." Maya shivered. "We gotta walk by the zombies."

Sarah clung to her. "They're not zombies. Zombies are made up. They're just dead people."

She tiptoed forward, covering less than an inch each step, staring at the Fade victims on the right.

A rotting woman's arm twitched.

Maya screamed her lungs empty. In her mind, every corpse shifted to look at her. The giant rat laughed. She bolted forward, running toward the way out with barely open eyes. Every time she bumped or brushed a dead person's limb, she shrieked. She leapt a bloated man's body at the entrance to the corridor and ran eight steps before a patch of semidry gunk took her sneaker out from under her. She came down hard on her butt, rolling to the right and wound up facing back the way she'd come.

Sarah hopped over the fat dead man at the start of the corridor, moving quick but placing her feet with care not to come near any of the bodies. The pain from landing on her backside stunned Maya long enough for panic to dissipate. Why wasn't Sarah running? It took her a moment to realize the soft surface she landed on was a dead person.

"Eww!" Maya leapt up and swatted at herself.

None of the bodies near her appeared leaky—yet. In fact, most looked recent.

Lightheaded and sick to her stomach, Maya waited for Sarah to approach close enough, then grabbed her arm in both hands. "Ugh. I'm going to puke."

"They're not getting up. That woman didn't move. A rat was nibbling on that arm."

"Stop." Maya pressed a hand into her gut and gurgled.

"I wanna get out of here."

Maya leaned to the side and coughed up bile. "Yeah."

Clinging to Sarah's hand, she hurried to the leftward corner and gazed up a round-roofed tunnel. Six sections of stairs separated by stretches of flat with vending machines long devoid of food led up to street level. At the top, a barricade of boards and plastic sheeting offered a few gaps that looked wide enough for them to squeeze through.

Maya raced up the stairs, thankfully devoid of more bodies. At the top landing right inside the barricade, she doubled over, hands on her knees, gulping down fresh air. Sarah collapsed, out of breath, beside her.

"What the hell," gasped Sarah, "was that?"

The reality of having touched dead people pierced the shield of panic she'd erected. Maya held up a finger in a 'wait a moment' gesture, turned to the side, and threw up.

Sarah clamped a hand over her mouth and nose. She crawled to the barrier and slipped out between two slats, tearing plastic to make a hole. Maya coughed up half-digested egg sandwich, spat a couple times, and wiped her mouth. Two breaths later, her head stopped spinning. She stared down the stairs, realizing she remained inside the 'cavern of death' alone, probably with fifty zombies about to come after her.

With a squeak of terror, she dove headfirst out the hole Sarah made, crawled a few feet away, and sat on the ground breathing hard. The subway entrance let out to an extra-wide section of sidewalk containing a row of decorative trees planted in square patches of dirt. Pedestrians went back and forth nearer the road, a few glancing in their direction with raised eyebrows. Behind her, a row of identical yellow signs on the barrier read, 'Do Not Enter: Fade.'

"Sorry." Sarah scooted closer. "I shouldn't have said anything about zombies. Didn't know you were so scared of them."

Maya spent a few minutes taking slow, calming breaths while watching cars go by. "Zombies are scary. Especially when we've been talking about them in a dark cave and find a room full of dead people."

Sarah squatted. "So, what was that?"

"Tomb."

"They just throw them down there? That can't be safe." Sarah fanned herself. "I'm never going to forget that stink."

"It's not. Rats... they're going to—well, not the rats. Their fleas." Maya got up, fuming angry. "They're doing it on purpose so people keep getting sick. Authority is watching for drone-released Fade. Those 'bioassay' units? I bet they weren't really checking the air; they used them to spray Fade. No one's watching for fleas."

Sarah glanced around at the city, shivering. "Do you know where we are?"

"Don't worry." Maya grinned. "The power of your butt will save us again."

Sarah turned bright red in the face but laughed. She shimmied, waving her rear end at the sky.

"I don't think that's going to help the reception." Finally somewhat calm, Maya reached up and pulled the scrunchie off, allowing her hair to fall free.

"So, do we just wait?"

"Umm." Maya looked around, experiencing a strange sense of familiarity. "I think I've been here before. I dunno how long they'll wait for us at the pipe end before they start looking for your butt." She headed to the right, drawn to an alley that she almost remembered.

Sarah laughed, but sounded nervous. "Where are you going?"

"I wanna see something. If I'm wrong, we sit down and wait."

"'Kay." Sarah caught up in a few quick steps and fell in stride. "What do you think is down there?"

"Someone who can help us."

[29]

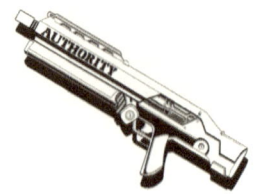

A NECESSARY SERVICE

Weaving among the oncoming crowd of pedestrians, Maya headed for the opening of an alley a block or so from the old subway entrance. They waited for a traffic signal to flip, crossed the street, and rounded the corner.

A giant yellow sign marked 'Integration Ward 4' hung on the brick wall of an old warehouse, with a flashing amber light on either side of it.

"Oh, shit. Don't go in there." Sarah pulled her back.

"It's okay. I've been here before. And we're both vaccinated, remember?"

Sarah whined, and stared at her for a few long seconds. "It's still scary, you know. I grew up terrified of getting sick."

Maya's enthusiasm waned. She couldn't comprehend how frightening that must've been. As much as she hated Fade for knowing what it did, the closest she had come to it affecting her on a personal level had been the emotional weight of meeting a five-year-old on the verge of death. Never in Maya's life had getting sick from Fade been as much as a slight worry. Until a few weeks ago, Sarah had lived with the fear every day of her life that at any moment, a chance swing of fate might infect her with a disease she would not have survived.

I wonder if her father would've gotten off his ass to take her to the VA hospital if she got Fade.

"I can't imagine how scary that was. I'm sorry."

Sarah attempted to act casual, shrugging. "It's okay. I mean, I guess it wasn't as bad as I thought, right? Dad's a vet, so I'm technically a Citizen. Would the VA have paid for Xenodril for me?"

"I don't know. Probably as long as they didn't know you helped, umm, certain people." *They were going to shoot Sam because Genna was wanted Brigade. The Dad wasn't involved with them, was he? Is that why he avoided the Sanc? Nah, the Brigade wouldn't have recruited him—he had too much mental damage. Sarah's innocent. Wait, no, she did stuff for them, but did the Authority know that?*

Another pair of 'Integration Ward 4' signs hung from a high chain-link fence at the end of the alley. The Fade ward inside looked deserted, far from how it had been when they dropped off Xenodril only weeks ago, and no Authority officers tried to keep people away.

Maya walked up to the gate and slipped past it.

The empty courtyard echoed her footsteps. All the tents remained, pale white fabric fluttering like ghosts in the wind. None had any people in them. On one hand, she hoped her video had forced Ascendant to stop releasing the virus, and Vanessa's 'oh shit' face-saving maneuver of handing out free Xenodril had emptied the rest of the Sanc's wards. On the other, she worried something more sinister may have happened. Those bodies in the subway station didn't look like they'd been there long.

"Umm." She halted in the center of the quad, turning in place. Late afternoon overcast sky added a supernatural bleakness to her surroundings that reawakened her fear of zombies. A memory of being chased by a swarm of Fade victims into a dead end alley got her shaking. "Maybe we should just go back to the street and wait."

"Okay." Sarah started to walk toward the gate but froze when a door squeaked open.

Maya whirled to face the office, the only non-tent structure in the place. A thirty-something woman with olive skin and black hair emerged, a pistol almost pointed at them. She hesitated, then lowered her arm and pulled the door open the rest of the way.

"What are you doing here? This ain't no place for children. You should get out of here right away."

Maya raised a hand in greeting. "We're sorry. I was looking for Doctor Janus."

The woman's caution shifted to concern. "Why, child? Are you... sick?"

"No." She walked a few steps closer. "I'm Maya. I kinda got lost and wondered if she could help."

Sarah pressed close to her, staring fearfully at the spectral tents. "I don't like it here. It feels like a dying place."

"Oh, Maya!" The woman put the gun in the side pocket of her medical smock and hurried out into the courtyard. "It's so nice to meet you. I'm Mindy Khan, a caretaker. Doctor Janus is not here. After your broadcast, we had no need to pretend anymore. All the people who were treated with the Xenodril you and your friends brought went back to their lives. We have not had any new cases. Ascendant distributed more Xenodril to all the Fade wards. As far as I know, they're all empty now."

"Wow." Maya blinked. "It really worked?"

"For now." Mindy sighed. "The Authority is keeping the Fade Wards open on the off chance your information turns out to be false, and the disease is not coming from Ascendant."

"It's true, but it doesn't prove that *only* Ascendant could use it."

"Why would anyone bother?" Mindy shrugged. "It's not like World War Three *had* a winner."

Maya pointed at the alley. "There's another problem. There's an old subway station down the street full of dead people. I think they had Fade. Rats are all over them. Fleas."

Mindy blinked. "Oh, no!"

"Yeah..." Maya nodded. "That's a serious problem. Is Doctor Janus okay?"

"She's doing fine, working at the hospital."

"How's Ashley?" Maya smiled, hoping for good news.

"Last I heard, still weak on one side, but she's improving, and Fade-free. She can walk again. Doctor Janus has decided to take her in."

Maya grinned.

The quiet whine of protesting e-motors came from the alley. Headlight shine danced across the wall.

Sarah put her hands on her butt. "Please!"

Mindy raised an eyebrow.

"Tracker," said Maya.

The grey van rolled to a stop outside the gate. Genna shoved the passenger door open and jumped out.

"Thank you." Maya waved to Mindy. "Mom's here. Gotta go."

Mindy smiled. "You two take care of yourselves."

"Mom!" yelled Maya. She ran across the quad and slipped between the gate and the fence before leaping into a hug.

Sarah walked over, smiling, but kept a little distance.

"What the hell happened down there?" Genna picked her up, cocked an eyebrow at Sarah, and held out her arm. "What you doin'? Get over here."

"Sorry." Sarah leaned into the embrace.

"The pipe had a huge hole in it," said Maya "We tried to get past it, but it broke and we fell into a subway tunnel."

Genna carried the girls to the door and lifted them in one by one. Maya scrambled over the passenger seat, pausing long enough to smile at Pope, and jumped on the middle bench. Sarah followed, Genna climbing in last.

"Butt-dar for the win," said Sarah.

Pope laughed. "Yeah. Zero already had a tracker online once you two got cut off. As soon as he saw your blip appear, we knew something went wrong, but Genna didn't panic too much since the blip meant you weren't underground."

Genna gave him a look. "I kept my cool, thank you very much."

"That poor guy on the bike would have an alternate opinion of that exchange." Pope winked.

"What happened?" asked Maya.

"Dude was riding a bicycle in the street," said Genna. "Slower than we wanted to go."

The girls giggled.

Pope backed the van out of the alley and pulled onto the road.

"Are we going home now?" asked Sarah.

"Almost. Gotta stop at The Hangar real quick. Figured we'd grab something to eat there too."

"Uhh." Maya held her gut with both hands. "Maybe I'll be hungry if I smell food."

Genna leaned around the seat, fixing her with a 'you left something out' stare.

"The subway station... it's full of dead people who had Fade. Someone dumped a lot of bodies down there."

"Rats and fleas," said Sarah. "That's bad for some reason."

"Fleas can carry Fade to new victims, and the rats will spread the fleas all over the place," said Maya.

"Nothing some fire won't fix." Pope clucked his tongue. "Or a lot of fire."

Maya nodded as she worked her way out of the harness. "I told Mindy at the Ward. Maybe she'll have them cremated."

"Brigade's gonna wanna look into it just ta make sure." Genna pulled out a minicomputer and wrote herself a reminder.

THE RIDE TO THE HANGAR TOOK ABOUT TWENTY MINUTES. POPE parked in a spot near the building, their van only the third vehicle in the lot at a touch past noon. Genna checked Maya over for contamination from her contact with the dead and, finding none, took her by the hand. They headed around the building to the street-facing entrance, Pope and Sarah behind them.

A sign above the door made to look like riveted steel letters read 'The Hangar' in a military font. Inside, a handful of people sat at tables, most of whom appeared to have popped in for lunch. Ancient weapons, bombs, missiles, machine gun ammunition, and such hung from the ceiling and walls. Large portraits of veterans, platoons, or warplanes covered almost every spot big enough for a frame. A waitress in a pre-war Air Force uniform walked by, smiling at them.

The bartender, a big dark-skinned man with a shiny bald head, waved as they went by.

"Hey Rodolfo," said Genna. "They trust you behind the bar?"

He laughed. "Only in the afternoon. No one drinkin' yet."

"Heh. I might need one in a few minutes." Genna winked and kept walking to the kitchen.

She crossed a wood-floored area full of small, round tables and pushed a flapping door out of her way. The smell of cooking food drew a growl from Maya's stomach. The two cooks looked up at Genna in annoyance, but once recognition set in, they went back to their work without a word.

In the storeroom at the end of the kitchen, Genna pressed a hidden switch behind the shelves. Unseen electric motors groaned. The shelf rose an inch up and slid to the left, exposing a stairwell leading to the basement and a hallway lined with fat green pipes.

Maya darted down the steps to the corridor, rounded the corner, and skidded to a stop by a thick grey door with an eye slot. She knocked.

A metal strip at eye level to an adult slid open and a man peered out. A second later, he shut it.

Maya knocked again. "Hey!"

He opened it again, this time peering down at her.

Genna, Pope, and Sarah came around the corner.

"Oh. Heh," said the man. "Didn't see you."

The eye slot closed, and after a few metallic *clunks*, the door opened.

Maya strolled into the Brigade HQ lounge. It hadn't changed since last time: three sofas, a television, a pool table, bookshelves, and a number of chairs surrounded an octagonal table littered with rifles, gun parts, hand grenades, and ammo.

Two women, one pale with snow-blonde hair down to her shoulders, the other Indian, sat next to each other at the giant table to the right of Harlowe. His silver brush cut glimmered like steel wool in the glare of a lone light bulb hanging above the table. At Maya's approach, he smiled, nodded, and gave her a quick salute.

Maya returned it.

"Captain." Genna walked up behind Maya and rested her hands on her shoulders.

Sarah scooted around to stand next to her, and Pope stopped at Genna's right.

"Unorthodox, but it worked," said Harlowe. "Zeroice obtained the package. He's whining about data encryption, but he thinks he can crack it. Might be a little while though."

"We found something on what you asked about." The snow-blonde sat straighter. "It looks like there's an internal faction within Ascendant that's using the current unrest and distrust caused by the evidence we released to attempt a coup."

"Let me confirm that," said Maya. "They tried to kill me."

The room fell quiet. A few people in the rear of the basement working at computers stopped typing and leaned back in their chairs to look at her.

"Kill you?" asked Harlowe.

Kris, the white-haired woman, gasped.

"Vanessa's got a will. If she dies, guess who winds up owning Ascendant. Only, I'm a little kid so it would go into trust, controlled by someone on my behalf. They don't want that, since they don't know if they can control whoever it is. So if they kill me, I guess they think they can kill Vanessa and have the company. Vanessa believes it too, which is why *she* kidnapped me from them." Maya explained her encounter with Mr. Needle and re-abduction by Vanessa.

"How long is this investigation of the Authority going to take?" asked Ravi. "It's already been two weeks and this woman is still on her throne."

"Be right back," muttered Pope. "Gonna grab some chow."

Genna nodded at him.

"We haven't been able to determine why it's moving at such a monolithic pace." Harlowe grumbled. "Best guess is that money changed hands, or she's got friends in the government who're blocking for her."

Maya furrowed her eyebrows, thinking. *Shen...* "Captain?"

"Hmm?" He looked at her.

"Can you set up a video call that can't be traced here? I want to try something."

"All right. What's on your mind?"

Maya raised her arms up and let them flap against her side. "Maybe more evidence against Vanessa. Maybe something we can use on her."

"So you're throwing poo at a wall and hoping it sticks?"

"Huh?" Maya tilted her head.

"Never mind. That's just an expression." He chuckled. "I suppose it's worth a try. Brennan, set up a secure outbound."

"On it," yelled a blond man in his mid-twenties.

Maya walked around the table to the back corner of the room which held a group of five cubicles.

Brennan opened a software phone client, dragged it onto his third monitor, and maximized it before pointing at a spot on the floor. "Stand there."

She did.

He tapped a few keys and she appeared on the screen. A few more clicks and taps changed the background of the Hangar, leaving her surrounded by a bright green field. He mumbled to himself while scrolling down a list of text. Eventually, he clicked on one and the scenery behind her shifted to a grungy-looking industrial building. The shadowy forms of huge machines appeared to lurk behind Maya.

"That's a bit too scary. Can you make it look like I'm at my old apartment? Or a fancy home?" *Crap.* "Mom!"

Genna walked over. "What's up?"

"Can you please go get that dress from the van? They're not going to believe me if I look like this."

"All right." Genna trotted to the door, turning sideways to slip past Pope, who reentered with a tray. Maya's mouth watered at the sight of chicken fingers and fries.

"One sec, kid." Brennan opened two more windows and typed at a dizzying rate for a short while. The background shifted to a place similar to her former penthouse. "Okay. Go ahead."

"Not ready yet." She squatted, undid the Velcro on her sneakers, and stripped down to her underpants.

Brennan's eyebrows went up. "Uhh?"

"Sorry for making you uncomfortable. I used to have to swap outfits twenty times in an hour with a whole crew around." She looked down at herself. "I suppose I should have waited for Genna to come back with the dress, but I'm in a hurry." She raked her fingers at her hair, trying to make it look neater.

"What's the rush?" asked Pope, munching on fries.

"That smells awesome," said Maya. "I wanna eat, but I don't wanna burp on camera."

Chuckling emanated from around the room.

Genna returned in a few minutes and handed over the purple dress. Maya wriggled into it; Genna zipped her up.

"Ugh. I think this is the first time in my life that I *wanted* to put one of these on."

"What are you doin', baby?" Genna brushed at the dress so it fell straighter.

"Improvising. Okay." She nodded at Brennan. "You're going to record this, right?"

Genna fussed over her hair for a few seconds before backing out of frame.

"Yep." Brennan winked.

She tapped at the touchscreen holding the video call software and dialed the number for the Ascendant auto-attendant. A box popped up with options. She poked the button for the company directory, sorted by last name, and scrolled down to S. The listing held three people with the last name 'Shen.' One, a man, she disregarded. Of the remaining two, Tian Shen's listing listed her as 'Senior Vice President – R&D. The other, Baozhai Shen, appeared to be a 'Marketing Analyst II.'

"Tian Shen," said Maya to herself.

She backed out of the menu system and dialed a private internal number she'd had to memorize years ago, which connected to the executive coordinator at Ascendant. The same woman she always called during business hours whenever she tried to reach Vanessa—when that woman had still been Mom.

Mrs. Kerry answered in three beeps, pale, a little heavy on the makeup, and smiling. She appeared more exhausted than usual, but brightened within a second of the video feed starting. "Oh, Maya! Hello sweetie!" She gasped. "Are you okay? Are you hurt? There's so many rumors going around. Did someone kidnap you? Are you being forced to make this call?"

Maya offered a pleasant smile. "I'm all right, Mrs. Kerry. Can you please connect me to Miss Tian Shen? Vanessa Oman wants me to give her a surprise call for her birthday on behalf of Ascendant."

"Oh, that's adorable. Your mother's so thoughtful."

You poor, confused woman. "Yes." Maya flashed a big smile.

"I believe she's here. Hold on a moment, I'll put you through."

The screen shifted to an Ascendant logo.

"Who is Tian Shen?" asked Genna.

"The woman who tried to have me killed," muttered Maya. "Poison needle man was talking to her on the phone."

A Chinese woman, later forties, long straight hair, black suit, appeared on the screen, her expression bewildered.

Maya's over-saturated smile faded to a serious face. "Hello Miss Shen. As you can see, the men you hired to murder me have failed. Unfortunately for you, they're also stupid. They forgot to take my mini-computer away when they abducted me. I have a recording of everything, including when Mr. Winnow called you to apologize for Ruiz being late."

Miss Shen blinked, shaking her head. "Maya, I have no idea what you are talking about."

"Oh, I think you do, and I also think you're about to listen to the terms of my offer."

"Why would I listen to your terms?" Miss Shen smiled. "Even if anything you say happens to be true, you would be like a mouse attempting to negotiate with the cat."

"Because my offer makes sense for you. It saves time, money, effort, and reduces risk. Also, we both get what we want." Maya folded her arms. "I don't want Ascendant. I know you're the one who's trying to take over. Mr. Winnow couldn't even go to the bathroom without you on the phone telling him how to do it. I won't take what you tried to do personally. I know you would've killed Vanessa and left me alone if I wasn't in her will. But I don't want the company. You can have it. I also don't want to die."

"I am not hearing any proposals, little girl." Miss Shen quirked an eyebrow. "Only someone walking in circles."

Maya smiled, as false as Vanessa's 'overjoyed mother' act would've been. "Do whatever you have to do to. The company becomes mine due to the will. I sign documents transferring ownership to whomever you want. Then, I walk away, and no one ever learns of your involvement in my attempted murder or that you had anything at all to do with whatever unfortunate event happens to Vanessa Oman."

"Hmm." Miss Shen rubbed a finger back and forth across her lips.

"There's one more thing I need." Maya held her head up. "I want the formula for Xenodril. Detailed production specifications."

Miss Shen gasped. "Are you mad, girl? That is a flagship product."

"Ascendant produces at least thirty medical products that no one else does. Medical supplies vital for life that are not cheap. The only reason Xenodril is a flagship product is because Ascendant is releasing Fade all over the world. It's not aliens; it never was. It's a pay-us-or-die profit scheme on a global scale. In exchange for me giving you Ascendant, there is no more Fade. Xenodril becomes a common market drug that everyone makes, so there is no gain in killing people."

"You don't understand, child. Ascendant is cleansing this sick world. We are serving a vital purpose. We are the flies that clean the carcass this planet has become. That there is profit to be made when wind shifts is a pleasant side effect."

Maya glared. "So you'd continue releasing Fade even when you are running the company?"

"Of course." Miss Shen looked at her as if she'd said the most idiotic thing imaginable. "There's no reason not to. Especially since war is brewing with the California-Washington Commonwealth. I would consider sparing you only out of pity since you are so young, but I am not willing to negotiate on Fade. That is—"

Bang.

Maya jumped as the screen lit with a flash.

Miss Shen stood frozen for a second before a trickle of blood ran from her lip. She emitted a faint wheeze and fell straight down out of frame. A blurry form in the background of the office walked closer, resolving into the visage of Vanessa Oman.

"That took longer than I thought it would," said Maya.

"Well, dear." Vanessa almost smiled, one eyebrow slightly raised. "I suppose I should thank you for exposing the traitor."

"I said your name on purpose, knowing your listeners would trip."

Vanessa leaned back, her haughty laughter reverberating in the basement of the Hangar. "I knew you had it in you to keep the company strong, in the family."

"Stop releasing Fade," said Maya.

"Oh, Maya." Vanessa sighed. "You're too soft-hearted. Perhaps someday you will understand how things work in this world. There are those of us at the top... and everyone else. Your little bout of unabashed idealism has made it problematic for certain operations to continue in this region. As a token of my gratitude for this little favor, I may decide to focus Xenodril sales away from the Eastern Seaboard for the foreseeable future. The Authority is weak, you know. There's only so many left with any sense of—what is that they call it? Duty or honor?" She stifled another conceited laugh. "Ascendant will control the ECS soon enough, Fade or no Fade. Their 'government' is a mere re-enactment of the same petty and weak-minded fools who burned the world to ash. They had their chance and failed. The old government does not deserve to exist."

Maya trembled with anger. "It's wrong to kill people just to make money."

"Is it?" asked Vanessa. "Violence will occur no matter what. Would you rather people kill each other over mythological gods, a sense of national identity, or slight variances in genetics?"

"No one has to die at all!" yelled Maya. "The global population is only eighteen percent of what it was before the war. There's been *enough* death. Please, stop!"

"Ahh. My little idealist." Vanessa flashed a patronizing smile. "Since you have helped me secure control of my company, I'll leave you to your little safari if that is what you really want. When you get tired of living in the slum, you're welcome to come home. You know the number. I'll even let you bring your little friend."

Glaring, Maya breathed in and out hard through her nose, her chest heaving. Everything she thought to say sounded childish, so she only fumed.

"Try not to catch too many fleas out there." Vanessa leaned in. "Oh, and do not cross me again, child."

The vid call dropped, her image shrinking to a white line that collapsed to a tiny dot.

Genna took a knee behind Maya, arm around her back. "You'd have a much better life there, baby. I can't give you the kind of things you're used to."

"Not better. Richer. More comfortable, but not better." Maya spun into a hug. "That place is lonely, hollow, and superficial. I'd get depressed. Maybe I'd turn into a bitch like her after years of being ignored. Maybe I'd end up wild, on drugs, and be dead by twenty."

"Whoa." Brennan leaned back. "This kid's morbid."

"That's not morbid. That's cynical." Maya smiled. "I watched too many movies." She peeled off the fancy dress and changed back into her t-shirt, BDU pants, and sneakers before darting to the big octagon table and taking the seat next to Sarah. "I'm starving!"

Pope had brought down a giant basket of breaded chicken fingers and French fries. Before she could grab any, Genna scruffed her and lifted her out of the chair.

"Go wash your hands. You crawlin' over dead people." She set Maya down on her feet and gave her a prod toward a basin sink.

Grinning, Maya complied, then rushed back to have dinner with her family.

[30]

END OF WATCH

At a small memorial service company, in a cube-shaped room with walls the color of burnished pewter, Maya found herself once again wearing her expensive purple gown. Sarah stood at her side in a charcoal dress they'd picked up on the way. The store didn't have anything black in her size. Besides, dark grey, she might actually wear again. Sneakers felt disrespectful for the setting, rubber-soled sandals even more so.

In the Sanctuary Zone, limited manufacturing produced modern apparel, but no company bothered making formal wear, especially in kid sizes. Only a small handful of executives had any interest in such things anymore, while everyone else merely tried to survive. Everything Vanessa had stocked Maya's old closet with had been custom ordered from individual makers in Europe, the only explanation for its cost. Despite Sarah's protest at 'wasting money,' Genna got the girls plain black ballet flats.

Among a small group of veterans wearing a mixture of camo, combat boots, and ordinary street clothes, Maya felt conspicuously overdressed, a glimmering butterfly perched on a branch among moths. Only one vet, a fiftyish man with a scar down the left side of his face and a military haircut, had worn a suit—rather a dress uniform. Wrinkled and with a small rip or two, it appeared to predate the war, but he'd kept it in good enough shape for a funeral. The man approached to offer his condolences to Sarah.

Maya stared at his cufflinks, gold discs depicting a bird perching on a globe with an anchor behind it. A thin gold nameplate by his suit jacket's pocket bore the name 'Cabrera.'

"So sorry for your loss." He held Sarah's hand for a moment. "Sergeant Hawthorne was a good man and a fine soldier."

"Thank you," said Sarah.

Cabrera took a step to the right, exchanged a few words with Pope, which included some chuckling, and moved on.

For the better part of two hours, Maya sat in the front row of a bank of padded chairs, with Sarah beside her, staring at a small black table bearing a silver urn with an engraved US flag above the words: 'SSG William R. Hawthorne – US Army. Oct 3 2059 – Jul 17 2094.'

She'd expected Sarah to be a mess, but the girl remained calm and quiet.

A silver monolith, a slab the size of a door, had a monitor at head level displaying a continuous series of images. All showed The Dad at various places and times in his military career. He looked like a teenager in most of them. Maya watched it until the pictures looped.

"It's all Army stuff," whispered Maya.

Sarah nodded. "My mother disappeared when I was five. Dad never talked about any other family. No one had any pictures except the soldiers."

"Sorry."

"It's okay." Sarah tucked a lock of hair behind her ear and sighed at the urn. "Who has time to take pictures when they're trying to stay alive?"

"He did the best he could for you, even with, umm, mental issues." Maya glanced left at an eruption of subdued laughter among the soldiers. "I'd rather have had him for a father than Vanessa for a mother. Twice over."

Sarah managed a weak smile.

They sat in silence for a little while more until another man, well into his sixties, walked in wearing a sharp Army dress uniform and carrying an actual paper book. He circled around to the space between the seats and the urn, looked left and right, and approached the front row.

"Excuse me, are you Sarah?"

"Yes." She looked up at him.

He took a knee, and her hand, patting it. "I'm sorry for your loss."

"Thank you," she half whispered.

"My name is Liam Anderson. I was the unit chaplain where your dad spent a few of his years over in that abominable place. He whiled away many hours talking to me, trying to figure out what God's plan for him was."

Maya glanced at him. *If God exists, he's an asshole for letting us nuke ourselves.* She kept a pleasant smile but said nothing.

Sarah sniffled, nodding.

"Would it be all right with you if I said a few words?" asked the chaplain.

"Yeah. Dad would like that." She looked down.

He bowed his head, stood, and took two steps back before clearing his throat. "Hello, everyone. I'm Lieutenant Anderson. I served as a base chaplain for the 7th Cavalry based at Pujon."

A few hats came off.

"I won't take up much of your time. Sergeant Hawthorne, as were many of you, was thrown into an awful situation when he wasn't much more than a boy. They say that most people these days don't have a lot of use for what God has to say about anything, but Billy always looked to Him for hope. I suppose it came with his Irish blood"—chuckles emanated from the gathered—"but there aren't too many people who can go into a situation like that and not at least hope He is watching out for us.

"Billy and I spent quite a few hours talking about the whys of things. Why was there war, why were we still fighting after command went silent, why were we still even in Korea. There's a lot we don't know. But I do know that Billy was a fearless protector of the freedoms we all hold dear. Not once did he ever wish he could just go home and forget his duty. He did not enjoy having to kill, he did not savor the fight, but he believed that our way of life was worth defending."

Murmurs of agreement filled the room.

"So, if you'll put up with me for a moment more, I'd like to offer a prayer for him."

Maya put an arm around Sarah, noticing tears on her face. The chaplain opened his book and read from it, stuff about welcoming into a kingdom and whatnot. She tuned most of it out, focused on trying to make her best friend feel better.

Eventually, Lieutenant Anderson thanked everyone, closed the book, and mingled with the small group of soldiers.

HAD THEY TAKEN THE VAN, MAYA WOULD'VE CHANGED OUT OF THE dress on the ride home. The funeral service had been an arduous three-hour process. The two hours spent afterward at The Hangar watching the adults drink had been worse. Sarah spent the whole time hiding under a booth table, alternatively staring into space and crying. Maya remained at her side, content to evade the attention of everyone else.

They rode an e-bus packed with commuters back to the Habitation District. People kept staring at Maya, making her feel conspicuous. As soon as they got home, Maya ran to the bedroom and changed. Even though the dress reminded her of Vanessa, it didn't seem right to leave something so expensive lying on the floor. She hung it up in the closet, alongside her mother's camo tops, black T-shirts, and a body armor vest with a dimple in the chest.

With a gasp, Maya picked at the spot a bullet had struck, lost to a momentary tremble at how much of a difference in her life that vest had made. She ran out and sprinted down the hall to the living room where Pope and Genna had collapsed on the sofa, still rambling about old Army stories.

Maya dove into a hug, clinging.

"Baby?" Genna raised an eyebrow. "What's wrong?"

"I saw the armor in your closet." She snuggled tighter.

"Aww." Genna kissed her atop the head and put an arm around her.

They continued sharing—edited for children—stories of things that happened in Korea, mostly about watching dumbasses do stupid things. Their memories varied from the whimsical (someone losing a Kevlar helmet down a latrine) to the OMG (someone smoking in the wrong place and almost setting off a fuel depot explosion that would've destroyed half a base).

After a while, Maya's reawakened fear of losing her mother calmed enough for her to realize Sarah hadn't come back. She sat up straight and looked around. "Mom? Where's Sarah?"

"She was right behind us up the stairs," said Pope. "Think she might be down the hall."

"Should we leave her alone?" asked Genna. "She's only eleven."

"Thought you planned on taking her in?" Pope raised an eyebrow.

Genna slugged him in the shoulder. "Jackass. That's not what I mean. I mean alone right now. Not livin' on her own."

He grinned. "She needs a little time, I bet. The girls have had a rough week."

"I'm going to check on her." Maya slid to her feet. "Okay?"

Genna nodded and leaned against Pope. "All right, but I want the two of you back here before dark."

Maya walked out into the hall. Banging, drilling, and hammering echoed in the main stairwell, the workers still repairing the giant hole on the ninth floor. Eager to get away from the noise, she hurried down to the corner apartment and found the door halfway open. Fearing another fake worker had done something, she rushed inside.

Her growing worry burst into a cascade of sadness at the sight of Sarah on the couch, curled up on her side in the middle of The Dad's well-worn spot, crying into a small green pillow. She hadn't even taken her shoes off. Maya pushed the door closed and approached, easing herself to sit beside her. After a few minutes of Sarah not reacting in any way to her presence, Maya crawled up to lay behind her, putting an arm over her.

Sarah let go of the pillow with one hand and grasped Maya's.

Perhaps an hour passed, the silence trading places on and off with construction upstairs and Sarah's sniffling. Maya continued to hold her. A few times, she opened her mouth, but changed her mind. All the words that came to her sounded either cold and clinical, or stupid. She hoped her presence would be enough to make Sarah's pain more bearable.

"Is Genna looking for me?" whispered Sarah.

"She is worried about you, yeah." Maya shrugged the shoulder she didn't lay on. "I think they want a little time together. She didn't send me. I was worried."

"Thanks." Sarah sniffled. A few minutes passed without words before she let out a teary chuckle. "Guess I won't be feeding everyone cheese sandwiches anymore. They only came over to eat when no one else had food anyway. I'm the only one who liked those things."

"I think they're good too."

Sarah scratched at her shin. "So, they like each other?"

"I think so." Maya leaned close, whispering at Sarah's ear, "Genna and Pope could still get cheese sandwiches. They're vets too."

Sarah burst into a fit of cry-laughing. "Yeah...."

"Hey." Maya glanced around. "Would it be okay if we all stayed here instead? Genna's apartment is tiny. Only one bedroom."

"Huh?" asked Sarah.

"That way, this is still your home. We'd have our own room instead of having to sleep on the floor. Genna wants us home before dark. She's your mom too now."

Sarah shifted, peering back at her. "Really?"

"Yes." Maya nodded. "You're officially my sister now."

"Wow," whispered Sarah. "That's so nice of her."

Maya prodded her. "Come on. What else would we do? You didn't think we'd leave you living on your own, did you?"

Sarah shrugged. "I didn't wanna assume, but, I hoped."

"So, do you want to keep this apartment? We don't have to. It's okay if it makes you too sad to be here... or too scary."

"Scary?" Sarah let go of the pillow and wiped her face with her free hand. "Why would it be scary?"

"'Cause of what happened. The shooting."

Sarah took in a big breath and let it out slow. "It's a little scary, but Dad didn't die here. The sofa still smells like him. It's like he's still around. I'd like to stay here if Genna doesn't mind moving."

"Okay. The other apartment is smaller than this, and the fridge still stinks."

"Genna could've asked me if it was okay for her to move in here. She didn't have to send you. I'm not afraid of her." Sarah again looked back over her shoulder at Maya.

"Yeah, she could have." Maya grinned. "But she doesn't know we're moving yet."

fin

THE STORY WILL CONTINUE

Maya's story will continue in book 3 - *Ascendant Revolution*

Nine-year-old Maya dreads living in the Habitation District with her new family. It's not the lack of video games or her shabby clothes, or even wondering *if* she'll eat from day to day—it's the giant target on her back.

Her ex-mother's offer of a truce scares her more than any threat the woman could have made. Both her new parents are former Special Operations soldiers, but even that provides little sense of safety. Barely a week goes by without an abduction attempt over her connection to Ascendant Pharmaceuticals.

After one such random attack, Maya discovers information that leads the Brigade to come up with a risky plan: use her unique combination of small size and large brain in an operation that could end the Ascendant threat for good. Hoping to peel the target off her back, Maya accepts the mission.

Her Brigade friends assure her it's completely safe.

Freakishly intelligent kids can do many things well, but commando raids aren't on the list. Her idealism leads to real bullets flying, crushing her hopes to live like a normal child.

She'll be happy to live at all.

ACKNOWLEDGMENTS

Thank you for reading Ascendant Revolution!

I'd also like to thank Ricky Gunawan for the amazing cover and interior art art!

Many thanks to Olivia Swenson for her wonderful assistance editing this novel.

ABOUT THE AUTHOR

Originally from South Amboy NJ, Matthew has been creating science fiction and fantasy worlds for most of his reasoning life. Since 1996, he has developed the "Divergent Fates" world, in which *Division Zero, Virtual Immortality, The Awakened Series, The Harmony Paradox, and the Daughter of Mars series* take place. Along with being an editor at Curiosity Quills press, he has worked in IT and technical support.

Matthew is an avid gamer, a recovered WoW addict, Gamemaster for two custom RPG systems, and a fan of anime, British humour, and intellectual science fiction that questions the nature of reality, life, and what happens after it.

He is also fond of cats.

Visit me online at:
    Facebook: https://www.facebook.com/MatthewSCoxAuthor
    Amazon: https://www.amazon.com/author/mscox
    Pinterest: https://www.pinterest.com/matthewcox10420/
    Goodreads: https://www.goodreads.com/author/show/7712730.Matthew_S_Cox
    Email: mcox2112@gmail.com

OTHER BOOKS BY MATTHEW S. COX

Divergent Fates Universe Novels

Division Zero series

- Division Zero
- Lex De Mortuis
- Thrall
- Guardian
- Harbinger

The Awakened series

- Prophet of the Badlands
- Archon's Queen
- Grey Ronin
- Daughter of Ash
- Zero Rogue
- Angel Descended

Daughter of Mars series

- The Hand of Raziel
- Araphel
- Ghost Black

Virtual Immortality series

- Virtual Immortality
- The Harmony Paradox

Prophet of the Badlands Series

- Prophet's Journey

Divergent Fates Anthology

(Fiction Novels - Adult)

The Roadhouse Chronicles Series

- One More Run
- The Redeemed
- Dead Man's Number

Faded Skies series

- Heir Ascendant
- Ascendant Unrest
- Ascendant Revolution

Temporal Armistice Series

- Nascent Shadow
- The Shadow Collector
- The Gate to Oblivion

Vampire Innocent series

- A Nighttime of Forever
- A Beginner's Guide to Fangs
- The Artist of Ruin
- The Last Family Road Trip
- The Phantom Oracle
- How Not to Summon Demons
- Ordinary Problems of a College Vampire

Standalones

- Wayfarer: AV494
- Axillon99

- Chiaroscuro: The Mouse and the Candle
- The Spirits of Six Minstrel Run
- Sophie's Light
- The Far Side of Promise anthology
- Operation: Chimera (with Tony Healey)
- The Dysfunctional Conspiracy (with Christopher Veltmann)

Winter Solstice series (with J.R. Rain)

- Convergence
- Containment
- Catalyst

Alexis Silver series (with J.R. Rain)

- Silver Light
- Deep Silver
- Silver Quarrel

Samantha Moon Origins series (with J.R. Rain)

- New Moon Rising
- Moon Mourning

Vampire For Hire series (with J.R. Rain)

- Moon Master
- Dead Moon

Maddy Wimsey series (with J.R. Rain)

- The Devil's Eye
- The Drifting Gloom
- Dark Mercy

Samantha Moon Case Files series (with J.R. Rain)

- Blood Moon

Immortal Operative series (with J.R. Rain)

- Broken Ice

Young Adult Novels

The Eldritch Heart Series

- The Eldritch Heart
- The Cursed Crown

Evergreen Series

- Evergreen
- The World That Remains
- The Lucky Ones

Standalones

- Caller 107
- The Summer the World Ended
- Nine Candles of Deepest Black
- The Forest Beyond the Earth
- Out of Sight

Middle Grade Novels

The Adventures of Ubergirl series

- My Dad is a Mad Scientist

Tales of Widowswood series

- Emma and the Banderwigh
- Emma and the Silk Thieves
- Emma and the Silverbell Faeries
- Emma and the Elixir of Madness
- Emma and the Weeping Spirit

Standalones

- Citadel: The Concordant Sequence
- The Cursed Codex
- The Menagerie of Jenkins Bailey